A COMPANION TO WOLVES

A COMPANION TO WOLVES

Sarah Monette

AND

Elizabeth Bear

A TOM DOHERTY ASSOCIATES BOOK

NEW YORK

A COMPANION TO WOLVES

Book design by Mary A. Wirth

A Tor Book
Published by Tom Doherty Associates, LLC
175 Fifth Avenue
New York, NY 10010

www.tor.com

Tor® is a registered trademark of Tom Doherty Associates, LLC.

Library of Congress Cataloging-in-Publication Data

Monette, Sarah.
   A companion to wolves / Sarah Monette and Elizabeth Bear.—1st ed.
      p. cm.
   "A Tom Doherty Associates book."
   ISBN-13: 978-0-7653-1816-9
   ISBN-10: 0-7653-1816-4
   1. Wolves—Fiction. I. Bear, Elizabeth. II. Title.
   PS3613.O5426C66 2007
   813'.6—dc22

                                                            2007021243

First Edition: October 2007

Printed in the United States of America

0 9 8 7 6 5 4 3 2 1

This book is for Amanda Downum
and Beth Meacham.

The Wolfheallan, the Wolfcarls, and the Wolves

❧

ARAKENSBERG WOLFHEALL
Ulfsvith, wolfjarl
Vethulf, brother to Kjaran

BRAVOLL WOLFHEALL
Asvolfr, wolfcarl

FRANANGFORD WOLFHEALL
Kari, brother to Hrafn

KERLAUGSTROND WOLFHEALL
Osk, wolf

KETILLHILL WOLFHEALL
Aslaug, konigenwolf

OTHINNSAESC WOLFHEALL
Brokkolfr, brother to Amma
Othwulf, brother to Vikingr

NITHOGSFJOLL WOLFHEALL
Aurulfr, brother to Griss
Clorulf, brother to Vith
Eyjolfr, brother to Glaedir
Fostolfr, brother to Guthleifr
Frithulf, brother to Kothran
Grimolfr, wolfjarl, brother to Skald
Hringolfr, brother to Kolgrimna
Hrolfmarr, brother to Kolli
Hrolleif, brother to Vigdis, konigenwolf

Isolfr, brother to Viradechtis
Randulfr, brother to Ingrun
Skirnulf, brother to Authun
Skjaldwulf, brother to Mar
Sokkolfr, wolfcarl
Thurulfr, brother to Egill
Ulfbjorn, brother to Tindr
Ulffred, wolfcarl
Ulfgeirr, brother to Nagli
Ulfmaer, brother to Hroi
Ulfrikr, brother to Skefill
Yngvulf, brother to Arngrimr

Asny, wolf
Eitri, wolf
Frar, wolf
Frothi, wolf
Hallathr, wolf
Hannar, wolf
Harekr, wolf
Havarr, wolf
Ingjaldr, wolf
Isleifr, wolf
Nyr, wolf
Olmoth, wolf
Surtr, wolf
Thraslaug, wolf
Valbrandr, wolf

THORSBAER WOLFHEALL
Leitholfr, brother to Signy, konigenwolf
Stafnulf, brother to Ormarr

Groa, wolf

VESTFJORTHR WOLFHEALL
Bekkhild, konigenwolf

AUTHORS' NOTE

There are many worlds in the branches of the tree, and legends do not stay untouched as they move from place to place. The world of the Iskryne is not Earth, but certain of its human cultures are not unlike certain historical Terran cultures. We have chosen to recognize this kinship by rendering the language of the people in this story in a melange of Norse, Anglo-Saxon, and other Germanic languages—making our choices in each case by ear rather than striving for a spurious consistency—in the hopes that this alien familiarity and familiar alienness will help readers as they enter into this cold and perilous world.

A COMPANION TO WOLVES

ONE

N jall could not stop looking at the wolf.

She lay on the flags before the fire in his father's hall at Nithogsfjoll and panted, despite the chill. Njall was sixteen, almost a man, even if he was hoping for just one more spurt of growth, but her head was as broad as the span of his palm between her eyes. His arms couldn't have circled her barrel, and if she rose on her long racer's legs, she would—almost—be able to look him in the eye, were her attention not reserved entirely for her master.

She was big even for a trellwolf, and more, she looked tired. Her winter coat was shedding in hanks and clumps, like handfuls of dirty rags gray with scrub-water, and he could see her ribs under the skin like sprung staves. Her midsection bulged with the promise of pups, and her heavy black nipples leaked watery fluid on the stones where she lay, infinitely patient, waiting for her master to finish his business with Njall's father.

Njall didn't know what the business was, exactly, but he did know his father wasn't pleased to be doing it. Njall had been exiled—not to the boys' dormitory but to his mother's empty solar—and fed his noon meal in isolation and bid *stay* like a puppy. Which he was not, and it rankled. Perhaps it was the insult that sent him, once the ale and bread and cheese and wizened last-winter apple were gone, edging down the long ragged curve of the stair to peer around the corner into the hall, stone rough under his palms, and learn what business his father had that his heir was excluded from.

And perhaps it was curiosity, too, for the men of the wolfheall almost never came to the keep. They were not welcome here, and they knew it.

The wolf had noticed him, for her ears flicked toward him now and again, but she never moved her firelight-hazel eyes from her master's face.

Njall had seen her master before—had even seen her at his side—among the cottages that clustered around the roots of his father's keep like goslings huddled at their mother's feet. The wolfcarl was a big man, almost as tall and stocky as a troll himself, wild-bearded, his graying red hair braided back from his temples; the edge of the axe he carried was bright with nicks and sharpening. He was Hrolleif, the Old Wolf, high-ranked in the werthreat, and Njall knew the villagers—and the manor—owed him obedience and fear.

Obedience, for he and the trellwolves and the werthreat were all that stood between the village and the trolls and wyverns of the North. And fear, for he was of the Wolfmaegth, the Wolf-brethren, and not quite human anymore. The more so because he had bonded a bitch, a Queen-wolf, with all that that implied.

Njall had heard stories about the werthreat and the trellwolves all his life; when he was a little boy, his nurse had threatened him that if he wasn't good, his father would tithe him to the wolfheall. Everyone knew the men of the wolfheall were half-wolf themselves, dark and violent in their passions, that they drank the blood of their fallen enemies and nursed from the teats of their she-wolves. No decent man, said Njall's father, wanted anything to do with them.

Njall didn't want anything to do with Hrolleif. He just wanted to look at the wolf.

His father's voice rang across the hall: "And I'm telling you there *are* no boys of an age to give to your tithe. You won't take them little but you don't want them once they've come to be men, either. We do not have that many children, wolfheofodman, and I cannot conjure them out of the fire for your asking."

"I thought your eldest son was of an age, Lord Gunnarr."

"My son is not for the tithe!"

Njall flinched back at the vehemence in his father's voice, and the wolf's head turned. For a dizzying moment her eyes caught him, pinned him like a spear through the gut, firelight and autumn leaves and a clarity he'd never seen in a dog's eyes, and then she looked back to her master, and Hrolleif laughed.

"Come out, then, pup! Let us see this boy who is not for the tithe."

Njall heard his father curse, and if it had just been Hrolleif he wouldn't have moved. Obedience was owed to his father, as jarl and as sire.

But the wolf had looked at him.

Njall came the rest of the way down the stairs, not looking at his father. Not looking at Hrolleif. He kept his eyes fixed on the trellwolf, and although she did not look at him again, her ears monitored his movements.

"So," said Hrolleif, and Njall had to look at him now, tilting his head to meet the Old Wolf's eyes. "My sister says you might be fit to join our threat, youngling. What think you?"

Sister? Njall was bewildered; the only people in the arched and gloomy hall were his father, Hrolleif, and himself, and why would the wolfheofodman be taking a *woman's* advice? But then the wolf turned her massive head to give him another look, this merely in passing, not the breath-stealing blow of before, and he knew that Hrolleif had meant *her*. *His sister.*

He gulped and said, "I do not know, Lord Hrolleif."

"An honest answer, at least. I do like a boy who doesn't swagger."

Hrolleif stepped forward, swiftly and with such power that it took a conscious effort for Njall to hold his ground. He caught Njall's jaw in one broad hand, turning his face toward the firelight. Peeling calluses scratched Njall's face. "Handsome lad. He takes after your lady wife, I see."

"Damn you, Hrolleif—"

"Lord Gunnarr." All the easy amusement was gone from Hrolleif's voice, although his fingers stayed gentle against Njall's face. "You know the laws. You owe the wolfheall tithe, and as you yourself have said, there are not many lads of the right age in manor *or* village. We cannot farm when we are fighting, and if we are not fighting, you are jarl of—" His free hand rose in an expansive gesture "—nothing."

"Thorkell Blacksmith's son," Njall's father said, and Njall was embarrassed at the note of pleading in his voice.

"Is simpleminded," Hrolleif said flatly. "As this one is not. What's your name, pup?"

"Njall, Lord Hrolleif."

"Njall. You will fulfill your house's duty to the wolfheall, will you not?"

Fear blocked Njall's throat. *Wolfheall.* There were stories—he turned away, pulling against Hrolleif's grip, so he would not have to look into the wolfheofodman's eyes or at his father's rage. He owed a duty to his father. To the village and the manor. He was the jarl's son, raised to be heir. There was a girl, Alfleda, whom he'd half-promised to take as a paramour once he was married, and there was a betrothal to a jarl's daughter he'd never met, and there was his father's gaze, resting on him now with an iron weight.

And there were the stories of what the men of the wolfheall did with each other, with the boys who went in tithe.

But as he turned, the trellwolf lifted her head again and caught him with a gaze of such piercing, knowing sweetness that he swallowed the fear.

He couldn't stop looking at the wolf.

And he owed a duty to the wolfheall, too.

Because Hrolleif was right; if the wolfheall did not fight, there would be nothing left worth fighting for.

"Yes, Lord Hrolleif," Njall said, and his father the jarl turned away and slammed his fist against one of the great supporting beams.

"All is not lost, Gunnarr," Hrolleif said, releasing Njall and turning to go, his wolf—*his sister*—coming slowly to her feet to follow him. "He may not be chosen. It is a spring litter, after all, and spring litters are small." He paused, and traded a glance with the wolf. "Send him with the wagon tomorrow, when you deliver the rest of the tithe. I'll not take a boy from his mother without a kiss."

Njall swallowed again as the door closed behind Hrolleif. At another time he might have protested the implication that he was still a child, still tied to the woman's world of kitchen and solar. But now, his hands shook and his knees trembled. The more so when his father, staring at the banded door, did not raise his voice at all but only said, gently, as if to a woman, "Njall."

"Father?"

"I cannot stop you. You've sixteen summers, and were you not to be jarl after me, you'd be a year or three 'prenticed. But think a moment. What if that wench of yours is with child? What of your mother, and your sister, too? If I were lost on the hunt or the field, who would care for them and keep the town strong?"

"Father—" Njall said. His hands clenched in the fabric of his trews. He shook his head, but Gunnarr stayed him with a hand before he could answer, whatever he might have said.

"Think about it," Gunnarr said. "Before you sell yourself to be some . . . unclanned bastard's catamite. Or worse." He shook his head, and turned to stare Njall in the face. "Go to the dormitory, son. You have until morning to change your mind."

❧

Of course Njall couldn't *stay* there. At this hour of the day the older boys were all at weapons-practice—as Njall should have been if his father had not chosen to try to hide him away like the child he wasn't—and the younger boys were giggling over some elaborate game among themselves. There was neither comfort nor counsel to be looked for from that quarter. He found himself shivering with delayed reaction, rubbing his hands across his face and then sniffing the fingers as if the smell of Hrolleif's wolf could have somehow transferred from skin to skin. He paced, and threw himself on the bed, and rose to pace again. He sent one of the younger boys to look for Alfleda, but the child returned to say that she had left the keep, and had said to tell Njall that she could not be found.

So was a woman's opinion made plain.

Eventually, inevitably, Njall's pacing led him out of the dormitory, across the courtyard, and up the stair toward his mother's solar. Perhaps he was not thinking clearly, but he had heard what Hrolleif had said—*tomorrow, with the rest of the tithe*—and, even be it womanish and weak, childish, he did not wish to leave without bidding his mother farewell.

Chosen by a wolf, he thought, and felt again the brush of the trell-wolf's amber eyes.

He was halfway up the stairs when he realized that he had seen not a single servant or waiting woman—as if they had all vanished or been sent away—and that the keep, rather than bustling with dinner preparations, was silent as moonset. Hiding from Gunnarr's temper, no doubt; it could be formidable when there was cause. Njall knew the back of his father's hand well enough, although never without reason.

He had hoped that, when his own time came to inherit, he would make such a lord, so just and so strong.

Raised voices paused Njall's footsteps in the antechamber to his mother's domain. He pressed back against a tapestry, breath short, because one of the voices was his father's.

"We must send him away, Halfrid. Send him to the monks at Hergilsberg, away from Nithogsfjoll. Better a monk than a *beast*."

"Gunnarr." His mother's voice, smooth and level. Njall could picture her, tall and stalwart in her white kirtle and indigo surcote, her hips broad with childbearing and the corners of her eyes crinkled with smiles. It *hurt* to think of her, of how she smelled of barley-and-mint-water, of her fingers quick with a needle and a silver thimble. "You cannot send him away."

"I'll tell the wolfheofodman he ran."

"And when the wolf-bitch cannot find his trail over new snow? The wolfheall will not protect us if we do not tithe, my husband. As is only just. It is the law. Besides, I do not think you will convince him to flee. He knows his own honor." Gentle, implacable, and Njall felt something uncomfortable twist in his belly.

Perhaps sometimes it was wise to listen to a woman. Not that he would have to learn, unless he wasn't chosen. Wolfcarls did not marry. But for a woman's voice to speak reason when a man's counseled cowardice—there was shame.

"Damn you, Halfrid." But surrender filled Gunnarr's voice, although his next words fell cold as stones. "You know what they do to those boys."

Njall heard footsteps, his father's footsteps; he slid between the tapestry and the wall, holding his breath.

"You must warn him," she said.

The footsteps stopped shy of the door. The stone was dank against Njall's back. The tapestry smelled of cedar and smoke and mildew. "Warn him that they'll make a wolf-bitch of him? Warn him that I am handing him over to be some beast's nithling and toy? Warn him of what he already knows?"

"Hrolleif does not seem less than a man to me," Halfrid said, after a hesitation.

Njall's father snorted harsh laughter through his beard; the sound was almost a sob. Njall drove his nails into his palms, willing himself silent and still.

"Perhaps—" The sweep of her skirt across rushes. She sighed, and there was a rustle of cloth. Njall imagined she drew his father into her embrace. "Perhaps he will not be chosen. Perhaps he will be chosen by a male, and he will lead the werthreat someday himself. Perhaps he will grow to be a powerful ally to you, my lord. Your son, a wolfheofodman—"

"Perhaps is a cold word, Halfrid," Njall's father said, and then there was only silence through the doorway, until Njall slipped away.

❦

The other older boys had returned to the dormitory, Njall's brother Jonak included, but he found he could not face them and walked out into the cold dusk instead. He crossed the courtyard once more to seek solace in the stable. His old pony Stout had been given to his sister Kathlin when he grew strong enough to handle a man's steed, but the little mare was still a friend, her shaggy wire-harsh gray mane drifting over gentle eyes. He leaned against the bar of the box she shared with two other ponies and let her drape her neck over his shoulder, steaming breath snuffing his cheek.

Kathlin found him there. She was a slip, an alf-seeming thing with the promise of their mother's looks, and all their father's temper. He wasn't surprised when she strode across the packed earth floor, stared at him for a moment, her chin lifted defiantly, and kicked him hard in the shin.

She got her hip into it. "Ow!" he protested, and was about to grab her and pick her up off her feet when she lunged forward, dissolving into sobs with the immediacy of a child. "Kathlin," he said, hopelessly. She cried harder, thumping his chest with both hands doubled up around the leather jerkin.

"You're leaving," she accused between sobs. "Father says you won't come back and I'm not to visit you. And Alfleda said she won't ever come back—"

"Did he say I was forbidden?" Njall asked, stroking her shoulders. She shook her head, her face pressed into his shirt. The tears soaked the cloth so cold bit through. Stout nickered and nosed Kathlin's hair, which made her laugh, and sniffle, finally, although she didn't step back.

"Don't go."

He hugged her tight. She was warm, but shivering. Her bones were too big for her flesh—she was growing, and felt stretched out over them. "I have to." He brightened, though. "I'll come visit you. When I can. If they let me."

"Won't they let you?" She stepped back, smoothing her dress, self-conscious enough to give him her shoulder. Younger than he by summers, but suddenly like a woman grown. "They can't keep you locked up, can they? I mean, wolfcarls aren't supposed to have families. You can't marry, you can't . . . It's in all the songs. You're just going to fight the trolls until you *die*."

"They may not even take me," he said, and reached out to grab her shoulders. "Come on, Kathlin," he said, when he felt that she was shivering still. "Come inside before Nurse finds you missing, or you freeze. They probably won't take me. And if they don't, I'll be home by harvest, and our debt to the wolfheall will be paid."

She glanced at him under her lashes, her eyes startlingly blue. "Promise?"

"Promise," he said, and squeezed her tight before he hurried her inside.

❧

He slept little and uneasily, rising well before dawn to wash and dress. His father had not sought him out, neither to tell him he was being sent to Hergilsberg—and Njall knew, with some surprise, that his mother was right: if his father had proposed that plan, he would have refused—nor to speak with him plainly, as man to man, about the customs of the wolfheall. Njall was not sure if he was glad or sorry, as he was not sure if he was glad or sorry that his father had not come to bid him farewell. The one thing he did know was that he would not have his house's duty to the wolfheall unfulfilled through *his* cowardice. No matter what they did to him, it would be better than knowing himself craven.

The tithe-wagon was in the courtyard, thralls loading it with sacks of turnips, barrels of salted herring. Halfrid stood beside the great, patient horses, stroking their noses while the tired-eyed wagoner swallowed the last of a hasty breakfast.

"Mother," Njall said awkwardly, and she turned and smiled at him, her eyes as warm and steady as ever.

"Are you ready, Njall?"

"I suppose," he said and then in a low-voiced rush, "Ready for *what?*"

"To attend the tithing. To become a man of the werthreat if you should be chosen. To defend Nithogsfjoll, keep and steading, with your life." She sighed and pushed an escaped tendril of wheat-fair hair behind her ear. "It is not the path to manhood I would have chosen for you, but it is an honorable path."

"Father said. . . ." But he could not speak the word "nithling" to his mother. He blushed, and mumbled at his boots, "Father said it was my choice, but I fear I have chosen wrong."

The thralls were almost finished loading the wagon, the wagoner making some joke and swinging onto the wagon-seat. Njall looked up and saw his mother's face grim and rather sad. "You've heard stories, of course. Boys talk."

"Yes. But it's not—you said it was honorable, to go to the werthreat. I could protect you. I could—"

She kissed his brow swiftly and said, "You must decide what your honor is, Njall, and hold to it. I know men who have gone to the wolfheall and made a warrior's life there. You can too. Or you can come home, and we will have you."

"Father won't," Njall said.

"Your father has his own trolls to hunt," Halfrid said, and might have continued if the wagoner had not interrupted when she took a breath.

"Begging pardon, Lady Halfrid, but we haven't got all day. They like you to be timely at the wolfheall, so they do."

"Go on with you, then," Halfrid said to Njall. "You have your mother's blessing."

"Thank you," Njall said and climbed up into the wagon.

All the way down from keep to wolfheall, he pondered his mother's words. *You must decide what your honor is.* But honor was honor, wasn't it? It wasn't something you could pick and choose about. Yet she would not have wasted her breath with meaningless words.

But they reached the great barred gate of the wolfheall's wall before he had puzzled out her meaning.

Even as the wagoner was drawing his horses to a stop, the gate was opening, and a man came out, his hair iron-black and his face like something carved from flint, a trellwolf beside him that seemed the size of a bear. Even the great carthorses shied and stamped at the sight of that monster, and Njall's palms grew clammy. This wolf's eyes were more orange than those of Hrolleif's bitch and his heavy pelt rippled like water over his muscles. Njall recognized the man, just as he had recognized Hrolleif: Grimolfr, the wolfjarl, who ruled the wolfheall as Njall's father ruled the keep. Njall swallowed hard.

"So," said Grimolfr, while his wolf sat beside him and let his tongue loll. "You are Njall Gunnarson. It seems I owe Hrolleif a forfeit. I wagered you would not appear this morning."

Njall slid down from the wagon. "My house honors its duty to the wolfheall," he said.

"As well it should. Did you bring anything?"

"No."

"Good. That's less we have to get rid of. Come along."

He turned on his heel and strode into the wolfheall compound, calling for the thralls to come unload the wagon. His wolf moved with him as swiftly and surely as his shadow. Njall followed him, because whatever his honor might be, it certainly didn't include succumbing to the childish impulse to plant his feet and refuse to budge.

The wolfheall wasn't a grand stone keep like his father's. The walled compound was halfway flagged—and a good thing, too, because the feet of men and trellwolves had churned what wasn't paved into a springtide mire—but the central building was a roundhall in the old style, wooden, roofed in slates, a thick stream of smoke ascending from its center. The whole bustled with activity: wolves and men and thralls at work all about. Njall saw two men enter at the postern gate, a pole slung over their shoulders with a dead buck dangling from it. Two wolves paced them, one a red so pale he was almost tawny, the other dark as smoke, like Grimolfr's gigantic male. *Will my wolf be gray?* Njall wondered. *If I am chosen?*

He snuck a glance sideways at Grimolfr's male, and wondered if it was the father of Hrolleif's bitch's pups. And then he thought of the shocking things that were whispered by older boys to younger in the dormitories at night, thought of his father's brutal words; he looked up at Grimolfr and blanched at his imaginings.

"Vigdis won't whelp tonight," Grimolfr said, without returning the stare. "Tomorrow, perhaps. Have you eaten, pup?"

The wolfjarl's voice was not unkind, and Njall decided to risk honesty. "I haven't been hungry, sir. Are . . ."

"Speak, whelp. Wolves say what they think when they think it; we have our politics, but they're not devious ones."

"I was going to ask where you were taking me."

"To Ulfmaer, the housecarl, and his brother. They have charge of pups, wolf and man, until they're bonded. Any other questions?"

Njall had thousands, but he settled for the first one to come to mind. "Is Vigdis the name of Hrolleif's bitch—I mean, sister?"

"One of her names," Grimolfr said, unexpectedly soft and fond, allowing a little smile to curl his lips under his beard. He did glance down then, and Njall found himself pinned on the man's dark-brown gaze as surely as he'd been pinned on Vigdis'. "My brother is called Skald. His own name—" The wolfjarl gestured, and Skald turned his head, staring into Njall's eyes with his own sunset-colored ones.

Njall smelled ice and cold wind, a musk like serpents, the dark metal of old blood. "Like a kill at midwinter," he said, coughing, and then realized what it meant. "Their names are smells."

"Aye," Grimolfr said, sounding pleased although he did not smile again.

"And Vigdis? What is her name?"

It was the scent of a wet dawn in late autumn, bare trees and pale sunrise and the leaf-mold sharp and crisp at the back of Njall's sinuses. He drew a deep, hard breath, and sighed.

"You like that, whelp?"

"Yes. Sir." No, no point in lying. None at all.

"Hmh." A grunt, a dog-sound, almost animal. Njall startled, but Grimolfr didn't seem to notice. Instead, he jerked his chin at the buck, dripping icicles of blood from a slashed throat as its bearers went past, the wolfcarls who bore it nodding respect to their jarl. "Well, you'd best eat when that game is served, pup. We hunt tonight and you'll need your strength."

They had all but crossed the yard. Njall sighed relief when they entered the wind-shadow of the roundhall. "Hunt, sir? What do we hunt at night?"

Grimolfr paused with his hand on the great copper-sheathed door. "Foolish puppy," he said, and showed Njall his teeth. "We hunt trolls."

⚶

Njall was relieved that the meat he was served for noon meal was cooked—and not, he judged, actually the buck that the wolfcarls had brought home that day. This was seasoned meat, hung until tender and roasted sweet. The wolfheall's cook knew his—or her—business.

Njall shared his trencher with a slight blond boy, Brandr, who'd arrived a few days earlier and who was full of gossip and good cheer. There were six boys in all, and Njall was sure that Ulfmaer thought that too few to give Vigdis' pups good selection. The stout gray-haired housecarl traded doubtful glances with his gray-faced trellwolf throughout the meal, his uncertainty making Njall feel gangly and grimy and much younger than his years—but the hall itself wasn't unlike his father's hall, except larger, and wood instead of stone, and the dogs gnawing bones and squabbling over their portions alongside the tables weren't dogs at all but wolves as big as men.

Njall did notice that Grimolfr sat at one end of the long table and Hrolleif at the other, just as Njall's father and mother sat—and that Skald stood guard over Vigdis while she lay by Hrolleif's chair and ate, and permitted no other wolf or man near her. Nor was it lost on him that the fond looks Grimolfr sent the length of the table included not just wolf and bitch but red-bearded Hrolleif as well.

Njall found himself pushing the meat on the trencher over to Brandr's side. Brandr accepted with a glance and a shrug. Njall watched Brandr make short work of the venison, because it allowed him not to look at Hrolleif, until Ulfmaer's knotted hand descended on his shoulder.

"Njall. Nerves about the hunt?"

"Yes," Njall lied, twisting his head to look up at the housecarl.

Ulfmaer smiled, a gap-toothed grin, and squeezed his shoulder.

"We'll find you weapons after the meal," he said. "In the meantime, you must eat, lad." *Lad*, and not *pup*. That one word unknotted the tangle of fear in Njall's breast a little. "I know something you can think on to distract yourself."

"What?" Not meaning to sound so eager, but there it was.

"If you are chosen—and Vigdis has at least four pups in her, so the odds are good—you'll need a name."

"A—sir, a name?"

Brandr elbowed him. "Idiot. You don't think they're *all* born named 'Wolf.' Ow!"—as Ulfmaer cuffed the back of his head.

"Respect for your packmates, whelp," he said, and stomped off.

Brandr waited until he was out of earshot and then slid Njall a sly look, and grinned. "Old bastard. You know Hroi's his second wolf?"

"You can have more than one?" Njall blinked, surprised.

"Even wolves get killed by trolls," Brandr said. He made a long arm that would have gotten Njall or his brother clouted, and ripped a wing off the goose three places down the table. "I hear his first wolf was a bitch, and he misses it. Makes him cranky."

"Oh," said Njall, and blushed. "What will you . . . I mean, have you thought of a name yet?"

Brandr made an expressive face. "My uncle's a wolfcarl—not here, in the wolfheall at Arakensberg. He made me promise I'd call myself Frithulf, after a friend of his who died."

"And will you?"

"I promised," Brandr said with a shrug, and Njall was relieved to realize that meant *yes*. Maybe honor would not be so difficult to hold here after all.

He was still thinking about that, chin on his fist and brow furrowed, when Brandr nudged him. There was—not a commotion, but a disturbance—at the head of the table, and Brandr bounced on the bench. Njall looked up; a tall spidery dark man was rising from his seat. "Skjald-wulf," Brandr hissed, leaned so close to Njall's ear that Njall could feel him jitter. "Skjaldwulf Snow-Soft, they call him. We're in luck."

"*Soft!* That's a name for a wolfcarl?"

Brandr snorted. "Soft as a knife in the ribs. He nearly never talks," he explained. "But he can *sing*."

The tall man pushed black braids behind his shoulders and picked his way over snoring wolves on the rush-and-fur-strewn floor. When he had found a clear place to stand by the fire, he scuffed his feet wide and settled comfortably, eyelids lowered. One of the older tithe-boys brought him a horn of ale. He quaffed it and handed it back, and took a deep breath, running his gaze across the wolfcarls and tithe-boys and thralls spread around the hall.

The room went silent, as Njall was accustomed when someone was about to declaim. And Skjaldwulf Snow-Soft spoke in a resonant, carrying baritone that sounded as if it rose from the depths of the earth, carrying smoke and rain.

"Winter is long, and the nights are cold. There was a time when men maintained mere dogs to guard their cattle, when there were no wolfheallan and no wolfcarls, when trellwolves were troth-enemies of true-men. When fell trolls, terrible tyrants, walked in winter as they willed it, and our forefathers shuddered in shallow scrapes. This was the time of Thorsbaer Thorvaldson, who first knew a konigenwolf and swore to serve her for salvation.

"I took this tale from Red Sturla in his age, and as he told it me I tell it you. This was the time—"

Njall listened, enraptured. There had been better skalds at his father's hall, now and again, but not many—and there had been worse, as well. Skjaldwulf's voice rang like a brazen bell when he raised it, and the alliteration tolled from his tongue with heavy power. And Njall had not heard this tale before.

Skjaldwulf—Snow-Soft, and now Njall saw another reason for the kenning-name, for he was subtle and chill in his wit, as well—told it with precision and deftness. How Thorsbaer Thorvaldson had been cast out for sorcery, for playing at women's magic, and how he had found—alone—a daytime encampment of trolls.

It would have been worth his life to attack them. And he could not return to his jarl's keep, even with a message of grave urgency—he'd die on the point of a spear before he spoke three words.

But perhaps he could send a message somehow, or raise a warning. Perhaps he could spoil their ambush, when night came.

He waited.

And with sunset—not that the sun ever rose but briefly, so deep in winter—the wolves came. When he saw that they had come to hunt the trolls, Thorsbaer Thorvaldson fell in with the pack.

And the pack, to his shock, permitted it. He'd half-expected to be pulled down with the trolls, treated as prey. Instead, he found himself moving with the wolves, dreaming—so said Skjaldwulf—with the wolves.

Until all the trolls were dead.

Thorsbaer's jarl would not take him back on the strength of that. Most certainly not with a snarling she-wolf by his side, when he was already suspected of sorcery. He had lived with the wild packs until he died, and fought the trolls on behalf of men who would not have him.

But something strange had happened.

As the pack settled close, and Thorsbaer spoke for them, and it became noticed that trolls did not travel unmolested through their territory to attack the human steadings—other men joined him. Disaffected men, younger sons, disgraced men. Men who practiced unmasculine arts—weaving, seithr—or some who were lovers of men. They came among the wolf-pack, and to Thorsbaer's rude cottage they attached a timber hall.

And the wolves chose from among them.

And together they hunted the trolls.

⚬᛭⚬

Ulfmaer and Hroi took the six tithe-boys out to the practice-field that afternoon, accompanied by four young men only a year or so older and three amiable half-grown wolves. They'd be bonding soon, Brandr told Njall in an undertone, and then the odd boy out would have to decide what to do.

"Won't he go home?" Njall said.

"Maybe, maybe not," Brandr said with another of his expressive shrugs. "*I* wouldn't."

"Why not?" And then he caught himself. "I'm sorry, I didn't mean—"

"It's all right. I'm no jarl's son, Njall Gunnarson, and I can do a good sight better for myself in a wolfheall than I ever could on my father's steading."

"They'll let you stay? Even if you don't bond?"

"Who says I won't bond?" Brandr said, grinning, and Njall couldn't help grinning back.

He found he knew rather more about the use of the quarterstaff than most of the boys, and remembered the way Brandr had said, *I'm no jarl's son*, not resentfully but with resignation. "You've been trained with the axe, lad?" Ulfmaer asked him.

"Yes, sir," Njall said.

"Well, that's a mercy. I'm always afraid these clumsy young idiots will lop their own ears off." And he glowered at the older boys, who grinned back affectionately. "For today, though, will you help the other lads? I hate to lose boys before a tithing."

"Does it happen often?" Njall asked, pleased that his voice didn't squeak.

Ulfmaer exchanged a look with Hroi—Njall had noticed how frequently that happened, even though Hroi, unlike Vigdis the day before, did not watch Ulfmaer constantly. He had his own work with the half-grown pups. But trellwolf and man always knew where the other was, and they were never out of each other's line of sight. Ulfmaer sighed. "'Tis no tourney you go to tonight, youngling. The trolls do not care if you be unpracticed. But Grimolfr says we can't protect those who must learn to protect others, and I fear he's right."

"I'll help," Njall promised, wanting suddenly to make Ulfmaer look less tired, less worried.

"That's a good lad," Ulfmaer said, and wheeled, bellowing, "Fastvaldr, an axe is not a flyswatter!"

Njall went to help the other tithe-boys.

They were inclined to be uncomfortable at first, almost resentful, but he deliberately let the smallest of them, Hlothvinr, catch him a glancing blow alongside his skull, and grinned and said, "Perfect. But you'll have to hit me harder than that." And the other boys laughed and listened more willingly.

They were all limping and favoring bruises by the time the lengthening shadows prompted Ulfmaer to call a halt. He and Hroi herded them back to the roundhall and, unyielding to blandishments and protests, into the bathhouse. "The first lesson to be learned, boys. The wolves can smell you. It's only polite of you to try to smell good."

"Who says they don't like the smell of honest sweat?" Brandr said, and Hroi shook himself with such vigor that all of them laughed.

"*They* do, Brandr Quick-Tongue" said Ulfmaer, "so scrub up."

The wolfheall's bathhouse was bigger than that of the manor; Njall guessed that maybe half the werthreat could bathe at once, if they crowded on the benches. The ten boys were able to spread out more than that, but Njall still found himself grateful that Ulfmaer did not leave, but stripped to his breechclout and stumped up and down the aisle scattering water on the rocks to make steam, grumbling at them to scrub behind their ears, and passing pitchers with snide comments: "Yes, you do have to get your hair wet, Svanrikr. Otherwise you can't get it *clean*."

Njall shared with Brandr and one of the older boys, Sigmundr: the Stone Sigmundr, a good byname for a lad as self-contained as a keep's high walls. Sigmundr was silent except for politely answering when Brandr asked him questions. Njall concentrated on washing, and stealing sideways glances at the scars that marked Ulfmaer's torso, forearms, and thighs. Scars that looked like the marks of teeth and claws.

There were clean clothes when they were done, and then back to the hall for supper. The food was again plentiful and well-cooked, and even nerves could not prevent Njall from eating heartily. Brandr sat beside him again and told him the names of the werthreat and their trellwolves, at least as many of them as he knew. Njall listened with half an ear, but mostly watched the trellwolves, red and gray and dark brindle, eyes golden, amber, orange—there were even three or four wolves whose eyes were almost green. He wondered if those wolves all had the same father and asked Brandr, "Is Vigdis the only bitch in the wolfheall?"

Brandr snorted into his ale. "It's your own wolfheall—you've only lived nigh it your whole life."

Njall hunched a shoulder uncomfortably. "My father doesn't like it spoken of."

Brandr's eyebrows went up, but he said only, "Well, Vigdis *isn't* the only bitch in the wolfheall. She's just the konigenwolf—the top bitch."

"Oh," said Njall, and couldn't help his eyes going from Hrolleif to Grimolfr. Happily, Brandr didn't notice. He said, "There's three or four other bitches, I think. I know the pups who came out with us today were whelped by Ingrun," and he nodded down the table to a young man, blond and ruddy-faced and laughing at something his trencher-mate had said. "Randulfr's sister. We're lucky we're getting a shot at Vigdis' pups."

Njall watched a moment, to see if he could tell which of the wolves near Randulfr was Ingrun. And yes, a tawny-gray wolf, gnawing on a deer-rib, looked up at Randulfr just as he leaned back from the table to pass her a tidbit. Brandr prattled on beside him. Njall looked at Hrolleif, and then at Vigdis and Skald, and knew that Brandr was right.

They set out across the snow at moonrise, well-armed and outfitted as became warriors, all afoot, including Hrolleif and Grimolfr, because even battle-hardened horses would not stand before a wyvern. They divided into three parties and cast out: Njall's group included Ulfmaer and Hrolleif and traveled north and east toward the rising moon, over snow so cold it creaked under their boots.

Each man had a wolf beside him except Hrolleif—Vigdis being too gravid to hunt—and the four unbonded boys. Besides Njall, there were Brandr Quick-Tongue, Svanrikr—whom Brandr called Un-Wise, but not where Svanrikr could hear him—and the Stone Sigmundr—and one of the three adolescent wolves, Eitri, although Njall noticed that the men and grown wolves kept the boys and pup in the center of the group, and Eitri did not look at Sigmundr the way Hroi looked at Ulfmaer.

The trees they moved through were still gaunt, although the tips of their branches swelled with the promise of spring and life. After a little, it struck Njall that they passed through the dark with very little conversation—the wolves wove among the men, ranging out and back, and the men cast out among the trees but seemed to find each other effortlessly. Njall fingered the edge of the axe slung across his chest, his feet slipping slightly in his too-new boots, and realized that he was moving with the rest, as much a part of the pattern as a goose flying in a wedge. He could smell the night around him—the snow and the dark and the sap running up branches, the first green tang of spring. He could smell Sigmundr beside him, smell the wolves and the men, each individually, smell Brandr's sour fear and his determination, smell his own confidence—for, unlike the other young men, he was a jarl's son and this was not his first time in battle—and he thought if he closed his eyes and concentrated, he might be able to pick out the scent of the moonlight on snow. Moving, all moving, like a great, coordinated dance, and he bit his lip to keep from laughing in delight.

He glanced around, wildly aware of the sound of his own heartbeat, and found Ulfmaer at his elbow. "You feel it," Ulfmaer whispered, barely more than the motion of his lips, and Njall nodded, *yes.*

"It's the pack," Ulfmaer said, his eyes glimmering excitement in the sharp blue moonlight, where everything laid hard-edged shadows. "You have the pack-sense already. Aye, lad, you'll bond, and well—"

His head came up, as if linked to Hroi's, and Njall smelled it the same moment—a sharp, bitter odor, wood-smoke and oil of terebinth, and that musk as of serpents that had underlaid Skald's name. Ulfmaer stepped back and put his shoulder to Njall.

"The scouts have cornered it. Time for that axe," the housecarl said, unnecessarily, as—somewhere in the darkness—a trellwolf howled.

The leather axe-bindings were sticky on Njall's palms when he shoved his hands out the slits in his mittens and gripped the weapon. His father preferred the shield-wall—a shocking weight of charging men with their bucklers interlocked, swords at the ready, a rank of spears behind—but Njall had learned axe too, and he believed Ulfmaer when the old man said that swords were no good for troll-necks. Troll-necks needed hewing.

Njall had heard stories of this as well, of course. Villages raided, the men strung up with their guts in puddles on the ground and left to watch as the women, still alive and screaming, were eaten—although nothing like that had happened in his lifetime. The wolfheallan stood between men and the cold North, a thin determined line, and Njall had never seen a troll, much less a wyvern, and had never spoken to anyone who had seen one—before today. He tightened his grip, and the wolfcarls and their wolves moved forward, toward another eager hunting cry.

Two wolves stood guard before a cliff face and a thicket, crouched low, obviously well back from their quarry and waiting for the rest of the pack. Njall had seen wood wolves, trellwolves' smaller cousins, hunt elk, and dogs bring deer to a stand; this was no different from hunting deer behind his father's rangy coarse-furred deerhounds, except that arrows would not pierce trellhide, or a wyvern's scales. This was killing that had to be done at hand, with jaws and axes.

The stories had not prepared him for the long quick shape that slid out of the darkness as they approached, snow hissing against its belly scales as against the runners of a sleigh, small wings paddling the air frantically as its head swayed and snapped on a long neck, lithe and un-gainly as a goose and with the same beady, evil-tempered eyes. Njall's eyes had adjusted to the dark, and a quarter-moon shone bright on all that snow. He saw the wyvern clearly, and he saw the stumplike human-ish shape beside it.

"Only one?" he asked Ulfmaer stupidly.

Ulfmaer grunted. "One's enough. Come on, lad, it's on our side," and stamped forward with Hroi on his left hand and his axe unlimbered in his right.

Njall hesitated. He glanced over his shoulder, saw the Stone Sig-mundr start forward in his footsteps and Brandr Quick-Tongue drawn back, away from the sally, by a wolfcarl whose name Njall didn't know. "Sometimes they circle," the wolfcarl said, and Njall understood the wis-dom of it; some would fight, and the others would watch, so that the cliff against which the wolves had cornered the troll did not become the cliff against which the wolfcarls were brought to bay.

Hefting his axe, he went to cover Ulfmaer's flank, and felt Sigmundr and the two wolfcarls whose brothers still crouched, grinning death up at the troll, start forward.

Five men, three wolves, one troll and one wyvern. And the only thing that saved them was the pack-sense, the knowledge of where the wolf-brothers would be, smiling, snarling, dancing their dance a half-step faster than the snakelike pattern of the wyvern's flat-iron head. They wove before it, harried it, leaped one another stiff-kneed and came down in unexpected places, decoyed it away from the cliff while the other four men faced the troll and Njall stalked, waiting for the wyvern to overreach itself, to turn its back from the wall, to give him a chance to move inside that weaving net of teeth.

He heard bronze clank on steel and knew the others had engaged the troll—the gross creature with its stony, knotted hide wielded a bronze axe twice the size of Njall's—but his whole attention was for the wyvern, its pale silhouette dangerously indistinct in snow and moonlight, its mouth snapping after the trellwolves as full of teeth as a lamprey's.

It did not seem overly impressed with Njall. Among the smallest of the pack, after all, and he didn't dart in, snapping, and dart out again while sharp teeth *snicked* shut on cold air and the mist of panting breath. He just crouched, coiled, waiting, ready to spring, and did not take his eyes off the wyvern even when he heard an impossibly fast passage of arms beyond, heard the troll ululate in agony and a wolfcarl shout in pain. The sickening *snap* was not branches—

Njall did not shift his gaze. He saw Hroi crouch, heard him yowl more like a cat than a wolf, saw him throw himself at the wyvern's throat. And Njall knew in his bones, the pattern of pack, that Hroi's attack was the distraction, and that his own place—

He charged, biting back a shout, and felt a trellwolf running at his side, shoulder to his hip where he could know its presence without having to look. Njall threw himself forward, boots slipping on snow and the slick dead grass and leaves beneath, and swung his axe high and boldly with all the force of his shoulder and his mass behind it. At his side the wolf leaped, and Hroi snarled and lunged at the wyvern's head this time.

Njall's axe hit hard, bit scale just in front of the wyvern's haunch, slipped down and sideways. He turned the cut into a looping curve, kept the momentum, brought the blade up and around again and back into the same place, just as the trellwolf's jaws closed on the wyvern's hamstring. The thing could not shriek; snakes have no voice. But the little wings beat as if it could fly and it hissed like a steaming kettle forgotten over the fire. The troll shouted once more, and there was a sound of metal on bone and of bone breaking and the blood was hot, musty and serpent-sharp over Njall's hands, his arms, salty and thin across his face, in his mouth, and the wolves were snarling, and he hacked again and again as Hroi got the wyvern's neck between his jaws and dragged its head away from Njall's back, and this time the hot gush of blood across his arms brought slick, wrist-thick ropes of intestine with it.

If Hroi hadn't grabbed Njall's arm, in jaws that could snap a bull's leg like a brittle reed, and hauled him safely clear, Njall would have still been under it when it came down, because he didn't think to stop hacking.

⁘

Ulfmaer died two hours after they travoised him to the Nithogsfjoll wolfheall, surprising no one. The blood staining his beard had been red, bright with froth; the snapped ribs had driven into his lungs. Hroi lay beside the body in its place against the wall of the roundhall. The old wolf's chin rested in the groove between Ulfmaer's thigh and groin, Ulfmaer's fingers softly curling across the mammoth skull. Hroi's green-gold eyes were watchful; he would not bear the body touched. Not on that night. Not until the morning.

The pack gave him his mourning in private, and took theirs into the snow, around a bonfire built on the flagstones. Njall held warmed ale in a horn and barely touched it; he'd seen death before, of course, and death in battle was kinder than the death of age and illness and blindness and fouling oneself in senility, so he knew his sorrow for pure selfishness at having lost his family and his new teacher and guardian, all in one day.

He didn't speak to them, but he was grateful when Sigmundr and Brandr came and sat on either side of him, and leaned their shoulders against his for warmth. Sigmundr didn't talk much—just helped him stare into the fire. Brandr told the dirtiest jokes he'd ever heard, under his breath, in a monotone, until even Sigmundr couldn't quite keep his lips from cracking into a smile.

"How many boys were tithed with you, Sigmundr?" Njall asked, finally, when Brandr paused for breath.

The older boy sipped his mulled wine and shook his head. "Nine," he said, his eyes on Eitri and one of his brothers, where they lay staring into the fire.

"But there are four of you—" Brandr, who stopped himself short, and left Njall infinitely grateful that Brandr had been just a little bit faster to be stupid this time.

He felt Sigmundr shrug. "We have been unlucky. Ulfmaer said that it's a bad tithe when they lose one boy before bonding, a *very* bad tithe when they lose three."

Njall didn't speak, but the other two boys must have felt him shiver, because both of them pressed close. He was grateful, actually, that they were not put to bed and expected to sleep that night, because a great loneliness welled up in him when he looked across the fire at the drinking men and thought of his sister and parents warm in their beds, of the boys in the dormitory. *Homesick, cub?* he thought scornfully, and knuckled his eyes. He didn't think Brandr noticed.

The men were still drinking and the wolves were still whining when Skald emerged from the warmth of the roundhall to bring Hrolleif and Grimolfr within.

Vigdis' cubs—two gray dog-pups, a cream-colored dog-pup, and a bitch-pup brindled black and red like the fabled Tyger—were all born hearty and hale by dawn. "A bitch," Brandr said with a bitten lip when Hrolleif brought the boys in to meet the blind, snuffling velvet grubs, and glanced sideways at Svanrikr. "I wonder who she'll choose."

Svanrikr shrugged. Njall looked into Vigdis' laughing, self-satisfied eyes and said loyally, "She's the prettiest."

"It's good you think so," Svanrikr Un-Wise snickered, tilting his head so Njall could just hear him. "So're you."

Njall didn't dare hit him. The wolves were watching.

TWO

Life in the tithe-boys' dormitory of the wolfheall was not so different from life in the boys' dormitory of the keep, although no one looked askance at how much they ate or told them it was time they started behaving like men. The werthreat knew they were men and simply expected that they would behave accordingly. It was the wolves they waited for, not their manhood.

The new housecarl, Ulfgeirr, and his brother Nagli were both redheads: Nagli's pale tawny-red coat striking next to Ulfgeirr's long copper-red braids. Ulfgeirr put up with a good deal of teasing on the subject with perfect equanimity, although he was quick enough to anger over matters pertaining to the peace and safety of the roundhall. He was also, as Brandr found out and reported gleefully to the other boys, the lover of the wolfheall cook. "They would marry, if the werthreat could allow it. Jorveig is heall-bred and understands about—"

He closed his mouth abruptly as Ulfgeirr came over to them. "I could wish, Brandr Quick-Tongue," he said, "that your hands worked as swiftly as your mouth."

Brandr crimsoned and fell silent for nearly a quarter hour.

With Vigdis' litter suckling and squeaking and learning how to use their legs, everyone began to watch the adolescent wolves very carefully. They would bond soon, and Njall noticed the way that Sigmundr and his tithe-mates were taking elaborate pains to be near Eitri and Authun and Harekr—not touching unless invited, but yearning. Njall found he could not watch them, and wondered if the same look was in his eyes when he went to visit Vigdis' pups. And the young wolves watched the boys in return, but did not choose.

It was two weeks after the birth of Vigdis' pups that Ulfgeirr told Njall and the five other young men of his tithing that they would be going out on a long patrol with Randulfr and Ingrun and a handful of other wolfcarls and wolves. He seemed tight, on edge—unlike his usual easygoing self.

"When do we leave?" Njall said, because somebody had to say something. He had not intentionally taken command of the group of tithe-boys, but habits bred since birth were hard to break, and the others were grateful, even if heall-bred Svanrikr grumbled about it.

"Tonight," Ulfgeirr answered, in a tone that brooked no argument. "Jorveig will have packs for you. Expect to be gone three days at least, perhaps a week."

"Yes, sir," Njall said and kicked Brandr's ankle to keep him from adding his contribution. Ulfgeirr was tetchy enough.

Jorveig the cook, a big, rawboned woman with a grip like a blacksmith's, was clearly worried when they went to the kitchen at sundown to get their packs. Njall had witnessed three fistfights that afternoon, and all the wolfcarls seemed distracted, snappish. The wolves were no better, snarling and pacing. Njall dared to ask her, "What's going on?"

"Ulfgeirr didn't say?"

"Just that we're going out on patrol. For a week."

She tsk'd impatiently and adjusted Hlothvinr's jerkin with brusque fingers. "I'll have to speak to him about that. There's no reason for you not to know, no matter how badly Nagli wants to get his ashes hauled. Asny's coming into heat."

"Oh," said Njall, not usefully.

"So the housecarl and the wolfjarl together make sure that Asny's kin and Ingrun and Kolgrimna are at a safe distance. You mind your manners, boys, and do what the wolfcarls tell you."

They agreed, raggedly, and walked down to the gate where Randulfr and Ingrun were waiting for them. The other wolfcarls had gone on ahead, Randulfr told them. "It's harder for them to think, this close to Asny, and we don't want bloodshed."

"Yes, sir," Njall said and did not ask, *What about you?*, no matter how badly he wanted to.

Randulfr laughed. "I'm not *sir* to you, lad. Tell me your names again."

"I'm Njall." He pointed to the other boys, one by one. "That's Brandr Quick-Tongue, Hlothvinr the Brown, Svanrikr Un-Wise"—Njall pretended not to notice when Svanrikr, not fond of the byname, glowered— "the Great Leif, and Johvatr the Younger."

The wolfcarl made a tolerant face. "And you are Njall the Not-Jarl, I see," he teased, and when Njall blushed he patted him on the arm. "I'm Randulfr. Not *sir*. I hope soon I'll be your brother in the werthreat. And this is Ingrun." He glanced down at the tawny bitch beside him, and she looked up, first at Randulfr with bright love shining in her eyes, and then at Njall. He smelled her name: moss in a stream of ice-melt water. Then she looked past him at the other boys. Njall noticed, because he'd been learning to watch for it, that Brandr, Hlothvinr, and Leif clearly "got" Ingrun's name. Johvatr didn't. Svanrikr knew how to look as if he did, but Njall wasn't sure if he was faking or not.

Randulfr and Ingrun shared another look, and Njall wished he knew what they were saying to each other. Then Randulfr turned and with a wave at the boys to keep up started away from the wolfheall and into the wild wood.

It was one of the most grueling weeks of Njall's life, worse even than the campaign of his fourteenth summer, and that had been bad enough. The wolfcarls were all on edge, even Randulfr, although he controlled it better than the others—or felt it less. The wolves squabbled among themselves, and the tithe-boys were witness to demonstrations of the brutal and effective nature of trellwolf discipline. Ingrun did not hesitate to use her teeth if she felt she needed to.

They were lucky; they encountered trolls only twice, and one was half-grown. They did not find any wyverns, and Njall, remembering that hissing twisting nightmare, was not sorry. It made the wolfcarls uneasy, though; Njall heard them muttering to each other, "Where *are* they?" "They should have smelled us coming two days ago." "There's *always* trolls along the river." The boys kept their mouths shut and jumped when the wolfcarls said *frog*. Njall couldn't even begin to guess at the amount of ground they covered; he only knew that by sundown each day his calves and thighs were burning. He wasn't the only one who found himself awake in the smallest hours of the morning with cramps knotting his leg muscles; he and the Great Leif spent the better part of an hour, their third night out, massaging each other's legs.

By the end of the week, Njall knew his tithe-mates better than he had ever expected to and was beginning to be able to think of the wolf-carls as potential brothers, as Randulfr had said. Brandr's quick, malicious tongue was matched by the quickness of his brain; Svanrikr swaggered about being heall-bred but was no better prepared for the arduous nature of a long patrol than the other boys. Johvatr was nervous of the wolves and stayed nervous, although how anyone could be truly nervous of them after watching Hrolfmarr use his brother Kolli as a pillow Njall did not know. The Great Leif was quiet, steady, observant; he was going to be a massive man when he finished growing, and live up to his byname—he was already half a head taller than the tallest of the wolfcarls. Hlothvinr the Brown was shy and wary, but chattered like a magpie once he was comfortable. Ingrun seemed to think he needed mothering; Randulfr twice had to call her away from washing Hlothvinr's face with her great pink tongue. But Hlothvinr glowed with delight at the wolf's attention.

Njall told himself, in a memory of his mother's voice, not to count his chickens before they hatched, but he could not help the way his speculations were edging toward certainty. Hlothvinr would be chosen; Leif would be chosen; Brandr would be chosen. He himself wanted to be chosen so badly it was like a perpetual ache in his chest, but, imitating Halfrid again, he reminded himself that pride went before a fall and it would be fitting if he had to stand by and watch Svanrikr bond with Vigdis' bitch-pup.

The thought did not make his own mood any sweeter.

But they came back to the wolfheall to find the tension washed out like mudstains from the laundry that billowed joyfully across the yard. Asny's mating had gone well, and one look at Ulfgeirr's ear-to-ear grin told Njall that Nagli had indeed gotten his ashes hauled, although Njall wondered a little at Ulfgeirr's skinned knuckles and blackened eye, and the swollen bite-mark on Nagli's cheek. And in the aftermath of Asny's heat, two of Ingrun's pups had chosen their brothers. Eitri and Harekr had bonded with two of Sigmundr's tithe-mates, and it was clear that Authun was going to choose the third, although he was flirting, coyly, and leading poor Fastvaldr a merry chase.

Njall and Brandr found Sigmundr in the armory, patiently mending torn leathers, with Hroi watching from the open doorway as if to assure himself that the work was done properly. Njall knew the wolfcarls were worried because Hroi had not yet picked a new bond-partner, instead pacing the roundhall and outbuildings as if looking for something he could not find.

Njall and Brandr sat down and began work themselves. After a long silence, Njall said, "What will you do?"

"Stay here," Sigmundr said without surprise or hesitation. "Hrolleif thinks I have another year before I'm too old for a first-bonding."

"Will you try for one of Vigdis' pups, then?" Brandr said and managed to sound casual rather than fiercely jealous.

Sigmundr smiled a little. "I don't think so. Maybe one of Asny's. I thought Eitri and I. . . ." He sighed, and all three boys looked up in surprise as Hroi echoed the sigh.

"Hroi?" said Sigmundr, an odd note in his voice.

The old wolf tilted his head, his ears pricking, his green-gold eyes bright.

Njall and Brandr watched, hardly daring to breathe, as Sigmundr cleared the leather off his lap, stood up, and advanced a couple paces toward the door. He sat down then, hard, more as if his knees had given way than with any intention.

Hroi stood up and came across to him, shoving his massive gray-muzzled head into Sigmundr's hands, demanding plainly to be scratched behind the ears. Sigmundr's smile dawned slowly, but it was so radiant that Njall had to look away, blinking hard.

"You asked the wrong question, Njall," Brandr said into the silence. "It's not what he's going to do, it's what he's going to be named."

෧ᛉ෧

The Stone Sigmundr chose to be named Sokkolfr, and Njall came to realize that in many ways Sokkolfr was lucky to be bonded to Hroi. The old wolf was gray-muzzled, it was true, but he was strong and deft and canny to a fault, and he complemented quiet, thoughtful Sokkolfr very well.

As for Njall—from the time Viradechtis' eyes opened, there was never any doubt whom she would choose.

He sat in a circle with the other tithe-boys on the deerhide rug beside Vigdis' nesting box and watched Hrolleif lift each pup, say its name—Kothran, Viradechtis, Skefill, Griss—and set it in the middle to crawl to whomever it listed, and when Viradechtis crawled to him, he was lost. Utterly, hopelessly lost, as breath-stolen as a child reaching for the moon. She squinted at him with cloudy blue eyes, and—with a glance at Vigdis for permission—he lifted her to his face. She yipped with bold excitement rather than fear, and tried to suckle the tip of his nose until he laughed so hard he was afraid he'd drop her.

"Love at first sight," Grimolfr said, almost sadly; Hrolleif elbowed him hard enough to make him stagger, and came to crouch at Njall's shoulder.

"See if she'll tell you her name," he said, and laid one hand on Njall's shoulder.

It was a comforting touch, and Njall leaned into it. He looked into the pup's blue eyes and frowned. Her speech was a confused jumble of impressions, milk and mother and Hrolleif's big warm hands that smelled of oil and leather, warm puppy bodies and Njall's own warm, gentle hands and his smell, a *good* smell, an alluring smell—

She yipped again, a fierce imperative puppy-bark, and licked his nose.

"I don't think she knows it yet, Hrolleif"—and it was still an effort to call him that, and not *sir*—"but she's hungry."

"Pups that age are always hungry," Hrolleif said. "You'll get used to it. Ask Vigdis her name."

Njall held the puppy close to his chest and looked her mother in the eyes. And Vigdis laughed at him—she was always laughing, that one—and gave him the scent of sun-warmed pine boughs, sharp and clean and full of summer.

From that moment, Viradechtis was his world, and he was hers. When she wasn't terrorizing her littermates, she stuck to Njall's heels, and he had to place her bodily back into the box beside her mother at night before returning to his own bed in the tithe-boys' dormitory. And even then, half the time Brandr wound up shaking him awake on their shared pallet, because he was reaching about him in his sleep.

He knew Vigdis was watching him smugly, and if she were a woman and not a wolf he would have said she was gloating over having found him lurking in the shadows of the stair. Hrolleif was watching him as well, with a quizzical expression, trading frequent, headshaking glances with Grimolfr. None of that could affect Njall's happiness.

Spring gave way to dawning summer, and when the pups were four months old—just as another batch of tithe-boys was being sought for Asny's litter—they were allowed to sleep where they wished. Viradechtis chose to sleep beside Njall, rousting Brand from his place without so much as a by-your-leave. And the tight ache of homesickness in his chest finally lifted for good.

The next afternoon, although Njall's duties were still with the tithe-boys, Ulfgeirr came to tell him that his sleeping quarters were being switched to the roundhall, for the sake of Viradechtis and the other boys.

It wasn't too strange to sleep in a huge hall full of snoring men and wolves who whined and ran in their sleep. It wasn't so very different from the boys' dormitory, although much bigger, and besides, Viradechtis was there beside him, her blunt puppy muzzle buried in Njall's armpit, her thoughts clearer and sharper to him with every passing day. Even the sounds of sex, whether solitary or companionable, were familiar, and he contributed his share. He missed Alfleda; none of the wolfheall's thrall-women took his fancy, and he was reluctant to go into the village, afraid that the villagers would react as Alfleda had and scorn him. In any event, with Viradechtis too small to follow him he wasn't going anywhere, which left him alone with a restless drive that would *not* be sublimated into weapons practice or patrolling and tracking lessons.

He'd somehow expected the wolves would speak in words, and of course they didn't; that had been a child's fancy and foolishness. What Viradechtis gave him when her gold-velvet eyes met his was a sense of humor so sharp it was almost malicious, coupled to a thousand details of scent, of hearing, of the world moving around her and the pack moving through the world. He was never certain, exactly, when the bond happened—not like Sokkolfr and Hroi—but soon he couldn't remember a time when he hadn't been able to reach out with his heart and feel his wolf-sister's attention: warm, wry, and deadly sardonic.

It was an idyll, a precious summer where he threw himself into his wolf and the business of the wolfheall and his friendship with Brandr Quick-Tongue and the Stone Sokkolfr—and the entirely surprising mentorship that grew up between himself and Hrolleif, starting that night in the circle by the birthing den.

☙❧

The summer evenings stretched almost to morning, the sky light even after the sun went down. Njall walked with Viradechtis in the half-light, letting her run because it was not fair to the older wolves to bring her like a whirlwind into the roundhall when all they wanted to do was sleep. Sometimes Brandr came with them, although mostly these days Brandr was spending his free time as near to Viradechtis' littermates as he could get. Sokkolfr and Hroi would walk with them, too, and Njall was grateful to Hroi for teaching Viradechtis.

"It's his nature," Sokkolfr said. "He is very well suited to be the brother of a housecarl."

"Is that what you want to be?"

Sokkolfr was silent for a time. "I don't know if I would be any good with the tithe-boys," he said at last. "But I like orderliness."

"I think you'd be just fine with the tithe-boys. You wouldn't do it like Ulfgeirr, but that's not the same thing as doing it badly."

And then Hroi and Viradechtis came back from a long elaborate game of chase, their sides heaving, very pleased with themselves, and Njall said, feeling a great warm glow of happiness spread through him at the words, "Let's go home."

He liked walking with company, but he most frequently went out alone, just he and Viradechtis and his thoughts. On the solstice-eve, he found himself positively glad to escape from other people, for the wolfheall was like a kicked-over anthill with preparations for the solstice-fest, and Njall had been ordered about and snapped at and teased—Not-Jarl, Gunnarson—all day. And he had thinking he wanted to do.

Grimolfr had said two days before, when Njall was helping him scrape deerhides for leather, "Have you thought about your name yet?"

"My name? But I'm not . . . she isn't. . . ."

"Don't try and tell me you're not bonded, pup," Grimolfr said.

"I thought she had to be older."

"Bitches bond earlier—unless they're froward, as some bitches are. But that's not your little girl."

"No," Njall agreed helplessly, happily, and half-grown Viradechtis looked up from where she was wrestling with her father; for a second Njall was enveloped in pine-boughs-in-sunlight and knew that that was her way of saying: *Mine*. Skald and Grimolfr traded a look, and Grimolfr burst out laughing, a thing which Njall had never witnessed before.

"Well, that's settled," the wolfjarl said.

So Njall had been trying to think of a name. He'd asked Brandr, whose suggestions made his face burn, and Sokkolfr, who said, "It's *your* name, Njall." And out here, just himself and his sister, feeling peace well up and spill over, it occurred to him that the sensible thing to do was ask her.

She thought the question extremely funny. But she cooperated, enough that he got a strange, momentary, dizzying view of what he looked like through her eyes, precarious and fragile and pale, skin and hair and eyes all pale, like snow, like ice.

Oh, thought Njall. *Isolfr.*

It was, in the end, as simple as that.

Njall walked back to the wolfheall pensively—although not so pensively that he did not lose a good stretch of time to a game of Viradechtis' invention—and when he reached the courtyard, he dodged two tithe-boys, five wolfcarls and their brothers, three thralls, and a flock of goats, entered the roundhall, rich with the scent of Jorveig's cooking, crossed through to the back and opened the door to Grimolfr's records-room, which was also the wolves' birthing den. And there, on the deer-hide rug—

He stopped. Stared, pressing one hand instinctively over his mouth to keep from making a sound. Stepped back and closed the door, as quietly as he could.

And turned and fled.

He found Brandr in the bathhouse, along with the usual assortment of wolfcarls and tithe-boys, and dragged him into the back corner where they could talk without being overheard.

"What?" said Brandr. "You're white as new snow."

"I saw . . . I didn't mean to . . ." He swallowed hard. "Hrolleif and Grimolfr . . ." And because he couldn't quite bring himself to use any crude word for it, he dropped his voice to a whisper and said, "*Mating.*"

Brandr snorted laughter, and then again at the look on Njall's face. "What were you, born yesterday? Hrolleif's lucky Vigdis is konigenwolf, and he only has to lie down for Grimolfr. Some of the other bitches breed to six or seven dogs in a heat."

Njall didn't say, *But Hrolleif was on top—*

"You'd better get used to the idea," Brandr said. "'Cause that's going to be you in another couple years."

"Thank you, Brandr," Njall said, as witheringly as he could, and set himself with shaking hands to clean away the day's grime, wondering *Can I do that? Could I lie down for that?*

It was in the long lazy hours after supper, while Viradechtis and her littermates and Ingrun's three, who were still young enough for puppy-games, went tearing around roundhall and courtyard, knocking over wolfcarls when they could and swarming Skald every second lap, that Hrolleif came up to where Njall was sitting, helping Sokkolfr comb through Hroi's dense coat looking for ticks, and said, "Njall, do you have a moment?"

"Go on, Njall," Sokkolfr said. "Hroi and I can manage, can't we, brother?" And Hroi sighed happily and rested his head on Sokkolfr's thigh in a way that would send the leg to sleep in a matter of minutes.

Njall got up, feeling his stomach knot. Viradechtis was there, pressing against him, bumping her broad head up under his hand, and he sank his fingers into her ruff and was comforted.

He followed Hrolleif through the drowsy cheerful crowd of the werthreat and into the records-room, where Vigdis thumped her tail in greeting. Hrolleif sat down on the bench along the inner wall and motioned Njall to sit next to him. "Vigdis says you saw, earlier."

The blush felt like fire. Viradechtis dropped her head across his lap and he looked down, watching his own fingers worry gently at her ears. "I'm sorry. I didn't mean to—"

"Nothing to be sorry for," Hrolleif said. "We were due to have this conversation anyway. Njall—oh. Grimolfr said he spoke to you about choosing your name. Have you?"

"Yes," and really it would be easier if he just burst into flames right now. Died of embarrassment.

Viradechtis disapproved emphatically, nudging her head into his stomach in a way that she knew perfectly well made it hard for him to breathe.

"That's why . . . I was coming to tell Grimolfr . . ."

"Ah," said Hrolleif and courteously did not laugh. Vigdis had no such scruples, but Njall found he didn't mind her laughter; it was so much like her daughter's. "Then what is your name to be, Njall Gunnarson?"

Njall thought, oddly and very clearly, that that was the last time he would ever be identified as his father's son.

Everything for the wolfheall.

"Isolfr," he said.

"Isolfr," Hrolleif repeated thoughtfully, weighing the name in his mouth. "Yes." He extended one hand, broad, callused, and after a moment's blank confusion, Isolfr returned his grip. And dared to look up at Hrolleif and return his smile. "We'll name you tonight then."

It was a quick ceremony, no different from the naming of a babe. A sprinkle of water, the shape of Thor's hammer marked on one's forehead, and one was born again. A brother to wolves, now, and no longer a wolf-less man.

Pleased, Viradechtis let him breathe again unencumbered by wolf-skull. Hrolleif said, "You've got a strong-willed wolf there."

"Yes."

"She'll make up her own mind on most things, you'll find," Hrolleif said, and traded a loving look with Vigdis. "And you need to be prepared."

"Yes," Isolfr said and swallowed dryly.

"You've heard stories, I take it. So had I, when I became brother to Vigdis. But how much do you *know*?"

"I . . ." He was blushing again. Viradechtis was pushing love at him, and Vigdis got up and came over to put one heavy paw on his knee, even as she leaned into Hrolleif.

"Vigdis says I am not to bully you." And Isolfr caught a sharp picture of a red wolf shaking a white wolf puppy by its scruff. "Isolfr, there is nothing to be ashamed of, no matter what your father may have had to say on the subject." When Isolfr looked up, Hrolleif smiled rather ruefully. "We've heard a great deal over the years about Lord Gunnarr's opinion of what he calls the 'goings-on' in the wolfheall. Do you agree with him?"

"N-no," Isolfr said. "I mean, I don't know. But . . ." He watched his own fingers stroking across Viradechtis' broad head and down into her ruff. Then he looked up defiantly and said, "She's worth it. Whatever it takes, I can do it."

"You're frightened."

"If . . . you won't think me womanish to say it." Hrolleif's eyebrow arched under his braids, and Isolfr regretted his choice of words immediately. "I mean—"

"Hush, lad. It's not so terrible as all that." Hrolleif came to him, and threw an arm around his shoulders, and squeezed hard. "No one's daft enough to throw a virgin boy—"

"I'm not—!"

"Oh I'm sure you've bedded your share of willing maids. But have you ever bedded a man?"

Isolfr shook his head, and wished he could stop blushing.

"Nor ever thought of it, I reckon. Then you are virgin in this, and *no one* is daft enough to throw a virgin boy into the middle of a mating frenzy, no, nor a virgin wolf neither. She won't come to heat for another year"—a glance traded with Vigdis, and Isolfr looked down into Viradechtis' eyes and breathed in warmth and wood-smoke, comfort, dried herbs by the hearth—"and we don't breed a bitch her first season. It's not good for them when they're still growing; they need that strength for their own teeth and bones."

"What do you do with them, then?" Hrolleif's arm was warm around his shoulders, but Isolfr couldn't fight back the image of his body, straining so hard that every muscle, every vein stood out in sculpted relief, poised over Grimolfr's while Grimolfr arched himself up into it like a man in a seizure. It shortened his breath in his throat with something that felt like fear but wasn't, exactly, and Isolfr—not really meaning to—tugged away.

"Isolate them," Hrolleif said, and didn't let him pull free. "At first. And when they are older and a little more experienced, and the bitch is ready for a litter, we send them away with another young pair, to learn." He grinned, and turned Isolfr by the shoulders to face him. "You won't be expected to contend with the pack until you've had some experience, Isolfr. And Viradechtis will take care of you. Even in heat, she'd not risk her brother."

Somehow, Viradechtis wasn't between them, anymore. Instead, her mother had her backed into the corner by the fire, and was determinedly washing her ear. Isolfr's breath came a little easier, but not quite smoothly. Hrolleif's eyes were sun-faded blue; he squinted inside lines carved by the glare of sun on snow. "What you have to ask, ask it."

"How are we supposed to . . . gain experience?"

Hrolleif smiled, and pressed a kiss to his mouth—chaste, whiskery, but it nevertheless left Isolfr's lips tingling. "Time enough for that when you and the little girl are older, I think."

⟨◈⟩

The next morning started badly, with a sudden, snarling, bloody fight between Vigdis and Egill. Pups and tithe-boys fled to the sides of the hall, while Hrolleif and Thurulfr, both tight-lipped and sweating, stood from their seats and stared, not at their wolves, but at each other. Isolfr felt them in the pack-sense, through the anger-fear-jealousy-greed miasma that Vigdis and Egill were throwing off. Egill and Thurulfr were incomers, traded from another wolfheall; they had been scarcely longer in Nithogsfjoll than the boys of Sokkolfr's tithe. And Egill was a dominant male—not as dominant as Skald, but clearly too dominant for Vigdis' liking. Isolfr couldn't follow all of it, but he got, very clearly, Hrolleif warning off Skald and Ingrun and Asny and the other wolves who were ready to join in to support Vigdis. And just as clearly, Thurulfr warning away the wolves who might have supported Egill. It was stark in Thurulfr's mind that the konigenwolf could kill Egill, and she would if she felt she had to. He had seen it happen in Bravoll wolfheall. Isolfr shuddered away from the memory, vivid in the pack-sense, and saw that Vigdis and Egill had come to a halt, Vigdis with her teeth brushing Egill's throat, Egill, bleeding from long gashes on his flanks, whining submissively, his head turned aside. It was a long, long moment before Hrolleif said, very gently, "Sister," and Vigdis looked up at him for all the world like a man jerking alert after his mind has wandered. Her ears came forward, and she let Egill up, and the werthreat collectively began breathing again.

Isolfr noticed that before Egill would let his brother catch him to doctor his wounds, he cuffed, subdued, and mounted Ingjaldr. And felt it in the pack-sense, that Egill accepted the konigenwolf's authority, but that did not mean he would let other wolves dominate him.

The day did not improve from there, with Svanrikr Un-Wise wondering loudly how long it would be, now that Viradechtis was bonded, before she came into her first heat. Although it helped a little that Brandr told him to shut up. Then, that afternoon, as Isolfr was helping Ulfgeirr with some of the most recalcitrant cattle either of them had ever seen, Johvatr came skidding around the corner of the outbuilding and said, "Nj—Isolfr. Lord Grimolfr wants you at the front gates."

Ulfgeirr's red brows drew down, but he said, "Go along, lad. Don't keep the wolfjarl waiting."

Isolfr went, Viradechtis at his heels, and he was not even within sight of the gates when he knew what the trouble was.

His father.

Gunnarr had a warleader's voice, trained to carry, a great bass roar, and every word was as sharp and distinct as ice picks through Isolfr's eardrums. "I won't have it, Lord Grimolfr! I won't have my boy made a bitch for men twice his age!"

And Grimolfr's answer, laudably calm, "He has bonded, Lord Gunnarr. The choice is no longer yours to make."

"Bonded to a bitch! And you knew it would happen! You *let* it happen!"

"I could hardly stop it," Grimolfr said, very dryly.

"He's my *son*, Grimolfr," Gunnarr said, and Isolfr stopped dead in his tracks, horrified at the note of pleading in his father's voice. "The heir of my house."

"He is not your only son."

A beat of hard silence. Gunnarr said, "He is my firstborn. And no nithling fit for your perversions, wolfjarl. Let him go."

Isolfr swallowed hard, realizing simultaneously that nothing Grimolfr could say would appease his father, while it was amazing that Gunnarr had not already provoked the wolfjarl's unamiable temper, *and* that the resolution of this nightmarish situation was squarely on his shoulders. He was the bone of contention.

Viradechtis liked the thought of bones. Isolfr, waking up quite sharply to the awareness that Viradechtis' presence would make an already horrible situation just that much worse, told her to find Sokkolfr and Hroi, and they would get her a bone. She hesitated, clearly torn, and Isolfr was touched at her desire, however unformulated it was, to protect him. But he said, again, *Go,* and assured that it was what he wanted, she went, carrying the thought of *bone* with her like a flag.

Isolfr squared his shoulders and stepped forward, around the bulk of the hall, just as Grimolfr was saying with awful politeness, "I am afraid you misjudge the situation, werjarl. I do not hold your son prisoner, nor—" He broke off when he saw Isolfr and said, only the faintest lightness of relief smoothing his furrowed brow, "But here is Isolfr now."

"Njall," Gunnarr said.

"Isolfr," Isolfr said, coming to stand beside his wolfjarl. "It is as Lord Grimolfr says, Father. He does not keep me here against my will."

His father stared at him, his face dark with anger. "It is true, then? You *wish* to be a bitch for these men? You know what they will do to you?"

Isolfr thought of Hrolleif's kiss and felt himself blush. But he said, as steadily as he could, "Father, you do not speak fairly."

"I don't speak *fairly*? Tell me, Njall, what *fairness* is there in this choice you have made? What honor? What *manhood*?"

Halfrid had told him he would have to choose his honor, and Isolfr felt that choice now like the wrench of a dislocated joint. He thought, miserably, that his father's idea of honor was too small, too confined. He could not hold honor as his father saw it without dishonoring himself, without dishonoring the wolfheall and the wolves. He said, "My name is Isolfr, Father. And I do not believe that any of my brothers in the werthreat is less of a man than you are."

"Well spoken, Isolfr," Grimolfr said, with a clout on the shoulder that nearly knocked him over.

Gunnarr's glare was murder, and it took all Isolfr's will not to flinch. He couldn't have done it if it hadn't been for Grimolfr beside him, and Grimolfr's obvious pride in him.

"You refuse to honor your duty to your father?"

"Our house owes duty to the wolfheall," Isolfr said. "That does not change merely because it is . . ." He hesitated, searching for a word. "Distasteful."

It was the wrong word. Probably, there was no right word. Gunnarr said, his voice icy, the tone that Isolfr had learned to dread in babyhood, "You dare to lecture me on duty, boy?"

"Father, I—"

"No." Gunnarr cut him off with a sharp gesture. "If you wish to bring shame upon me, upon your mother, I cannot prevent you. *Isolfr*. But understand. If you do not leave with me now, as you ought, you will not be welcome in the keep. I do not want you corrupting your brother and sister."

"Then I will abide by your wishes, Father," Isolfr said. "But I will not leave the wolfheall."

"To think that such a creature could come from my loins," Gunnarr said, turned his head, and spat in disgust. He said to Grimolfr, "Good day, wolfjarl," and turned and strode away.

Isolfr shut his eyes against the sting of tears, swallowed hard.

"Lord Gunnarr does not mince words," Grimolfr said, and Isolfr was grateful for the detachment in his voice, grateful that he was not offering sympathy or concern.

"No," he said, and they both ignored the wobble in his voice. "He never has."

THRee

At the solstice, there was feasting. Two days later, after Jorveig the cook had dispensed heroic quantities of her herbal tisane to counteract the heroic quantities of ale the werthreat had consumed and the hangovers were mostly memory, a man and a wolf Isolfr did not know staggered weary and footsore to the heall, the man tall and red-haired, the wolf angle-shouldered, odd-eyed, and leaving red-splotched prints on the snow.

By a trick of fate, Isolfr was the first to see them. He and Viradechtis had been departing on one of their restless rambles, and he had seen the dark shape against the drifts as he crossed the meadow, the man breaking trail for the limping wolf. Isolfr had bolted back into the wolfheall, uncertain if the strangers were friend or foe, and dragged Hrolleif and Ulfgeirr from table to attend it.

Man and wolf—Vethulf and Kjaran were their names—had come

without stopping from the wolfheall at Arakensburg, with news that would not wait. The village of Jorhus had been overrun by trolls.

Grimolfr gathered the werthreat together in the roundhall to tell them; Isolfr sat next to the Stone Sokkolfr, the dense heat of trellwolf bodies pressing against them, and listened as Vethulf described, grimly, the complete annihilation of a village of two hundred souls.

No survivors.

It answered the question of why the long patrols during Asny's heat had found so few trolls, and Grimolfr said frankly, bitterly, "We are stretched too thin. There are too few wolfheallan, and no way to remedy that except by the passing of time." Isolfr gulped and told himself it was coincidence that Grimolfr's eyes met his just then. But he couldn't believe it.

"Then what shall we do?" said Randulfr. "We must do *something*."

"Long patrols," Grimolfr said, and nodded to the red-haired man sitting on the hearth with his odd-eyed wolf, cupping a horn of ale in his hands now that he had finished speaking. "Vethulf Kjaransbrother brings, along with news, the counsel of the Arakensbergthreat. The wolfjarl of Arakensberg says, and I agree with him, that we must cover more ground as best we can. You will all be going out, two weeks at a time. A week out and a week back."

There was uneasy muttering among the wolfcarls. A week was farther than most of them had ever been from the wolfheall, certainly since their bonding. Hrolfmarr, Kolli's brother, asked, "How many to a patrol?"

"Ten wolves and their brothers. Two patrols out at a time, two remaining here. We cannot leave the wolfheall unguarded, either." The muttering darkened as the wolves thought vividly of Asny's unborn pups; the hair on the back of Isolfr's neck rose as Nagli and Arngrimr and the other possible fathers of those pups began to growl.

"Peace, brothers," Grimolfr said, and Skald seconded strongly. "We will draw up the rosters today; the first two patrols will leave tomorrow morning."

Dismay colored the pack-sense.

"The jarls are frightened, and rightly so. We have sworn to protect them, we of the Wolfmaegth, and that is what we must do."

◌⳿◌

Grimolfr and Hrolleif were very careful about balancing the patrols between older wolves and younger. Isolfr noticed that Sokkolfr and Hroi counted as "older" for these purposes, and supposed with rather wry amusement that Hroi could be depended on to keep more boys than just his own out of trouble. He himself was not on the first two rosters, and although he knew he would feel foolish and childish for it, he could not keep from going to Grimolfr to ask why.

"Viradechtis isn't big enough," Grimolfr said, as if that should be the end of it.

"We're bonded," Isolfr argued. "I'm part of the werthreat."

"And that is why you will be taking on some of Hrolleif's duties when he and Vigdis go out in two weeks' time."

Isolfr felt his jaw sag.

"Isolfr," Grimolfr said, putting a hand on his shoulder. "Your little girl has more promise than I've seen in a pup any time these past ten years. Vigdis throws good wolves, and good bitches, but this time I think she's thrown better than good. She's thrown *true*. You and Viradechtis will have to patrol, of course, and show your strength, and learn the pack. But later, when we have a better idea of what awaits. We can't risk her without intelligence."

"You think she's . . ."

"She'll be konigenwolf of her own pack in another few years," Grimolfr said. "I didn't mean to tell you yet. But you aren't the sort to get a swelled head, and Hrolleif says he's been talking to you about what you're going to face as her brother."

"A little, but he didn't say anything about . . ."

"Don't worry about it now," Grimolfr said, without his usual gruffness. "She's young, you're young. She won't even come into her first heat for another year, most likely." He turned away, for the wolfjarl was a man whose duties rarely allowed him to rest, adding over his shoulder, "And talk to Hrolleif."

Isolfr didn't think he would be able to keep from worrying, but talk to Hrolleif he could and did.

"Grimolfr said . . . her own pack?"

"We need to establish new wolfheallan," Hrolleif said. They were taking inventory in the armory. "And it's not every bitch who can be a konigenwolf. Asny, for instance. She's a fine wolf and bids to be a fine mother to her pups, but she'll never be able to stand up to her mother. And Ingrun and Kolgrimna wouldn't be here if they could be konigen-wolves themselves."

"I don't understand."

"You will," Hrolleif said dryly. "Isolfr, who rules the wolfheall?"

"Grimolfr," Isolfr said reflexively. "The wolfjarl."

"Meaning Skald is the leader of this pack?"

"No," Isolfr said, and then his mind caught up with his mouth. He said slowly, "Vigdis rules the pack."

"Yes. She is konigenwolf."

"But you . . ."

"I am Vigdis' brother," Hrolleif said simply. "As Grimolfr stands to the men of the wolfheall, the wolfjarl, so I stand to the wolves, the wolf-sprechend. Or, rather, so Vigdis stands, and I stand at her side as Skald stands at Grimolfr's. It is a weaving, like a net, do you see?"

"I . . . yes, I think so."

"It will become clearer to you as Viradechtis becomes older. She's still a pup, and pups are granted a good deal of license. I've seen you watching the men in the roundhall, and someday you will tell me what you have observed. But for a while, try watching the wolves."

⚬⟊⚬

Try watching the wolves. A simple command, and one that Isolfr intended to follow, but time to do it was suddenly in very short supply. He spent his waking hours glued to Hrolleif's side, soaking up the knowledge of everything the wolfsprechend did in a day's span and trying to understand *how* he did it. It wasn't the everyday tasks of household management—those fell to Ulfgeirr and Jorveig, the housecarl and the mistress of the kitchens—and it wasn't the choice of where they would patrol and fight and when they would claim tithe, because Grimolfr—with the counsel of the werthreat and the consent of the wolfthreat—made those decisions.

What Vigdis did was keep order among the wolfthreat, and what Hrolleif did was make sure that no detail of the wolfheall's daily rhythm escaped Grimolfr's attention. No matter what task was at hand, he was there, dirtying his hands at butchering pigs and at raising outbuildings, talking to everyone from the blacksmith to the milkmaids in the village—and it was to Hrolleif, and Vigdis, that man and wolf alike came with complaints.

It *was* very like what Isolfr's mother did in his father's keep, but he put that thought aside, and comforted himself with the warm breadth of Viradechtis' shoulder and the strength of her neck when she shoved her head against his hip. She was Vigdis' daughter, and—now that Isolfr was looking for it he could see—Vigdis was a konigenwolf among konigen-wolves, queen of queens. Even the top wolves of other wolfheallan de-ferred to her when their brothers came to meet with Grimolfr and plan the defense of the wolfless men, and that meant, Isolfr realized slowly, that the wolfjarls of those wolfheallan deferred to Grimolfr and Hrolleif. *Strength grows from the pack*, he understood, and concentrated harder.

He was a jarl's son. He had been raised to lead men.

Surely he could learn to lead wolves as well.

He fell onto his pallet beside Sokkolfr's in dull exhaustion every night, and it was half a day's length before he learned that Brandr Quick-Tongue had bonded the gray-mantled ivory dog-cub Kothran and be-come Frithulf—he only found out, in fact, because the new Frithulf Quick-Tongue pitched his pallet next to Isolfr's, grinning at the startled look on Isolfr's face.

Blood and determination did not matter. A fortnight was not enough time; he was not ready to stand in Hrolleif's boots when the Old Wolf and his sister made ready to go. It was high summer; the woods were full of game. The wolfsprechend need not carry much beyond his axe, a knife, his tinder, and dry socks.

Still, Hrolleif clasped Isolfr about the shoulders before he went, and Vigdis pinned Viradechtis with a halfway playful growl. "Keep care of my pack, cub," the wolfsprechend said, and squeezed a little harder before he stepped back.

Isolfr's fear tightened his throat; he knew better than to wish them luck. "Keep an eye out for tithe-boys," he said, as if he wasn't a bare finger's breadth removed from a tithe-boy himself. "Ulfgeirr says Asny's packed with pups. He can feel six heads, maybe seven."

"Fall litters are always larger," Hrolleif said, and clouted Isolfr's shoulder before he went. Isolfr closed his eyes and turned his head away, so there was no way he could accidentally watch Hrolleif out of sight.

It was unlucky.

❦

Within hours of Hrolleif's departure, Isolfr discovered the difference between a wolfsprechend and a boy pretending to be a wolfsprechend. He had no authority with either wolfthreat or werthreat, and wolves and men were more or less polite about letting him know it. He had Grimolfr and Skald to back him up, but he was painfully aware that Hrolleif didn't need that, that it was *Hrolleif* who backed up *Grimolfr*.

That became more and more apparent as the days crawled past, and Isolfr began to notice certain men in the werthreat eyeing Grimolfr with a hard, speculative look that he did not like at all. And their brothers began scuffling with Skald more and more often, in encounters that sometimes looked like play and sometimes did not.

And Isolfr had not the first idea what to do about it.

He kept remembering, miserably, what Hrolleif had said: *Keep care of my pack, cub.* He was failing; he knew he was failing, and it was only made worse by the fact that Grimolfr was not looking to him for help. He didn't want to be indebted to a boy, and Isolfr understood that, but he also understood that by *not* relying on him, Grimolfr was showing the werthreat that he, Isolfr, was *not* wolfsprechend and did not have to be regarded.

He lay awake most of one night, listening to Viradechtis' contented snuffling breathing on one side and the twinned snores of Frithulf and Kothran on the other, and came to a reluctant but inescapable conclusion. He had to talk to Grimolfr. Privately.

He had paid careful attention all that day, noticing which wolves seemed to be intent on turning play-fighting with Skald into the real thing, and admiring the way that Skald kept sidestepping the point where that would have to happen. They would gang up on him if given the excuse, and even the massive Skald couldn't hold his own against three or four or five wolves. But if he could keep them from making it serious. . . . Isolfr wondered despairingly what Grimolfr imagined he was going to do. Were the wolfjarl and his brother just planning to play a waiting game until Hrolleif and Vigdis returned?

While the discipline of wolfthreat and werthreat crumble to nothing around them.

Arngrimr seemed to be the most aggressive of the lot. His brother Yngvulf, called the Black, was a man Isolfr did not know particularly well. Although the werthreat was the werthreat, there were definite factions within it, and Yngvulf was one of the men who looked to Kolgrimna's brother Hringolfr Left-Hand. And no matter what Hrolleif said about the wolfthreat giving license to pups, Isolfr would have had to be blind and deaf to the pack-sense not to know that Kolgrimna disliked Viradechtis intensely. Isolfr was not welcome in Hringolfr's circle.

Kolgrimna was a means to an end; Arngrimr had designs on Skald's place as Vigdis' mate, and a number of the lesser wolves backed him. And Glaedir—a great yellow-eyed silver creature with a mask and shoulder-mantle like smudged charcoal, not yet grown into his adult bone and muscle—was not ready to tackle Skald on his own yet, but if Arngrimr moved, Glaedir would back him. And if Glaedir moved, black Mar would fight him, in part to support Skald, and in part because Mar, Skjaldwulf Snow-Soft's brother, was ambitious, and Glaedir and Mar were jockeying for the same space among Kolgrimna's suitors. And if Mar moved against Glaedir, Isolfr knew which wolves would follow him, which wolves would see their own chances. One of his father's vassals had shown him once the trick to building walls without mortar, how the stones fit together—and how, if you moved one stone, the whole wall came down. The wall was the threat, and the stones were men and wolves.

Although Isolfr knew it was stupid, he was hurt by Glaedir's eagerness. Glaedir's brother Eyjolfr was Randulfr's lover, Glaedir one of the sires of Ingrun's litter, and it seemed wrong that he and Glaedir should move against Grimolfr and Skald, when neither Randulfr nor Ingrun would dream of doing such a thing.

But that was thinking like a wolfless man, and useless besides. He thought Randulfr might step in if things got too unpleasant, but watching the wolves had taught him that Ingrun and Kolgrimna had only an uneasy truce; if Randulfr tried to intervene between Eyjolfr and Yngvulf the Black, he might as easily precipitate a fight between the bitches as prevent a fight between the males.

This is what the wolfsprechend is for, Isolfr thought, rising in the early-morning quiet and making his way to the bathhouse, Viradechtis padding sleepily at his heels. *And this is why the wolfheall must* have *a wolfsprechend.* Because the politics of the wolfthreat were the politics of the werthreat as well, and Isolfr could not believe that he had taken so long to understand it.

He bathed with grim thoroughness. A few wolfcarls were beginning to come in as he finished, rubbing the sleep from their eyes and making the sort of early-morning conversation that Isolfr usually found comforting and now found almost unbearable. He knew that Grimolfr would be awake and in the records-room, making his plans for the day.

He left the bathhouse, let Viradechtis lick the moisture off his back as she loved to do, dried himself, dressed. Plaited his hair as befitted a man of the werthreat. And went, not happily, to talk to Grimolfr.

⟨◦⟩

Grimolfr was waiting for him. Isolfr wasn't sure *how* he knew that Grimolfr was waiting—the headache tingle of the pack-sense, his own awareness of Skald's awareness of his presence in the passageway before he opened the hide-hung door—but he was unsurprised to find both Grimolfr's dark eyes and Skald's sun-orange ones already trained on him as he came through the door, Viradechtis at his side.

Urging him, in fact: she was already a bit of a bully, and she nudged the door out of his hand and swung it closed herself while Grimolfr watched with his brows crawling up his forehead.

And then that gaze switched back to Isolfr, and Isolfr froze like a rabbit under the shadow of a hawk, waiting for Grimolfr to speak. The silence twisted between them, and Isolfr clenched his hands together behind his back. It was how he would have stood before his father when expecting punishment, and as soon as he realized that, he forced his hands to fall naturally at his thighs, squared his shoulders, and drew a calming breath. Grimolfr still did not speak, but waited expectantly, patient as a wolf.

Patient as any wolf except Viradechtis, that was; the bitch puppy yawned sharply in the continued silence and plopped into a sit, curling her brush around Isolfr's ankles and leaning heavily against his calf and thigh.

Chagrined, Isolfr glanced down at her, and caught her sharp eyes laughing up at him out of her ruddy, black-masked face. She shook her striped ruff into a semblance of order, and leaned more heavily, her every gesture betraying profound boredom. Isolfr snorted, and when he looked back at Grimolfr, was comforted to find one corner of the wolfjarl's mouth twitching upward. "She makes her opinion known," Isolfr said, apologetically, and Grimolfr rewarded his feeble effort with a chuckle.

"She wouldn't be a konigenwolf-in-waiting if she didn't. Sit, Isolfr. The tale in your eyes looks a long one in the telling."

Blushing, Isolfr hooked a three-legged stool away from the wall and sat. That it was Hrolleif's usual chair only made him feel smaller and less prepared. He took a deep breath, Viradechtis' head draped heavily across his knee, and busied his hands on her ears as she groaned and leaned into him. "I'm worried about the wolfthreat."

Grimolfr chewed his lip and, when it became evident that Isolfr couldn't make his voice heard without prompting, nodded and said, "Continue."

It took less time to spill the whole slippery tale than Isolfr had realized it would, and when he stopped, he was embarrassed by the paucity of his information. ". . . I'm sorry," he finished. "I don't know any more. But I think they'll move against Skald soon. Arngrimr and Glaedir are both ambitious, and I don't think he can stand against both of them—"

Skald shook out his ruff and dropped to his elbows, ears pricked. Isolfr looked at the big wolf and spread his hands apologetically.

"What do you think set this off, Isolfr?"

For a moment, he could fantasize it was Skald talking. Certainly, the gray wolf's quizzical expression fit the question. Isolfr sighed and looked back at Grimolfr. "Hrolleif and Vigdis being away for so long."

Grimolfr frowned. "They've been on long patrols before."

"But not—oh." He bit his tongue, and then, knowing the rule of the werthreat, forced himself to continue before Grimolfr could gesture him impatiently on. "But not with a new konigenwolf in the wolfheall."

Grimolfr's lip curled up again. "Correct. So what are you going to do about it?"

"That's the problem, Grimolfr." Still an effort to say the name. "I don't know what to do, or—"

"You would have done it."

"Aye."

"You will need to know this," Grimolfr said, stretching out his legs, "because someday you will have a wolfjarl of your own to contend with, and it is unlikely that you will be so fortunate as Hrolleif and I are. We were boys together and shield-brothers; we are both heall-bred. I know Hrolleif, and Vigdis knows Skald, as you will not have the luxury of knowing your wolfjarl. Am I plain?"

Isolfr swallowed. *He is telling me I will have to lie down for a stranger, and support him even if I find him repulsive.* "You are plain, wolfjarl."

Grimolfr nodded, and continued. "Vigdis has mated elsewhere in her time, and if Skald were not strong enough to keep her, she might very well again—but it is, you understand, not like men squabbling over a maid when wolves compete for a bitch. A bitch has teeth, and a bitch with a will like Vigdis—or Viradechtis—will not hesitate to put them to a wolf she does not care for, even in her heat."

"Oh." Then he glanced up, eyes wide. "*Oh*. You're saying I should let Viradechtis handle it. Since it's her, as much as her mother, that they—"

"Hope to impress. Yes. Kolgrimna will not like it."

"No," Isolfr said, as much to himself as to Grimolfr. "Kolgrimna won't. But Kolgrimna is not a konigenwolf. What does she hope to gain?"

"Status in the pack, the same as any wolf. She's not a konigenwolf, but that does not stop her from wishing to be one, and Viradechtis threatens her place as second among the bitches. Kolgrimna is top bitch when Vigdis is not here."

"Viradechtis is a puppy."

"Viradechtis"—and Isolfr did not miss Grimolfr's fond glance at the puppy, who had flopped onto her side and was unceremoniously chewing the webbing between her toes, moaning and mumbling under her breath—"is a very unusual puppy."

Isolfr rocked back on the stool, but his wolf had his foot pinned under her shoulder. "You're saying Viradechtis leads a faction, as surely as Kolgrimna or Skald."

"I'm saying that if it is obvious that Viradechtis favors her sire, the wolves will understand that there is nothing to be gained by attempting to unseat him. And the ambitious males will be content to bide their time until she is older, because when Viradechtis founds her own pack, she will look favorably on the dogs who have impressed her." Grimolfr coughed against the back of his hand. "So, you see, it's not what you do, so much, as what Viradechtis does. Or doesn't do. But she's inexperienced, and she needs your help to read the werthreat and the wolfthreat. You must teach her, as your father taught you."

They sat silently a time, Isolfr looking thoughtfully at Skald, who looked back at him steadily. Then he said, "I am afraid that if I fail . . ."

"Skald did not make me wolfjarl only because Vigdis favors him," Grimolfr said, resting one hand on his brother's massive head. "But the problem is between Kolgrimna and Viradechtis. It is not of Skald's making, and it is not of his solving."

"Why did you say nothing to me? If I had not come to you, would you have spoken at all?"

"You are not wolfsprechend for this wolfheall," Grimolfr said. "It is not your place to question the wolfjarl." The small room was close with hostility, something that was not quite a growl threading the air between Skald and Viradechtis.

"Then how can I do the wolfsprechend's job?" Isolfr demanded. "They see that you think me only a boy, wolfjarl, that I have no true authority. Hringolfr thinks me as much a puppy as Viradechtis."

"You *are* a puppy." And Isolfr supposed that to a man of Grimolfr's age, a boy who had only just seen his seventeenth summer seemed no older than Viradechtis.

"I am asked to do a grown man's job." He did not look away from Grimolfr, no matter how much he wanted to drop his eyes. The trell-wolves' hackles were up, and the growl was getting clearer. Part of Isolfr's mind was coldly aware that if it came to a fight, Viradechtis would lose and might be hurt badly. But he also knew he had to hold his ground, that if he was to be the brother to a konigenwolf, he would have to learn to face down wolfjarls. "I cannot support you if you do not support me. Grimolfr."

For a moment, it hung in the balance, both wolves showing their teeth, Grimolfr's face stony, unreadable. And then the wolfjarl looked away and Skald's ears came up.

"I do not look to take Hrolleif's place," Isolfr said. "But he asked me to look after the pack in his absence, and I wish to be worthy of his trust."

"And I begin to see that you are," Grimolfr said with a reluctant quirk of a smile. Skald yawned alarmingly and Viradechtis came to lick fondly at her sire's face. "Very well, Isolfr Viradechtisbrother. Do you deal with this problem among the wolfthreat, and I will not treat you as the pup your face shows you."

He stood, rolling tightness out of his shoulders, and said, "Let's go, brother. We've work to do." He stalked out, Skald pacing him.

In the silence after their departure, Isolfr looked at Viradechtis and felt an absurd, helpless surge of love. "We must work too, little sister," he said. "You have learning to do."

She cocked her head at him. He was not perfectly sure how much human conversation she—or any of the wolves—understood, but she thought of Kolgrimna, and he knew she'd followed at least a little.

He had to work slowly, showing her what she was too young to see for herself. He suspected darkly that a mature bitch who had felt the madness of rut would have understood instantly. But Viradechtis *was* a little girl—for all that she showed promise to match her sire's size—and it was hard for her to understand why Kolgrimna should be jealous of Vigdis or why Glaedir should wish to replace Skald. She thought of Vigdis and Skald, he realized, not merely as konigenwolf and consort, but as the parents of the wolfthreat, and that was the surest sign of how close she still was to her babyhood. He'd watched Asny with Vigdis, watched Ingrun and her pups, who were only half a year older than Viradechtis, and knew that this was something that would be changing, and soon. Had maybe begun to change today, even, because Viradechtis would have fought Skald if Isolfr had asked it of her. Fought and lost.

It was easier to make her understand that Kolgrimna was jealous of her. That was only natural, Viradechtis said, and laughed at him with her great gold eyes. And he managed to lead her backwards from that to at least a dim grasp of why Kolgrimna did not like Vigdis.

She understood, more keenly than he had expected, the factions among the wolfthreat, although for her it was a simple matter of which wolves would play with her and which would warn her off. Glaedir played with her willingly—she had vivid, delighted memories of the silver wolf playing keepaway with her in the rain—and Isolfr thought that with him, it would only be a matter of making it plain that Viradechtis did not wish her sire challenged.

But Arngrimr and his wolves would have to be dealt with through Kolgrimna, because it was in large part Kolgrimna's enmity to Viradechtis that made those males restive. *Nothing like an absence to teach the value of something*, Isolfr thought, for he could see plainly, although it was not something he could explain, how Vigdis' absence had caused this upheaval.

Well, that and Kolgrimna being a silly bitch.

Viradechtis agreed with him, which made him laugh, and he said fondly, "Let's find some breakfast."

◦❦◦

he got lucky, finding a place at the long table beside Eyjolfr, an eagle-faced ash-blond who was not so very much older than Isolfr—a young man of twenty-one, rather than a grown boy of seventeen—and inclined to be friendly. *Courting favor with the konigenwolf-in-waiting, indeed,* Isolfr thought and then was ashamed of himself, but he couldn't shake the feeling of expectation in the way Eyjolfr's eyes sometimes lingered—as if Eyjolfr were measuring him, as well.

He enjoyed the conversation with Eyjolfr more than he had expected; Eyjolfr was sharp-eyed, and he had some keen observations about the differences between this wolfheall and the one where he and Glaedir had first bonded. Having learned the politeness of wolves, Isolfr did not mention the wolfjarl and Eyjolfr didn't either. But Viradechtis threw herself willingly into the pack-sense between herself and Glaedir, and Isolfr could feel the knot untangling as he and Eyjolfr spoke and Glaedir and Viradechtis, their hunger sated, wrestled behind their seats. Ambition was not the same as enmity, and Eyjolfr was quick to see that if he had ambitions toward becoming wolfjarl, his odds were better with the young konigenwolf than with the old. Glaedir—Isolfr felt it suddenly, strongly, and knew it was coming from Glaedir himself because Viradechtis could not understand it to relay it—Glaedir wanted to get laid, and if he couldn't get that, then he wanted a fight. Isolfr thought of the long patrol, of fighting trolls and wyverns, and Glaedir seemed at least slightly mollified. If a fight started, he'd be in it, but Isolfr could feel that he'd rather fight trolls than other wolves.

Glaedir was, indeed, *very* young.

Isolfr made no attempt to find Hringolfr and Kolgrimna that afternoon. There were other chores that needed attending to, and Viradechtis still had a puppy's span of attention. But after supper, Isolfr listened to the pack-sense and knew that he could not put it off any longer, no matter how much he wished to. *There will be fights among the wolfthreat,* Hrolleif had told him. *You can't prevent it. But you can prevent it becoming more than just a fight.* He hadn't fully understood that at the time, but he did now. If Arngrimr and Skald lit into each other, that was one thing, and Skald could handle it. It was that underlayer, the dark current running between Kolgrimna and Viradechtis and the absent Vigdis. *That* was what the wolfsprechend—or, in this case, the wolfsprechend's inadequate stand-in—had to divert.

If a trellwolf could be pretty, then Kolgrimna was a pretty wolf. She was smaller than average, fawn-brindled, her eyes pale yellow. Of the four adult bitches in the wolfheall, she was the most inclined to flirt with the males, and Isolfr wondered, now that he was considering her more carefully, how many of the fights among the wolfthreat could be traced back to her. Hringolfr, by contrast, was a bulky, dark man with arresting blue eyes. It was hard to imagine him lying down for anyone. Certainly he did not bow his head readily, and he watched Isolfr's progress through the vaulted darkness of the smoke-scented roundhall with open amusement.

It didn't matter, Isolfr told himself. What was at stake here was not between himself and Hringolfr Left-Hand; he was in fact only approaching the wolfcarl because he wanted what was about to happen to be open, not a secret or a surprise. Viradechtis had had no doubts about how to deal with Kolgrimna, and although it was not what Isolfr would have chosen, he also knew that he would do no favors for either wolfthreat or werthreat by trying to force the wolves to behave like men.

He murmured a polite greeting to Hringolfr and Yngvulf and the other men of their circle.

"What can we do for you, boy?" Hringolfr said.

Do not call me boy, Isolfr thought, but said, "For me? Nothing."

Yngvulf's black brows were drawing down, Hringolfr was opening his mouth to ask what Isolfr thought he meant, when there was a sudden snarl, a rising shriek, and they all, Isolfr included, whipped around to see a wild, rolling, squalling ball of fur and claws and teeth: Viradechtis and the much bigger Kolgrimna. Isolfr turned back, caught Hringolfr's eyes, and stared him down as he started to rise. It was easier than it had been with Grimolfr.

The fight was over quickly, Kolgrimna showing Viradechtis her throat without any real injury being done. And Viradechtis stood over her opponent, her lips drawn back and a snarl rolling like thunder, and glared at Arngrimr and his two closest confederates, who had been considering entering the fray to defend the older bitch.

Isolfr felt, distinctly, what it meant that Viradechtis was a konigenwolf. Because the three males, each of whom outweighed her by a considerable margin, backed away. She swung her head, looking to see if any other challengers wanted to announce themselves, and then simply stepped over Kolgrimna and sauntered off. Kolgrimna was under the bench behind Hringolfr's legs almost the instant Viradechtis began to move.

There was silence, uneasy, awkward. Isolfr looked at Hringolfr and knew he had not made a friend. And then Yngvulf the Black laughed and said delightedly, "Your girl's got spirit, Isolfr!" and extended his hand.

Isolfr clasped hands with him and listened to the pack-sense, felt the shift rippling outward.

Kolgrimna was no longer top bitch in Vigdis' absence. And when Isolfr turned away from Yngvulf and Hringolfr, he saw Eyjolfr watching from a bench along the wall by the rolled furs of the sleeping pallets, speculation warming his cool gray eyes.

❦

After that, even Grimolfr had to admit that Viradechtis could take care of herself. "A troll's not a wolf," he warned Isolfr. "Wolves mostly don't fight wolves to kill." But along with the warning came a promise; Viradechtis and Isolfr would be permitted to join the patrols.

And a fortnight thence, they did.

Eyjolfr had command of the patrol. Viradechtis was the only bitch.

The rest of the pairs ranged in age from Mar and Skjaldwulf, experienced adults, to Frithulf Quick-Tongue and Viradechtis' littermate, white Kothran.

The nights were harsh, the travel exhausting despite skis, and as they journeyed north and toward the inland mountains the summer was no barrier to snow. They slept by day, adapting to the habits of the trolls they hunted. Isolfr managed not to complain chiefly because he had too much pride to be first to whine about cold food and cold weather. Viradechtis relished the snow and the exercise, but as Isolfr huddled in the warmth of his bedroll, his wolf curled sleeping by his side and Frithulf warming his back, he could not help dreaming of his father's fireside and mulled wine served steaming hot.

He wondered at Grimolfr's choice to send black Mar and silver Glaedir on patrol together when they were rivals—and when their rivalry so clearly affected their brothers. Skjaldwulf, spare-framed, coarse-skinned and dark-haired, silent still to the point of being worrisome, might have been Eyjolfr's shadow-twin, and there was no ease between them.

The two men stayed well apart, taking far ends of the line as the patrol moved through the forest, ranging their wolves in opposite directions. Isolfr and Viradechtis kept to the middle of the line, protected from flanking attacks—and, Isolfr slowly came to realize, equidistant between the two most dominant wolves.

Mar was interested in Viradechtis too, although the court he paid was very different from Glaedir's. The older wolf did not flirt or tease or bring Viradechtis dainty tidbits. He hunted, when he hunted, without fanfare, and brought down animals of a size to feed a swift-traveling party without waste or the nuisance of butchering something big. He kept order among the young wolves, and at camp he sometimes came and lay beside Viradechtis, shoulder to shoulder and hip to hip, sharing warmth.

Sometimes she let him stay there, and on those days Glaedir's solicitations became more strenuous.

"Your girl knows her power," Frithulf commented, as he and Isolfr haggled strips of meat from the ribcage of a snow hare Kothran had presented them with. It was the fifth night of the patrol, and they had found neither trolls nor trellsign. Viradechtis was calmly gnawing on the hare's skull, bone splintering under her teeth. Mar had curled around her, his big dark head draped over her haunches, and Skjaldwulf occasionally glanced up from toasting flatbread on a rock at the fireside; he almost seemed amused, but never commented.

"We're quite the commodity," Isolfr answered, wiping grease off his cheek and onto his hand. He thought of his blood-sister and frowned; Kathlin's fate, he knew, wouldn't be so different from his own. Bargained off to seal an alliance or placate an ally, like the girl he would have married if he'd stayed in the keep.

He wouldn't think of Kathlin now.

Isolfr lowered his voice. "Can you really see Skjaldwulf as a wolfjarl?"

Frithulf shrugged. "People surprise you." Then he lifted his chin as Kothran's ears pricked, and the pale wolf started to his feet. "He hears something," he said, unnecessarily.

A moment later, and Viradechtis started up as well, followed in quick succession by the rest of the wolves.

The third time, even the men heard it: a long, eerie ululation, carried on and tattered by the wind. "Trellwolves," Eyjolfr breathed, one hand out to restrain Glaedir.

"Wild wolves," Skjaldwulf agreed, rising to his feet as Mar whined at the back of his throat. The two men exchanged glances, and Skjaldwulf rubbed his beard.

Isolfr could only stand the silence for so long. "Are they coming here?" *Will there be a fight?*

"We're off our heall's range," Eyjolfr said. He looked down and smoothed his wolf's ruffled hackles, then used the same hand to gesture to Skjaldwulf. "We'll sing to them for our passage."

Skjaldwulf nodded. He dropped back into a crouch to retrieve the scorching crispbread, and without looking up from his task he began to sing.

Isolfr had never asked, but he thought the tall, thin man might have chosen his name because he had been a skald's apprentice before he was given in tithe. In any case, as he relaxed his throat and let the music roll out, it rose clear and sweet into the brief winter dawn. Only moments later, the trellwolves joined him, their long, cool voices rising in harmony and counterpoint against the night.

Isolfr couldn't sing. He stayed where he was, and strained to hear if the other pack answered. He cupped his hands to his ears and opened his mouth to concentrate the sound, turning this way and that.

There was no answer, but they were not visited by wolves while they slept, and as much as Isolfr was disappointed not to see them, he had to admit it was all to the good.

Four days after that, they stumbled across trellsign.

⚜

There were three of them, moon-prints of cloven hooves that dented the snow with every step. The tracks were ringed around with feathery traces like the marks of a fox's brush; Eyjolfr said they were from the wolf or musk ox leggings that trolls bound about their calves.

Ten wolves and ten men were more than a match for three trolls. The traces were less than eight hours old, and the patrol skied through the twilit summer night to catch up with the troll band.

They reached them at sunrise.

The trolls had bedded down in a copse of young pine, the trees drifted high enough with snow to serve as a natural windbreak. The men removed their skis, and they and the wolves, moving single file and silently except for the creak of snow under boots and paws, entered the snow-walled corridor the trolls had broken. White breath wreathed faces and froze on whiskers and in beards. Isolfr carried a troll-spear, his axe still bound across his back for the time being, and the leather was cold and slick under his hands when he poked them out of his mittens for a better grip.

The battle was more of a slaughter. Secure in their snowy stronghold and the knowledge that they were far outside the range of any of the wolfheallan, the trolls had posted no guard. Two of them died before they could rise; Mar and two younger wolves savaged the third before any of the men got close enough for axe work, and when it staggered Isolfr transfixed it with his spear.

The shock of the troll's weight knocked him back three steps, even though he had braced the butt against the snow as well as he could manage. The troll bellowed, waving its wickedly curved bronze blade, and charged him up the length of the spear, slaver dripping from gilded tusks.

The haft slipped in his hands, but he held his ground, sidestepping a wild swing of the monster's weapon. The crosspiece would stop it—had to stop it—and if he let go of the spear, there was nothing to keep it from pursuing him.

The crosspiece splintered under the troll's weight. Isolfr ducked, levering the butt of the spear off the ground, trying to force the troll to its knees. It didn't work; the thing's piggy eyes glinted as it took one more step, and then another, driving broken wood into its own flesh.

Viradechtis struck the troll high on the shoulder, a beautiful leap that fouled its weapon arm as she snapped and clung. Her teeth found meat, her back feet scrabbling, leaving long blood-dewed scratches on the troll's flank. But she was too small, half-grown, her weight not enough to overbear it, and the troll twisted under her and passed its weapon to its right hand, hauling back for a looping underhand blow that would sever her spine behind the shoulders if it landed.

Mar's teeth met in the troll's forearm. He dragged its arm back, away, *his* weight enough to bring the creature to its knees. It went down hard, a shudder that Isolfr felt all the way up the length of the spear, and Eyjolfr appeared behind it, his axe buried in its thick, knobbed skull.

The troll toppled forward, the remains of the troll-spear shattering under its weight. Isolfr jumped backwards and fell, landing on his ass, the troll's brains spilling over his boots. Eyjolfr's eyes met his over the body.

"Bravely done," Eyjolfr said, and glanced down.

Before Isolfr could answer, Frithulf and Skjaldwulf called them to look at one of the other corpses: a sow, her massive body strung about with amulets, a pectoral of bones and bronze weighing down her dugs and shoulders.

"A witch," Eyjolfr said, tugging one of her greasy braids up to display the silver and leather ornaments worked into it.

The patterns made Isolfr queasy. He stepped back. "I've never seen a female before," he said.

"Not surprising," Skjaldwulf answered, and then continued, startling Isolfr. It was a rare moment when he strung more than two words together. "I'm fifteen years in the heall, and I've never seen one out of a warren at all."

He fell silent, but the look that passed between him and Eyjolfr said more. *This is a new thing.*

And not a good one.

Isolfr was surprised when Skjaldwulf squeezed his shoulder lightly, in passing, before he went to see about fuel for a pyre on which to burn the troll bodies.

❦

Over the month that followed, Isolfr found himself more and more busy. Ulfgeirr had him drilling both the remaining boys of his own tithe—Svanrikr, Leif, Hlothvinr, and Johvatr—and the eight boys who came as tithe to Asny's pups. As the white nights of summer gave way to early autumn, Isolfr found himself amazed that those boys, fifteen and sixteen—his own age, near enough—seemed to him no more than children. They deferred to him as the dog-pups and the other bitches deferred to Viradechtis, and it was Sokkolfr and Frithulf who sat down with him at meals—and once in a while Eyjolfr and one of his friends, but they were polite, almost courtly, and their wolves made a point of feting Viradechtis. *I am being courted*, Isolfr realized, and it sent a cold, hard shiver up his spine.

Svanrikr Un-Wise was trouble. Viradectis' remaining littermates, the gray brothers Skefill and Griss, were alike as twins and both growing into the image in bone and color of their gigantic sire. And they remained unbonded. That meant four boys to two wolves, and while Isolfr's other three tithe-mates were content to hide their irritation at his luck and Frithulf's, Svanrikr made no bones of the fact that he considered it a personal insult that a jarl's son had been chosen before heall-born, and by a konigenwolf.

Frithulf Quick-Tongue received less resentment. Kothran was the runt of the litter, the palest-coated wolf in the wolfheall, and fine-boned to boot. "He'll never be top wolf," Frithulf said with affected sourness, watching Hroi knock the impudent pup aside when Kothran tried to drag a bone from under Hroi's big paw.

"No," Isolfr said, without looking up from the trencher they still shared, as he was intent on eating fast enough that Frithulf would not get *all* of the duck in late summer gooseberries this time. "He'll be a scout. He has the best nose and ears in the wolfthreat, barring Asny."

Frithulf blinked at him, a ragged hunk of bread forgotten in his hand. "How do you know?"

How do you not know? Isolfr almost asked, but bit his lip and shrugged. "The wolves know."

❧

That night, as the werthreat diced and lied on skins by the fire, Hrolleif made Skjaldwulf Marsbrother sing. Skjaldwulf, Isolfr thought, was not just a fair enough singer to have made a skald; he must know more songs and stories than any singer in the North. Because he knew the familiar chants—the first one he gave them, that night, was one of Kathlin's favorites, a funny song about Sven Peddlar, who tried to trade between the svartalfar and the liosalfar, and wound up swindled of his gold, his feet, his stones, and his eyes. But he also knew other stories, ones the wolfcarls must hold to themselves, for Isolfr had heard none of them.

Such was the second and melancholy saga Skjaldwulf shared, a fragment of the epic tale of Hrolljotr Hognisbrother and Freyulf Alfdisbrother, who had been wolfjarl and wolfsprechend at Franangford in the time of Isolfr's great-great-grandfather, when the winters had been worse than any in memory, and the trolls had come down from the Iskryne in fell waves, starving and savage.

This piece of the saga dealt with the death of Alfdis, Franangford's then-konigenwolf, and Freyulf's choice to stay in the heall as a wolfless man and Hrolljotr's lover, even when he did not bond again. Hogni, a wolf still remembered for his strength and cleverness—and a distant ancestor of Grimolfr's Skald—had been chosen consort by the next konigenwolf as well, and Franangford had found itself in the peculiar position of having, after a fashion, two wolfsprechends . . . one of them unwolfed. It proved wise, for by the time the winter ended, the new konigenwolf was dead birthing her first litter, and Freyulf was the only wolfheofodman left to that heall, for he had bonded Hogni when Hrolljotr fell to trolls.

The story did not comfort Isolfr. He found himself reaching surreptitiously to rub Viradechtis' ears, trying not to imagine what it would be like to lose her.

"I couldn't do it," Isolfr said to Sokkolfr, who sat tailor-fashion beside him, elbows on his knees and chin on his fist. "If Viradechtis—" he swallowed. "I couldn't stay. And I really couldn't take another wolf, not after—"

"It was his duty," Sokkolfr said, moving so his knee brushed Isolfr's thigh.

And then Frithulf leaned around Sokkolfr and said with all the worst of his arch disdain, "He loved Hrolljotr. What was he supposed to do, run away like a coward and leave the wolf alone?"

෨෴ඁ

Asny littered on a cold full moon night when the first frost lay over the loam under the pine trees. Isolfr was not there to see it; Hrolleif had taken him, with Vigdis and Viradechtis in eager companionship, on a long patrol east of Nithogsfjoll. Older wolfheofodmenn did mentor younger ones, as Ulfgeirr the housecarl mentored Sokkolfr—tacit acknowledgment that Sokkolfr would be a steward in his turn—but Isolfr thought there might be a reason Hrolleif chose to do some part of his teaching away from the wolfheall and the pack-sense.

He remembered the kiss.

His apprehension was not allayed when, after a cold camp and a colder supper, Hrolleif sent Vigdis and her daughter to hunt fresh meat for breakfast and then turned to regard Isolfr though the chill twilight. "Kolgrimna will come into season soon," he said, and Isolfr nodded, his mouth dry as if he sucked pine-pitch.

"You will need to know . . ." Hrolleif stopped, came to stand next to Isolfr, and Isolfr could feel the wolfsprechend's heat like the fire they had not built. "Ingrun and Vigdis will go out. Asny has her pups, as Vigdis did when Asny's season came on her."

"When you sent us all out," Isolfr said.

"Yes. We will be taking the tithe-boys out again, for it is not something they should see, not until they have the pack-sense to understand it. But, Isolfr, you need to witness."

Because it will be your turn soon enough.

He swallowed hard, although it did not help, and managed to nod.

"You and Frithulf, and the others who are bonded to pups still too young for the madness, you will have to hold household, because the werthreat cannot. Do you understand?"

"Yes." Barely a whisper.

"Ah, lad, don't be so frightened." And Hrolleif hugged him roughly. "I promised you we would not throw you out of the nest with your wings still unfledged, did I not?"

"Yes," but there was no more strength in his voice. No strength in him anywhere, and when Hrolleif's fingers caught him under the chin, he looked up obediently.

"It is time for you to learn," Hrolleif said gently, "what happens between werthreatbrothers when a bitch is in season." His mouth quirked. "And at other times as well." He leaned down, still gently, his blue eyes full of kindness as well as heat, and kissed Isolfr on the mouth.

This time it was not a chaste kiss. Hrolleif's mouth was strong, demanding, and Isolfr found himself parting his lips, welcoming Hrolleif's tongue into his mouth, his hands coming up to steady himself against the wolfsprechend's shoulders.

He knew the heat in his lower belly as it started to kindle and spread, had felt it many times before in Alfleda's bed at the keep, and sometimes in the dark of the roundhall as well. He and Sokkolfr, he and Frithulf, had helped each other, as boys do.

But this was not what boys did.

After a time, Hrolleif broke the kiss, leaned away a little. Brushed a loose strand of hair away from Isolfr's face. "Will you lie down for me, Isolfr?" And his voice was still gentle, still kind, and burning in Isolfr's mind was that single glimpse of Hrolleif and Grimolfr and the ecstatic look on Grimolfr's face.

He had been waiting for this, he realized, and from somewhere he found his voice and managed to say, "Yes," and was thankful—beyond thankful—that his voice did not crack.

Isolfr lay down for Hrolleif, and Hrolleif taught him carefully, patiently. Lying flat on his back, staring up at the stars, Isolfr said, "They won't all be as kind as you, will they?"

"No," Hrolleif said, one hand stroking Isolfr's sex, warm and callus-rough, while two fingers of the other, slick and burning, moved inside him, making him ready. "I will teach you how to prepare yourself before Viradechtis has an open mating. But, no, you may not be lucky in your wolfjarl at first." Isolfr cried out, his hips bucking, as those fingers, relentless, found something inside him he had never imagined the existence of.

"But I will tell you something else," Hrolleif said, and Isolfr could hear the warm, self-satisfied smile in his voice. "Wolfjarls can be taught."

☙❧

Later, on his knees, his face pressed into the thick wolf-smelling blankets of their bedrolls, his fingers digging desperately into the earth beneath him, Isolfr learned that which his father had feared, learned what it was to submit to a man—and learned, hearing the rough cadence of Hrolleif's breath, hearing his low, sweet moans as Isolfr moved against him, that he could take as well as give, that like the politics of the wolfthreat, this heady darkness was richer, earthier, more complicated than it seemed when you had not tasted it for yourself.

He came for Hrolleif, and Hrolleif came for him.

Afterwards, wrapped together in the sleeping roll, they heard Vigdis and Viradechtis return with their kill, felt their triumph. And moments later there was a rush of massive furry bodies, and the men were flanked by their sisters.

Viradechtis licked Isolfr's face carefully, snuffled in his ear. "Go to sleep, little sister," he said, and Hrolleif said, his concern bright through the pack-sense, "Are you all right?"

Isolfr considered. He was sore, but that was not what Hrolleif was asking. "I am . . . grateful. That it was you." And then a sudden, horrifying thought, "Grimolfr isn't going to kill me, is he?"

Hrolleif laughed, a purring, delighted chuckle. "No. Grimolfr knew before we left."

"Oh."

Hrolleif's arm reached across, drawing Isolfr close, breath moving against his ear. "I know it is not easy, Isolfr. You need not fear that I will think you craven or . . . 'womanish,' as you once said, if you are doubtful, or hurt. Or angry."

"I . . ." His throat was threatening to close; he swallowed hard. "I don't want you to think you hurt me."

"I understand."

"But . . ." He couldn't explain, couldn't find words that even got near the tangled lump of fear and sated pleasure and shame and delight, power and weakness, the terrible feeling of having come adrift from what he had been and not knowing how he was going to become what he had to be—for the wolfthreat, for the werthreat, for his family, for Viradechtis. One made choices in going to war, and sacrifices. Because one had to. Because the alternative was *not* to stand between Halfrid and Kathlin—and even his father, and Alfleda, and those who wouldn't forgive his choice—and the cold north and the trolls.

"No one will force you to remain with the wolfheall, Isolfr," Hrolleif said. "Though we will mourn you if you go, and none so more than Viradechtis. And I for one think she's chosen well."

Hrolleif's voice trailed off, embarrassed, and Isolfr realized that the wolfsprechend was babbling, trying to make things all right. Finally,

Isolfr took pity on the man and answered, because there was nothing else he could say, "She's worth it."

And Hrolleif said, "Yes," and held him tight in the warm dark between wolves, until he slept.

FOUR

The strange part was coming back to the wolfheall—coming *home*—and realizing that no one could tell to look at him that anything had changed. That nothing had changed, that he was still Isolfr, wolfsprechend-in-waiting, and Hrolleif was still Hrolleif, as much elder brother as wolfheofodman, and that there was no private message in Grimolfr's arm-clasp to either of them, no, nor in the one he offered Randulfr Ingrunsbrother or Hringolfr Left-Hand, either.

That nothing had changed, and that everything had changed instead.

Kolgrimna, as if contrariness were mined so deep into her nature that even her body was intransigent, failed to go into heat in the autumn, or in the easy part of winter. Instead, she waited until Asny's pups were eye-open and staggering, and eighteen inches of snow overlaid the ground.

The whole of the wolfheall knew it was coming. Thralls and free servants alike took liberty in the village when the tithe-boys, Kolgrimna's close kin, and the other bitches took their leave. Asny and her pups remained in the record-room; Viradechtis' unbonded brothers went with the patrol. Before he left, Hrolleif took aside each bonded boy whose wolf was too young for the madness—the three of Ingrun's litter, Frithulf, and Isolfr—and spoke some words to him.

"This is the werthreat and the wolfthreat," Hrolleif said to Isolfr. "This is the brotherhood of wolves, that I give my pack and my wolfjarl into your keeping, brother, and know you will hold it as I would, for your hands are mine, and my hands are yours."

And Isolfr looked into Hrolleif's eyes and shivered, dry mouthed, and nodded although his jaw clenched so hard his teeth ached.

Isolfr did not think that Hrolleif kissed the other four farewell.

The first day was quiet. The wolfthreat quarreled and the werthreat diced and combed winter lice from their beards, and the lot of them ate cold shoulder and pease porridge toasted over the embers of the fire.

The pack-sense awakened Isolfr at moonset. Skald was not sleeping; the big wolf moved through the heall like a shade from the grave, the last embers reflecting in his eyes. Isolfr caught a breath as Skald's eyes stroked over him, but Skald had no time for puppies now. Isolfr felt the fever in the pack as if it ran under his skin, felt it as he'd felt Hrolleif's kiss in the pit of his belly and the join of his thighs.

This is it.

Isolfr reached out in the warmth under the furs as Viradechtis stirred against his leg, and took Frithulf's hand on one side and Sokkolfr's on the other before he remembered that *Sokkolfr's* wolf was not a cub; Hroi was awake, watchful in the darkness as the pack's leader paced his domain. Sokkolfr came alert with a start, gasping, and put his free hand to his throat as if he felt teeth prickle his skin. Frithulf, curled around Kothran's warm, pale body, had to be shaken into wakefulness, but he too stirred and lifted his head, understanding what was happening with a glance.

"This is it," he whispered. "Nothing to do now but watch, and hope they don't kill each other, then—"

Everywhere, wolves were rising. Hroi, Arngrimr, and Kolli. Nagli, red as beaten copper. Glaedir, silver as steel. Hallathr, Valbrandr and Frothi. Isleifr, Guthleifr, Egill, Havarr, Surtr, Ingjaldr, and black Mar. Wolves upon wolves, the smallest of them thirteen stone and the greatest half again that size. Viradechtis lifted her head, crowded back against Isolfr, and whined low in her throat. The wolfthreat was on the move, and single in its mind.

Someone who was not a wolf rose naked from his bedclothes; Isolfr recognized the sturdy shape as Hringolfr, and shivered. A dim red glow caught the shine of sweat on his skin, revealed the ridges of scars and the swell and fall of muscle. Kolgrimna stood out of the furs beside him, facing Skald, her haunches to Hringolfr, her lip curled in a silent snarl, her teeth gleaming with firelight as if with blood.

Skald just <i>looked</i> at her, all the pack—allies and enemies, brothers all—arrayed behind him. Kolgrimna growled, low and thready, and Skald lifted his chin, pricked his ears, wagged his tail as if to show that really, it was not all so serious—

—and pounced.

She snapped at him, and Hringolfr grabbed for his scruff, but even Isolfr could see that the protest was a matter of form. He couldn't have said where Grimolfr came from, but the wolfjarl had Hringolfr's arm and was dragging him away from Skald as Skald mounted the bitch, powerful forelegs clutching her barrel. She growled and yelped, snapping over her shoulder at him as his hips began to thrust, seeking her vulva, but Isolfr could see that her tail was twisted to the side, and her hips were not tucked down.

Grimolfr shouted something—not words, a snarl, a wolf's voice twisted in a human throat—and wrenched Hringolfr's arm behind his back. The bigger man went to his knees, flickering firelight turning them into a series of red-limned statues as the wolfjarl shoved him forward, leaned over his body, and buried both hands in his hair.

And Sokkolfr shook himself free of Isolfr's grip and started forward, following Hroi.

Kolgrimna's yelp when Skald found his mark sent Isolfr lurching backward into Frithulf's arms even as Viradechtis shoved herself roughly into his. Hringolfr cried out once, falling to brace himself with his hands as Grimolfr moved savagely against him, and then Isolfr could not tell whose whimpers were whose, man's or wolf's. He shivered in Frithulf's arms, waiting for the cutting comment, the crack at his cowardice. But Frithulf Quick-Tongue failed his name and just pulled Isolfr close, wrapped in their bedclothes in the shadow of the wolfheall's massive timber wall, and dragged Isolfr and wolf-cubs all further into the darkness.

Men stood among the wolves now, moving forward, pushing and shouldering like cattle at a trough. Someone snarled. Someone shoved. Someone's bright teeth flashed, and Glaedir and Mar were on one another, snarling, rolling, the sound of snapping teeth and thudding bodies like a rockslide crashing down a hill, punctuated by Hringolfr's short, bitten cries. Skjaldwulf, long-reached and fast as a wyvern, lunged for Glaedir's brother, fingers grappling, wrestling, trying for a bear-hug that Eyjolfr sidestepped as Glaedir pinned Mar, enormous silver jaws tight on a black-furred throat. Eyjolfr hopped on one foot and kicked Skjaldwulf hard behind the ear with an unshod heel; Skjaldwulf went down on his elbows and gagged, and Eyjolfr kicked him once more for good measure before turning to survey the rest of the werthreat, as if to ask who would be the next to try him.

Kolgrimna cried out again; Viradechtis whined, ears flat, crowding herself into Isolfr's lap like a pup half her size. He wrapped his arms around her chest and hauled her close, aware of Frithulf behind him and Kothran backing them all, aware of Ingrun's cubs and their boys huddled against the far wall, where they had slept, aware of Sokkolfr knotting both hands in Hroi's ruff, as if to steady himself or hold the old wolf back. Hroi shook against the grip, irritated, but leaned against his boy's legs and belly as if to say *I am too old for this foolishness, but I will bear witness—*

"Bear witness," Isolfr said, and gagged on it. "Oh lord, oh, Othinn, god of wolves, oh, god—" Frithulf, murmuring nonsense, squeezed him tight. Kolli moved toward Glaedir, and Glaedir held his ground, and

Hringolfr cried out again, harshly, to a chorus of yelps from his bitch, and Isolfr knew, somehow, terribly, that he'd found release. The pack knew, and Isolfr knew what the pack knew. Grimolfr was still on Hringolfr, though, still moving, moving with Skald as Kolli and Glaedir fought, and Glaedir, dripping red from a gash across his face, again held the field. Kolli, limping heavily, welling blood, dragged himself into the darkness beneath the long tables. Isolfr tugged at Frithulf's hands, wanting to crawl to the big gentle wolf who let his brother use him as a pillow and see if his leg was broken, but Frithulf held tight and yanked him back.

Glaedir followed Skald, and Arngrimr—who had not fought Glaedir, canny thing, but who had fought and defeated the next three wolves after him—followed Glaedir, and Hallathr followed Arngrimr. Long past sunrise, Guthleifr's brother Fostolfr mounted Hringolfr, who had moved past weeping and swearing and into a low, exhausted moaning that would not stop, while other wolves and their brothers—those who had fought and lost—scuffled or mounted one another in frustration about the heall.

Isolfr turned away over Viradechtis' shoulder and vomited on the pine-strewn floor, half a cup of frothy yellow bile that left him choking and sore as if he'd been kicked in the gut.

"I didn't know," Frithulf said, pulling Isolfr's pale hair out of his face, holding Isolfr steady while he turned himself inside out and Viradechtis whined and washed his neck and ear, her own fear forgotten in worry for her brother. "I didn't know, Isolfr, by Othinn I would not have mocked you if I had known—"

Isolfr gagged one more time and wiped the strings of snot and saliva from his face onto Viradechtis' fur. Unmindful of the burn of acid, she turned and licked his mouth, licked his tears, wriggled worry and delight against him as Frithulf squeezed him until he almost couldn't get air.

"It's all right," Isolfr said, breathing like a failed runner, his head fallen back against his werthreatbrother's shoulder, his hands knotted in Viradechtis' fur. "I can do this." And he said, as he had said to Hrolleif, because he did not have any better words, "She's worth it."

Frithulf nodded and held him close as a brother, and with the politeness of wolves, neither of them mentioned the tears tracking the other's face.

Later, they discovered Hrolfmarr curled around the soft gray body of his wolf.

Kolli had died of his wounds.

⚬⟆⟍⚬

They burned Kolli at dawn, on a warrior's pyre. It had taken both Frithulf and Authun's brother Skirnulf (who had been Fastvaldr) to drag Hrolfmarr away, and then it fell to Isolfr to hold Hrolfmarr's broad hands, to try to keep those glazed eyes focused on him while Frithulf and Skirnulf and Sokkolfr prepared Kolli's body for the fire.

Hrolfmarr did not weep, did not speak. He allowed Isolfr's touch, allowed Hroi and Viradechtis and Authun and Kothran to press around him. It was clear through the pack-sense that Hrolfmarr was still part of the pack. The wolves did not grieve Kolli exactly, not as men understood grieving, but his death was heavy over the wolfthreat, and men and wolves alike were aware, terribly aware that Hrolfmarr had lost something precious.

There was no blame apportioned. It was not Glaedir's fault Kolli had died, any more than it was Kolgrimna's fault she had gone into heat. It was the way of the wolfthreat, and when Eyjolfr, ashen-faced but determined, came to keep vigil, Hrolfmarr seemed more glad than otherwise.

Cremation was a matter of the werthreat; the wolves accepted this madness of their brothers philosophically. All the werthreat who could stagger followed the boys as they carried Kolli's body to the pyre beyond the practice field. This was where Ulfmaer had been immolated, and Asny's pup who'd been born dead, and others, wolves and men, whom Isolfr had never met but found he mourned. Eyjolfr stood by Hrolfmarr, Glaedir pressed anxiously against his brother, and Viradechtis and Kothran, Eitri and Authun and Harekr, like frightened children, made a small anxious wolfthreat of their own as their brothers lit the stacked wood and resin and stood shoulder to shoulder, their faces scorched by the heat.

No one said anything, but Hrolfmarr's shoulders were straighter when the fire died to blowing ashes, and Isolfr could feel something shift in the pack-sense, like a stressed muscle releasing its tension.

Isolfr threw himself into the business of holding household with grim determination because doing was better than thinking. He and Sokkolfr between them organized Frithulf and three or four others into dragging out meat for the wolfthreat, although none of them had the first idea how to cook for the werthreat and could provide no better than cheese and pease porridge and winter apples. And ale. Lots of ale. The werthreat did not complain.

He could not bring himself to go near Hringolfr Left-Hand, cravenly asking Sokkolfr to find out how Kolgrimna and her brother did. Sokkolfr gave him a thoughtful look, but did as he asked, reporting back that man and wolf were fine, and that Yngvulf the Black and Arngrimr stood guard over them.

"Arngrimr will be happier," Sokkolfr said. "He can't have Vigdis, but Kolgrimna favors him over Glaedir, and at least some of her pups will be his. He stands higher in the wolfthreat after this mating."

"Yes," said Isolfr, and realized too late how bleak he sounded.

"Isolfr?" Sokkolfr sounded worried and Isolfr had Hroi's warmth bumping against his back, pushing Viradechtis aside. She snarled, but it was a puppy snarl, and Hroi ignored her while she dragged at his ruff.

"I'm fine," he said to Sokkolfr, and "I'm fine, old man," to Hroi. "Truly."

Hroi whined in the back of his throat, manifestly unconvinced, and Sokkolfr said, "Hringolfr is unhurt." He studied Isolfr a moment and added, "Hringolfr says there is no shame in fearing Viradechtis' season. He says the only shame is if you let your fear hurt your sister."

Isolfr felt his face burning. "Thank you, Sokkolfr," he said and turned away.

❧

The magic of the mating worked its trick; when the first of the long patrols returned, Hlothvinr had bonded Griss, becoming Aurulfr the Brown, and Svanrikr—surprising Isolfr—had bonded Skefill and chosen to be called Ulfrikr. ("Ulfrikr Un-Wise," Frithulf crowed, delighted.) Johvatr did not return, and at first Isolfr's heart beat hollow in his chest, but Aurulfr assured him that Johvatr had decided to leave the wolfheall rather than remain as an unbonded man.

The Great Leif, though, returned, more massive and silent than ever, and Isolfr noticed that the smallest of Asny's pups, who had shown no interest in the new tithe-boys, would stagger purposefully after Leif whenever he saw him.

And that was hopeful.

Briefly, Isolfr thought of his father and mother, of Jonak and Kathlin, and then pushed the thought away. He was not welcome in the jarl's hall; his father had made that clear. And if he had lost blood-sister and blood-brother, he had gained werthreatbrothers in their stead.

More restless than he would admit with the events of the past few days, he skied out in search of game with Viradechtis running broad-pawed on crusted snow beside him. In the cold shade of the fir wood, a brace of snow hares at his belt, they came upon the second long patrol, and even from a distance Isolfr could see that something was wrong. Someone—Hrolleif, to judge by his size and his twin red braids—trudged on snowshoes before a travois. Isolfr could not see who was missing at first, but the wolf who floundered beside the makeshift litter was Ingrun. Too heavy to run atop the snow like Viradechtis, she plowed through it on a trail broken by Vigdis, and she whined and nosed the hand of the man in the travois. Tithe-boys skied behind, their faces grim, and two dog-wolves and their brothers brought up the tail.

Randulfr. Forgetting his dignity, Isolfr skied to them, calling through the trees. Viradechtis barreled to meet her mother, and Hrolleif looked up at his name. The creases of his squint deepened when he saw Isolfr's face.

"Kolgrimna and her brother?" he asked, when Isolfr was close enough that they would not have to shout. The tithe-boys drew together in a worried knot, and Kolgrimna's kin and their brothers came forward, still giving Hrolleif and Isolfr a certain respectful distance as Viradechtis climbed onto her mother's shoulders, sniffing and licking.

"Well," Isolfr said. "Five wolves covered her: Skald, Glaedir, Arngrimr, Hallathr and Guthleifr. Man and bitch are fine. Randulfr—"

"I'm fine, Isolfr," Randulfr said from the travois, his voice only slightly strained. "The second troll had a club, but my leg will heal. A little crooked, maybe, but Hrolleif set it well."

Isolfr exhaled in relief, and only knew then that he had been holding his breath. Hrolleif shifted his grip on the travois; his heavy hand fell on Isolfr's shoulder. "Someone was hurt," he said. It wasn't a question.

"Kolli," he said. "Glaedir—" He couldn't move any more air. Hrolleif squeezed his shoulder hard, and then jumped at a sudden, meaningful snarl as Viradechtis piled into Isolfr's legs hard enough to knock him off his skis. He went down, and found himself sprawled on the snow between two angry wolves.

Vigdis' teeth had snapped shut on air, but her ears were flat and her hackles up, her amber eyes fixed on her daughter. Isolfr did not know how Viradechtis had overstepped but he knew without a doubt that she had. He could see it in the way her ears and tail drooped and she skulked forward, whining submissively, to lick and paw at her mother's mouth. Vigdis arched her neck up, her ears forward; the puppy rolled on her back on the snow, showing her cream-colored belly, and all was well.

Except Isolfr looked up to see Hrolleif regarding Viradechtis steadily, worried contemplation plain on his face. Isolfr closed his hands on the snow hard enough to press icy pellets through the slits in his mitten palms. He braced against the drift and stood, then knelt to fix the bindings on his skis, without daring to glance at Hrolleif again.

⊙⌇⊙

Viradechtis came into season in the green warmth of spring. She was by then already larger than either Kolgrimna or Asny, and Hrolleif said, lifting one massive paw after another to check the bones of her legs, "She will have Skald's size."

"Like Skefill and Griss."

"Skald sired true with that litter," Hrolleif said, a little ruefully, while Viradechtis slobbered genially into his hair. It was Vigdis more than her daughter who had signaled Viradechtis' approaching heat, becoming ever more snappish and rough with the younger wolf, growling when she came too near Skald.

"Except Kothran," Isolfr said, smiling at the thought of Frithulf's frequent, insincere complaints about Kothran's size. Kothran was small, but he was fast and a canny tracker, and like Viradechtis, he had his mother's sharp intelligence. He suited Frithulf perfectly, and man and wolf both knew it.

"Clearly he gave it to his litter-sister. Go on with you, little girl. You're strong as an ox." He shoved her with his shoulder and she went, skirting cautiously around her mother, who watched with baleful amber eyes. Hrolleif stood up, said, "Patience, sister," to Vigdis, and to Isolfr: "Watch for limping, though. She's of the age to hurt herself just because she doesn't want to stop running."

Isolfr nodded.

Hrolleif hesitated, said, "We will have to be careful, when you return. She is not ready to be konigenwolf yet—"

"But she's already too close, isn't she?"

Hrolleif nodded, unhappily, then clapped Isolfr on the shoulder. "We will talk," he said. "Go now, and safe journey."

This time there was no farewell kiss, and Isolfr was aware, not only of Vigdis' implacable stare, but of Grimolfr watching from the doorway of the roundhall, his face unreadable.

He and Viradechtis set out briskly, for they had a good deal of distance to cover to reach the shelter Hrolleif had told him of, that was known to all the wolfheallan of the North as a place not to disturb. Isolfr was glad to have purpose, glad of a reason to drive himself hard, because he began, as the sun climbed in the sky, to feel heat sparking in his groin and belly, something that was not quite an ache in the long bones of his thighs. Viradechtis seemed not to feel anything of that sort, but he noticed she was as distractible as she had been as a small puppy; it was the first time he'd ever had to call her to keep her by his side. Her thoughts were scattered, racing, full of heat. They slept piled together that night, as they always did, but he was awoken long before dawn by a faint muttering snarl that sounded like nothing so much as a man cursing under his breath; he came up blearily on one elbow to see her pacing back and forth across their campsite. Her head swung round at his movement, and for a moment he was pinned by molten gold fury.

He saw her for the first time not as Viradechtis whom he loved but as a trellwolf: fifteen stone of power and blood-lust that could rip his throat out here, now, in this small clearing, before he could so much as sit up. And then he smelled pine boughs warm with the sun, and she was herself again, the low snarl shifting to a whine of distress, and he thought, *She knows even less than you do of what is happening to her.*

He sat up, raked his fingers through his hair, said, "Come here, little sister." And she came gladly, gratefully, and tried to bury her head in his armpit. The thought came, sharp as a stabbing knife, *She trusts you.*

He got them moving as quickly as he could, and it was mid-afternoon when they sighted the shelter—a lean-to against the face of a cliff, but better than nothing and with a good supply of firewood laid in. Most of Isolfr's work while they were here would be replacing the wood he burned.

He took a moment, both of them shivering a little, to test Viradechtis' legs as Hrolleif had. But there was no soreness, no sharp pain of injury, and he ruffled her ears and said, "Go hunt, sister."

She did not wait for him to tell her twice.

❦

It took four days for Viradechtis' heat to run its course. She and Isolfr were both fretful, uncomfortable, and Isolfr was deeply grateful that Hrolleif and Randulfr had both, separately, warned him about the blood, for he knew otherwise he would have panicked, and here in the wilderness panic was the same as death.

Viradechtis hunted, taking out her mating anger on rabbits, deer, even a winter-skinny bear. She and Isolfr ate very well, but he noticed that both of them were always hungry. He chopped wood, repaired the lean-to's roof and walls, began the process of curing the skins of Viradechtis' kills, all the while painfully aware of the fire burning in her, a fire that kept him half-hard for hours at a time. And at night, while Viradechtis ran, he lay beside the banked fire and brought himself to release with his hands, twice, three times, using himself more and more brutally until he was able to sleep.

He was glad there was no one with him.

On the fifth day, he woke sometime in the afternoon to find Viradechtis sound asleep, curled around him as if she were a child and he were her doll. He was exhausted, aching in every limb, but that sensation of prickling, scathing heat was gone. *Thank you,* he thought vaguely, although he did not know whom he thanked, and fell back asleep.

It was a full week after they had left the wolfheall before they began the return journey. Isolfr found himself reluctant to hurry; he needed time, still, to feel his way through the changes in his sister. She was still Viradechtis, still sunlight-in-pine-boughs, and she was still a very young wolf.

But she was not a puppy. Her eagerness was tempered now, her gold eyes deeper, something darker behind them that had not been there before. She had always been dictatorial, but now there was a weight behind it, a sense of strength. He realized, with a shiver of anxiety, that she would not reflexively roll over for Vigdis now. *We will have to be careful,* Hrolleif had said, and Isolfr knew it for an understatement.

So he did not feel that there was any rush to return to the wolfheall, where life would only become more difficult. He walked slowly and let Viradechtis roam as she pleased. And about noon of the first day, when she called to him, sharp and urgent, he turned aside without hesitation.

She had found a trellherig, a place of sacrifice. There wasn't much left of the victim, and Isolfr was just as glad, but Viradechtis' emphatic images in his head told him that she had caught the trolls' scent, and it was recent.

Isolfr thought pointedly of the wolfheall, and the strength of wolves and men within it.

But Viradechtis shook him off, already running along the trolls' route.

The only thing stupider than tracking an unknown number of trolls would be to leave his sister to track them alone. Isolfr cursed and went after her.

The shelter was remote from any wolfheall, but it was south of them, not north, and inside the long patrols. There should be no trolls here, and no trolls *anywhere* with summer coming on and the days lengthening toward white nights and the midnight sun. It was too far for them to travel in a night, and trolls were not fond of the sun, even the weak sun of winter.

So the broad, careless trail of many hooves, the crushed underbrush, the ease with which Isolfr could track them even without the pack-sense, were not simply unsettling. They were *impossible*. But nevertheless, even he caught the musty reek of trell-bodies, dozens of them.

He put his head down and ran.

Trellwolves were sprinters. Their gait over distances was a lope, and a fit man could run faster for longer. Isolfr had finally hit that hoped-for growth spurt, and though he would never be a tall man, he was of a height with Sokkolfr. And life in the wolfheall had made him strong, stronger even than the jarl's son he had been; a jarl's son might practice at arms and ride long hours, but it was nothing compared to running with wolves and the hard physical labor of the life of a wolfcarl.

It wasn't long before he saw Viradechtis' brush and haunches flickering through the ancient trees ahead of him. Soon, he was running beside her, and he thought she slacked her place a little to let him catch up—or perhaps she was tiring. Her tongue slipped between her teeth, at least, and her long-legged canter slowed. As he drew up beside her she stopped at the base of a slope leading up the back side of a bluff. She whined low in her throat and lifted her muzzle to the wind.

He could have picked the rank scent out of the air even without Viradechtis' assistance. He dropped a hand to her ruff, smoothed her thick-coated ears. She leaned into him, her ribs rising and falling on heavy breaths, and took a hesitant step up the long hill before them.

Footsteps silent as his wolf's, Isolfr crept forward. There was a village at the base of the bluff, Ravndalr, a little hamlet of some five families that subsisted on charcoal-making and clay mined from the bluff. It was beholden to Gunnarr Sturluson, and Isolfr, when he had been Njall Gunnarson, had known it well.

It was hard to believe that that had been only four and a half seasons gone by.

He knew before they came to the top of the hill what they would see. Viradechtis scented no blood, no death, no fire—no fire at all, not even the fire of hearths—and over it all hung the appalling reek of troll, and, what was worse, the serpent-musk of a wyvern.

And wyverns could see in the daylight.

This time, Viradechtis listened when Isolfr asked her to stay. She dropped her elbows, not quite lying down, hovering a finger's width over the pine needles. Isolfr was not so dainty; he pressed his belly to the damp ground and crawled, moving away from the trellpath. When he reached the bluff, he rolled behind the tangled roots of an undercut tree, steeled himself, and looked out over Ravndalr.

Ravndalr was not there.

Isolfr saw the small clearing where it had been, the friendly, bowering pines. The cottages that had clustered around a central well were so much wreckage. Heaps and layers of strewn earth lay over the pine needles and the cattle paths, red clay annealed in lumps on the timbers of destroyed cottages.

Clean-picked bones lay piled in the center of the clearing, but Isolfr could see no sign of trolls. Just the smell of them, thick as if he lay in the center of the whole warren. And then, horribly, he understood where they were.

They had chosen Ravndalr because of its prized clay bluff, and when they were done dining on the inhabitants, they had simply burrowed trell-caves into the sticky earth itself, and gone to ground there. A whole warren indeed—and only a long day's ride from the keep that held Isolfr's own mother, his father, his brother Jonak, rising twelve, and his ten-year-old sister Kathlin, who might by now have retired the rag doll she had still slept with when he left.

He thought it was Viradechtis who whined, but when he glanced over his shoulder to quiet her, he realized it was himself, his own breath hissing through his painfully tightened throat. *Grimolfr has been hiding from us how bad things are*, he thought, and let his forehead fall down on his hands. He drew a breath between fingers sticky and black with pine tar, the scent of clean loam and pine needles clearing his head of the fear-miasma of troll.

I need the pack.

I cannot do this alone.

But the pack was a day away—a day there, and a day back. And there were wolfless men within striking distance. He couldn't leave; if the trolls began to move, there might be something he could do. *Die like a babe*, he mocked himself, and bit his fingers, hard, for the focus of the pain.

Then Viradechtis was beside him, pack-warmth and the scent of pine needles that were not fallen and brown. She nudged his armpit with the point of her nose, and Isolfr blinked at her and bit his lip, and wondered.

Help, he thought, experimentally, reaching out to the pack-sense, surprised to find it there, not just Viradechtis but the whole pack, all the knowledge of the wolves, their presence and awareness. *Feel me. Please. Feel me.* Not words, of course, but need, *needing* his brothers and willing them to find him—

And to his absolute surprise, the wolfthreat felt him, and took notice.

⊙ᛉ⊙

Night was on them before the pack arrived, and the troll warren stirring. Isolfr and Viradechtis lay together still on the bluff, watching. He had identified two main entrances to the warren and knew that the lower, the one farther from the bluff and what remained of Ravndalr, was the wyvern's lair, for not even the largest troll would need a hole of that size. He felt the pack before he smelled them, and he didn't hear them at all; even in the midst of his fear for his family and his father's liegefolk, his grief for Ravndalr, and his choking, all-consuming hatred for the trolls, he felt a warm ember in his chest that this was *his* pack, these his brothers.

He felt Grimolfr belly-crawling beside him, and did not startle when the wolfjarl said in his ear, "The pack says trolls."

"They've . . ." It was hard to say it, even though he'd been staring at it for hours. "They've destroyed Ravndalr and warrened the bluff. There's a wyvern, too, farther entrance."

"Do you know how many?"

"Enough?" Isolfr said hopelessly. "There's been movement, but they haven't really come out yet. Ravndalr was not . . . was not very large."

"No, I remember it." Grimolfr hesitated, then laid one hard hand on Isolfr's shoulder and said, "You've done well. Come now. We must plan our attack."

And Isolfr wriggled back to where the rest of the pack waited, and felt for a moment giddy-headed with relief that it was not *his* burden any longer, that he could now do what he was told and let older, wiser heads do the thinking.

He pushed away the little voice that said, uneasily, *But Grimolfr has not been telling us the truth.* That was a different matter; tonight was simple: a battle to fight, people to defend, the dead to avenge, brothers to stand beside.

Communicating mostly through the pack-sense, trusting the wolves to carry the meaning of his murmured words to their brothers, Grimolfr said, "As we don't know how many of them there are, we can't let them get out in the open. But we don't want to let them lure us into the warren, either. In those tunnels, the advantage will be theirs." He divided the threat quickly into two groups—the smaller, but with more seasoned warriors, to take the near entrance, the larger to take the wyvern's hole. The key to beating a wyvern was distracting it, and thus the more moving bodies, the better. Isolfr found Frithulf beside him and gave his friend a half-smile.

"I'm glad *you* found *them*, instead of the other way around," Frithulf said, and clouted Isolfr companionably on the shoulder. And they moved with the pack down into what had been Ravndalr.

It was ugly, dirty, brutal work, and it took them all that night.

When daybreak came, there were three men dead, and five wolves, but the wyvern had been hacked horribly to pieces, and Yngvulf, Grimolfr, Ulfgeirr, and Skjaldwulf, their brothers with them, were searching the halls of the warren to be sure they left no surviving trolls. Sokkolfr had Frithulf and Skirnulf helping him examine the wounded, and Isolfr, troll blood under his fingernails and matting his hair, labored with Hrolleif and the rest of the werthreat to drag the dead trolls together so that a pyre could be lit. You couldn't leave troll corpses to rot; they poisoned the ground, and even ten years later plants would be stunted and sickly.

At noon, Sokkolfr and the younger members of the werthreat started for the wolfheall, travoising their injured and dead behind them; Hrolleif sent Isolfr and Viradechtis with them, because he and Grimolfr needed Hringolfr—and Randulfr, who still limped, but not as badly. It was already plain to both Hrolleif and Isolfr that Viradechtis was more than capable of keeping order among a dozen wolves, especially when those who weren't injured were exhausted. Unspoken was the further consideration that this would keep Vigdis and Viradechtis separated a little longer. Isolfr knew that they were merely putting off a conversation that was going to be painful to both of them, but he was bone-weary and selfishly glad that the conversation *could* be put off a little longer.

"We should be no more than a day behind you," Hrolleif said to Sokkolfr and Isolfr, and they nodded and set out for home. The werthreat's shoulders sagged; the wolfthreat's tails were dragging. The brothers of injured men kept the pack-sense roiling with their anxiety, and the men whose wolves were hurt were little better. Isolfr found his nails digging into his palms, found himself wanting to turn and howl at them all to shut up. He felt flayed with exhaustion, raw and a-twitch.

Sokkolfr touched his shoulder gently. "Isolfr? Did Viradechtis' heat go badly?"

"How should I know? We'd never done it before." He was appalled at the bitterness of his words even as they came out of his mouth. "Sokkolfr, I'm sorry. Truly. I didn't—"

"Hush," Sokkolfr said. "You have as much right as anyone."

"To snap your nose off? No, I don't think—"

"Isolfr." Exasperated now. "No one expects you to behave like a wolf-less man. What you have to say, say it."

Isolfr ducked his head, so that Sokkolfr wouldn't see him blushing. "Sorry."

"Forgiven," Sokkolfr said fondly, and Isolfr found the fretting of the pack-sense easier to bear after that.

They reached the wolfheall staggering with weariness, well after dark, guided the last mile and a half entirely by the wolfthreat's land-sense. But the gates were open when they got there, and Asny's brother waiting in the gateway to welcome them. He kissed Isolfr on both cheeks, as werthreatbrother to werthreatbrother, and Isolfr was so astounded it took a sharp nudge from Frithulf to keep him from simply standing there like a man struck to stone.

Two hours' worth of mad bustle, and the injured were settled, the dead laid out to wait until dawn for burning, the hale—or relatively hale—fed and bathed and settling into sleep, and Isolfr could make his way to the bathhouse and finally, *finally* wash away soot and blood and mud and the clinging grime of the wyvern's foul death.

He was close to drowsing with the heat and the blissful relief of cleanliness when a voice said, amused, "If you fall asleep in here, it'll just mean Viradechtis has to drag you out."

He startled, catching his head a sharp knock against the wall.

Eyjolfr was standing in the aisle, looking at him with his head cocked to one side.

"Eyjolfr." Isolfr floundered to his feet, excruciatingly aware of his own nakedness when Eyjolfr was wearing shirt and trews, his hair lank with steam and his face shining with sweat. "I . . . I didn't know you were there."

"I could tell," Eyjolfr said dryly. As Isolfr came level with him, he reached out and laid his hand along Isolfr's cheek, turning his head gently so that they were looking at each other.

Isolfr's heart was pounding; he could not read the expression in Eyjolfr's eyes.

Eyjolfr smiled and said, "You are very beautiful, you know. Now go to bed before you fall asleep standing up." His hand lingered a moment longer, an unmistakable caress; then he let Isolfr go and stood aside.

Isolfr bolted like a spooked deer.

❦

L ying in his furs and blankets that night, with Frithulf's back fitted warmly against his own and Viradechtis sprawled out like a wanton, her ears twitching against his chin, he tried to think on it like a konigenwolf's brother, not like the virgin Hrolleif had called him. Would it be so bad, if it was Eyjolfr?

Viradechtis adored Glaedir, and the silver wolf was not so much older than she that he had lost his humor. If he ever would: there was an enduring sparkle to that one. Moreover, Isolfr had not forgotten the arrogant power with which he had fought for the right to sire Kolgrimna's pups. He was worthy of Viradechtis—more worthy than Arngrimr.

And in a moment of selfishness, Isolfr thought of Eyjolfr's hand on his cheek, and remembered Hrolleif's words. *Wolfjarls can be taught.*

Yes.

He thought Eyjolfr could be taught. If Randulfr had not taught him enough, already.

But that thought led to other thoughts, a different wolfjarl and a different kind of teaching. As soon as he could, he resolved, he would speak to Grimolfr. He might not be wolfsprechend, but he was Viradechtis' brother. And she had found the trellwarren. They had acquitted themselves well in the battle. And Grimolfr had sworn that he would treat Isolfr as a wolfcarl rather than a cub—

Yes. When the wolfjarl returned to the wolfheall, he would speak with Grimolfr. And find out what else the wolfjarl had been keeping to himself.

❦

I t almost had the air of ritual about it now. Isolfr came upon Grimolfr as Grimolfr was crouched beside Tindr, showing giant, purposeful Leif some detail of the pup's design, and waited respectfully until the wolfjarl stood and met his eyes. "You wish to speak with me, Isolfr?"

"Yes," Isolfr said, and forced hands that wanted to clasp behind his back to relax at his sides as Tindr—freed—bounced up and planted both feet on Leif's belly, wriggling. Meeting Grimolfr's eyes wasn't easier than it had been, but it was more practiced, and perhaps—perhaps—Grimolfr did not lean quite so hard as he once might have. Isolfr lowered his voice, trying for the fair tone his mother used when she disagreed with his father, and came a step closer. "Wolfjarl, why have you not spoken before of how far south the trolls have warrened?"

"Have you considered that I have spoken, perhaps, and simply not to you?"

Isolfr hid his startle, but he couldn't stop his eyes from widening. Viradechtis bumped his knee; he noticed that Skald was nowhere to be seen. "I—" Then he firmed his jaw, and didn't care that his tone went sharp. "Haven't I proved myself?"

Grimolfr smiled. "It has nothing to do with proof. It has to do with not troubling you with a problem that is not your concern, when there are many, *many* problems that do require your attention."

Isolfr swallowed. "But how am I supposed to—"

"You're not." Another man would have cut Isolfr silent with a gesture, a flat-palmed hand. Grimolfr did it with the touch of his eyes. "You are not a wolfheofodman yet, Isolfr. But you have the instincts of one. You're like your little girl, a heart full of the need to be doing and not yet the sense to know what must be done—no. Listen. You do not need to know because your place is not to choose for the wolfheall; your place is to learn what you must know when it will be your duty to keep the wolfheall strong. And then fighting trolls will be the *least* of your problems."

Isolfr pressed his palms to his thighs and considered, chewing his lip lightly. It made sense; he could *see* the sense in it. But something in him chafed at backing down so easily, and he squared his shoulders and asked, "And when will that be, wolfjarl?"

Grimolfr shrugged. "Three, five years or so?"

Isolfr crossed his arms, uncertain whether he should say *so soon?* or *so long?* and anyway uncertain how he and Hrolleif would keep Vigdis and Viradechtis from killing each other in the meantime. "Three years?"

"At the earliest," Grimolfr said. "It depends on Viradechtis. And when she comes back into season." He crossed his own arms and permitted himself a wicked, unsubtle grin. "And whether she gives you one year or two between matings."

❧

He thought about Grimolfr's words for the rest of the day, in between a thousand and sixteen other things that somehow needed his urgent attention. Skirnulf shyly came to talk to him about the trouble Authun was having with Frar; Frar was an older wolf, a gray-muzzle like Hroi, and he seemed to have decided Authun was a threat to him. Skirnulf didn't know why, assuring Isolfr anxiously that Authun didn't want to hurt Frar at all, and Frar's brother would only laugh and say, "Let them sort it out themselves, pup."

Skirnulf's pride was hurt, Isolfr thought and felt the sting of too-close empathy. And through the pack-sense, he caught a memory of Kolli's scent and understood that Skirnulf was afraid for Authun, who was a big gangly creature without an ounce of vice or malice in him. He listened more widely, letting Skirnulf tell him about Authun, and felt Frar, old and wise and angry.

Why angry? Isolfr did not ask, exactly, and the wolfthreat did not answer, exactly, but he felt the gaps the dead wolves—six now, after Ravndalr—had made in how the wolfthreat thought of itself, and he could see that Frar stood too close to the edge of one of those gaps, and Authun too close to its other side. And Frar, disliking change and feeling himself too old for fighting, was trying to back Authun off from threatening his place in the pack.

"Frar doesn't want to fight, either," he said to Skirnulf. Skirnulf was all but deaf to the pack-sense, and Isolfr abandoned after only a moment's thought any attempt to explain to him exactly what was going on. "You'll have to be patient. It's part of Authun growing up, and you can't stop that, or help with it, either."

"Oh," Skirnulf said. And then, "Oh! You mean Frar thinks Authun's an adult now."

"Yes."

"Oh!" Skirnulf was almost beaming. "I thought we'd done something *wrong.* Thank you, Isolfr."

For what? Isolfr thought, watching Skirnulf call to his brother and stride out into the beautiful spring day. *I told him exactly what Frar's brother told him.*

Viradechtis, resting her chin on his shoulder, pointed out that dignity was something wolves and men both needed, and Isolfr grinned and said, "What do you know of dignity, sister?"

She laughed back at him and licked his ear.

But that was how his day went, that day and the days that followed. He had less and less time for himself, between drilling the tithe-boys, talking with those members of the werthreat, mostly the youngest, who did not want to bring their problems to Hrolleif, and learning everything he could from Hrolleif—even though he had to send Viradechtis away with Sokkolfr or Frithulf to do it. He and Hrolleif could not talk with Vigdis and her daughter both beside them, for every hint of dissent or dissatisfaction between them was immediately caught and magnified by the konigenwolves, and it took no more than minutes for the snarling to start.

Isolfr had been right; Viradechtis didn't roll over.

She hated to be sent away from him. She thought it was punishment and was anxious and clingy with the need to understand what she had done wrong. But Isolfr could not explain it to her; her instincts were too deep and too clear. And even if he could have, he would not have ordered her to submit to Vigdis, firstly because Viradechtis was konigenwolf as much as her mother and she might do as he asked but it would rip her heart out, and secondly because Vigdis was konigenwolf as much as her daughter and there would be no way for Viradechtis to submit *enough.*

So he told her to go play with Kothran, or sleep with Hroi, and Vigdis relaxed and even liked him a little again. She appreciated his understanding of her place in the wolfthreat.

He knew now what Grimolfr had meant, as Hrolleif talked to him more and more openly about what the wolfsprechend's job entailed. It was too big for him, too big for his sister, and he could admit that. Spring warmed to summer, and Asny's pups chose their brothers—Tindr choosing Leif, as everyone had known he would, and the last of Isolfr's tithemates became the Great Ulfbjorn and laid his bedroll in the roundhall. Isolfr concentrated on taking as much of the load off Hrolleif's shoulders as he could.

And in dealing, most often scarlet-faced and flustered, with the increasingly obvious attempts of certain members of the werthreat to court him.

Eyjolfr led them, but he was far from the only one. Fostolfr and Skjaldwulf—and also Ulfgeirr, which so consternated Isolfr that even Sokkolfr could not help laughing. Other men, the brothers of young wolves, strong wolves, wolves who wanted standing in the pack—men who would like to be wolfjarl and knew it would not happen while they were wolfcarls under Grimolfr and Hrolleif. Men who saw in Isolfr their way to power.

It terrified him, and only partly because it forced him face to face with a destiny he wasn't sure he could stand up to; Viradechtis was konigenwolf, he would be wolfsprechend, and he could do nothing but pray he would not fail. But more than that, what made his hands icy and his face hot was that the men courting him were not simply courting a wolfsprechend-in-waiting. They were courting *him*. Isolfr. *You are very beautiful,* Eyjolfr had said, and he saw that same truth in Skjaldwulf's eyes and those of some of the others. They wanted him, and he thought of Hringolfr and felt cold fear like deepest winter in his bones.

He did his best to keep it to himself, not to let it influence Viradechtis. She wasn't afraid, but showed lively interest in each of her suitors. He thought she liked Glaedir best, but she liked Mar as well, and sometimes scorned them both in favor of another wolf.

"Your little girl's a flirt," Hrolleif said in his ear one late summer afternoon.

"I know," Isolfr said helplessly. "I thought she'd . . . *choose.*"

"Like Vigdis and Skald? It is not the only way of doing things in a wolfheall, although it suits us very well. Viradechtis knows what she wants."

"Yes," Isolfr said, and could not help the note of long-suffering in his voice.

Hrolleif laughed and tugged gently on one of his braids. "Do not worry so much, Isolfr. I think you may be sure that your wolfjarl, whoever he is, will wish to please you."

And Isolfr found himself blushing again.

❧

The long summer offered a reprieve from troll raids on into autumn, and Viradechtis' second season came on her just before the equinox. This time, she recognized its coming and woke Isolfr from a sound sleep, very early one morning, with an emphatic thought of *male-wolfness*.

As Hrolleif had said, she knew what she wanted.

Isolfr was awake on the instant, rolling out of his blankets. Frithulf made a small complaining noise and cuddled closer to Kothran without waking. Sokkolfr and Hroi were nowhere to be seen. Isolfr, not waiting to find his boots, crossed the roundhall to the records-room, where he found Hrolleif awake and placidly awaiting him.

"How . . ."

"Shut the door behind you," Hrolleif said, and when Isolfr had done so, he said, "Vigdis has been konigenwolf for twenty years. And she is very aware of her competition." He smiled as Viradechtis bumped his knee, demanding attention. "Yes, you, little girl." He looked up at Isolfr, one hand gently stroking Viradechtis' massive head. "I will be glad when she is grown, though saddened that it means you must leave us."

"Yes," Isolfr said, to all of it.

Viradechtis snorted, impatient, and that insistent *male-wolfness* hit Isolfr again—and, to judge by his startled blink, Hrolleif as well.

"Don't be pushy, sister," Isolfr said, and Hrolleif laughed and rumpled Viradechtis' ears.

He said, "We want a litter from Hroi."

"Hroi?" An iron weight seemed to fall away, and only in its absence did Isolfr realize how frightened he had been. "You mean, Sokkolfr?"

"Who is Hroi's brother, yes," Hrolleif said dryly. "We also thought you could use a respite from your eager suitors, and I must say Sokkolfr was very pleased to be asked."

Stop blushing, Isolfr said furiously to himself, though it did no good. "Sokkolfr"—a deep breath, to settle his gut, as Viradechtis whined—"does Sokkolfr know already?"

"Sokkolfr's gone on ahead." Hrolleif reached out and gave Isolfr a rough hug before he quite realized he was gaping. "Go, get your boots and your bedroll, Isolfr. I think you know the way, and your sister won't wait for sunrise. Besides, Ingrun's season is due, and your sister isn't yet konigenwolf enough for her scent to put a stop to it."

"Hrolleif?"

"Don't hurry back," the wolfsprechend said with a grin, and pushed him toward the door.

The frost lay heavy on the swell of the earth; man and wolf left footprints like dark pearls in silver as they ran across it side by side. He did know the way, and his wolf's urgency drove him. He felt her heat, familiar now, a craving need that sparked along his spine and made his testicles ache. She whined, running ahead, pacing to and fro when he did not move fast enough to suit her, ranging out and back, and for the first time he wondered what *his* need felt like to her.

She ran him through the tail-end of the night and into morning, her desire gnawing holes in him, so strong that even when he was staggering with weariness, he could barely force himself to stop long enough to suck cold water from the summer-dried streams they crossed. This was nothing like her first heat; there was no tentativeness in her this time, no fear of the unknown—only desire. And it worked in Isolfr, too, until he found himself strangely eager.

He smelled smoke before they came up on the lean-to. They were met by Hroi, bounding to them, ears up and tail waving like a king's banner in greeting, his scent-name, freshly turned forest loam, like a benediction in the pack-sense. Viradechtis took one look at the old wolf and fled, running flat-out with her long brindled body stretched low to the ground. Hroi laughed at Isolfr and took off after her, flashing through the trees in the dappled sunset light. Isolfr drew up, panting, limbs leaden, and watched them until they vanished over the breast of the rise. Then he turned down the long slope to the lean-to, and Sokkolfr.

The apprehension had returned, but the need burned stronger than ever. He found himself hurrying, and he was grateful—insanely grateful—to find Sokkolfr waiting for him in the shelter of the lean-to, propped on his elbows on a bed of cut pine boughs, his bare shoulders pale and freckled against the blankets.

There was no room for embarrassment. No *time* for embarrassment: Isolfr yanked off his boots and socks, stripped off his trews and tunic and jerkin, tossed his clothing and bedroll into the back corner of the lean-to, and slithered under the blankets beside Sokkolfr before the autumn chill could prickle his skin to gooseflesh. He was sweating anyway, lightly, as he turned to Sokkolfr and drew a breath full of the scents of damp wool and sex.

Sokkolfr still hadn't spoken, but his eyes were wide, pupils dilated, breathing light and fast and high in his throat. Somewhere, Viradechtis was running, moist soil denting under her nails, Hroi's breath at her flank, making the old wolf work for what he wanted—what she wanted too. Hesitantly, Sokkolfr reached out, touched Isolfr's cheek with the back of his hand. Isolfr shivered at the touch, almost moaned. Sokkolfr, startled, drew back.

Words seemed very far away. There was the scent of the forest, the scent of the big male who gave chase, the weight of his shoulder against her hip. There was the rasp of blankets and the ache in his loins and the hard, seductive warmth of Sokkolfr's lean body just inches away. He needed to touch that body, needed to feed the heat inside him. The fire would consume him if he didn't give it something else to burn.

He reached out, not gently, and grabbed Sokkolfr's fingers. Sokkolfr flinched, but didn't snatch his hand back, and frantically, Isolfr clawed after the words. Now, *now*, because Hroi was about to catch him, and he thought he couldn't bear to evade the big wolf again, and if Hroi caught him before Sokkolfr did, he thought—he was *certain*—the pain of the need would kill him then and there.

Words. He had words. They were stupid, bootless things, but he had them, and he needed them—

"You know what to do?" Through gritted teeth, and almost not words at all, but somehow Sokkolfr understood them and nodded. And then Sokkolfr grabbed him, savagely, as if a cord had snapped and freed him. Isolfr moved into it, rolled onto his belly, arms crossed under his chest, legs spread and knees braced as Hrolleif had showed him, feeling Sokkolfr's hands, his fingers, hasty, striving to be gentle and failing as Hroi's legs clasped Viradechtis' barrel. She pushed back against him, clumsy, inexperienced, then panicked at the touch of his sex on her vulva and jerked forward, yelping, twisting to snap at his face as he ducked away.

Sokkolfr cried out his wolf's frustration, clutching Isolfr as if Isolfr would try to wriggle away as well, but Isolfr was braced, trembling, his hands knotted on his own braids, the pain an anchor. Viradechtis snarled, tail clamped between her legs, her haunches to a fallen pine as Hroi minced up to her, ears pricked, tail up, head tilted just a little to show the konigenwolf his throat. She displayed long teeth and he paused, and through the pack-sense Isolfr could feel his hurt as well, his need and Sokkolfr's too as Sokkolfr froze in place.

"Show her," Isolfr managed, somehow, shaking.

"Show who?" Sokkolfr's voice sounded very far away, as far away as Isolfr's own. The snarls and whines of their bondmates were closer, vibrating their throats, caressing their tongues.

"Show my sister what to do," Isolfr said, and hollowed his spine, offering himself, and braced himself with his hands.

He felt Sokkolfr's hands pressing his buttocks apart, tried to relax, to remember Hrolleif's advice—

—and yelped like a puppy when something warm and wet and soft ran along the cleft between his buttocks. He was pushing back into the touch, frantically, even before he realized it was Sokkolfr's tongue. And then Sokkolfr's hands were hard against his hips, and his tongue was . . . his tongue was . . .

. . . his tongue was against her, lapping a wide wet path, and her hips were up, her tail canted aside, and the desire was there, hard and hot and needful . . .

. . . and Sokkolfr's tongue was pushing inside, easing the muscles, making ready for his fingers, which were slicked and strong, and his tongue moved lower, letting the fingers work but not relinquishing a single shred of the pleasure he was creating, and Isolfr keened between his teeth, unable to keep his hips from rocking, unable to tell his need from Viradechtis', and when Hroi mounted her, she was ready, unafraid, and Isolfr was crying out—no words now, only desperate begging cries, and when Sokkolfr's mouth and hands moved away, he wailed, his raw need overwhelming Viradechtis as well, so that this time at the touch of Hroi's sex she did not pull away.

Sokkolfr's hands were on his hips, Hroi's legs around her barrel. "Oh," said Sokkolfr, a breath, a whine, and Isolfr felt him, felt slickness and heat and heaviness, felt Sokkolfr move *into* him, slowly, felt Hroi's sex inside her, felt the knot swell, locking dog and bitch together, and something trapped in Isolfr's chest was suddenly released. He did not know what to call it, love or care or desire, but it was there between them and it rode the pack-sense from Isolfr to Hroi, from Sokkolfr to Viradechtis, and they moved together, and the scent of pine-boughs and earth was strong around them.

֍

Wolves are not men. They do not mate like men; they do not love like men. Isolfr knew that, knew that Viradechtis' need and Hroi's stamina would outlast his and Sokkolfr's. He knew as well that this would not be like the first time; the act of mating would bring Viradechtis' estrus to a close within a day or two, and he had, in fact, felt some relief at the knowledge that it would not drag on in endless prickling heat and frustration.

But knowing is not the same as understanding. The strength of night came down around them while he was still stretched, half-drowsing, under the leisurely, rocking weight of Sokkolfr's body as they shadowed Hroi's slow, languorous tie with Viradechtis. Isolfr had long since sprawled on his belly, face cradled on his crossed arms, relaxed and half-drowsing as Sokkolfr nibbled his shoulder and nape and moved against him without urgency, without sharpness.

They were past that, *those* needs long seen to; this was about the wolves, and the pack. This was the heartbeat of the world, creation, destruction, brothers of the wolfthreat and werthreat, until Sokkolfr drew breath hard and flexed taut against Isolfr, not for the first time, and finally fell against his shoulders, sighing out bliss.

One minute, two, and Isolfr moved against his werthreatbrother restlessly, seeking in Viradechtis' stead—a reflex, a low driving thread of desire. Sokkolfr laughed against his neck and kissed him behind the ear, and said softly, in almost-human tones, "You know, they'll be at it all night."

"Mmmm," Isolfr said, pushing into Sokkolfr's warmth. He couldn't help it; his body moved with his sister's, and the heat was still driving her, low, and sweet, and unfinished. He whimpered complaint as Sokkolfr moved back, stroking his shoulders, and Sokkolfr laughed again. "How would you like to be on top for a while, Isolfr?"

"*Me?*" Isolfr said. He rolled onto his back under the bridge of Sokkolfr's body and set his hands on Sokkolfr's waist.

"There's no reason you can't," Sokkolfr said reasonably. "*They* won't mind."

"But . . ."

Sokkolfr stroked his hair back from his face. "Please?"

"You want me to?" His voice was nothing more than a whisper, his eyes wide. He had never imagined such a thing being *offered* to him, not unless he was as lucky as Hrolleif in his wolfjarl. And he certainly hadn't imagined Sokkolfr would . . . would . . .

Would lie down for him.

He sat up, said, "I don't know what to do."

"Well, Ulfgeirr explained it to me very carefully," Sokkolfr said in his dry, straightfaced way. "So I imagine I can explain it to you."

"Oh," said Isolfr, and of course Ulfgeirr had explained, had shown, as well—"Sokkolfr, I don't want . . ." But he couldn't explain, couldn't find the words, and the heat was growing in his belly and thighs. "I don't want to hurt you."

"You won't," Sokkolfr said, and moved easily to hands and knees, arching his back down.

A silence, and then Isolfr said in a small voice, feeling himself blush, "Do you know where the salve's gotten to?"

Sokkolfr snorted laughter into the blanket. "It's around here some-where."

They both ended up looking for it in the uncertain firelight, and found it at last under the pine boughs that made up their bed. Sokkolfr said, "Ulfgeirr said, don't worry that you're using too much. Because you won't be."

"All right," Isolfr said. His breathing was faster, his own eagerness like a fire sweeping through his body with every beat of his heart.

Sokkolfr went to his knees, resting his forearms on the blanket. "And put it on yourself as well as on—in me."

"Yes," said Isolfr.

The salve was something Jorveig made, the smell medicinal but not unpleasant. Isolfr was lavish with it. Sokkolfr said, slightly muffled against the crook of his elbow, "Ulfgeirr said, go slow."

"We didn't do very well with that part," Isolfr said, teasing a little, and felt more than heard Sokkolfr's laughter.

"It's different, with a bitch. I mean, in heat. It's not like . . ."

"Had you done it before?" He was working slowly, the conversation helping to distract him from his own need, from the dense animal plea-sure saturating the pack-sense.

"Not very often," Sokkolfr said. "But yes. The wolfheofodmenn make sure of it, you know, that no one comes virgin to mating."

"Wise of them," Isolfr murmured. Sokkolfr was relaxed with the hours of their lovemaking; he opened easily, his long body willing and pliant, and Isolfr had to bite hard on his lower lip to keep from saying anything stupid.

"Yes," Sokkolfr said. "Isolfr, I wish—"

"Hush," Isolfr said gently, and just then he found within Sokkolfr

what Hrolleif had once found within him and marveled at his own satisfaction as Sokkolfr cried out in pleasure. There was no talking after that,
need simmering in both of them, partly theirs and partly their wolves',
but Isolfr was slow, careful, and Sokkolfr's sigh when Isolfr at last pressed
close against him was of satisfaction, not of pain.

They rocked together, their wolves with them, within them, and
made something new in the world.

Five

The winter was war. The trolls pressed southward, as relentless as the snow from the mountain heights, and Ulffred himself, who was older even than Hrolleif, was heard to comment that there had never been so many in living memory, no, nor in the memories of any wolfcarl he'd known in his long life. It was not a hard winter, no colder than most, and game was thick in the wood. The wolfheofodmenn were helpless to explain the reason behind the inundation of trolls. Fortunately, they were not helpless to *fight* it, and they were likewise fortunate that—as if they had suffered casualties enough in the spring—wolves and men alike emerged scatheless from battle, again and again.

It was a miracle, Othinn's gift that could not last.

Viradechtis, growing fat with cubs, chafed for the hunt but was spared it, and Isolfr chafed with her. He paced the hall, fretful in their confinement, and showered his sister with treats and attention when

Hroi was not present to spoil her. Glaedir did also—not a tremendous surprise, but a meaningful one, that he paid court to Viradechtis even when she was great with another wolf's young.

As Eyjolfr paid *his* court to Isolfr, between battles. A polite, understated sort of court, it was true, and one suited to a wolfcarl and not a woman—Isolfr chuckled to think of his mother or sister offered the beaten bronze rings from a troll's gnarled fingers as a curio—but it was court nonetheless. Viradechtis betrayed no interest beyond the companionate, and Isolfr understood. It was not the way of the wolfthreat to seek pleasure in their mating when there were no young to be made.

It *was* the way of the werthreat, and his time with Sokkolfr had reawakened something in Isolfr that he had almost forgotten, among the business of his new life as a wolfcarl. He had his admirers among the camp followers and the thrall-women of the wolfheall, and he took himself to them when desire was on him, in a sort of casual way, less finicky as a wolfcarl than he had been as a jarl's son. He remembered rejecting that option when Viradechtis was a puppy, but could not remember why. The women of the wolfheall were warm and willing, and they understood the ways of wolves as much as anyone not bonded could. But they could not help his loneliness, and so he also had a different, sharper awareness that Eyjolfr's courtship had as much to do with himself as with Glaedir and Viradechtis—and that Eyjolfr's lover Randulfr, whose Ingrun might be second bitch to Viradechtis when she was only fourth under Vigdis, was not opposed—and with that knowledge weighing him, he once or twice permitted Eyjolfr liberties he might otherwise have refused.

And at night, he slept between Sokkolfr and Frithulf, Viradechtis great-bellied and snoring beside him, and that gave him comfort.

❧

One of Hrolleif's particular ideas was that wolves and wolfcarls needed to accustom themselves to going among wolfless men—and that wolfless men needed to be accustomed to seeing trellwolves so that they would not think them monsters as terrifying as trolls.

In practice, this meant that when the wolfheall did business in Nithogsfjoll village, it did so with wolves in attendance, and the wolf-carls, especially those with young wolves, were encouraged to take their exercise in that direction. Ironically, now that Isolfr belonged to the wolfheall, he spent more time in the village than he ever had when he belonged to the keep.

Viradechtis enjoyed the village, and as her girth slowly expanded with her growing pups, she and Isolfr walked there more and more often. It was easier on her than the tangled thickets and steep ravines of the forest, and Isolfr noticed that even those villagers who were most uneasy with the wolfheall did not seem to be frightened by the gravid young konigenwolf. Several of the village matrons would rise from their spinning or sewing and come to their doors when they saw Isolfr's flaxen head, to ask about the progress of Viradechtis' pregnancy and share wisdom from their own, sometimes far more explicit than he was prepared for. The younger ones especially seemed to delight in making him blush.

But it was Hjordis Weaver who asked him boldly one afternoon, "Does she like to be petted, as dogs do?"

Hjordis was nearly twenty-five, a grown woman, unmarried only because Einarr Skeggason had died of a pleurisy three winters back. She was tall, big-boned, her hands strong and callused from spindle, wheel, and loom. But her eyes were bright and merry as a girl's still, wickedly teasing, and Isolfr knew he was blushing when he said, "Yes."

He didn't need to say anything at all, he thought, his embarrassment lessening when he saw that Viradechtis' ears had perked. She knew the word "petted."

"Would she let me, do you think?"

"Give her your scent," Isolfr said. "She will not bite you, that I promise."

Hjordis smiled at him and extended her hand. Viradechtis snuffled it, her tail waving cheerfully, and then nudged—gently by her own standards, but hard enough to stagger anyone not braced for it. Hjordis laughed, mingled startlement and delight, and then began to scruffle

Viradechtis' ears in a way guaranteed to make a trellwolf melt like butter in the sun.

"Don't lean on her, sister," Isolfr said and, shyly, to Hjordis, "She still knocks me down sometimes, when she forgets she's not a puppy."

"How old is she?"

It took a moment for Isolfr to reckon. "It must be more than six seasons by now."

"Not so far removed from a puppy, then. And yet already a mother. Do young creatures grow up so fast in your wolfheall, Isolfr?"

His gaze, startled, came up to her face. She smiled, blue eyes dancing, both hands now rubbing just behind the hinge of Viradechtis' jaw while the konigenwolf moaned and made silly faces of delight. He swallowed, and gave her a smile he might have given Alfleda, once. "Aye. Aye, they do."

Her expression warmed, and she said, "Would you and your lady like to step inside out of the cold?"

His heart hammered. She was not beautiful—long-nosed, raw-boned—but she wanted him. She cared nothing for the politics of werthreat and wolfthreat, cared nothing that he was brother to a konigenwolf. Her smile was for him, and he said, "Yes, we would like that very much," and was astonished at his own daring.

Hjordis Weaver smiled and welcomed him into her house. And not very much later, into her bed.

❧

Ingrun littered first, and Isolfr worried, but Hrolleif patted his shoulder and told him it was often so, with first litters, and that some bitches simply took longer than others.

Viradechtis' time came with the thaw. The restlessness was on Isolfr with the first spring rains; he and Viradechtis paced the roundhall together, scarcely noting the sidelong looks from the werthreat. The wolfthreat watched with grave interest, and he was astonished by the fondness that permeated the pack-sense, not merely for Viradechtis, but for himself. They wished him well, wished her well, and even as it amazed him, it made the restlessness, the aches and twinges, easier to bear.

Viradechtis chose a corner in the kitchen storeroom behind the hearth for her den, inconveniently, but not surprisingly. Ingrun and her three pups—big males, all of them—were already ensconced in the record-room, and bitches would rarely share a den when their pups were new.

Isolfr wished that Hrolleif could have helped him, but it had been perfectly clear that Viradechtis would not tolerate Vigdis near her birthing den, and they both knew it would only get worse when the puppies were actually born. So Isolfr was left with Grimolfr as his guide, and all Isolfr could think of was Skjaldwulf's old stories and how many bitches in them died littering.

"I've helped with more litters than Hrolleif has," Grimolfr pointed out, coming upon Isolfr and Viradechtis in the storeroom, she pacing in small, fretful circles, he sitting in the corner watching her, feeling such anxiety it was hard to breathe.

Isolfr knew it was true, that the wolfjarl sat with every littering wolf, whereas the wolfsprechend could sit only with his own. But it did not help. There was no ease in his relationship with Grimolfr. He wished he could have Sokkolfr beside him, but it was unwise to have too many men in the room, especially with a first litter.

"She is young, strong, and not so crowded with pups as Asny was. Do not fear until there is reason for it."

Sound advice. Isolfr only wished he could follow it. He sat with Viradechtis that night as she lay down, panting, rose, paced, muttering again as she had at the onset of her first heat, talking in almost human tones. Grimolfr sat with him, speaking occasionally of trivia, small things. Then, quite abruptly: "I hear you are keeping company with Hjordis Weaver."

Isolfr startled. "Aye. Is that . . ."

"Oh, 'tis no problem. Hjordis is her own woman, and all know it. But if you lie with her, then you may get her with child. Yes?"

"Yes," Isolfr agreed, feeling himself go red.

"'Tis a thing that happens," Grimolfr said, more gently. "And in sooth it is a good thing, for village and heall both. For wolfcarls are strong men, and their blood is vigorous. But what you must know is that the wolfheall owes duty to your children as much as it does to your wolf-sister's."

"Oh?"

"Sometimes the woman wishes to keep the child, and we are too wise to come between a mother and her cub." A flash of a grin. "But if she does not or cannot, as also sometimes happens, then the child comes to us. It is not a bad thing to be heall-bred, as both Hrolleif and I can tell you."

"What if the child is a girl?"

"Then we dower her. Many jarls are happy to wed the good will of the Wolfmaegth. And any wolfheall needs women like Jorveig, or Hilde who is mistress of the flocks. And boys can be apprenticed, if they do not wish to follow their father. It is not thralldom, Isolfr."

"No, I see that. And thank you for—"

He had been watching Viradechtis, because it was easier than trying to meet Grimolfr's eyes, and he saw another contraction ripple across her belly. She turned her head, ears up, as if startled by it, and whined low in her throat. Isolfr's hands went to his mouth like a girl's at the rush of fluid that followed, soaking her tail and hocks, and he started forward, but Grimolfr's hand on his shoulder stayed him. "It's her water breaking. It won't be long."

And of course Isolfr knew that, couldn't be a jarl's son in a keep full of cows and pigs and serving-wenches, and the eldest of three children, without knowing that. But it was different, now, because it was Viradechtis, and he could feel her contractions rippling her belly, feel her urgency and her nervousness and her desire to be *done*.

Isolfr sat back, and waited for her to come and shove her great head roughly against his chest, her coarse, slick coat warm between his fingers. He held her tight, chin between her ears, and she leaned into him when she strained again. "It's not bad for her to be walking around?" Just to be saying something, *doing* something, although the only one there to hear it was Grimolfr.

"Trust the wolf," Grimolfr said, his voice rough with some emotion Isolfr couldn't identify. "The pack knows how to birth pups."

And they did, Isolfr realized, unfolding into the pack-sense, feeling dogs and bitches—present and absent—aware of Viradechtis in her labor, ears tuned, hearts laboring in time. Ingrun was there with her, calm and satisfied, knowing, experienced, and behind her were Vigdis and Asny and even Kolgrimna. Isolfr squeezed Viradechtis tight, awed and terrified at the thought that he could have gone his whole life without knowing this, a wolfless man—

And then she whined and pulled away from him, and lay heavily on the folded blankets piled under the bottom shelf, panting, her flanks rippling with effort, and Isolfr glimpsed bloody white membrane and dark fur before the pup slipped back inside. Grimolfr went to her side, gesturing Isolfr forward impatiently. "When he breaches again, hold him—gently—and help. It's less work for the bitch if she doesn't have to start over again with every push, and once she gets the shoulders out he'll come fast."

Isolfr nodded, his hands spread, ready to catch. When the puppy appeared again, he grabbed the slick, tiny paws in trembling hands and held them, not so much pulling as resisting the pup's tendency to slip back in. Viradechtis whined and *pushed*, the will of the wolf-pack behind her, and Isolfr's hands were full of slimy puppy.

"Clear his mouth," Grimolfr said, as the wolf curled curiously around to see what was happening. "And then give him to his mother so she can bite the cord."

Isolfr did, although his hands were shaking. Viradechtis snuffled her first-born, bit through the cord, and then cleaned him with two swipes of her tongue. And Isolfr watched, wide-eyed, as the pup struggled forward, pushing with his almost useless legs, and found his mother's teat. "Good boy," Grimolfr said softly, and Isolfr did not ask if he meant the newborn pup or the shaky-handed wolfcarl. Grimolfr showed Isolfr how to deal with the afterbirth, and advised him not to watch while Viradechtis ate it.

It happened three more times between the midpoint of the night and the dazzling glory of midday. The second of these, Grimolfr rocked back abruptly on his heels as the pup came into the world, and swore.

"What?" said Isolfr, busy with the tiny body in his hands.

"Your little girl's thrown us a bitch," Grimolfr said.

Isolfr looked again, even as the pup squirmed and bleated and Viradechtis made a sharp gruff noise demanding her third-born child. Isolfr gave her her daughter and turned his head to look at Grimolfr. "I thought . . ."

"You thought correctly," Grimolfr said. "Trellwolves are warriors. They do not throw bitch-pups very often . . . we were amazed that Vigdis threw two in ten years. Asny and Kolgrimna have never thrown bitches at all, and Ingrun has only once. We sent her daughter to the wolfheall at Vestfjorthr, where I believe she does very well."

He was babbling, Isolfr realized incredulously, and Grimolfr realized it himself. He ran his hand down the side of his face and swore again. "Your sister is full of wonders."

"Yes," Isolfr said and looked at Viradechtis, who laughed back at him. Her daughter was already at a teat, working eagerly, and Viradechtis was unmistakably smug.

The fourth pup, a dog, was born near noon, and Viradechtis and the wolfthreat knew there were no more. She flopped down on her side with a great sigh, and the two men crouched beside her. Two brindled dog-pups, a gray dog-pup, and the red bitch-pup.

"You have done well, wolfthreatsister," Grimolfr said, and she thumped her tail tiredly against the flagstones.

The wolfjarl stood up, stretched and grimaced, and said, "Come, Isolfr," offering him a hand. "Let your sister and her children rest. You need to eat and bathe, and I think to sleep yourself."

Isolfr glanced at Viradechtis, who gave him a fond but exasperated look.

"You're right," he said and accepted Grimolfr's hand. "My mother always said there was no place for men in a birthing-room."

He looked at Grimolfr; Grimolfr looked back at him. For a moment they were both straight-faced, as befitted wolfjarl and brother to a konigenwolf. Then Grimolfr's lips twitched, and he and Isolfr fell against each other, laughing too hard to stand on their own.

Viradechtis thumped her tail against the floor and laughed with them.

⚬⚭⚬

Viradechtis wouldn't allow Hroi into the narrow warmth of the store-room, so he lay on the earthen floor beside the door and would not be moved, watching from under arched brows as Isolfr and the tithe-boys went in and out. Isolfr found, to his surprise, that it was his responsibility to give the pups their wer-names—although he wasn't sure where he'd thought they'd come from otherwise—and he chose Hannar, Olmoth, and Nyr for the dogs and Thraslaug for the bitch.

He felt a little pity for the tithe-boys. Two litters kept them busy, and they regarded both him and Randulfr with almost superstitious awe. It was hard to remember that only two years ago, that had been him.

What was harder was being chained to the camp in the rising spring, and he knew Viradechtis felt it too. They both breathed a sigh of relief when the pups legged out a little—Ingrun's and Viradechtis', both—and the whole mad pack of them could be left in the care of one bitch while the other enjoyed a hunting expedition or just a long ramble with her brother. Not long after *that*, the pups were old enough to be taught to hunt, and Isolfr sometimes had two days in a row when it was like old times, himself and his sister, Frithulf and Sokkolfr and their wolves, rambling the forest when their duties didn't hold them to the camp. Sokkolfr continued to be Ulfgeirr's right hand, and Isolfr's duties were divided between weapons-mastering the tithe-boys and assisting Hrolleif, despite the uneasy awareness between them that Vigdis would come into season soon, and the rivalry between herself and her daughter would be pushed to a peak.

The one relief was that Thraslaug showed no signs of having the instinct of a top bitch. Even her brothers bullied her, to the point where the tithe-boy who seemed sure to bond her was obliged to feed her away from the others to ensure she got some supper. Randulfr took that boy under his wing, and Isolfr was grateful to be spared the embarrassment of giving advice when he himself was still so uncertain.

That summer, as last, the threat of the trolls continued long past the spring equinox. Grimolfr's wolfheall was fortunate to lose only two wolves and a man; east of them, Thorsbaer lost an entire long patrol. Isolfr and Viradechtis were among the wolves and men sent to assist in hunting down the trellthreat responsible. The Thorsbaer wolfsprechend did not join the patrol, as his bitch was on the edge of season, and Isolfr was less surprised than he might have been at how easily Viradechtis dominated the pack. The Thorsbaer werthreat eyed him and Viradechtis thoughtfully, and although no one had time or energy for courting, Isolfr noticed which men took particular pains to be pleasant. Everyone knew a new konigenwolf meant a new wolfheall, and Eyjolfr was not the only wolfcarl who could plan ahead.

Vigdis' season came while Isolfr and Viradechtis were on patrol. By the time frost fell, man and wolf were as blooded as any of the Wolf-maegth, and not even Grimolfr called him *cub* any more.

At the dark of the solstice, the village of Kallekot was overrun.

Grimolfr, haggard, his eyes red-rimmed, bloodshot, both he and Skald worn near to nothing, left in the early darkness of the morning a few days later, heading in the direction of the keep. He was back by noon, livid, swearing foully, and it swept through the werthreat like a brush fire that he had gone to petition Lord Gunnarr to raise a militia among the steadholders and artisans.

And Lord Gunnarr had refused.

Isolfr tried to stay out of Grimolfr's way, especially as the wolfjarl had started drinking the moment he got back and by suppertime was drunk, the first time any of the werthreat could remember seeing such a thing except at wakes.

But the pack-sense meant you couldn't hide from anyone, even if you wanted to, and Isolfr felt no surprise, only apprehensive resignation, when Grimolfr cornered him.

"Your father," the wolfjarl said, "thinks I'm bedding you. Thinks that's why I won't let you leave." He snorted unmirthful laughter. "As if I could *make* you leave, eh, Isolfr? Says he's given . . . given enough to the wolfheall, so why can't we do our proper *work?*"

"Grimolfr, I—"

"Maybe I *should* be bedding you. Maybe I should lay you out on Gunnarr's damn table there in the great hall. Think your father'd like that?"

"No," Isolfr said, crowded against the wall, watching Viradechtis and Skald watch each other, awash in the ale-stench of Grimolfr's breath and sweat.

"No," Grimolfr agreed, and then his hand was in Isolfr's hair, knotting behind his ear, jerking his head back so that they were face to face. Isolfr held still, met Grimolfr's eyes steadily. The pack-sense was tight around them; he could feel Ulfgeirr and Hrolleif both heading their way and knew Vigdis wouldn't be far behind, and if Vigdis entered this already precarious situation, there was going to be a very bloody, very ugly, and very, very pointless fight.

So he did the only thing he could think of.

He yanked forward against the wolfjarl's grip and kissed Grimolfr. On the mouth, not subtly, and hard.

And Grimolfr released him, staggering back; Skald was there, supporting his brother, letting Grimolfr's fingers clutch at his ruff, giving Isolfr a dismissive look with his smoke-orange eyes, and Isolfr thankfully edged two steps sideways to where Viradechtis was waiting for him and threw his arms around her, burying his face in her familiar smell. She gave him pine-boughs-in-sunlight and licked his ear and neck, and her pups came and clambered anxiously on both of them.

He heard Hrolleif say gently, "Come to bed, wolfjarl."

☙❧

In the morning, Grimolfr was ashen-faced with hangover but grimly steady on his feet, grimly measured in his words. He did not apologize, and Isolfr did not expect him to. He was not sure there was anything to apologize for, and if there was, he rather thought it was his place to be apologizing for his father, and that he could not bring himself to do.

Isolfr sat and watched and listened as Grimolfr called eleven men of the werthreat before him, bid them go to the wolfjarls of the North and summon them to a Wolfmaegthing. "We cannot hide the truth any longer," he said, "and the truth is that we are being overrun."

Wolfmoots, Isolfr had gathered from Eyjolfr, were not uncommon among the other wolfheallan. Nithogsfjoll, the most northerly wolfheall, was also the most isolated and needed more than the excuse of a fine spring day to meet with another threat. Their closest neighbors were Gunnarr's keep and Gunnarr's steading, and—

And Isolfr hoped he was worth it to the Wolfmaegth.

He had never forgotten his mother's quiet comment about honor, and those twinned thoughts lent him a stern sense of purpose. Unfortunately, it was a purpose without direction as yet, and so he resigned himself to wait for the Wolfmaegthing with good grace, even when Ulfrikr Un-Wise mocked him that—if there *had* been any doubt that every wolf and man who was not needed to patrol would come—that doubt was removed by giving them the opportunity to ogle Isolfr and Viradechtis.

Isolfr *did* manage to bloody Ulfrikr's pretty nose on the practice field, however, so he was not entirely without satisfaction.

Travel times were long, and with the trolls loose in the world far fewer wolves and men could come than otherwise; steadings could not be left undefended merely so the wolfheofodmenn could unify a course. It was a fortnight and a week until the Wolfmaegthing, and Isolfr fretted every instant. In the days before, Nithogsfjoll wolfheall assumed the aspect of a bazaar, and in the roundhall itself they slept packed together like pups in a den.

Isolfr was fascinated by the wolfjarls who arrived and by the wolfcarls they chose to bring with them. And especially by their wolves. He could see, more easily than he would have thought—if he had thought about it beforehand at all—the bloodlines of the various wolfthreats, and in fact recognized the wolfjarl of Kerlaugstrond by his brother, who was of the same dam as Vigdis though of an earlier litter.

Although the pack-sense of Nithogsfjoll remained cohesive, comfort like a heavy blanket in the back of Isolfr's mind, the trellwolves of other packs were quite willing to talk to him. Most of the wolfjarls had brought their young wolves, and Isolfr was appalled and embarrassed to realize that, no matter how crudely he had put it, Ulfrikr had been right. The wolfjarls could talk about trolls, but their threats were interested in the young konigenwolf and the promise of a new wolfheall. There were fights: young wolves, and young men, and for one heart-stopping moment Vigdis and Signy—the konigenwolf of Thorsbaer, who was half-term and snappish in her discomfort—almost lit into each other. They stood nose to nose, lips curled, amber eyes and green unflinching, a low rumble rolling from Signy's throat and Vigdis' head down, silent, hackles raised, showing teeth as long as two joints of a woman's finger.

Isolfr plunged both hands into Viradechtis' ruff and made fists hard enough to creak the bones in his hands. If she piled in, in defense of her mother—

Then Grimolfr, calm as if he did not risk maiming or death, stepped between the konigenwolves, and Signy's brother Leitholfr had his hands on Signy, and after a moment long enough that Isolfr's chest hurt with holding his breath, Signy turned her head aside and began washing her brother's face. And Grimolfr tilted his head and caught Isolfr's eye, pushed his gray-brindled braid behind his ear, and sighed relief—a gesture that was meant for no one but Isolfr and the Thorsbaer wolfsprechend.

It was a conspiracy of sorts—the conspiracy of wolfheofodmenn presenting a front to the pack—and Isolfr was startled to find himself on the inside of it.

In the first raw days of spring, the threat of the last wolfheall arrived. The men and trellwolves of Othinnsaesc were cold and exhausted; their road had brought them all the way from the rough cliffs and fjords of the wild north sea, and they had been fourteen days traveling. Less of their threat had journeyed even than those of the other wolfheallan. There was only the wolfjarl and wolfsprechend and a handful, six, of the strongest and canniest of the wolfthreat. Isolfr lined up with the rest of the wolfheofodmenn of Nithogsfjoll wolfheall to greet them, clasping arms as the wolves whined and licked and sorted out who would defer to whom.

He was halfway down the line when he found himself looking into Gunnarr Sturluson's gray-blue eyes. He blinked, and almost stepped back, but the other man's clasp on his arm and strong hand on his shoulder steadied him long enough to note that it was not his father's face, just one very much like it, under wheaten braids shot through with ash. And the other man was staring at him with a similarly startled expression. "By Othinn, you have the look of her," the strange wolfcarl said, and squeezed his arm hard before releasing it. "Isolfr, is it not?"

The wolf at his side was a massive male, a charcoal-black as tall as Skald and broader at the shoulder, with cool green eyes. He sat politely, his head at the level of the blond wolfcarl's ribs, and smiled at Viradechtis through grooved yellow teeth.

"Yes. Isolfr Viradechtisbrother. And you—"

"Othwulf," he said, and bumped the big trellwolf's head with his elbow. "And this is Vikingr. You have the look of your mother Halfrid when she was young."

Isolfr stepped out of the line, away, where they would not block the muddy gateway. Othwulf followed, his brother at his side. Vikingr's muzzle was roaned with gray, but he still moved with the grace of a cat—a cat the size of a child's pony. Isolfr put his age at perhaps eighteen or nineteen years: a wolf in the mature prime of his life. Isolfr stole a sideways glance at the tawny Othinnsaesc head-wolf, whom Vikingr dwarfed. *That wolf must have a will of cast iron. Or perhaps the konigenwolf prefers blonds.*

He bit his lip on the grin. "You knew my mother."

"I was betrothed to your mother," Othwulf said, his thin lips twitching into a smile. "I'm your father's brother, Isolfr. I was Sturla Sturluson before I was a wolfcarl."

"Oh," Isolfr said. Viradechtis leaned heavily against his hip, making coy eyes at Vikingr. He was grateful for the warmth; he didn't think he was shivering because of the biting wind—despite the break of the stockade—or the crunch of mud freezing under his boots.

"Oh?" Mildly, an expression that Isolfr could never remember having seen on Gunnarr's face arching Othwulf's brows and pursing his lips.

Isolfr swallowed. "It—explains a great deal." Othwulf didn't answer immediately, and Isolfr shook himself, trying to break the terrible quiet that had settled over him. The motion startled Othwulf into laughter. "Come inside," Isolfr said, when he could think what to say next. "You've journeyed far, and you'll want hot ale and meat and the bathhouse."

Othwulf grinned and clasped his shoulder, and gave him a squeeze. "In just that order, too."

Twelve wolfjarls sat to the Wolfmaegthing, and ten wolfsprechends— the konigenwolf of Bravoll would litter at the equinox and did not travel, and the wolfheall of Franangford, hard-hit that winter and still reeling, could not spare both wolfjarl and wolfsprechend. But, as the wolfjarl of Bravoll said a shade ruefully, it was not as if they did not already know and agree with what the absent wolfsprechends would say. Meanwhile, the Wolfmaegth of the North sprawled across the Nithogsfjoll wolfheall's compound, a vast, noisy, squabbling family, and waited their wolfjarls' decision.

They were not idle while they waited. Ulfgeirr and wolfcarls of similar authority from the other wolfheallan were dickering like farmers' wives at market, using the opportunity of the Wolfmaegthing to shake up their threats, get new blood. Thraslaug went to Franangford with two of Kolgrimna's pups, Harekr to Bravoll, Olmoth and Eitri to Kerlaugstrond, two of Asny's pups to Ketillhill. In return, wolves from Vestfjorthr, Kerlaugstrond, and Thorsbaer joined the Nithogsfjollthreat. They did not trade with Othinnsaesc, Ulfgeirr said when Isolfr asked, because both Vigdis and Skald came from Othinnsaesc lines.

"And Arakensberg?"

Ulfgeirr snorted. "Ulfsvith, the wolfjarl of Arakensberg, is crossgrained—although if you tell anyone I said so, you're a dead man. He and Grimolfr have been scuffling for power like Mar and Glaedir these five years past. And Ulfsvith Iron-Tongue does not like it that Grimolfr called the Wolfmaegthing rather than leaving it to the discretion of Arakensberg. We would get nothing but troublemakers and weak wolves from Arakensberg this season, were I fool enough to ask, which I am not."

Isolfr nodded, and paid closer attention to the Arakensberg wolves courting Viradechtis. Two were older wolves, one Skald's age, one probably fifteen or so; the third was a pup younger than Viradechtis herself. "Puppy-love," his brother said resignedly, and he and Isolfr laughed.

Viradechtis was indulgent toward the pup, as she was indulgent toward her own children; she was polite but unenthused about the oldest wolf. Isolfr only wished she would show the same restraint with the third wolf, Kjaran—or the scent of snow carried on a bitter wind. He was an odd-eyed gray, not as heavy-built as Viradechtis or her sire, but agile and fast and very, very smart. He and his brother were the indomitable runners from Arakensburg who had brought the news of the destruction of Jorhus what seemed a lifetime ago.

The problem was not the wolf. The problem was Kjaran's brother Vethulf, a tall, arrogant blue-eyed redhead of about Eyjolfr's age. Vethulf-in-the-Fire his werthreatbrothers called him, apparently for his temper as much as his hair—and for his love, demonstrated many times over the days of the Wolfmaegthing, of a fight. Isolfr had vivid memories of the young man struggling across the frozen fields, of the sharp and concise manner in which he'd spoken of the devastation of Jorhus. He seemed far more like a wolfheofodman than Isolfr could ever hope to be.

He tried to stay away from Vethulf, but that merely put him in the thick of things with the wolfcarls of the other wolfheallan, and Viradechtis made trouble wherever she went.

"You're as bad a flirt as Kolgrimna," he told her, and she ignored him. And he understood that where Kolgrimna merely flirted out of boredom or malice or whatever it was that went on in her thick little skull, Viradechtis was thinking like a konigenwolf, encouraging competition among the dog-wolves so that she could judge their skill and speed and craftiness, so that she could choose her consort.

But it was disruptive, annoying to other konigenwolves, and inappropriate to the business of the Wolfmaegthing—and Isolfr himself was unnerved at the way she seemed to favor Vikingr. He tried not to imagine himself lying down for his uncle, tried especially not to imagine what his father would say when he heard of it, but he could not help knowing that there was nothing to stop Othwulf putting himself forward as a candidate for wolfjarl when the time came—it was not as if Vikingr and Viradechtis shared unhealthily close blood and not as if the bloodlines of wolfjarl and wolfsprechend mattered at all.

In desperation, he went to Ulfgeirr and begged to be put to work. And Ulfgeirr smiled, not unsympathetically, and set him to stirring glue for the tents that needed mending. Hot foul-smelling work, but Isolfr was comforted by the thought that no one was likely to try to court him over it.

He reckoned, however, without the persistence of a stubborn wolf. Or two wolves. For Viradechtis followed him, and Kjaran followed Viradechtis, and inevitably Vethulf-in-the-Fire followed Kjaran—and found Isolfr. Who—red-faced, his hair lank with sweat, his hands spotted with burns—had never felt less capable of dealing with someone like Vethulf in his life.

Vethulf took in the scene, his eyebrows going up. And then, instead of doing the charitable thing and going away again, he came and stood beside Isolfr while Kjaran tried to lure Viradechtis into a game of tug-o-war with a scrap of waterproofed bullhide.

"So, I hear you are Othwulf Vikingrsbrother's brother-son," Vethulf said, with a sidelong glance. "It must have been very different, growing up in the keep of a jarl."

His tone was amiable, but the blue eyes were coolly mocking. Isolfr wondered with a sudden, horrible pang, if Vethulf had been talking to Ulfrikr. "Different from?"

Vethulf's gesture took in the yard of the roundhall, the packed men and beasts, the fire Isolfr sweated over, shirtless and smoke-smudged. "It can't be what you expected your life would be like."

"Meaning what, exactly?" Isolfr said, wiping sweat off his face.

"Well, you're willing to turn your hand to any work."

He has *been talking to Ulfrikr.* "And why should I not be? Am I not a wolfcarl?"

A few feet away, near where Ulfgeirr crouched on a stool, draped in leather, Nagli raised his head and whined.

The wolf might show concern, but there was no law of pack or man that said Isolfr must stand and be insulted by a wolfcarl, even if Viradechtis favored his brother. He leaned his weight on the paddle, stirring the stinking mess in the cauldron harder.

Vethulf said, "I only meant—"

"I don't care what you meant," Isolfr said untruthfully. "I have work to do, so if you'll—"

Vethulf made an exasperated noise and pulled the paddle from Isolfr's hands, leaving Isolfr staring at him, bewildered. "Aye," Vethulf said, beginning to stir the glue savagely, "and I see they're right that say you've prickles like a porcupine. Go find a stream to dunk your head in, Isolfr, and perhaps you'll be better company."

Dismissed like a child, and Isolfr did go to the forest for most of the afternoon, though he and Viradechtis came back with little enough to show for it. The game was picked thin, wolves hunting anything, down to deer mice. It kept him away from the wolfheall, though, and so he did it more often—even, cravenly, fleeing altogether and hunting for several nights out. The scarcity of local game was a good enough excuse. He had not realized before how strongly he needed time to himself.

So he hunted; it was useful work, and it allowed him to roam as far as he pleased. He returned with game and went out again. Frithulf came with him. Kothran and Viradechtis made a formidable team. Sokkolfr looked wistful, but he and Ulfgeirr had their hands more than full with the Wolfmaegthing; Frithulf teased him that that was what he got for making himself invaluable.

The fourteenth day of the Wolfmaegthing—and all of them hoping it would be the last, before Signy and Vigdis caused a riot—Isolfr and Frithulf were kneeling together, companionably butchering a deer while Viradechtis and Kothran fought grand mock-battles over the entrails, when Frithulf said, abruptly, "When you go to start a new wolfheall . . ."

"Yes?" said Isolfr.

He looked up when Frithulf did not answer immediately, and was surprised to see his friend blushing hotly. "Will you take me and Kothran with you?"

Isolfr's jaw dropped. He said stupidly, "Kothran will never be top wolf with Viradechtis."

Frithulf snorted and glanced fondly at his brother, currently playing keep-away with some unsavory portion of the deer's innards. "Kothran's never going to be top wolf, no matter what wolfheall we're in. And that suits me fine." He grinned. "You may find this hard to believe, but I don't *want* to be a wolfjarl. You know Sokkolfr's planning to follow you, and Ulfbjorn, and several others?"

"I . . ."

"And I want to be where you and Sokkolfr are." For once, the expression in Frithulf's bright blue eyes was perfectly serious. "You're my pack."

Isolfr nodded, his heart too full for speaking, and bent his head again to his work.

When they returned to the wolfheall, lugging the deer and a brace of rabbits, they found the doors of the roundhall still barred and the werthreat looking tired and grim. No decision had been reached. No solution had been found. And Isolfr didn't need to see Hrolleif to know what the issue was.

The issue hadn't changed.

There simply were not enough wolves, and there were not enough men, and they did not know what—if it were more than some dim, trellish instinct to expansion awakened after hundreds of years of border wars—was pushing the trellmaegth southward into the lands of men.

Isolfr and Frithulf delivered the meat to the kitchens, where a delighted and harried Jorveig greeted them with warmed ale and coarse rye bread smeared with bear fat, and then Isolfr scratched his light beard, made his excuses to his werthreatbrother, and went in search of somebody whom he had been taking pains to avoid.

Othwulf was making himself useful by the byre, doctoring the fevered hoof of a spotted cow while another man held her head. Their wolves were not in evidence, for which Isolfr was deeply grateful, and he sent Viradechtis away as well before he approached the unhappy animal. Wise to the ways of skittish cattle, Isolfr made sure she could see him plainly as he walked up. He did not think Othwulf would thank him for a kick in the ear if the cow spooked, and it was already agitated enough about what the wolfcarl was doing to it with a heated knife.

The cow lowed and jerked hard. Othwulf must have gotten the angle he wanted, because he was rewarded—if that was the proper term— by a spurt of bloody, putrid pus across his hands and the smack of a befouled cow-tail across his skull. He swore and set the cow's hoof down, grinning as she lowed again, irritably, and put her full weight on the hoof apparently without noticing that it didn't hurt. "Ungrateful woman," Othwulf said, and, holding his knife's pommel as if it were the tail of a dead rat, looked around for something on which to wipe his stinking fingers. For an instant, Isolfr could see his father's face in Othwulf's satisfaction at another problem seen to.

Mutely, Isolfr led him to the wellhead in the courtyard, hauled up a bucket, and sluiced the rot off Othwulf's hands and knife.

"Thank you, Isolfr."

"You can thank me with answers, uncle."

Othwulf laughed. "I'm not your uncle here."

Which was, of course, its own small part of the problem. "I need you to be, for a moment." He noted with gratitude that Othwulf's sardonic smile deserted him, and that the wolfcarl waited silent for what Isolfr would say. Isolfr gulped air and forged forward. "My father hates the Wolfmaegth."

Othwulf nodded, drying his knife carefully on his jerkin before putting it away. "I suspected as much. And knew it, when I saw you here. He didn't want to marry Halfrid, you know. Didn't want to be jarl and raid and quarrel and raise cattle and worry about there being enough hurdles woven to keep the sheep in pasture—" The wolfcarl sighed. "Those were to be my duties. Gunnarr talked of going viking, bringing home a king's ransom and a princess from across the sea."

"He's jarl. He could go if he wanted—"

Othwulf's eyebrow rose. "And leave Nithogsfjoll, of all places, without a lord all summer? He might as well carve runes on the door inviting the trellmaegth for dinner and maybe a circle dance." And Othwulf looked up, over Isolfr's shoulder, a squint that Isolfr knew by Othwulf's smile had the big wolf Vikingr pinned on its other end. "He was not happy to lose you."

"He was not happy," Isolfr agreed, falling into step beside him as Othwulf began walking toward the pack of wolves among whom Vikingr dozed. "And when Grimolfr went to ask for men-at-arms—"

"I understand."

Isolfr laughed, although it scoured his throat. "Not the half of it. He told the wolfjarl that he had given enough to the wolfheall already, and asked how Grimolfr liked bedding me."

Othwulf snorted laughter. "Does he like it?"

A shrug, as they drew up beside the wolves. "He wouldn't know," Isolfr answered, as dryly as he dared. "And Hrolleif would have his balls if he tried. Theirs is a closer than usual partnership, or so I am told."

"Aye, they're shield-brothers as well as wolfheofodmenn," Othwulf said, crouching beside Vikingr where the big wolf sprawled on the flags, soaking up the thin springtime sun. "It's not unheard of, and makes a strong pack when it works. There's other options, you know, for all a wolfcarl cannot marry." He regarded Isolfr steadily, and Isolfr knew that Othwulf had seen through him as if he had no more substance than the scraped membrane of a sheep's gut. "Widow-women are grateful for a strong protector, a strong provider, and they say men who know wolves are more gentle than those who do not."

Isolfr snorted mirthlessly, remembering Hjordis soft and willing in his arms. "And do they ask why that is, Othwulf?"

"Not in my experience. Nor do they wish to know what pertains when a man returns to the wolfheall and his brothers there. But women—it's good to remember women, Isolfr, although not many a warrior will say it. It reminds us why we fight. And there are not so many women in a wolfheall as for that. And there are other things—if the blood runs strong, it's a shame to spill it unbred. I've two sons of my own. The younger, I'll wager, will be a wolfcarl himself." Othwulf smiled, rising and crossing his arms. "Maybe even one like you."

Isolfr stepped back, wishing Viradechtis were beside him. "How can I shift him?" he asked plainly, hoping for some spark of knowledge in Othwulf's eyes, but Othwulf shrugged and spread his hands.

"Scare him," Othwulf said. "And show him that you are no less a man for what you have become."

Before Isolfr could speak, the doors of the wolfheall swung open, and twenty-two wolfheofodmenn emerged. Every one of them looked grim. But the pack-sense carried determination as well and the resolve that came with having settled on a course of action. One that, looking at their faces, Isolfr thought they half-knew was doomed, though it would be glorious in song. He knew what the answer was before Grimolfr raised his voice to announce it.

With summer, they would take the war to the trolls.

Somehow, Isolfr had to earn his father's forgiveness before then.

⁂

He thought about it that night, lying wakeful and cramp-limbed among fur and flesh and the dense heat of the sleeping pack. Thought about his father's pride and his mother's solemn patience, thought about the specter of Othwulf-who-had-been-Sturla that had hung, without his knowing it, over his childhood. Thought about his brother Jonak, now his father's heir, and wondered if his own shadow was lying cold across Jonak's shoulders.

He rose as soon as there was light enough to see. Bathed and dressed and braided his hair carefully, and with Viradechtis padding at his heels, slipped out of the compound. No one saw him leave, and even if they had, they would only have assumed he was going hunting.

He supposed, with bitter humor, that they would not have been entirely wrong.

Viradechtis liked the village and was happy to go there, but he didn't feel the sharp force of her interest until they were starting up toward the keep. They passed by the cottage that Hjordis shared with her sister and brother-in-law, and Viradechtis was disappointed; he promised her a visit on the return. But the keep renewed her excitement.

Here she had not been—here, as a pup, she had in fact been forbidden to go—and although she had always been sensible about the matter, her curiosity was wide-awake and eager. Her enthusiasm eased some of Isolfr's own apprehension, and he reminded himself that no matter what his father might say, he, Isolfr, was a man of the werthreat and, moreover, had sixteen stone of trellwolf to guard him. *After all,* he said to himself, as they rounded the last curve of the switchback, *he has already refused his help to the wolfheall. There is nothing you can lose.*

The scrawny young armsman on guard at the gate did not know what to make of him, and was hard pressed to keep his gaze on Isolfr's face instead of on Viradechtis, standing in the sunlight with her tail waving good-humoredly, clearly capable of eating the armsman in two bites if she felt like it.

"Tell Lord Gunnarr that Isolfr Viradechtisbrother wishes to speak with him," Isolfr said and watched, carefully not smiling, as the boy's eyes widened and he squeaked, "Yes, sir!" and bolted.

"Come, sister," Isolfr said to Viradechtis, and they stepped together into the courtyard of the keep.

It was much as Isolfr remembered it, clean and orderly, the walls gleaming with whitewash and the cobbles swept clear. Viradechtis leaned against him, interested in what she saw and smelled, a little puzzled by his thoughts. He gave her a memory of the birthing-box she had spent her first few months of life in, and she tilted her head, bumping up into his armpit, and thought of puppies playing catch-me across these clean, clean cobbles.

Isolfr was smiling at the thought when someone said, from the main door to the keep, "Njall?"

He turned and for a moment had no idea who the girl was. But he saw Halfrid in her face, and said, "Kathlin?"

"It *is* you!" She came down the steps, her blue eyes very wide. "Is this your wolf?"

"This is my sister, Viradechtis," Isolfr said. "Viradechtis, this is my sister Kathlin. And I'm Isolfr now, sister."

"Oh." Her dismay was plain. "I forgot."

"It does no harm," he said smiling. "You're lucky I remember *your* name at all."

"You didn't come," she said, and he heard all her hurt piled up in her voice. "You said you'd come, Nja—Isolfr."

"I am here now," he answered, without looking down. "And if Father will permit it, I may come again."

She bit her lip and glanced down at Viradechtis, in patent avoidance. "Will she . . . may we clasp hands?"

"I would hope you might have a hug for your brother," Isolfr said, and she blushed and sidled close enough to hug him hesitantly.

"I have *missed* you," she said, as shyly as if she spoke to a stranger. Isolfr was not sure who he hated more at that moment, his father for forbidding him the keep or himself for making no effort at reconciliation.

"Would you like to pet Viradechtis?" he offered. "She'll love you forever if you scratch her ears."

"Oh, may I?" Sincere delight, and he nodded. "Give her your scent first, as you would with a dog."

She did, and Viradechtis snuffled her hand, licked her fingers— *sausage* she said happily to Isolfr—and ducked her head invitingly. Kathlin took the invitation, and smiled blindingly when Viradechtis' tail began to wave back and forth.

"I'm glad you have her," Kathlin said. "I worried about you, when you went and Father was so—"

"*Kathlin!* Get away from that beast!" It was a roar; Kathlin, Isolfr, and Viradechtis all startled and turned. Gunnarr Sturluson stood in the doorway of the keep.

Kathlin hesitated; Isolfr said, "Please, tell Mother I would speak with her before I leave," and she gave him a quick, grateful nod and fled.

Isolfr looked up at his father and was bewildered to find him so small; he was accustomed to think of his father as imposing, stern and knowing as a god, but that had been before he learned to look Grimolfr Skaldsbrother in the face.

Isolfr wondered how he could not have noticed, that spring day four years ago, that his father was afraid of Vigdis. Afraid, but willing to stand up to her to protect his son.

Isolfr licked dry lips.

Viradechtis did not care to be called *beast*, and she did not care, either, for men who smelled like Isolfr but not as nice. Isolfr caught a twitch, there and gone, of what his father smelled like through Viradechtis' nose, and was reminded with sudden painful humor of what Ulfmaer had told him his first day as a tithe-boy, and of Hroi's emphatic agreement.

He coughed instead of laughing and said, "Father. Greetings. It pleases me to find you well."

"Does it?" Gunnarr growled. "And I suppose you want me to tell you it pleases *me* to see you in the company of that—"

"I should warn you, Father, that Viradechtis understands our speech tolerably well." The blood drained from Gunnarr's face, but he continued forward, and Isolfr remembered his duty—both the duty of honor he owed his father, and the greater duty he owed the wolfheall—and said, "I do not ask your blessing, Father, only your help."

"Help?" For a moment, there was light in Gunnarr's eyes. "You mean you want to come home?"

"Help for the wolfheall," Isolfr said patiently and told Viradechtis that if she moved so much as a paw, he'd put her to hauling firewood all summer long.

"You're here on the wolfjarl's errand," Gunnarr said, face darkening again. "Is it not enough that he's made you his wolf-bitch? Must he make you his errand-boy, too?"

For a moment, the matter hung precariously in the balance. Isolfr's fists were clenched so tightly he could feel his nails digging into his palms, and Viradechtis was growling, a low oscillation of menace, just barely at the threshold of audibility.

Gunnarr heard and went up on his toes, too proud to step back; Isolfr heard and reined his temper in. "Father, I will tell you once and tell you truly. Lord Grimolfr does not bed me, nor would wish to. And I come on the business of the wolfheall, not at his bidding. I come to tell you that what Lord Grimolfr told you is true. The trolls are coming south in greater numbers than the oldest man in the wolfheall can remember seeing. The wolfjarls have held Wolfmaegthing, and come summer, they will march north. And I tell you also, Father, if the wolfless men do not march with them, then the Wolfmaegth will die in the mountains and you will have nothing standing between you and the trolls but these beautifully whitewashed walls. And your walls will not save you."

He stopped, panting for breath. He had never said so much to his father at one time—had never heard his father let *anyone* say so much without interruption. And his father was staring at him as if he had never seen Isolfr before.

Gunnarr said, abruptly, "I must think on't," and turned away, disappearing into the keep.

Isolfr wanted very much to go home; Viradechtis, leaning into him, agreed. He turned toward the gate, and his mother emerged from the shadows of the stables. "Isolfr."

"Mother." He crossed to her; they clasped hands as adults.

She looked at Viradechtis. "And this is your . . ."

"Viradechtis is her name."

"A beautiful creature," said Halfrid, and Viradechtis told Isolfr that she liked this one much better than the unpleasant-smelling man.

"She thinks well of you, too," he said to Halfrid.

"You have found your way to manhood, I think," she said, touching one of his braids.

"Maybe," Isolfr said, and they smiled at each other ruefully. "I remembered what you said about honor. It has helped."

"Good," said Halfrid. "It is little enough a woman can give her sons."

Isolfr hesitated. "Will Father—"

"I will speak to him. Give him a little time."

"A little time we have, but not a great deal."

"I heard." Her face was grim. "And I believe you. I . . . I honor the wolfheallan for the choice they are making, though I fear it."

"We all fear, Mother," Isolfr said, and in some part of his mind was astonished that he was admitting as much to a woman. "But fear doesn't . . ." He shook his head helplessly. "It changes nothing."

"Yes," said Halfrid. "So it always is. So it has been with your father. I will speak to him."

"If it will help . . ." He hesitated again. "Othwulf—my uncle Sturla—came to the Wolfmaegthing. I do not know if Father should be told or not."

"Not," Halfrid said calmly, decisively. "You do not want to be raking up old bitternesses, old injuries." And without the slightest change in tone: "Is he well?"

"Yes," Isolfr said and immediately banished forever a question he had been wondering whether or not to ask. "He is well. Happy, I think. He has two sons. His wolf-brother is named Vikingr; he's bigger than Viradechtis."

"Impossible," said Halfrid, laughing. "And in any event, he cannot be more beautiful."

Viradechtis liked this one *very* much.

◦⥝◦

bjordis was not alone at her spinning wheel when Isolfr came to her home. Her sister, Angrbotha, stood up abruptly, though, and went to stir the fire with only a cursory greeting to the visitor. Isolfr and Viradechtis came to Hjordis, padding across the rammed earth floor, and she held out her hand so he could help her rise. Her expression was a little pinched, as if she worried, and she shook her skirts a little more firmly than usual after he claimed his kiss. She still had a scratch and a cuddle for Viradechtis, though, and he noticed that Angrbotha made herself quickly scarce.

"What's wrong, Hjordis?"

She looked up from the wolf and back down as quickly, her hands never stilling. "I'm with child," she said, plainly, and stole another quick sideways look as if to judge his mood.

The words made no sense to him at first, but then Viradechtis whined and nudged him, encouraging him to join the petting, and he blinked himself out of shock. "My child?" he said stupidly.

Hjordis laughed and straightened. "No, it could be any of a dozen men—yes, your child, Isolfr." She had her pride. She didn't give ground or drop her chin. "If you want it."

It hung there quivering in the air between them for a moment. She wrapped her arms around herself, raw-boned, ungraceful, strong—a handsome country woman, unpretentious and merry. "Don't be a fool, wench," he said, and pulled her roughly into his arms. "Of course I want it."

It wasn't until she relaxed into his embrace that he realized she was shaking. He kissed her forehead, took a breath, and swallowed hard before he said, "But we go to war at the equinox, and I cannot say when I'll return."

She didn't step back, just took a vast breath and let it out again. "You'll live to name the babe," she said against his shoulder. "I demand it."

"I will," he promised, and hoped he did not lie.

SIX

Gunnarr Sturluson mustered thirty dozen men by the equinox, and marched them out to meet Grimolfr, Isolfr, and the traveling three-fifths of the wolfheall on a day when the sky was slanting fine needles of frozen rain down on the tawny and gray and red and dark heads of warriors and wolves alike. Grimolfr never said a word, but Hrolleif, who had ridden out with them on a stout yellow pony, shot Isolfr a sideways glance. Isolfr kept his face stern, as befit a wolfcarl, but Hrolleif gave his elbow a quick squeeze and Isolfr did not think he had fooled the wolfsprechend.

Then Hrolleif returned to the wolfheall, because while Vigdis' pups were old enough for her to travel, the tithe-boys were not of an age to be left without a wolfheofodman to instruct them, and in any case—

At least a few konigenwolves would have to survive, if things went poorly for the Wolfmaegth, and Vigdis and Hrolleif would be a greater loss to the Wolfmaegth than Viradechtis and Isolfr. Vigdis had fifteen years of litters left in her, and both she and Hrolleif were experienced leaders. Isolfr was painfully aware that his wolf was still little more than a great, gangling pup, and while he was a man, he was a young one and he had not Hrolleif's canniness.

Besides, Sokkolfr and Frithulf were traveling with the war party. Gunnarr or not, Grimolfr would have had to chain Isolfr to the wall of the roundhall to keep him in Nithogsfjoll, and everybody knew it.

Werthreat and wolfless men alike pressed north despite ill weather and cold. They made a wet camp in the lee of a rose-and-gray granite cliff below Ulfenfjoll. Sokkolfr thought the name auspicious, and Frithulf laughed about it, but Isolfr did not miss the way he tucked his bronze medallion inside his shirt. It was a Thorshammer and hung on a knotted rawhide thong around his neck. He'd had it as long as Isolfr could recall.

It was not easy to make fire under those conditions. Ulfgeirr and Sokkolfr finally made shift to keep the rain off with a hide stretched on peeled poles while Skjaldwulf managed flint and tinder. Once one fire was lit, the others were easier; wood could be dried in the heat of the flames to make it burn more adequately.

Isolfr paced the camp, speaking to no one at first. He nodded to Eyjolfr and Grimolfr, didn't even attempt to enter the part of the camp claimed by his father's men, and finally fetched up against the rocks near where the Great Ulfbjorn crouched, checking little Tindr's paws as if there could possibly be something wrong that his wolf wouldn't tell him about.

"And how fare you this night, tithe-brother?"

Ulfbjorn stood, his teeth flashing through rainy dark. "Wet," he said, succinctly. "Tindr is asking to hunt. He wants meat with blood in it. Will you join us?"

Isolfr had to crane his neck back to look Ulfbjorn in the eye. "I'd be honored."

They fell into step side by side, the wolves ranging ahead. "I'm glad Tindr chose you," Isolfr said, after a little while.

"I'm glad we're brothers too," Ulfbjorn replied, which wasn't what Isolfr had said. But maybe was what he had intended. "How are you—"

"Oh, Gunnarr?" Isolfr couldn't quite bring himself to say, *my father.* He shrugged. "The real entertainment will begin when we reinforce the Wolfmaegth at the base of the mountains and he meets Othwulf. We'll want a skald along to tell *that* tale."

Ulfbjorn's laugh was a bass rumble low in his throat, almost a wolf's mutter. He seemed about to say something further, but just then Tindr howled on the scent of a stag, and they were off through the mud and leaves and the half-melted earth.

❧

The character of the land changed as they toiled north, and they caught and passed the spring. Despite the cold, Isolfr was grateful; travel was easier over frozen ground, and it kept men huddled close to their fires at night, limiting the opportunity for mischief between wolf-carls and wolfless men. Gunnarr seemed content to ignore his existence, and as Grimolfr looked to Viradechtis to head the pack in her mother's absence Isolfr was kept almost too busy to worry. They proved more than a match for the few trolls they met, dispatching them with axes and the crossbarred troll-spears wielded by the wolfless men.

The paucity of enemies worried Isolfr more than if they had been nigh overrun. Possibly the trolls were smart enough to warren away from the easiest routes of travel, but Isolfr feared that the few they ran across were scouts, and a trellish army was massing elsewhere, as it had not in the hundred hard-fought years of relative peace since the days of Freyulf and Hrolljotr. So he was wary, and the wolves were unsettled and snappish, especially when they came out of the cold taiga forests and into the tundra where the earth froze too deep and too hard for trees to root. The biting flies were a misery, but there were reindeer to keep their ragged army fed, and they were able to save their dried provisions and pemmican against want. Morale was not high, but they were grim with determination, and quarrels among the men were fewer as the cold nipped their flanks like a hunting wolf and the days grew toward endlessness. On the horizon rose the mountains called Iskryne—the ice-lashed glittering crown at the top of the world, borne on the shoulders of the giant Mimir, so old he himself had become part of the stones he carried.

Isolfr wondered that he had lived so long, to walk cold and frost-kissed into the embrace of legend.

The men and wolves of Nithogsfjoll, having the shortest distance to travel, were first to the moot and made camp there among the gnarled toes of the mountains, around stinking fires fed with desiccated reindeer and musk-ox dung. At night, Isolfr huddled with Sokkolfr and Frithulf among their wolves, and none of them demurred when Ulfbjorn asked if he could join them.

Isolfr wondered, though, since Ulfbjorn had seemed content with Ulfrikr and Aurulfr and Skirnulf. Diffidently, he asked, and Ulfbjorn said, "I grow tired of Ulfrikr's prating tongue. It's as endless as the world snake," and would say no more.

It did not assuage Isolfr's worries. While Aurulfr and Skirnulf had no harm in them, Ulfrikr was another matter. Ulfrikr Un-Wise like Frithulf Quick-Tongue was a gossip, but where Frithulf's malice did not discriminate between targets—and any rumor he passed on was sure to be bolstered or undercut by his own observations—Ulfrikr was cunning and did nothing without reason. With the Iskryne looming bleakly over them, Isolfr did not like the idea that Ulfrikr had managed to rile the phlegmatic Ulfbjorn to the point of causing a break between them.

The way of wolves is to say what they mean. Ulfbjorn had clearly said all he intended to say on the subject, and Isolfr did not plague him further. He found himself unwilling to face Ulfrikr directly without more than his own uneasy instincts to tell him that there was something amiss, and this was not a matter in which the wolfthreat could be of any great assistance. Not all wolves cared to listen to human speech as carefully as Viradechtis did, and since Tindr still hunted and played happily with the enormous gray brothers Skefill and Griss, the problem was not—Isolfr thought and smiled at his own phrasing—a wolfish one.

He sought out Aurulfr the Brown in the weak sunlight of a high overcast afternoon and found him and Griss, along with several other members of the threat, constructing a windbreak along the camp's most exposed side.

It was a good idea, and Isolfr went to work himself, letting the rhythm of shared labor color the pack-sense between himself and Aurulfr—who was no longer the weedy boy Isolfr had first known, but tall and broad in the shoulders, his brown-blond braids thick as ropes. He'd had his nose broken in the fighting the previous winter, and the lump across the bridge made him look older, harder. His green-hazel eyes were the same, though, shy and rather wary, warming noticeably when he looked at Griss and Viradechtis, who had sniffed each other, exchanged wide yawns, and curled up in a pile of gray and red and black to sleep.

"Sensible creatures," Isolfr said, and Aurulfr smiled and said, "Yes. More sensible than men."

"Yes," Isolfr agreed, glancing at the Iskryne, as he found himself doing at random moments throughout the day, as if he thought he might catch Mimir stirring in his sleep. He said, "I'm concerned about Ulfbjorn's falling-out with Ulfrikr."

And watched Aurulfr color to the roots of his hair, knowing, not happily, that his instincts had been right.

He gave Aurulfr time to collect his thoughts; he was not a bully, and he did not want this conversation to be a fight, either openly or covertly. Aurulfr, who had been Hlothvinr, was his tithe-brother.

So is Ulfrikr, said a snide little voice in the back of his mind, but Isolfr pushed it away.

Aurulfr said, "He means no harm, Isolfr. It's just . . . we're all frightened, you know, and the waiting gets hard."

"Yes," Isolfr agreed, but refused to be placated or put off. "What is it, exactly, that Ulfrikr is saying?"

"He doesn't think it's right that you've taken Hrolleif's place," Aurulfr said, miserable but not shirking the issue. "He says that's Randulfr's place by right. Or Hringolfr's. Not yours."

"Neither Ingrun nor Kolgrimna is a konigenwolf. They couldn't hold the wolfthreat." He smiled, and saw Aurulfr's eyes light in return. "I've nothing to do with it, you know. Any . . . *place* I have is as her brother.

Besides, Randulfr's quite happy *not* to have to deal with the wolf-sprechend's job." He did not mention Hringolfr, and Aurulfr did not call him on it.

He said, "It's not that, exactly. Ulfrikr . . . Some men have to have something to complain about, you know."

"Yes," said Isolfr, who did. And did not ask, because it was not Aurulfr's fault, *But why does it have to be me?*

That night, as they ate the spoils of Hroi and Kothran's hunting, Isolfr said to Ulfbjorn, "Do you think Ulfrikr truly feels there is injustice being done?"

Ulfbjorn gave him a long considering look. "You talked to Aurulfr."

"Yes."

"If I'd thought Ulfrikr were serious in his complaints," Ulfbjorn said, "I would have told you. I wanted to spare you worrying about something that isn't worth your attention."

Frithulf snorted. "Spend some more time with Isolfr and you'll realize just what a lost cause *that* is. You can't spare him worry, Ulfbjorn. All it does is make him worry about why you're sparing him."

The thread of the conversation was lost in shouting and laughter for a while as Isolfr wreaked vengeance for that calumny, with the enthusiastic help of Kothran, who liked nothing better than to be allowed to stand on his brother's chest and lick his face. But eventually, peace restored and Frithulf muttering direly about ingratitude and treachery while Kothran shoved his head in Frithulf's lap, demanding—and getting—his ears rubbed, Isolfr said, "Probably you're right, Ulfbjorn, and I oughtn't to concern myself. I know what Ulfrikr's like. I just . . ." He shrugged helplessly. "We're so far from home and walking into such trouble, I hate to have things be ugly that don't need to be."

"Peacemaker," Sokkolfr said fondly. Isolfr grinned at him. He couldn't imagine anybody who was less like his byname, when you got to know him, than the Stone. "You can't make Ulfrikr happy, Isolfr, and I think I speak for all of us when I beg you not to try."

"Hear, hear," said Frithulf, and Ulfbjorn said, "Let him complain about something foolish. He will get it out of his belly, and we will be friends again."

"Yes," Isolfr said and added only to himself, *I hope.*

☙❧

The other threats arrived slowly over the next two weeks, Thorsbaer first and Othinnsaesc again last. Each wolfjarl brought a complement of wolfless men, and the two uneasy communities of the camp grew.

Everyone was being very careful. Isolfr had had Viradechtis watching the wolfthreat from the start, and each konigenwolf who arrived added her own watchfulness to the spreading pack-sense, as wolfthreat joined wolfthreat and they became Wolfmaegth in truth. But the waiting, as Aurulfr had remarked, bore heavily on all of them, and tempers were fraying, those of men and wolves alike.

The relief Isolfr felt at not having to negotiate the wolfthreat with Signy in the mix—Signy, like Vigdis, was holding household at her wolfheall—was immediately cancelled out by the enmity which sprang up between Viradechtis and Bekkhild, the konigenwolf of Vestfjorthr. Bekkhild had not been concerned with Viradechtis at the Wolfmaegthing, but now recognized her as a rival. Her wolfsprechend, a slender man with red-gold braids and merry blue eyes, was apologetic, but acknowledged with Isolfr that there was nothing they could do except try to keep Viradechtis and Bekkhild apart. "It will be easier when we are moving," he said, and Isolfr agreed. Easier when they were moving, easier when there were trolls to fight. By the time the Othinnsaescthreat arrived, Isolfr no longer even blamed Ulfrikr for turning to petty malice to pass the time. Anything was better than this endless, helpless waiting.

But they could not leave immediately, even when their company was complete. Wolves and wolfbrothers and wolfless men from Othinnsaesc alike were exhausted; they had found more trolls than the other groups, and although they had fought them without fatalities, they had not done so without injuries, some serious. They needed at least three days' rest, and the wolfjarl of Othinnsaesc admitted that a full week would be better.

"A week, we cannot give you," Grimolfr said reluctantly, "but three days you may have."

Isolfr barely had time for a cup of broth with Othwulf before his attention was taken up, nearly from the moment of Othinnsaesc's arrival, with sorting out a nasty snarl of dominance between the wolfthreat of Nithogsfjoll and the wolfthreat of Kerlaugstrond, because while konigenwolf-in-waiting and konigenwolf were as amiable together as one could ask them to be, Osk, the second bitch of the Kerlaugstrond-threat, did not feel that she yielded place to Viradechtis, and she was a strong enough force in the threat that several of the dominant males went with her.

It was an exhausting matter to resolve without either undercutting Viradechtis' authority or offending the wolfsprechend of Kerlaugstrond—or Osk's brother, a man as touchy as his sister, who clearly gave his wolfsprechend a good deal of trouble.

Isolfr spent two days up to his eyeballs in the pack-sense between the two threats, and the first he knew of any other trouble was when he was coming back from the Kerlaugstrond camp to the Nithogsfjoll camp and heard his father's voice saying with untrustworthy mildness, "I want a word with you, boy."

He turned, let his eyebrows rise, noticing that while Gunnarr did not commit the solecism of calling him Njall, he didn't seem able to bring himself to call him Isolfr, either.

"And if you don't mind," Gunnarr said and looked pointedly at Viradechtis.

Isolfr *did* mind, but he was also aware of the need to keep strife between the wolfheallan and the wolfless men at a minimum, so he said to Viradechtis, "Go on, sister," and she gave him a deeply dubious look, but went.

He watched her until she was nearly out of sight, wanting that moment to collect his thoughts, his temper, then turned to Gunnarr, saying, "Yes, F—"

The blow came out of nowhere; he was on the ground with his ears ringing and the entire side of his face throbbing before he even realized Gunnarr was swinging at him.

"You filthy, depraved *beast*," his father hissed at him, and Isolfr got his feet under him to scramble out of range before Gunnarr could kick him, his attention focused frantically on cutting himself off from the pack-sense, from Viradechtis, with a strong command to *stay away*, because the uneasy truce between keep and wolfheall would not survive a wolf of Nithogsfjoll attacking the jarl, no matter how egregiously provoked she was.

He stood up, wiped blood off his mouth, spat sharp copper. "Father, what is this about?"

"Don't call me that. You unnatural, perverted trellspawn. Don't claim bloodkinship with me, not today or any other day."

"What—"

"You don't lie down for the wolfjarl, oh, no," Gunnarr said, almost shouted. "But what about your *uncle*?"

"My uncle? Othwulf?"

"*Sturla!*" Gunnarr howled. "Yes, your uncle Othwulf," in savagely mocking, mincing tones. "Who I understand you have been *flirting* with since the Wolfmaegthing. Is there *nothing* too low, too dishonorable for you to embrace?"

"Flirting? Father, I don't—"

"*Don't call me that*," Gunnarr said with loathing, and it was then that Sokkolfr appeared, saying, "Isolfr? Viradechtis is—"

He broke off, seeing Gunnarr's fury. Isolfr didn't imagine he himself looked much better. "Lord Gunnarr," Sokkolfr said, nodding.

"Is this another of your conquests, Isolfr?" Gunnarr said, investing his name with so much contempt that Isolfr flinched. "I hear you're very popular in the wolfheall, that even the most *unnatural* practices don't dismay you. How many men have you let have you, boy? How many in a *night*?"

Sokkolfr was somehow standing between them, saying gently and firmly, "Lord Gunnarr, the wolfjarl will call upon you later to address your concerns. You will upset the wolves if you continue to flyte their wolf-sprechend. Please."

The jarl stood silent, fists clenched hard, and looked into Sokkolfr's eyes. But Sokkolfr was a young man, heavy-shouldered with hard labor, and Hroi stood watchful and wise at his heels, lip curled despite his silence. Long moments later, Gunnarr turned on his heel, and strode off, bootnails clattering on the frozen ground, as Isolfr wondered distantly how Sokkolfr had known what to say, how he had known that Gunnarr's terror of the trellwolves would silence his wrath.

Sokkolfr's arm was around Isolfr's shoulders, and he was urging him gently back toward the camp. Hroi was on his other side, a dense warm weight. "No," Isolfr said muzzily, "not when I'm . . . I can't upset Viradechtis."

"Viradechtis is already upset," Sokkolfr said. "You won't help matters by hiding from her. Come on."

Blindly, stumbling, Isolfr let himself be guided; he couldn't uncramp his mind into the pack-sense, not with that ugliness staining everything. "Are you one of my conquests, Sokkolfr?" he said, aware that his voice was pitched too high, but helpless to control it.

"Of course I am," Sokkolfr said sturdily. "Proud of it."

Isolfr found himself giggling and forced himself to stop. "It's true, what he said."

"And what is that?"

"I will lie down for Othwulf, if Viradechtis wants Vikingr. Depraved, just like . . . like Lord Gunnarr says."

"Isolfr—"

Isolfr found himself flat on the ground for the second time in short succession, this time with Viradechtis standing over him, licking his face and throat, whining anxiously. Isolfr knew she could taste the salt of his tears and the sharpness of blood and tried to pet her to reassure her, but his hands were shaking so badly he suspected it wasn't much comfort.

"Isolfr," Sokkolfr said, "I have to talk to Grimolfr. We have to kill this thing now, before it spreads. You won't leave Viradechtis, will you?"

"No," Isolfr said, and recognizing his friend's concern, added, "I promise."

"Good. I'll get Frithulf to come help you, but I really can't—"

The wolfheall came first, and that was a comfort. "I understand," Isolfr said. "Go on."

Sokkolfr and Hroi went. Isolfr sat up, put his arms around his sister, and sobbed into her fur like a child. And Viradechtis stood patiently and leaned on him until his pain ebbed enough to clear his head for thought. Implications crowded each other, and Isolfr was clutching Viradechtis' ruff, hauling himself to his feet in a near-panic, when Frithulf strode up, a skin bucket of melted snow steaming in his hands.

"Whoa there—"

"Frithulf. Grimolfr. You have to stop him before he does anything about Lord Gunnarr. He *can't* have it out with my father over me. The jarls won't understand that it's about the pack. They'll just see him interfering in a family matter, and the wolfless men are unhappy enough already to be here."

Frithulf stopped and cocked a hip to prop his burden against. "Isolfr, much as I like you," he said, a wicked grin curving his lips, "someday you're going to have to accept that Grimolfr knows at least as much about politics as you do."

"But—"

The grin widened. "Othwulf is . . . 'speaking' to Lord Gunnarr." At Isolfr's befuddlement, Frithulf shook his head, grin widening. "Keeping it in the family, as it were. The jarls *will* understand that. Now are you going to sit down and let me wash your face, or am I going to have Viradechtis knock you down?"

Isolfr sat. "Has anybody asked where my father heard . . . ?"

"Ulfrikr," Frithulf said sourly, warming a cloth in his bucket of water. He crouched, and began to bathe Isolfr's face. "Grimolfr is 'speaking' to *him*."

"Oh," Isolfr said, flinching away from the cloth and then forcing himself to be still before Frithulf could ask if he was a girl or just cried like one.

The thought of Ulfrikr on the receiving end of one of Grimolfr's tonguelashings didn't do his bruised dignity any harm at all.

❦

As promised, the Wolfmaegth marched three days after Othinnsaesc's arrival at the moot. They left the shaggy horses—skinnier now—with the injured men from Othinnsaesc and one or two others, and began the climb into the Iskryne, weighted down with weapons and provisions.

The trellwolves were as comfortable here as anywhere; this was the ancestral home of their race and they found the going not so difficult as did the men. Many could even be convinced to pack supplies, which was a relief. There would be little food and fuel in the mountains—not for so many wolves and so many men.

They climbed as they could, following the line of a pass that was storied to lead all the way through the Iskryne and into the fabled land of the svartalfar, the dark elves with their hammers and forges and grindstones, their jewels mined from the bellies of mountains, their unrivalled golden finery and their weapons of unequalled steel. Surely they must find trolls soon; trellish raiding parties always returned north in the summers, for summer to trolls was as winter to men, and after all their travel the Wolfmaegth and the allied wolfless men were coming up on the time of year when the sun revolved around the Iskryne like a spun top, and never yielded to night at all.

On the third day of their climb, as if in obedience to the prophecy Isolfr had made in the roundhall years before, it was wide-ranging Kothran who picked up the scent. His howl floated to them like the sound of a reed pipe, and every wolf and every wolfcarl knew what it meant.

Trolls! Kothran called. *Come, come quick! I've found the trolls!*

A shiver ran through Wolfmaegth and wolfless men alike. Some three thousand cold, trudging, miserable pilgrims straightened in their boots, shuffled off their packs and reached for their weapons, and became an army again.

Isolfr raised his voice with the others and charged up the slope on Kothran's tail. His boots slipped on icy rock; he shed his cloak in the snow beside his pack and scrabbled on hands and knees, other men climbing beside him, trellwolves bounding past like mountain sheep.

The trellwarren could not have been more obvious if it had been signposted with a crier at the gate. The arched entrance was raggedly gnawed out of stone, but as Isolfr came to a halt before it, surrounded by wolves and men, he was struck by the symmetry and some sense of decoration that seemed to knot the claw-furrows into a pattern that squirmed just outside Isolfr's ability to define. The stench was worse than the midden-pile at his father's keep; even in the cold, the trellwarren smelled of snake-shit and wormy meat and the heated reek of a forge.

"They're armsmaking," Grimolfr said, and Isolfr started. He'd been so intent on the trellwarren that he had not felt the wolfjarl come up beside him, close enough to touch. He looked up at Grimolfr, and Grimolfr glanced down at him with a twisted lip. "Smelting bronze," Grimolfr said. "Othinn help us all."

"God of wolves," Isolfr said, and Grimolfr nodded, passionlessly.

"God of wolves. It's butchery now, lad."

"Yes," Isolfr said. "Let's go."

∽❦∾

The god of wolves is the god of death. He is the all-Father, the god of wisdom and the god of war. He is the god to whom all are answerable, in the end, and he is the god who paid with his sight and hung on the Tree at Mimir's feet for nine days and nine nights and counted the cost well paid for the reward.

He is the god who knows that nothing comes without price.

Isolfr held the god's name as a prayer as he hacked into the trellwarren. This time they could not wait for the trolls to come out to them; this was a proper warren, years in the digging, and they could not hope to find and block all its exits. Grimolfr had had a few brutally brief pieces of advice about fighting in an old warren, which for all his experience Isolfr had not done before, and those words rang clear in Isolfr's head through the acrid stench of troll blood, the bitter copper bite of men's and wolves' blood, the dark and smothering heat, the howling confusion of metal against metal, the snarls of wolves, the shouts of men, and the strange yammering of trolls:

Never get separated from your wolf.

Never turn your back on a hole if you don't know what lies beyond it.

And most important:

Never follow a running troll.

Men who did, Grimolfr said, were never seen again, neither alive nor dead, and the wolfthreat could not find them.

Othinn, god of wolves, god of battles—he feinted and slashed, and a troll went staggering back, its face gone in a torrent of black blood. *God of memory and thought, god of the old wisdom.* The tunnels were uncanny, twisting at angles that seemed wrong, shadows collecting in odd corners, and there was more decoration, here below, that Isolfr did not dare to look at for fear of being enthralled, as it was said the prey of dragons were enthralled by their eyes.

Viradechtis lunged, sinking her teeth into the upraised arm of a troll before it could bring its hammer down. A sow, Isolfr noticed, her six teats heavy with milk, her tiny red eyes glaring with berserker madness as the arm Viradechtis wasn't rending came swiping forward, aiming for Isolfr's eyes. She wore bronze rings in her mane, and they chinked oddly against the blade of his axe as he took her head off.

When the massive body fell, he saw that she had been guarding a doorway; Viradechtis was staring through it, snarling in a low, terrible, incessant rumble, and Isolfr, having checked that there were no other trolls in this piece of tunnel, stepped forward to see what the trellsow had been guarding.

He nearly vomited: a nursery, thick with the mingled reek of carrion and troll, a litter of four shrieking spidery black troll kittens rushing at him, their red eyes as mad and hateful as the sow's. Viradechtis hunted them like rats, breaking their necks with vicious efficiency. Isolfr killed the last of them as it tried to sink its teeth into the leather of his boot. And although he tried not to look, he saw the gnawed sphere of a human skull among the offal of the kittens' nest. *And where would they find such meat in the mountains?*

Back into the tunnel, back into the red smoky light of torches and small fires already burning. Down a slope pitched too steeply and with a twist halfway down that was *wrong*, terribly wrong although he could not have explained how, and he found himself in a wider hall, filled with men and trolls and wolves. He realized, going to the aid of a wolfcarl who wore Franangford's device, that the fighters here were all sows, and judging by the smell, and the weapons they carried, and the heavy slabs of muscle that made their blows as devastating as the kick of a draft-horse, they were the metalworkers. He remembered the trellsow they'd found in his second battle with the creatures; he'd never imagined so many in one place before. He'd thought the one they'd killed was a camp follower like the women in the wolfheall compound. But these were not whores or hedge-witches or even women like Jorveig, whom Isolfr had seen deck a drunken wolfcarl when there seemed no other way of getting him out of her kitchen; these were warriors and artisans, and he felt a sudden pain of empathy, realizing that they were defending their home.

Kallekot, he said to himself, hacking his way forward grimly. *Ravndalr, Jorhus.* Others and others and *Othinn, god of death, god of war, god of carrion and blood. God of the screaming, god of the dying, god who weighs and listens.* He found himself fighting shoulder to shoulder with one of the wolfcarls from Kerlaugstrond who had been giving him so much trouble, and there was no hostility between them now, as they and their wolves worked together to wreak the ruin of this trellwarren.

Othinn, watch for us.

❧

It took the better part of two days for the army, Wolfmaegth and wolfless men, to clear the warren, and it was butchery—as Grimolfr had said. Their casualties were severe: a band of artisan-boys from Arakensberg's territory panicked and fled in the face of a concerted rush, and though all of them died for their stupidity, so too did seven wolves and ten wolfcarls. And that was merely the worst of the Wolfmaegth's losses.

Frithulf had been badly burned in the fighting with the bronze-workers. "You always were prettier anyway," he said to Isolfr, and they both knew he had been lucky not to lose an eye—or both of them. But the wound would be slow in healing even if it did not fester, and it would scar badly, a spill of shiny knotted flesh down cheek and jaw and neck. Kothran lay as near to Frithulf as he could get, his head in Frithulf's lap more often than not, and Isolfr knew, for he could feel it through the pack-sense, how much Kothran's presence helped with the pain and the sick aftereffects of being so burned. All the wolves with wounded brothers stayed close to them. The army's wolfsprechends were kept busy preventing dog-wolves from becoming as protective of their brothers as a bitch of her pups, allowing the wolfheofodmenn close enough for the rough doctoring at their command.

Vethulf Kjaransbrother did a great deal of that doctoring. Although his manner with the wounded men was brusque, his bandaging was meticulous, and he was kind and quiet with injured wolves—something that startled Isolfr, for he would not have thought the red-headed wolf-carl was capable of gentleness. More typically, it was Vethulf who started calling Frithulf "the Half-Burned," and that byname quickly replaced the old one, though Isolfr and Ulfbjorn were at some pains to make sure that Frithulf never heard it.

It was one more petty excoriation on top of dozens on top of fatigue and cold and endless responsibility, responsibility deep enough to drown in, and Isolfr surprised himself by retaliating one night, "accidentally" tripping Vethulf, quite spectacularly, while his hands were full of musk-ox dung cakes for the cooking fire. Wolfcarls did not duel; they were forbidden the hide and the holmgang for the sake of the wolves. But Isolfr would not have minded if Vethulf had taken a swipe at him. A fistfight would suit him fine, a couple of good swings and a scuffle to clear the air, nothing dangerous enough to involve the wolves. Just something raw and simple—a chance to black one of those mocking eyes, a chance, however fleeting, to meet Vethulf simply as man to man instead of this endless prickly skirmishing between wolfsprechend-in-waiting and one who would be wolfjarl.

What he got was Vethulf picking himself up, dusting powdered dung from his hands, and shooting Isolfr a glare that should have started that fire right then. Vethulf-in-the-Fire, indeed. But then he squared his shoulders and turned away without a word, as offended as a splashed cat. Isolfr tried to feel that he'd won a victory, but all he felt was a nauseating kinship to Ulfrikr.

❧

Isolfr found himself returning to the trellwarren whenever he was not needed, not merely to escape the miasma of pain and unhappiness and muted fear that overhung the camp, but because it troubled him. He did not see beauty in trellish patterns, or in the way they worked metal, or in the terrible angles and proportions of their dwelling place, but he could not deny that he saw purpose. "They intended this," he said to Viradechtis, running his fingers over a strange design, sinuous and jagged, wreathing an archway in the depths of the warren. "They work metal. They must have some language, mustn't they?"

Viradechtis cocked her head. She was uninterested in what trolls did when they were not dying under her claws and teeth, but she listened to Isolfr uncomplainingly as always.

"Could we talk to them, do you think?" he said, ducking through the archway. "Could we negotiate?"

That word, Viradechtis knew, having heard it a great deal in the recent tension with Kerlaugstrond. Her answer was emphatic: a vivid, brutal memory of the stench overlying Ravndalr, jumbled with images of the trellherig and other places where they had arrived too late and could only be witnesses to what the trolls had done.

"Point taken, sister," Isolfr said, and then he frowned, forgetting his train of thought, peering into a corner well back from the doorway. Viradechtis stayed close as he advanced cautiously into the room—a storeroom, it looked like, if trolls stored anything, but possibly a prison or a shrine or something he did not know enough about trolls to imagine.

"They didn't intend that," he said, and only when he jumped at the echoes of his own voice did he realize he'd spoken out loud.

There was a hole in the corner, between floor and walls, the sort of hole a giant mouse might chew—but not in solid rock. "Are there stone mice, do you think?" he said to Viradechtis, picturing them briefly, little granite beasts with bright quartz eyes.

The stench is making me light-headed. He needed to leave soon, he knew, but he stepped just a little closer. Those were worked edges, and not worked by trellclaws or the crude tools the trolls had. He did not—quite—reach out to touch the lip of the hole, but he did ask Viradechtis what she smelled.

Troll, she reported dryly, and then, cautiously investigating the edges of the hole—which he was relieved, in an odd way, to find unnerved her as much as it did him—*oldness, anger. Not-troll.*

But more specific than that, she could not be.

I t was the first warren, but it was not the only one. The second was much like the first, although Isolfr fought beside Sokkolfr and Ulfbjorn this time, because Frithulf Half-Burned had returned with the wounded to the camp among Iskryne's roots. This was a bigger warren, delved until no air moved at the bottom of its passages, older, and the strange ragged decorations were worked deeper in the rock of the gateways and walls. There were wyverns here, three of them, and it was siege and pitched battle to clear that warren. Despite a half-formed plan, Isolfr did not have the chance to search the deep caverns for stone mice. In fact, he barely made it out of the warren alive, for the trellsows—and it now seemed plain that the females were the artisans—collapsed the deep caverns rather than surrender them. It was Othwulf and Vikingr's sharp nose that led them out, and Isolfr pretended not to notice that Gunnarr Sturluson was among the fifty men they brought to safety up from the deeps. It was just as well, because Gunnarr Sturluson pretended not to notice Othwulf, or Isolfr either.

Much could be said of Nithogsfjoll's jarl, but not that he was a coward. He acquitted himself brilliantly in combat, time and again. Even Grimolfr acknowledged it, his teeth set on edge as he suffered Isolfr to bind a wound that had laid his forearm open almost to the bone. It should have been Hrolleif's place, to tend the wolfjarl's injuries, but Hrolleif was not there. And Vethulf was avoiding the entire Nithogs-fjollthreat.

The third warren was abandoned, and Isolfr found more of those mouse-holes gnawed in its deeps. Not big enough for a man, not quite. But big enough for the boy he had been.

And so the third trellwarren brought them to the fourth, and men and wolves that Isolfr had known and respected—and men that Njall Gunnarson had known, as well—laid down their lives in the cold of the mountains, and the sun climbed high overhead until it made a second, unceasing crown beyond the crown of the Iskryne.

The solstice was upon them. Grimolfr did not say, but Isolfr knew—from the meetings of the jarls and the wolfheofodmenn, to which he was not invited—that if they did not wish to die in the snows of winter, they would have to turn back soon.

The gates of the fourth trellwarren were barred.

The remains of Grimolfr's army—for all that there was not so much rank among wolfjarls as negotiation, Grimolfr's generalship had arisen as naturally as a curl of smoke from a heap of ash—drew up before the gates, and wolfcarls exchanged uneasy looks with wolfless men. Not only had there been no gates in the other warrens, but no sign that gates had ever been intended, and these were vast brazen things, worked with twisting designs. They could not have been improvised.

This was a new thing, and Isolfr did not like it.

Fortunately, the trolls were not so adept in the art of defense as the Northmen were; there were no arrow-slits to guard the portal, no holes for falling stones or boiling oil. And Gunnarr had the answer, damn him. Without consulting Grimolfr or anyone else, he sent a party to the second trellwarren, and there they pulled timbers from the rubble and brought them back, to be slung between chains to make a battering ram.

It was a good plan. Even Isolfr could admit it, although he wondered at the tenaciousness of trolls who would haul lumber all the way north from the taiga around Nithogsfjoll, which would be the closest source of trees.

The doors came down over what would have been a night, had it not been solstice at the top of the world, and the ringing was like hammer-struck bells. No one slept. Isolfr, missing Frithulf more terribly than he could have imagined, diced with Ulfbjorn and Randulfr while Sokkolfr played camp-master for Nithogsfjoll, buying Ulfgeirr and Nagli a precious few hours of sleep. He didn't care to remember that it had been four years since he left his father's house. He was a wolfcarl and a man of twenty summers, and that was enough.

He didn't care to be reminded of his father's house at all.

When the sun had swung round her post again, lower to the north than the south but never quite dipping low enough to darken the sky, the gates of the trellwarren came down, and men and wolves alike massed before the entryway. It was greater than the other warrens, the main tunnel leading in and down on a long easy slope, to all appearances unguarded. The air that rose from the deeps was warm, and smelled of blood and fire. Isolfr breathed deep despite the stench, soothing his cold-aching lungs. Someone passed up torches; as they cast light into the depths, Isolfr caught the glint of hammered metal. Something squealed like a pig; the cry echoed.

"They're down there," Gunnarr said, squaring his men and those of another jarl into a shield-wall, swords and bucklers before and troll-spears behind. The wolfcarls gave place without protest; the wolfless men were far, far better at taking a charge.

They didn't have much time. Something else squealed, and the steady trip-trop of hooved trellfeet on stone broke into a rising rumble, the sound of an avalanche. Behind the shield wall, Isolfr readied his axe and braced himself. There was no guarantee the wall would hold.

Then the men were tumbling forward, the slope of the cave at their advantage, and they crashed upon the charging trolls as the white sea crashes onto stone.

Neither line held. Isolfr found himself among trolls, hewing bulging black-green bellies and muscled arms, his axe leaving shining chips in trellhelms and armored shoulders, and carving limbs from bodies and heads from necks. He hacked deeper, harder, his wolf- and werthreat-brothers a wedge behind him, Viradechtis snarling, frothing blood at his left hand.

He wasn't sure how they broke through, but they were clear and behind the troll vanguard, surrounded by dark and relative quiet. Sokkolfr came up to him with a torch brandished high; behind them armor rang, men shouted, wolves snarled, and trolls squealed in rage and pain.

Down the corridor something flashed, a bright fleck of color, a glimmer like firelight on armor or jewelry. Isolfr looked at Sokkolfr, and Sokkolfr shrugged. "Never follow a running troll."

"Even when there's ten of us?"

Sokkolfr glanced over his shoulder; three other wolves, and three men. "Follow, then," he said, and the five men and their brothers and sister went down into the darkness, in pursuit of whatever fled.

It wasn't a long chase, though they heard the fighting follow them. They brought the troll to bay against a doorway like the one that had led into the nursery Isolfr remembered all too vividly, and when they had it revealed in the torchlight, Isolfr understood why it had not seemed to move like other trolls. "Priest," he said, guessing by the drilled stones hanging in the thing's greasy gray mane and the colored spirals tattooed blue and crimson on its face—and recognizing, horribly, the crude designs on its beaten copper collar as those written in blood at the trellherig near Ravndalr.

"Witch," another man said, a wolfcarl of Vestfjorthr whose name Isolfr did not know. "It's a sow."

"So it is," Sokkolfr said, and stepped forward, swinging torch and axe.

The old troll did not die easy, and her squeals brought more down on them, two, then a half-dozen. Isolfr stuck to Viradechtis' side like a burr in her thick barred coat, almost not recognizing his wolf in the frothing, raging creature who reared up and battled trolls fang to tusk, who slashed rubbery, great-thewed legs, who fought through to the nursery beyond the dead trellwitch and did slaughter there like a fox run mad in a chicken coop.

Half the kittens were dead already when they burst into the chamber, spread in a gory fan around one of the holes Isolfr still thought of as the work of stone mice. It was a bigger hole this time, big enough for a trellwolf, and once she had dealt with the rest of the kittens, the trellwolf in the room moved toward it, her brush slung low in determination.

"Sister," Isolfr said, warning. Viradechtis ignored him, showing no interest in the other door—through which Isolfr could still hear Sokkolfr's battlecries, among others. She circled piles of rags and nesting filth, stopping to sniff the body of each kitten as she passed—the ones she had murdered and the ones that they had found already dead.

Isolfr almost leaped out of his boots when the third one she nosed startled upward with a shriek. She lunged after it, and—frantic—the thing spidered toward the mouse-hole. "Sister, *no!*" Isolfr shouted.

He might as well have shouted into the void. She was gone, and there was nothing for it but that he go after her, into the dark of that unknown hole. Because *never follow a running troll,* Grimolfr had said.

But he had also said never leave your wolf, and Viradechtis was not any wolf. She was the future of the Wolfmaegth, rolled up in a barred red and black hide.

Gingerly balancing his torch, Isolfr followed his sister down into the dark.

Trolls had not dug this tunnel; that, he knew before he had gone three steps. It was too low, for one thing—a bigger man could not have squeezed through—and the grade, while steep, was not *wrong* in the way that trellwarren tunnels were wrong.

Stone mice, he thought. He could feel Viradechtis ahead of him, feel her fury at the troll kitten that scuttled just ahead of *her.* But it was not only his sister's nose telling him this tunnel did not belong to the warren; he could smell it himself, sharper, cleaner than anything dug by trolls. And then a stronger scent, pungent, musky, and Isolfr came to the bottom of the tunnel, falling over Viradechtis before he realized she was there. And found himself face to face with the kitten, freshly dead, black blood still oozing out of its maw—

—pinned to the tunnel floor by a weapon that bore the same resemblance to a troll-spear that Viradechtis did to a mangy village mongrel.

He rolled, instinct moving him while rational thought stared blankly, but before he could get to his feet, the spear came down again, hard, fast, and pinned his shoulder. Most of what it pierced was cloth and leather, but not all. His torch fell and guttered, but did not quite go out.

Blinking against pain and smoke, Isolfr looked up. He found himself regarding, from a not very great distance, a thin, bony face with a jutting nose, curling, tufted eyebrows, heavy sideburns and a mass of elf-locked hair in which metal and jewels gleamed, catching and reflecting the torchlight like stars. It put its head on one side to look at him, eyes small and bright. *Quartz,* Isolfr thought. *I've found the stone mice.*

Then it said, in a high harsh voice like the wind howling through the narrow defiles of the Iskryne, "Is this your beast?"

He realized, after a moment's blankness, that it wasn't talking to him. It was talking to Viradechtis, who was frozen by the wall, crouched and hesitating, Isolfr thought, because the weird gnarled little person with the spear was bent so close to his throat. She growled, low and soft, and coiled herself like a springing snake.

"I'm not a beast," Isolfr said, getting his left arm up to grab the shaft of the spear. He thought it had cut a furrow across the top of his shoulder rather than pinning through meat or catching bone, and that was good, because it meant he could probably still use his right arm if he got the stone mouse off him.

It cocked its head from him to Viradechtis, the beads in its ratted locks chiming like crystal, and leaned down into his face, its weight on the spear ripping a gasp of pain out of Isolfr's throat. "Not a beast, you say?" There were harmonics in the voice, under and overtones, like the far-flung challenge of a wolf's howl. It rang along Isolfr's nerves like the bright clatter of the beads in its hair. "And yet you come following your mistress the wolf-queen into the dark under Ice-crown like a *good* beast, and I see her as ready to defend you as if you were her cub. What then, if not a beast, who speaks with only half a tongue?"

Half a tongue. He thought at first it was a threat, and then he realized it meant his own voice, his speech, unaccented by harmonics. "She is my sister," Isolfr said. "Her name is Viradechtis, and mine is Isolfr."

"Isolfr?" It blinked, a big froggy blink for such sharp little eyes. "You're no wolf-get." It backed away, though, freeing the blade of its spear from his shoulder with a jerk that left his eyesight blurry. Hot blood spilled down his chest under his tunic; Viradechtis was instantly beside him, whining, trying to nose the wound through his jerkin as the bent little man retreated and Isolfr got his first good look at its weapon and the metal and trellbone ornaments on its leather apron. The craftsmanship was foreign, beautiful.

"Svartalf," Isolfr said, on a shocked breath. "I've come to Nidavellir."

"No," it said, and crouched back on its ropy haunches, balancing against the planted butt of the spear, its torch held casually in its left hand. "You've come to Trellheim. Or under it. Nidavellir is deeper still."

Using Viradechtis as a prop, Isolfr sat. His axe lay beside him. The svartalf's troll-spear had three times the reach, and *it* wasn't at any kind of a disadvantage. He left the axe where it was and tore his sleeve to staunch his wound. He had no idea what the proper form of address would be, so he guessed. "What's your name, then, Master Delver?"

The little man smiled, showing jagged teeth that glittered like jewels. That were *set* with jewels, Isolfr realized, and decorated with fretted latticeworks of silver that gleamed bright without a hint of tarnish. "No Mastersmith yet," it said. "I am called Tin, of the smith's guild and the Iron Kinship. My mother's name is Molybdenum; the eldest-mother of the line is Copper. If you say you're not a beast, then you must be a *man*."

"Not according to some," Isolfr answered bitterly, and then looked up and tipped his head at his host. "I'm a man. A wolfcarl; my name you have, my styling is Viradechtisbrother."

It nodded, and stood. "And what brings you to Trellheim, Isolfr Viradechtisbrother?"

"I come to kill trolls."

"Ah!" That smile again, the glitter of teeth, the chime of beaded elflocks as it—as *Tin*—half-scuttled, half-hopped forward. "Excellent. And the queen-wolf too?"

"We had no intention to invade the mountains," Isolfr said carefully. "We came because the trolls have been raiding our homes, killing our men and our cattle, and we wished to burn the infection out at the source."

"Then how unfortunate for you that most of the trolls are already gone," Tin said, gesturing with his spear for Isolfr to rise. Isolfr managed it, clinging to Viradechtis' ruff, and Tin did not comment when Isolfr bent down woozily and retrieved his axe. "Or perhaps it is *fortunate*, since some of your men and wolves will live to fight again, and I do not think it would be so if the warrens had been full." He gestured Isolfr along the corridor, and Isolfr, with a longing glance toward the tunnel he and Viradechtis had scrambled down, went. There was no way his wolf could go back up that slope, and—frankly—he doubted his own ability to make it with only one working arm, even if Tin would let him try.

"Where did they go? The trolls."

Tin shrugged. "Out of their warrens. I care not where."

"Why out of their warrens? Why at midsummer?" The torch in Tin's hand sent his shadow leaping before him. He had to duck and crouch, one arm slung over his wolf's shoulder for support, to enter the tunnel Tin's spear-jerks directed him toward. He turned back over his wounded shoulder to get a look at the svartalf, and blinded himself.

"Because we drive them out," Tin said, and rattled the butt of his spear encouragingly against the wall. "And take their warrens for our own."

"Oh," said Isolfr. And again, "Why?"

A strange noise. Laughter? "In sooth, you are no beast, for such unflagging curiosity can only belong to creatures who are awake, whether they can sing or no." And he was uneasily aware that those words, *awake* and *sing*, meant something to the svartalf that they did not mean to him. "But those reasons, wolfbrother, are not mine to tell you, even if I wished to."

"Where are you taking me?" Isolfr asked after a moment. The tunnel was sloping down again, and he could not help remembering what Tin had said about Trellheim and Nidavellir.

"To the—" Tin said a word Isolfr did not know, and the strange harmonics of the svartalf's voice made it impossible for him even to guess at its meaning. He glanced over his shoulder inquiringly, and Tin hissed through his jeweled teeth and said, "The . . . Master Harrier, I suppose you might say. The leader of this our expedition."

"*You* killed the kittens," Isolfr said and cursed his own slow wits. And—of course—that skull he'd seen in the first nursery hadn't been a human skull at all, but a svartalf skull.

"Kittens, thralls, artisans, priests . . . we open rooms and kill what we find within them. Then we retreat, and the trolls are too wise to seek us in the lower tunnels."

Never follow a running troll. Isolfr shuddered.

"We are a small people, wolfbrother. We rely on cunning where trolls rely on strength. And men, apparently, rely on wolves."

"We do not have tunnels to retreat to," Isolfr said, feeling a vague sense of defensiveness on behalf of his race.

"No, you live on the skin of the earth, yes? Or so I was told as a child."

"Yes," Isolfr said, a little uncertainly.

"And the bright goddesses watch you always?" Tin sounded genuinely curious.

"The sun and moon, you mean? Yes, I suppose so."

"The world is full of marvels," Tin said. "You will want to watch your head, I believe, for you are much taller, and although it is shameful to delve in haste, sometimes it is also necessary."

Isolfr, who was already ducked almost double, was about to say that watching his head more closely would require a second pair of eyes, when the hand he had in front of him for precisely that purpose jarred hard against a lump of rock hanging down from the ceiling of the tunnel like a tooth. He couldn't quite bite back a yelp.

"Chalcopyrite. Er. Copper ore, you see," Tin said, not quite apologetically, but as one who realized that strange creatures might not understand the natural and obvious. "We haven't time to mine the vein properly now, and it would be waste more shameful than haste to discard it in the rubble."

"Of course," Isolfr said politely and proceeded from there with even greater caution.

The way went downward until Isolfr swore he could feel the weight of the mountains like Mimir's knee on his back. Better Mimir's knee than Tin's troll-spear, though. Viradechtis seemed to agree—or, perhaps, to feel that there was no need for caution. She trotted forward boldly, nails clicking on the hewn stone underfoot, stopping every dozen yards to crane back over her shoulder and see what might be taking Isolfr so long.

Isolfr wished he were better reassured by her lack of caution, but he followed with what trust was in him and eventually they came to a tunnel that was greater than the first, where he could stand upright. His thighs and calves and his lower back protested when he straightened, to the point where he thought he might almost rather have stayed cramped. *This* tunnel was nothing like the rough-hewn one that led to the trellwarren; it was spacious, wide enough for five svartalfar or three men abreast, and tallow lanterns flickered every few hundred feet, casting warm yellow pools of light through panes that looked like smoke-ambered crystal. By the nearest, Isolfr could make out the fine fluted patterns that curled along the walls of the hall. Hall, because he could not in honesty call it a tunnel. Not after the trellwarren.

"Follow me," Tin said, striding past as if he no longer needed to keep Isolfr under watch.

That alone would have warned Isolfr that his behavior would be measured. The high queer resonance of svartalfar voices rang around corners and echoed from place to place, and Isolfr could no more say whence they spoke than he could say how many there were. He laid a hand on Viradechtis' shoulder, and as she seemed inclined to follow Tin, so he followed her.

Finally, he could tell that the voices—or some of them, at least— came from ahead. There was more light there, too, pools of it, and it occurred to him that there must be ventilation shafts somewhere because the air he breathed was cool and fresh, and the fires burned clear. "Hold your spears," Tin said and stepped forward through a narrow place in the hall. "I am accompanied."

Viradechtis was untroubled, and so Isolfr went boldly, comforting himself that if he died here, it would be with his wolf at his side.

What he found beyond the stricture in the passage was a cavern perhaps the size of a herdsman's hut, a dozen or so svartalfar gathered around a fire that flickered hot and ghostly close to the coals. They looked as like Tin as Isolfr looked like his threatbrothers—which was to say, to a type, but not a matched set—and somehow that simple hominess made it possible for him to draw a breath.

"Fellows," Tin said, standing aside as more than one of his companions laid hands on their weapons, "May I present Isolfr Viradechtisbrother, and his mistress, Viradechtis Konigenwolf."

The svartalfar tipped their heads to look at him, birdlike, first one eye and then the other. He could see now, in the better light, that they had long arms for their low stature. He could not tell the length of their legs, but he wondered if their lack of height was more a matter of twisted backbones. Certainly their reach—as one stretched a hand out, beckoning imperiously, jewels gleaming on his hand—was frightening. "Come closer to the light, creature."

Viradechtis regarded them all with lively interest, and Isolfr knew that *creature* had been directed at him. He swallowed hard against a mixture of indignation and anxiety, and stepped forward.

"So," said the svartalf who had spoken. "We have heard your racket echoing down through the trellwarren and wondered what manner of beast it was that sang so." And again, *sing* did not mean what Isolfr was accustomed to it meaning.

Tin coughed and said, "Not *beast*. He says he is a man."

Eyebrows went up around the circle, rendering the svartalfar's faces even more grotesque in the firelight. "There have not been men seen near Nidavellir since my mother's mother's time," said one of the other svartalfar. "What brings you north then, creature, or do you but follow where your mistress leads?"

"She is not my mistress," Isolfr said carefully, "any more than I am her master. She is my sister. And she and I and the Wolfmaegth and wolfless men of the North came into these mountains to kill trolls. We did not know that Nidavellir lay beneath them."

"Then where did you imagine it to lie?" He could not tell if their curiosity was honest, as Tin's had been, or if they mocked him.

"You say men have not been seen near Nidavellir since your grand-mother's time," he said, with a bow to the svartalf who had so spoken. "It is more generations of men than that since we last had any knowledge of the svartalfar. I knew of you—before today—only from stories."

"As it should be," another svartalf said. This one, he thought, was older than the others; it had something of an old man's querulousness. "We want nothing to do with men."

"Yes. Why *did* you bring it down here, Tin?"

"The queen-wolf would hardly have stirred without him," Tin said, unperturbed by the note of accusation. "And it is true, as he says, that he and his kind are killing trolls. The warren above us is no more."

That seemed to please them, if he was hearing the harmonics of their mutterings correctly. But, "We want no men in our delvings," the old svartalf said stridently over the others. "Just because it kills trolls, Tin, doesn't mean it's a friend."

"I do not wish to be an enemy," Isolfr said, and that made all of them laugh.

"With a queen-wolf at your side, we will believe you," said the svartalf whom he had tentatively identified as the jarl. It cocked its head at him. "Though we would believe you more readily if you would put down your axe."

Isolfr hesitated only a moment before complying. The odds against him were not substantially worse without the axe, and Viradechtis still seemed content to sit and observe. They might care little for him, but he thought they would not kill him in the face of Viradechtis' obvious favor.

The jarl leaned sideways—that terrifying reach again—and picked up his axe, turning it over in his long, knob-knuckled hands. "Primitive," he said, "though I imagine your smiths do the best they can, given what they have to work with."

A bright look under the eyebrows; trying to pretend the throbbing wound on his shoulder troubled him not at all, Isolfr said, "No smith of my people would dream of competing with svartalfar. That much, our stories have remembered for us."

That pleased them, and the svartalf holding his axe said, "I am called Silver." It seemed to be a cue, or a decision, or something that Isolfr could not read, for the others named themselves as well: Mica, Flint, Granite, Gypsum—even the cantankerous old svartalf grudgingly admitted his name to be Shale.

Isolfr bowed and asked the question now urgently uppermost in his mind: "Tell me, Masters, what will you do with me?"

That occasioned some muttering back and forth. Silver seemed to be in charge, judging by the way his long pointed ears flicked under his hair as the other svartalfar spoke in turn, and Isolfr felt more confident in thinking of him as the jarl. Earrings clattered one on the other, and Isolfr wondered how the svartalfar ever managed to sneak up on anything. He waited with concealed impatience while they discussed him, worried about his werthreatbrothers and what they would think when he did not reappear. And worried more about what Tin had let slip earlier—that the svartalfar were driving the trolls out of their warrens, and thus down upon the men.

At last, Silver straightened from his huddle with the other svartalfar. "We aren't certain it's safe to let you go," he admitted, shrugging. His long, broad hands made wings in the darkness. "But we can't take you deeper, and we can't very well keep you here until the last cold comes down on us all." It blinked at him shrewdly, long upswept strawberry-blond eyebrows gliding together over the top of a whittled-looking nose. "What do *you* think we should do with you, Isolfr Viradechtisbrother? Since our sister assures us of your good conduct—"

"Sister?" Surprised, he looked at Viradechtis. She had dropped her elbows to the floor and stretched out, clearly content to nap while the two-legs carried out their incomprehensible pack-games.

Silver laughed, a grating multitoned sound. "Not *your* sister. Ours. Tin." *Foolish man*, his tone implied.

Isolfr stared hard at Tin. Nothing about the svartalf said *woman* to him. "Forgive me," he said, very carefully. "I had thought him—her—a male. Your sexes seem very alike to me."

This seemed to amuse the svartalfar extensively, if their chiming noises were anything to go by. "You haven't answered the question," Silver said when they had finished laughing at him. Isolfr wondered now if Silver was male or female, but determined not to ask. Maybe the names were a clue—rocks for males and metals for females? In any case, it was hard to imagine a male svartalf wielding his troll-spear with any more deadliness than Tin.

"I must return to my people," Isolfr said. He kept his eyes on Silver's face, not on the axe he—she?—held. "As fast as I can. They need to know the trolls have marched south, because south is where our families are."

Silver rolled the haft of Isolfr's axe dismissively between his hands. "What are man-families to us?"

"There are wolf families too," Isolfr said, trying to keep the rising panic from his voice. He must have failed; Viradechtis was at his side, her ears up and the fur of her hackles slightly raised.

"Hmmm." Glances traded between the svartalfar, and more of that musical muttering. "But it's seen svartalfar," Shale said. "It's seen our tunnel—"

Silver was nodding, sagely, sadly. Isolfr's hands went cold with fear and he felt Viradechtis rumble—not out loud yet, but thinking about it. They would fight if they had to—

"Let him give his parole," Tin interjected, tapping the butt of her troll-spear on stone.

"Parole?" Isolfr and Silver both glanced at her at once, startled.

"He's a queen-wolf's pack-brother," Tin said, reasonably. "His word is no doubt good."

Raised eyebrows, thoughtful mutterings. He gathered that they did not particularly wish to kill him; they were not, he thought, a warlike people, for all their fearsome weaponry. And he understood then that they were frightened, and even why.

"I will bring no harm upon you," he said, interrupting their debate. "I swear it by Othinn's spear, by my sister's strength, and by my own honor."

"You will not speak of us to others of your kind?"

"I will not. I promise." And part of his mind asked him how he thought he was going to convince Grimolfr and the other wolfjarls without explaining how he knew that the trolls were fled south, but he pushed it away. He would think of something.

Another colloquy, muttered, crashing. Silver stopped it with a brusque sideways sweep of his long hand. "Enough. This creature has done us no harm, and I do not want its blood-guilt. It was brave enough to go rooting deep in a trellqueen's warren, and it companions a queen-wolf, and *she*, I believe, we can all agree to trust?" Said with deep irony, and the other svartalfar winced. And nodded.

"If I am wrong in my estimation of you, Isolfr Viradechtisbrother, do not mistake. Your death will be spoken of in hushed and trembling whispers for centuries to come."

Isolfr believed it. "You are not wrong," he said, meeting Silver's strange, bright eyes.

Silver nodded. "Good, then. Your axe." And the long arm extended, spinning the axe to present Isolfr with its haft. "Tin, you brought the creature in, you had best take it out. And do something about its bleeding while you're at it."

"Come along, Isolfr," Tin said, not unkindly. "Are you hungry?"

Viradechtis came to her feet, yawned mightily, and shook herself. Isolfr bowed awkwardly to the svartalfar around the fire and turned to follow Tin. "No, I thank you, lady."

She laughed, and the noise made him shiver. "I am no 'lady,' wolf-brother, if I understand the word correctly. I told you. I am a member of the smith's guild—not yet a master, though even old Fluorite has allowed I may stand my testing at the Midwinter Convocation. I rate no honor in your speech."

"I beg pardon," Isolfr said, feeling heat in his face. "I am not . . . among my people, women don't . . ."

"Women," Tin said thoughtfully, as if tasting the word and finding it not entirely to her liking. "Females, yes?"

"Yes."

"We do not have the word," she said, gesturing him through a narrow doorway and into a small room which had been painstakingly hollowed out around a fountain, clear water rising from a cleft in the rock, a bench-like shelf around the walls. "*Women.* It is an odd word. Sit down, wolfbrother."

He sat, propping his axe beside him, and she hopped up nimbly to crouch beside him. "But you are female."

"Yes?" she said, looking at him sidelong, her eyebrows rising.

"What do you . . . what do you call yourself?"

"Svartalf," she said. "Tin of the smith's guild and the Iron Kinship. What else *ought* I to call myself?"

"I beg pardon," Isolfr said again. "I do not know."

She bared her teeth at him; he hoped it was meant as a smile. "Take off your shirt, and let me repair the damage I have done."

He obeyed her, and she clicked her tongue against the roof of her mouth the same way Ulfgeirr did when faced with spectacular bruises among the tithe-boys. "Well, it does not need stitching, and that is good, for it would be hard to explain to your people, would it not?"

She cocked her head, and he realized she was teasing him. "It would," he said. Viradechtis thumped her head down across his lap with a resigned sigh.

"Does she often have to sit with you while you are repaired?" Tin asked.

"It happens . . . with some frequency. Ours is not a peaceful life."

"Neither trellwolves nor men are creatures of peace," Tin said. She took a folded square of linen out of a pouch at her belt, reached a long arm to dip it in the fountain, and then attacked Isolfr's shoulder briskly. He set his teeth and did not yelp at the coldness of the water.

"I am sorry that I injured you," Tin said. "But I did not want to kill you before I knew what you were, and it seemed safer . . ." She shrugged, a remarkable gesture on a creature as bony and gnarled as a svartalf.

"I understand," Isolfr said, and did.

"It does not seem to be a serious wound, at least." Isolfr tipped his head awkwardly and saw that she was right; it was more than a scratch, but not by a great deal. It was no longer bleeding, and wouldn't even leave a scar when it healed.

Whatever she dressed it with stung. She gave him a little pot of some herb-smelling unguent, and he recognized the texture of beeswax when he dipped a finger into it. "You keep bees underground?"

She laughed like the tinkle of cracked crystal. "No, don't be silly. Within the mountains there's a valley, warmed by the breath of Mimir, where water grows so hot under the earth that it boils and steams in pools and fountains. We of Nidavellir alone know the way. We cannot farm animals in the dark, and neither can we grow fodder."

"So you do not turn to stone at the first touch of sunlight?" he asked, and then flushed at how like an ignorant savage he must sound.

"Sunlight. Oh, the brighter goddess. Ah, no," she said, as if she did not find his question peculiar. "We do not. Although we don't like it much better than the trolls do, to tell you true." She sighed. "Fortunately, we are more cunning than they, because Mimir's breath is not so hot as it was, and our crops are failing as the ice drips down from Iskryne and into our valley."

"The glaciers," Isolfr said, realizing why the svartalfar would be pushing south, making the trolls push south in turn.

"Yes," she said, and tied the dressing with a jerk at the knot. "Come along, Isolfr Viradechtisbrother, and I will show you a tunnel that does not run so steep."

SEVEN

It was, at least, not *harder* than Isolfr had feared to convince Grimolfr that the war-strength of the trellmaegth had left the warrens and headed south—because he had feared it would be impossible. But Grimolfr had been wondering—as they all had—and he came around quickly when he understood that Viradechtis' conviction agreed with Isolfr's: the trellboars were not in the warrens because they had gone south, leaving the sows and priests behind. Grimolfr and Skald turned the Wolf-maegth easily enough, and the wolfless men were not about to stay in the mountains alone, not with high solstice over and winter on the horizon. Sooner they would have stayed in the mountains of the moon.

It took a day to get the army moving, and half as long to get out of the pass as it had to get in. Rested men and horses awaited them; they had seen no trolls. A hasty council of war determined that the army would retrace the route of Othinnsaesc, as they had seen and fought more trolls and wyverns than all the other wolfheallan combined.

They had the sun all through the night and the endless drone of mosquitoes. They had mud and tired men and wounded men and horses staggering from lack of rest, and every man grudged an hour spent sleeping, for all the need.

The charge south was the sort of feat that births epics.

It was Frithulf, his face still raw and pink with healing flesh, and Kothran, ranging wide, who stumbled across the path of the troll army. The Wolfmaegth followed, and Isolfr soon lost track of the days. Sokkolfr watched him, or sometimes he watched Sokkolfr, but it was Ulfbjorn who made sure that the two of them and Frithulf and their wolves had hot food and clean water when they stumbled to the fireside at night. The Great Ulfbjorn seemed tireless. He walked—he was not much of a rider, and argued that he might as well spare a horse his weight—and somehow he and Tindr were always where they were needed, with a foul joke and a swig from a flask, keeping the line moving, keeping a man or a wolf on his feet for one more league.

At least the trell-path was clear, churned mud down to permafrost, and the flat landscape meant there was little chance of an ambush. Isolfr was glad of the rib-sprung carthorse they gave him to ride. It was easier to catch snatches of sleep in the saddle, and at times he could force Frithulf to ride for a space if he led. He worried about his tithe-brother; Frithulf's wounds still pained and exhausted him, and he had neither rest nor good food to buy him healing.

Othwulf rode up beside Isolfr at one point, long legs tight around the barrel of a sorrel gelding whose shaggy neck shed clots of hair into the dry, never-ending wind. Viradechtis was even too tired to flirt with Vikingr; she just leaned her shoulder against the black wolf's and sighed, and they slogged side by side through the mud. Isolfr leaned likewise on the horse's bridle, toiling forward through mud as Othwulf leaned down and lowered his voice so as not to wake Frithulf, who had fallen into a fitful doze. "How do the trolls travel by daylight, Isolfr?"

Isolfr didn't know any better than anyone else, but he knew why

Othwulf asked. Othwulf asked because even inane speech was better than silence, when they could not know if they had any chance of catching the trellthreat before it fell upon heall and keep and steading at Othinnsaesc. Or if Othinnsaesc was even where it was headed.

"The same way we travel by winter, I expect," Isolfr said. "With little pleasure. They're moving slowly, for trolls; it must be difficult for them."

"I wonder what drives them to such desperation."

"Ice in the north," Isolfr answered, and then bit his lip before he could say too much, but he did glance up into the silence that followed to see Othwulf staring at him with considered respect. It wasn't the covetous look that Eyjolfr or some of the others gave him. Rather, it was the slow, thoughtful nod of a man who's just been shown the trick to a puzzle he himself could not fathom.

"I'll speak with you later," Othwulf said, and put his heels to his tired steed.

Later, while Isolfr slogged beside the mare that Frithulf slept astride, he smelled blood and flinched sharply. And then looked up, realizing he had been more or less dozing on his feet, and felt a warm hand on his shoulder. Vethulf, the quarrelsome, the fleet-footed, Vethulf-in-the-Fire walked beside him, his gray wolf slogging more like a carthorse than a predator.

Vethulf said nothing at first, just thrust a stake into Isolfr's hand. One quarter of a skinned raw rabbit was threaded on the pointed end; the blood smirched Isolfr's mitten.

"No time to cook," Vethulf said. "But I didn't see any signs of worms when I butchered it."

The meat was still warm, steaming slightly. Frithulf woke at the voices and looked around blearily. "Are we attacked?"

"You're fed," Vethulf said. He gave Isolfr another bony fragment of meat on a stick—"for your shieldbrother"—and a whole unskinned coney for Kothran and Viradechtis to share.

He fell away into the column before Isolfr could blink the thought of thanking him into his bleary mind, and Isolfr looked up at Frithulf in supplication. "What was that about?"

"Stay pretty," Frithulf advised, through a mouthful of meat.

Isolfr would have kicked him if he hadn't been out of reach on the horse.

⊙↯◌

They pushed hard, frantically, and Grimolfr sent Skirnulf and Authun, who were young and light on their feet and had had no serious injuries between them, to try to give warning to Othinnsaesc village. "Tell the fishermen not to fight, if there's any fishermen left to tell," he said, and Skirnulf nodded.

But when they were half a week from Othinnsaesc, they felt the tear in the pack-sense, and then two days later they saw the smudge of smoke against the sky, and Grimolfr swore exhaustedly, while the konigenwolf of Othinnsaesc made a terrible groaning noise deep in her throat, like a woman's cry of pain, and then threw back her head and howled.

And the Wolfmaegth of the North howled with her.

A few miles further on, they found Skirnulf and Authun—or what was left of them—and from there the day slipped farther and farther into nightmare, between grief, and the stench of death and trolls, and the ambushes, first from one side, then from another. By the time they came upon the ruins of Othinnsaesc wolfheall and the ruins of Othinnsaesc village, both still smoldering fitfully, there was no surprise left, no shock, only the weary horror of confirmation. Othinnsaesc had fallen into the hands of Othinn Battle-crow, and Isolfr prayed desperately, numbly, that the dead had been gathered up.

Later, Isolfr was never sure how long it lasted, how long they fought among the ruins, and the only glimmer of light in that nightmare was the last remnant of the wolfheall finding them. Brokkolfr, brother of Othinnsaesc's second bitch, had kept his head even as the wolfheall was burning around him. He and his sister had fought their way out, taking with them the wolfheall's third bitch and her four three-week old puppies, and the few wolves and wolfcarls who could rally to them in the chaos. And he had kept them alive, he and Amma, for the better part of a week, hiding in the woods amid trolls and hunting wyverns.

When Brokkolfr saw the wolfsprechend of Othinnsaesc he went down on his knees before him and wept with shame that that had been all he had been able to do.

The Wolfmaegth and wolfless men fought their way into Othinnsaesc, but it was apparent from the beginning that they were outnumbered. When, two days after they reached the ruins of the wolfheall, a scout came back to report, white-faced and grim, that the trolls had already found their way into the seacaves along the coast, beneath where the village had been, Grimolfr rested his head against his hands and said, "We must fall back."

Ulfsvith, the wolfjarl of Arakensberg, protested, but Grimolfr cut him off. "We have neither the strength nor the numbers to finish them completely, and we must look ahead to the winter."

The silence in their rough camp grew even thicker. *A man could choke on it*, Isolfr thought.

"We are too late for the people of Othinnsaesc. We must not allow ourselves to forget the people of Nithogsfjoll and Franangford and Arakensberg"—this last said pointedly—"who will now more than ever before need the wolfheallan to stand between them and the trolls. We must fall back."

"And leave Othinnsaesc a trellwarren?" said Gunnarr, and Isolfr's hands clenched painfully as he tried to decide if he should step between Gunnarr and Grimolfr before blood was spilled.

But Grimolfr looked at the jarl and smiled a bleak, uncompromising smile. "Only until summer."

⚭

Whatever his father might believe of him, Isolfr was childishly grateful that the carnage at Othinnsaesc meant that Othwulf and his threatbrothers would be needed at Franangford, which was both closest to Othinnsaesc and most sorely depleted by the long, dragging war. And it *was* a war, and one that everyone knew without discussion would enact a hideous cost over the winter.

The remaining wolfheallan reinforced Franangford with every man and wolf they could spare, made plans for long patrols, and retired in haste to heall and steading while there was still a chance to lay in some of the harvest against the winter. Wolfcarls and wolfless men worked side by side at Nithogsfjoll; Isolfr, who had not scythed grain since he had gone to the wolfheall, found the work a welcome distraction, especially as Hjordis' girth and discomfort increased each time he stole a visit. Her feet pained her, and her back, and her sister Angrbotha, a hale and child-less married woman five years older, was as busy in the fields as any man.

"It isn't so, with wolves," he said, as he knelt by her feet to massage her swollen calves.

She laughed, kicks rippling her belly. "I wish I were a wolf, then," she said, and he kissed her hands and said, "I don't."

He needed the distraction as well because Frithulf and Sokkolfr and their brothers were among those sent to guard besieged Franangford through the winter, and Ulfrikr was determined to make the unsettling wait for Viradechtis' season as much of a horror as possible. At least Ulf-bjorn and Tindr were still there to share blankets. The big wolfcarl's steadying presence and agile, unexpected humor made the waiting nearly bearable, although Frithulf's savage tongue or the Stone Sokkolfr's un-flappability would have been better. No, not *better*, exactly—but he re-membered Frithulf saying *You're my pack,* and knew that he felt the same.

Almost, Isolfr wished Viradechtis would just hurry up and get it over with.

When he wasn't wishing she'd be magically converted overnight into a dog-wolf.

"The first time's the worst," Hrolleif told him, in one of the rare mo-ments when Vigdis would let him near, and Isolfr gritted his teeth and reminded himself that anything Hringolfr Left-Hand could get through, he, Isolfr, could get through as well.

And at least he wouldn't have to worry about Ulfrikr doing *that* to him. "To think I would ever be glad he bonded one of your brothers," he said to Viradechtis, and she pushed her head against his stomach and de-manded to be petted. She knew he was upset, and it worried her, al-though he could tell she did not understand what he was upset about.

She, in fact, seemed almost gleeful at the prospect of mating with more than one dog, and he tried not to watch her flirting, assessing, tried not to wonder whom she would choose, whom he would have to . . .

He remembered Grimolfr shoving Hringolfr to his knees and could not quite keep from shuddering.

His mood was not helped when the gossip reached the wolfheall, circulating down as it did through the village, that Kathlin Gunnarsdottir had been betrothed to the jarl of Vigrithlund, a man nearer their father's age than Kathlin's own and one whom Isolfr remembered disliking. Kathlin had not even chosen her fate, as Isolfr had chosen his in agreeing to be tithed, in agreeing to stay—in falling in love with Viradechtis. At least, Isolfr thought, Viradechtis would not choose for reasons as cold as Gunnarr's.

But it was no comfort; it only made him feel sorrow for his blood-sister as well as anxiety for himself.

The day that Ulfrikr suggested, slyly and so loudly that Isolfr knew he was meant to hear, that Isolfr ought to practice beforehand—and that Eyjolfr would no doubt be happy to help—Isolfr's temper simply snapped. He was on Ulfrikr before either of them quite realized what he meant to do, and was making quite satisfying progress towards beating the wyvern-tongued malice right out of him when hands dragged him away; he struggled against them and swore, and Grimolfr's voice said sharply in his ear, "Isolfr, look to your sister."

He looked and saw that Viradechtis had Skefill down, that the big gray male wasn't fighting her, and yet she was still snarling, her fearsome teeth a fraction from her litter-brother's throat. Then he became aware of the circle of clear space, the silence surrounding him, Ulfrikr flat on his back on the floor, gasping for breath against a freshly-broken nose.

"Sister," Isolfr said, his voice a croak. She turned her head, then moved away from Skefill with deliberate, breathtaking arrogance.

"Let us talk," said Grimolfr, his iron grip not leaving Isolfr's biceps.

"There's nothing to talk about," Isolfr said.

"I'm your wolfjarl, pup, and I say there is. Come on."

Face burning, split knuckles throbbing, Isolfr let the wolfjarl herd him into the records-room, let himself be shoved down on the three-legged stool. Sat and stared at his hands. Viradechtis came and leaned against him as she always did, and he blinked hard against the sting of tears.

"It'll be soon," Grimolfr said, and although he was as abrupt as ever, his tone was not unkind. "It's playing hob with your temper, Isolfr, and if Ulfrikr were older, or had a lick of sense, he wouldn't be teasing you now." They sat a moment, and Grimolfr said, "I'm going to send the patrols out tonight."

"*Tonight?*" Isolfr's head came up at that. "You think . . ."

"I think the sooner Ulfrikr's out of your hair, the happier we'll *all* be," Grimolfr said dryly, and Isolfr looked back at his hands. "But, yes. It's harder to tell with a young bitch, and it's harder to tell with a koni-genwolf, flighty creatures that they are—" He felt Grimolfr's fondness for Viradechtis in the pack-sense and felt Viradechtis laughing back. He himself had never felt so little like laughing in his life. "But I'd rather take no chances."

"That means Hrolleif will be leaving."

"Vigdis certainly isn't staying."

"And you? Are you . . . ?" His throat closed, and he swallowed hard.

"I'm not putting Skald to his own daughter."

Of course not, he meant to say, but all that came out was, "Oh," in barely a whisper, and then Viradechtis was nudging at him, nosing aside his braids so that she could lick his face.

"Isolfr." Grimolfr stopped, and Isolfr patted Viradechtis, pushed her gently away, looked up at the wolfjarl. "No one wants to hurt you. I promise you that. None of your threatbrothers wants any harm to come to you or to Viradechtis."

"I know," Isolfr said. He did know, and it didn't help. He knew as well that wolves died, and men died, and any wolfcarl a hair smarter than Ulfrikr knew he might someday find himself standing is Isolfr's place. "Who are you leaving in charge?"

"Clorulf, I think. He's a good lad—and heall-bred, so he'll understand what he's seeing."

Isolfr nodded. Clorulf had bonded the most dominant of Vigdis' latest litter; he was sensible, thoughtful, and kinder than many young men that age bothered to be.

Grimolfr looked at him. "It is a hard thing you do, and I honor you for it. Now go get Jorveig to put something on your knuckles."

Gratefully, Isolfr fled.

⚓

The patrols left that night; although it wrenched at his heart, Isolfr stayed away from the gates. Hrolleif and Grimolfr both stopped to take leave of him, and so did Randulfr, a kindness which Isolfr had not expected.

"I know you've probably been given more advice than you can hope to remember," Randulfr said, blue eyes twinkling, "but I wanted to add my handful."

"I am grateful," Isolfr said carefully.

Randulfr sobered. "It's just this: whatever you do, don't fight. Viradechtis is going to make the choices. You can't change them, and all you will do if you try is hurt yourself. And her."

Isolfr nodded, and thought gratefully of Othwulf and Vikingr, safely in distant Franangford.

"You will do well," Randulfr said, clapped him on the shoulder, and turned away, striding to join Ingrun at the doors of the roundhall. It said something, Isolfr reflected, about the—was "friendship" the right word between wolves?—the fondness, certainly, between Viradechtis and Ingrun, that although Ingrun had not followed her brother to Isolfr's corner of the hall, she had not protested his going, and Viradechtis had not protested her smell on Randulfr.

Don't fight, he said to himself, and that night, alone in the records-room, he prepared himself the way Hrolleif had taught him. It was an unpleasant business, humiliating, and he had to do it twice more in the following days, as tempers frayed among the threat, and Isolfr himself felt something building, like a thunderstorm in his bones and blood, building and building and yet refusing to break.

He tried not to look at either wolves or men, tried not to speculate. Viradechtis sparked and encouraged several savage fights, and the boys bonded to Vigdis' yearling pups were busy, aside from trying to keep everyone fed and comfortable, in treating the wounds of wolves and men.

And still Viradechtis' heat rose and rose and did not crest. Isolfr slept only patchily and restlessly, and he was aware of the men watching him, horribly aware of what they were thinking about. He could not even meet Ulfbjorn's eyes now, for although Tindr would certainly not top Viradechtis in the coming rut, he was no less male than the other wolves of the threat, and Isolfr could not encourage. Could not. *Viradechtis is going to make the choices.* The sexual tension was worse; for most of the second day he was half-hard, and yet unable, even when he surrendered to it and tried, to achieve any kind of release. The youngest wolfcarls were attentive, and Clorulf in particular was more patient than Isolfr thought he deserved; he seemed to find nothing shameful or unusual in Isolfr's wit-shattered restlessness and uncharacteristically vicious tongue.

Then, finally, as dusk came down on that day, like a thunderstorm it broke. Isolfr, eyes shut, cursing under his breath, had prepared himself again only an hour before, hating the way his own fingers added to his unslakable arousal. The jar of salve was beside his blankets, where he had put it when he returned from that almost furtive trip to the records-room. He had been keeping it close, knowing that the older wolfcarls at least would make an effort to use it.

He was sitting, back against the wall, head down, trying either to think of something other than his wretched swollen sex or to think of nothing at all. There was a snarl, the unmistakable snap of teeth, the thunder of two trellwolf bodies rolling across the floor, and Isolfr, looking up to see Viradechtis standing in a circle of bright-eyed dog-wolves while one slunk away, realized that she had just spurned, emphatically and unmistakably, the advances of a suitor. And was waiting for the next contender.

And behind the wolves stood the men.

He didn't know who the rejected wolf was. He couldn't seem to see clearly, and the pack-sense was a maelstrom of anger and desire and blood-red madness. He knew what he had to do, because Frithulf would laugh at him if he actually had the clothes ripped from his body. He got up on his knees and struggled out of shirt and trews, unwilling to stand up lest he draw attention. When he got his clothes off, he looked down at himself: fully erect, and he couldn't deny it.

Another spate of snarls; he looked up wide-eyed. Two males fighting now, Glaedir and Guthleifr, and Viradechtis flaunting herself, taunting them, urging them on. Eyjolfr and Fostolfr behind them, fighting as savagely as their brothers, while Mar and Frothi circled each other warily in the background.

And Isolfr could do nothing but watch and wait and see who would win him.

He could not follow all that happened; he felt as fevered as he had as a child with the winter-cough, and the wolves' bodies seemed to merge and shift before his dazed eyes. But he knew who came to him first. It was Skjaldwulf, Mar's brother, the rangy silent man with the black scowl, who sang for anyone. Viradechtis was still flirting Mar away, and Skjaldwulf reached for the pot of salve before he stepped onto Isolfr's blankets.

He'd been told not to fight, and he didn't want to fight; he rolled over, presenting himself to Skjaldwulf, begging mutely to be touched, to be taken, at least to know that there was someone trapped in this burning with him. Skjaldwulf went to his knees, and Viradechtis let Mar catch her; Isolfr felt her triumph, her joy. She knew; she made her choices, and she gloried in them. Mar's forelegs on her barrel, Skjaldwulf's hands, unexpectedly kind, and then Mar thrust and Skjaldwulf thrust and although Isolfr had sworn to himself he wouldn't, he cried out, a howl wrenched from him by the perfection of the way Mar and Viradechtis pressed together. And the threat answered him.

There were no words, no awareness beyond the heat. He moved against Skjaldwulf as Viradechtis moved against Mar, his cries matching hers. And Skjaldwulf, though he drove hard against Isolfr, remained kind; one hand came around and found Isolfr's sex, and the second time Isolfr howled, it was with the release of climax sweeping through him.

Mar did not take as long as Hroi had; there were other brothers waiting, and Viradechtis was eager for them. Skjaldwulf climaxed with his brother, and Isolfr felt bewilderedly the soft brush of lips against his backbone as Skjaldwulf pulled out.

And then Skjaldwulf was gone, Mar was gone, and Viradechtis presented herself to Glaedir. Dimly, Isolfr wondered why she had not accepted Glaedir first; there was a reason, though it was too deep in the wolfthreat for him to articulate or even fully understand. Glaedir mounted Viradechtis, and Eyjolfr's hands were hard on Isolfr's hips, his thrust forward almost punishing. Eyjolfr was . . . angry? It was hard to tell, hard to tell anger from lust from savage triumph. But he could not quite bite back a whimper as Eyjolfr slammed into him, a whimper that transmuted to a warning snarl from Viradechtis; Glaedir whined softly, contrite, and Eyjolfr moderated his force. But there was no kindness in him, not tonight, and Isolfr would have apologized, if he'd had any idea of what he'd done wrong, or how. As it was, he bit his lower lip and endured, letting Viradechtis' pleasure saturate his own body's responses, feeling her joy in Glaedir, and through that finding the wider pack-sense, where this was hard and savage, but also beautiful.

Glaedir was followed by Ingjaldr, Ingjaldr by Guthleifr, Guthleifr by Nagli. Isolfr was barely aware of the men mounting his own body, barely aware of the long rocking back and forth between pleasure and pain and pleasure again. But he could not bite back his sob as Egill succeeded Nagli, and Thurulfr took Ulfgeirr's place. *Please let this be over soon,* the first coherent thought he'd had since Viradechtis' heat started; maybe that meant the end was near, but it also meant that he could no longer simply escape into the pack-sense. His awareness was more and more trapped in his own body, in the bruises and cramped limbs, and the pain. He sobbed as Thurulfr used him, racking, tearless wrenches of stomach and lungs. And he realized how grateful he should be, to Mar or Viradechtis or whatever alchemy between them it was that ensured Skjaldwulf had had him first; Skjaldwulf was gentle, and had had the control to be kind. Each successive mating had been more savage; some of them had bitten him, others raked his back with their nails. And he did not resent them for it, any more than he resented Thurulfr, whose hands were layering more bruises on his hips even now. They did but follow where their brothers led, as Isolfr followed where Viradechtis led. *She is worth it,* he thought, and held the thought to him as a prayer, as Viradechtis and Egill began to strive together with urgency, as Thurulfr leaned forward, as Isolfr, helplessly, screamed, and screamed again as Thurulfr tensed against him and growled his own release.

The wolf was gone, the man was gone. The konigenwolf padded over to her brother, nuzzled gently at his ear. He was waiting, waiting for the next set of hands, the next hard, thrusting sex, the next . . . the next . . .

Someone was saying his name. "Isolfr? Isolfr? It's . . . it's all right now." Someone's voice was trembling. "Can you move? Isolfr? I would help you, but I . . ." Someone's voice caught on a sob. Isolfr reached dizzily for a name. Clorulf. That was right. Clorulf, Vith's brother.

A hand was patting his shoulder, tentatively. "Isolfr, I think you're frightening Viradechtis. You're frightening me." Clorulf's voice broke, and Isolfr remembered he was barely a man.

He knew he should comfort Clorulf, should comfort Viradechtis, who was whining against his ear, washing his face with broad strokes of her tongue. He should say something, but language was a thing that had left him long before, and he didn't want to be touched, not by Clorulf and not even by Viradechtis.

He shoved the wolf and the boy away and curled into the blankets, praying to the god of wolves for sleep, and nothing else.

❦

He lay fevered for two days, and later deemed it a mercy, because when he awakened he was only stiff and sore and savagely marked with bruises, and Frithulf and Sokkolfr had returned. Later, they told him that Ulfbjorn had been the one to quiet him, pinning him down with main strength so that his injuries could be doctored when he had at first been unwilling to accept even Viradechtis' touch. In any case, he awoke in his usual place, Hroi packed close on one side and Viradechtis on the other, and opened his eyes to find Sokkolfr sitting propped against the wall sewing saddle leathers. He lay and watched the needle move for a while, wondering—incongruously—what svartalfar needlework (or svartalfar needles for that matter) would look like. Finally, it occurred to him that he was thirsty, in his cocoon under the blankets, and he sought his voice to ask for ale.

What came out was a croak, and he felt his throat in surprise. The motion brought sickening pain, but either his croaking or his whimpering caught Sokkolfr's attention, and Sokkolfr was beside him, cradling his head and tilting a leather cup to his mouth.

Isolfr managed a few slow sips before he choked, and Sokkolfr pulled the cup away. "Don't move," he said. "Be cautious."

Isolfr nodded, and tried his voice again. This time, the words were recognizable, if harsh. "Is everyone—"

"No one's died," Sokkolfr said, settling beside him. "Ulfrikr's nose set crooked from where you hit him, though. He breathes with a whistle now. I didn't think you'd be upset." He shaded his mouth with his hand. "No one else is, except his shieldmates, for the snoring."

Isolfr found a smile somewhere. It hurt his mouth, but he stuck with it, and in a minute it got easier. "I feel awful."

"You look awful. Want to try some broth?"

Shockingly, his stomach rumbled. "*Please?*"

He didn't miss the relief on Sokkolfr's face, and it warmed him. "I'll fetch it from Jorveig in a minute. Isolfr—"

"Yes?"

"Are you all right? I mean . . ." A sigh, and a helpless shrug, and that troubled, watchful spark deep in Sokkolfr's eyes. It surprised and warmed Isolfr to see his friend's care, even as Sokkolfr continued speaking. "I think even Hrolleif was worried, when you wouldn't let Viradechtis near."

Isolfr thought about it. He turned his head on his aching neck and looked the wolf in her unblinking yellow eyes. She whined low and reached out, tentatively, to nose his cheek. He *could* leave. It wasn't often spoken of, but he could forswear the wolfheall, forswear the wolf, and leave the pack. It had been done before. Isolfr imagined it would be done again.

But he had chosen this; he had gone into it knowing what sacrifices might be demanded. And he had survived it.

He slid one hand out from under the blankets and fisted it in Viradechtis' ruff, so she whined again and leaned into him. "I'll live," he said, and shivered. Then he looked at Sokkolfr and reached out and grabbed his hand too. "I'm glad you're back," he said, and squeezed hard.

Sokkolfr smiled at him, his rare, sweet smile, and said, "Let me fetch that broth."

But it was Frithulf who brought it, Frithulf who helped him sit, who held the bowl when Isolfr's shaking hands could not manage. Isolfr could not look at Frithulf, his own screams seeming to echo in his ears. Finally, Frithulf set the bowl aside and said, "Is it my face?"

"What?"

"You won't look at me. Is it my face?"

"No!" Isolfr's head came up at that; he turned to look at Frithulf squarely. The scars were ugly, and they were dragging Frithulf's mouth out of true, but they did not matter and Isolfr was horrified that Frithulf would think they did. "How could you think . . . ?"

"You wouldn't be the first," Frithulf said. "Well, if it isn't my hideous countenance, what is it?"

"You were right," Isolfr said; his nerve failed him, and he looked away. "Weak as a girl."

"*Damn* my cursed flapping tongue!" Frithulf said, with such vehemence that even Hroi's ears pricked, and Kothran whined anxiously and licked the scarred side of Frithulf's face. "Isolfr, as you love me, will you *forget* the stupid things I say?"

"But—"

"No." Frithulf was glaring at him, daring him to argue. Isolfr shut his mouth and waited. "Clorulf and Ulfbjorn have told us . . . what they can. Do you think I'm like Ulfrikr, to mock at you for being in pain?"

"I don't think you're like Ulfrikr," Isolfr said, shocked.

"Then stop expecting me to behave like him." Frithulf's face softened, and he reached out, very gently, to touch Isolfr's face, where his own face was scarred. "You knew what was coming, and you did not turn away from it. That's bravery, Isolfr, not weakness." His smile was crooked with scarring, but it was still Frithulf's smile, still as bright and wicked as a magpie's saucy glance. "And did Sokkolfr tell you, Ulfrikr whistles when he breathes? I don't think he'll be so quick to taunt you as womanish again. Not now that he has a closer acquaintance with your womanish fists."

Isolfr settled back, surprised to find that Viradechtis had arranged herself as a warm, pillowed chair. Her body eased his aches, and he suspected Jorveig had put some herb or root in the broth; warmth and a sort of numb fuzziness chased through his limbs. He sighed, and leaned his head back on his wolf's warm flank, and asked, "How goes the war?"

And fell asleep while Frithulf was telling him.

ଽଡ଼ୡ

Viradechtis made herself his shadow, even when he was able to rise from his blankets again and totter to the privy or the bathhouse on his own. She even came *into* the bathhouse with him, and the werthreat laughed and complained, but none of them asked him to make her leave.

Understanding that she was unhappy, he did not try.

It took time for the question to rise from her mind to his, from instinct and scent into words. Three days after he woke clearheaded, when he was sitting with Frithulf rewrapping axe leathers while Kothran dozed belly-up in the weak winter sunlight and Viradechtis paced the courtyard thoughtfully, the words were there, simple words, almost childish words: *mating hurt you.* It was more images than words even then, but it was as close as Viradechtis would ever or could ever come to speaking to him, as a man spoke to his friend.

It startled him. Shocked him. Trellwolves did not speak in words.

But she was Viradechtis, and she was not like other wolves.

Yes, Isolfr agreed, because there was no point in trying to lie.

She paced the length of the courtyard again, and he felt his answer

· 192 ·

sinking down into her understanding. Frithulf was telling him tales of Franangford, and he listened with half his mind while the other half waited for his sister's response.

When it came, it shocked him into dropping the axe hilt he was checking for damage: *I hurt you.*

"You're lucky I took the blade," Frithulf said, staring at him. "Isolfr? What's wrong?"

Isolfr held out his hands to Viradechtis, and she came to him willingly, tail wagging, but her ears down. "Sister, no," he said softly, trying to give it in her language as she had struggled to give her question in his. "I do not fault you."

Her concern had outstripped her small store of words, but he could feel her love for him with astonishing depth and clarity. He had known that she would die for him, as he would die for her, but he had not realized that she would as willingly die for his happiness as for his life, that her loyalty was so much larger and simpler than anything men's minds could comprehend. She understood that he had been hurt, but she did not understand how, and he could feel behind her that the wolfthreat did not understand either.

"Isolfr?" Frithulf said, and he shook himself awake to the fact that his friend was becoming as anxious as his sister.

"It's all right, Frithulf. I need . . . I think Viradechtis and I need to walk."

"And you don't want company."

"No." The politics of wolves: say what you mean.

"Don't go far," Frithulf said, leaning to pick up the dropped axe haft. "Or we'll have to send Kothran and Tindr to sledge you home."

Isolfr grinned at the image and got slowly to his feet. "Come, sister," he said, and Viradechtis followed him.

He had not gone deep into the pack-sense since the rut-madness had died away, but he took a deep breath, clearing head and lungs, and let himself open to it, let himself feel what he had been closing out. Pine-boughs-in-sunlight strongly, and then, with a strange formal feeling, the wolves who had topped Viradechtis: Mar, Glaedir, Ingjaldr, Guthleifr,

Nagli, Egill. An honor guard, he thought, dimly understanding that they considered themselves . . . bound? Was bound the right word? Bound to Viradechtis while she carried their pups. And if they were bound to her, then they were bound to him. To the wolves it was that simple, and he did not look beyond them to their brothers. Not yet. And past Viradechtis' males, the wolfthreat, its great warm awareness enfolding him, and he knew that if he had left the wolfheall he would for the rest of his life have been like a blind man yearning for the sight of sunlight.

With the pack-sense, it was easier to show her, because the wolves were certainly aware of their brothers' couplings with women, with other men, and Vigdis, from the distance of a long patrol circling back home, unexpectedly contributed her memories of Hrolleif and Grimolfr, showing her daughter—perhaps for the last time as mother to daughter rather than konigenwolf to konigenwolf—the difference for a man between a mating with one other and a mating with many.

Viradechtis listened; he could feel her thinking, feel her sharp mind striving to comprehend something that was entirely outside its ken. Then he blushed scarlet when she put forward her memories of *his* couplings with Hjordis and, previously, the thrall-women. Those encounters had made her uncomfortable, making her groom her sex irritably and sometimes driving her to mount her brother Kothran, although it was not the same and did not appease the itch Isolfr's couplings awoke. But it did not . . . her comparison was the bite of a horsefly, and he snorted embarrassed laughter, hoping that Hrolleif had his mind on something other than the pack-sense at the moment.

It took him several tries, but he found a way to show her that men did not rut as wolves did. She gave him a picture, unintentionally brutal: himself, on his knees, begging with every fiber of his body for Skjaldwulf's touch. And he said, as firmly as he could, *wolfbrother*.

Her version of Gunnarr, stringy and bad-smelling and conspicuously without a wolf by his side. And he agreed with her, biting his cheek savagely to keep from laughing, that Gunnarr did not rut. She showed him Grimolfr, whose wolfname Isolfr caught for the first time: the smell of cold black iron. And Isolfr pointed her back to Vigdis' sharing of

Hrolleif and Grimolfr. Grimolfr felt rut. *Wolfbrother*, he thought again, not in words, but in the feel of it, what it felt to be a man bonded to a wolf.

He had stopped walking as soon as he was far enough from the wolfheall to be safe from interruptions, stopped and sat down, a little more heavily than he liked, on a fallen tree. The sun was falling down the sky, the wind picking up, but he wanted this clear between them before they headed back. So he sat and shivered and waited while Viradechtis thought.

She laid her head across his knees and gave him another image of himself, this time a younger version, saying, *she is worth it*. He was astonished at her memory, that she could give him the sounds accurately, even though she did not entirely understand what they meant. But the feeling that went with them . . . there was her question, there was the root of her question, and there was another flash of memory, there and gone, of him turning away from her, refusing her touch, and he understood that he had hurt her as surely as he had been hurt.

But her question was not so easy to answer. He remembered his younger self, discovering that "honor" was not a simple daylight concept, and now he thought he was discovering that "worth" was not, either.

He doubted he would ever say again, so glibly, that she was worth it. But she was *his*, and he was hers, and whatever price he'd paid was paid already. There was no use in demanding it back—and was it any greater cost than Frithulf's scars, when it came right down to it?

"I belong to you," he said to Viradechtis, knowing that that was truth, that "worth"—whatever it was—was not even the point between them. "I love you."

Neither of those made any more sense to her than "worth" did. He went deeper into the pack-sense again, trying to find something that she could feel, something that would ease her. And he found it, found it in her own uncomplicated loyalty that did not care what he did or how he treated her. He gave that back to her, as clearly as he could, with as little taint of the overcomplications of his own relentless mind as he could manage.

She pushed her head harder into his stomach. Wolves did not apologize, for it was not their nature, but she was not quite a wolf any longer, just as he was not quite a man. She was sorry he had been hurt, sorry—though the concepts were as elusive as fishes to her—that her nature and his did not match. And she loved him, with such joy, such fierceness, that she ended up pushing him backwards off the log, to land with a thump in the dead leaves, the wind half knocked out of him and unable to catch his breath for some minutes because he was laughing so hard.

eight

It wasn't so hard to find tithe-boys after Othinnsaesc. The wolfless men were scared, and the boys, imaginations fired with tales of the campaign in the Iskryne, were eager. Viradechtis was fretful and snappish as her girth increased. Ingrun and Kolgrimna came into heat in quick succession, as if Viradechtis had set them off, which Hrolleif said wasn't unlikely.

This time, Viradechtis got the records-room. The litter was seven pups, all dogs. Isolfr stayed with her as much as he could, but there always seemed to be something demanding his attention—messages from Franangford, which Hrolleif insisted he listen to, and understand.

It was nearly spring and Viradechtis was outside, teaching her pups the skills they would need as trellhunters, when Hrolleif pulled Isolfr into the records-room and explained with the simple bluntness of wolves, "Your little girl's next heat will be her last one as second at Nithogsfjoll.

She's ready for her own pack, Isolfr, and you must be ready to be her wolfsprechend. Franangford will need strong pack leaders to take the place of the fallen."

Isolfr nodded, biting his lower lip. His beard was coming in heavier, a patchy, itching thatch that was long enough to plait, now, and the wolfheall's women had been letting the seams out of his shirts across the shoulders. And Viradechtis was unapologetically ready to be matriarch of her own pack. "We'll have to alert the other wolfheallan," he said, uncomfortably. "Before the mating. But that's a year or two hence—"

Hrolleif shrugged. "It could be six months," he said. "She won't fall neatly into her mother's pattern anymore, Isolfr. Ingrun and Kolgrimna are evidence enough of that." Isolfr must have blanched visibly, because Hrolleif laughed, and reached out to clap Isolfr's shoulder. "Don't worry. Next time, she'll be choosing her wolfjarl as well as the father of her cubs. It will be different."

"Different," Isolfr said, letting his lips twist wryly. "Aye. The strongest and best of eleven wolfheallan will be there, and every arrogant hopeful therein." He frowned, thinking of the hard way Eyjolfr watched him now, remembering the biting wit of tall Vethulf and Viradechtis' interest in his odd-eyed brother, and then he almost laughed when he realized that the most tolerable outcome would be Skjaldwulf and Mar. *At least they were gentle.*

And he knew and trusted them.

He didn't think Mar was the strongest wolf in the Wolfmaegth, though.

Hrolleif seemed content to let him contemplate his future for the time being, but their companionable silence was interrupted by a scratching at the records-room door. "Come," Hrolleif called.

It was Ulfbjorn, his broad shoulders brushing the doorposts. He glanced from Isolfr to Hrolleif, as if not quite sure where to begin. "There's a man and his brother from Franangford, with news of the war."

"Who?" Hrolleif dusted his hands on his trews, already moving toward the door.

There was a pause before Ulfbjorn replied, and Hrolleif stopped, his eyebrows rising.

"Kari. And his brother Hrafn," Ulfbjorn said.

"Well," said Hrolleif. He shared a glance with Isolfr, and Isolfr remembered where he had heard those names before—a bonded pair, and neither name the name of a wolfcarl.

The Wolfmaegth subsisted on gossip. Isolfr's own reputation was his despair, even subsumed as it mostly was in his sister's, and he knew werthreat and wolfthreat alike were waiting with undisguised interest to see what sort of pack Viradechtis would create. But Isolfr and Viradechtis were not the only ones attracting interest this winter; Kari and Hrafn had been the source of some very choice gossip indeed. "The wildlings," Isolfr said. Hrolleif nodded, preceding him through the door.

As the story went, Kari had been the sole survivor of the troll attack on Jorhus. He had fled to the woods, and when the burning of Jorhus spread—for trolls were careless with fire—he rescued and bonded with a wild half-grown trellwolf, whom he had named Hrafn. The two had lived on their own for the better part of a year before presenting themselves at Franangford, where they had been taken in. Kari, however, had flatly refused to take a wolfcarl's name.

Franangford had lost both konigenwolf and wolfsprechend that winter to a troll sortie—unexpectedly encountered less than five miles from the wolfheall—and had been all but annexed by Arakensberg. Frithulf had had things to say about that, and a wicked gift for acting out the bitter rivalry between Grimolfr and Ulfsvith Iron-Tongue; he'd even made Hrolleif laugh once. So Grimolfr's choice of this *particular* wolfcarl as messenger meant something, and Isolfr wondered just where Kari stood in the uneasy tug-o-war between Arakensberg and Nithogsfjoll.

Then he blinked and had to smile at himself, playing politics as if he'd been born to the Wolfmaegth.

Whatever his father might have done since Isolfr left the manor, Gunnarr had prepared his children well.

◦╪◦

Kari was neither tall nor stern, and if anything he was a summer or two younger than Isolfr, lightly mustached and not yet showing more than a trace of beard. But he had a wiry, wild sort of dignity, even with his mouse-colored hair worked loose from its braids to straggle into his eyes, sweat plastering stray strands to his cheeks and forehead. The rangy wolf crouched at his side was black, darker even than Mar, marked with a mask like a stippling of hoarfrost, watching the proceedings with pale yellow eyes.

"Hrolleif," the boy said, and then his eyes flicked curiously to Isolfr.

Hrolleif made no introductions, so Isolfr said his name, which seemed to satisfy the messenger. Around the wolfheall, others—wolves and wolfcarls—were watching, but Kari pitched his voice low, so that it would not carry. "Grimolfr bids you greeting, wolfsprechend—and Isolfr, as well."

It was obviously Kari's own addendum, but Isolfr found he appreciated the gesture. "The news is ill," he said, not quite asking, with a glance to Hrolleif for permission. Hrolleif nodded and shifted his weight back, folding his arms.

Kari said, "Franangford is holding, although not comfortably. But we must be ready to push forward in the spring, and retake Othinnsaesc, and the thaw is almost on us."

Kari looked at Isolfr. Isolfr looked at Hrolleif. "Grimolfr wants us to bring the rest of the pack to Franangford," Hrolleif said, with a quarter-quirk of a grin for Isolfr's refusal to take the lead.

"All but the cubs," Kari agreed, "and a home guard to keep Nithogs-fjoll safe in your absence."

"The bitches too?" Isolfr asked.

"Everyone. Messengers have gone to every wolfheall. The wolfjarls think to let the bitches and their brothers defend Franangford, and quartermaster. That way, more of the dogs will be free for Othinnsaesc. And with so many of the Wolfmaegth rallied—and so many wolfless men—we need the konigenwolves on the lines and in the rear."

Keeping order. It was what konigenwolves did.

Hrolleif uncrossed his arms and frowned. "So it will be. Isolfr, will you and Frithulf see to the comfort of Hrafn and his brother?"

"I will," Isolfr said, because there was nothing else he could have said—but inside, his gut twisted around the undercurrents, the things neither Kari nor Hrolleif were saying about what this new strategy meant.

Kari watched Hrolleif walk away in search of Ulfgeirr and Jorveig, then turned back to Isolfr with a half a shy smile shading his mouth. "They said you killed a trellwitch in the Iskryne," he offered, as if holding it out for inspection.

"Come on," Isolfr said, brushing the implied question, with its freight of awe, aside. "Let me introduce you to my shieldmates. You can bed down with us, if you like. And then we shall find you and Hrafn something to eat and some hot wine to drink."

The shy smile turned blinding. "I'd like that."

◈

Ulfbjorn, Sokkolfr, and Frithulf were gathered beside the central fire—Ulfbjorn and Frithulf dicing while Sokkolfr mended leathers, drank wine, and offered advice. They glanced up as Isolfr and his guest approached, and—startlingly—Isolfr realized that they gained something by association with him. Something that Eyjolfr wanted too, and Yngvulf would not be averse to . . . Isolfr glanced around the heall, and noticed that Eyjolfr was at the long tables with Randulfr, apparently paying no attention—but Skjaldwulf was watching. The singer gave Isolfr a quick sweet grin before glancing away, a moment before Eyjolfr noticed the interaction and very obviously schooled a frown. Viradechtis, who played Mar and Glaedir against each other like a master swordsman practicing against a post, was not going out of her way to make things easy for Isolfr.

But if she were conciliatory, she would not be a konigenwolf.

Hrafn flopped beside the fire with a groan before Isolfr had even made the introductions. He didn't miss Frithulf's glitter of avarice when he considered Kari, as rich a source of gossip as he could have imagined. "So," Frithulf said, patting the skins beside himself as Isolfr went to see about more food and wine, "tell us your story."

Which Kari did, eventually, under the influence of a good deal of wine and Frithulf's skilled prodding. He was clearly uncomfortable talking about himself—but grew animated when talking about Hrafn and how they had survived on their own.

"So why did you go to Franangford?" Ulfbjorn asked sometime later, after the horns of mulled wine had made several rounds and Viradechtis had come in, washed Isolfr's face thoroughly, inspected Hrafn—Isolfr noticed Kari almost holding his breath—and flopped down with a long-suffering sigh, her head resting across both Isolfr's thighs.

Kari shrugged. "Hrafn wanted a pack. And it seemed likelier that a wolfheall would accept us than a wild pack."

Isolfr was listening half in the pack-sense, as he found himself doing most of the time these days, and Hrafn said, *Cold*, meaning not just the cold of only having his brother to curl up with to sleep.

"But you didn't take a wolfcarl's name," Frithulf said, his nose almost twitching with eagerness. Sokkolfr met Isolfr's eyes over his head, and they smiled at each other.

Kari said, "I didn't want to forget who I was." He made a frustrated gesture. "I'm the only person left who can remember Jorhus. And if I let myself become someone else—"

"That's not what it means," Frithulf argued.

"Of course it is," Sokkolfr said. "Or are you trying to tell me that you're Brandr Erikson, just as you were before you were tithed?"

"Well, I—"

"I'm certainly not Njall Gunnarson," Isolfr said, and the name felt strange on his tongue, unfamiliar.

"Yes, but your father—" Frithulf stopped so quickly he must have bitten his tongue, flushing red to the roots of his hair.

"Have some more wine, Frithulf," Ulfbjorn said kindly.

"I'm sure I would have felt differently if I'd been tithed," Kari said.

Frithulf made a face and pushed the wine away. "Something tells me I've had enough."

Kari laughed—he had an easy laugh, at odds with his earlier shyness—and then looked up startled as Jorveig appeared by the fireside. Like Ulfbjorn, she was light on her feet for her size.

"Isolfr," she said, her hands twitching—as if she wished to reach out and straighten his hair—before knotting in front of her apron. The note in her voice brought both Isolfr and Ulfbjorn to their feet, the other three—even Kari—close behind. "Hjordis sends to tell you the baby is coming."

Frithulf and Kari stayed by the fire, but the other two came with Isolfr and Jorveig into the cold dark of winter night, walking with a company of ten wolves—Tindr, Hroi, Viradechtis, and all her seven cubs—over the frozen ruts. There was no moon, and the sky was clear. Stars throbbed in an indigo like velvet, and the aurora burned over that rich darkness, bright as amber held to the light. Isolfr caught a breath.

My woman is bearing my child. It seemed unreal, alien. He slipped his hand through the slit in his mitten and knotted it in Viradechtis' ruff. She moaned low in her throat and leaned her shoulder on his thigh as they walked, all her love and worry in her touch. She thought of newborn cubs, damp and milky, the thick, meaty taste of the afterbirth, and the warmth of straw. Your cubs, my cubs. Ours, our pack, ours to raise and teach. If they live, and are strong.

Yes, he answered, and she tugged free, then turned her head quickly and curled a slick muscular tongue into his palm. Ours.

If they live, and are strong.

The night was a blur. It was early, perhaps too early, and despite Isolfr's assurances that he had attended more than one birthing, neither the midwife nor Hjordis' mother nor her sister Angrbotha would permit him in the cottage for her lying-in. He paced outside the door, Viradechtis and her pups swarming around his boots in the frozen late-winter mud, until Jorveig, who had come as the wolfheall's representative at the birth of a heallgot child, told Ulfbjorn and Sokkolfr that the best thing they could do was take Isolfr out, find Angrbotha's husband, and get Isolfr too drunk to stand.

Isolfr fixed her with a look that he knew made the worst of his icy pale stare, and even Jorveig backed down enough to allow the three wolf-carls into Angrbotha's cottage. Not into the close-screened corner where Hjordis lay, where she moaned and occasionally shouted curses—and Isolfr felt pride on her behalf; his woman was no screamer—but by the fire, where Sokkolfr and Ulfbjorn stirred coals and kept the water hot, and Isolfr paced.

Hroi, canny old creature—*he* crept behind the screen and lay against the wall near the head of the bedstead, out of the way and almost forgotten. "Hroi says there's not much blood," Sokkolfr said softly, when Isolfr glanced at him. "Hroi says her heart is strong."

Hroi did not need to tell them when the child was born. The baby's piercing shriek managed that. Viradechtis whined and glanced about anxiously, counting her pups, until Isolfr soothed her with the information that human babies were supposed to wail that way.

She thought it was foolish to attract predators with such noise. Isolfr could not help but agree.

He rose from his crouch by her head when Angrbotha and Jorveig came toward him, a mite wrapped in white swaddling in Angrbotha's arms, Hroi padding behind. "Your daughter," Jorveig said, and took the child to give her to Isolfr.

He almost felt his werthreatbrothers hold their breaths as he extended his hands. The baby was light, light as a wolf cub, surely smaller than Kathlin or Jonak had been—or was it just that he was so much larger now? He looked at his own hands on the baby's tiny body, their coarseness pale over bone and rough and red with callus and chilblains and scars, and shivered, cold to his heart.

Cub, Viradechtis thought clearly, standing beside him with her long nose straining toward the babe. The child's face was a wrinkled red winter apple, her arms squirming under the swaddling cloths. "Is she—I mean, will she—"

"She's small," Angrbotha said. "But made of stern stuff, I warrant."

"And her mother?" He couldn't bring himself to say Hjordis' name.

"Fine," Jorveig said, Angrbotha nodding agreement. Isolfr sighed.

"My daughter," he said, very quietly, and almost glanced over his shoulder to look for Sokkolfr and see if it was real. But Viradechtis nudged his hand again, and Jorveig caught Angrbotha's arm to restrain her as Isolfr crouched beside the wolf so she could sniff the baby's face.

The babe didn't cry. She opened hazy unfocused eyes when the wolf's whiskers brushed her, her lips working as if she sought a nipple. Jorveig cleared her throat. "What's her name, Isolfr?" she said, as Viradechtis sat on her haunches and flipped her tail neatly over her toes.

Of course, she had to have a name. He rose again, cuddling the baby against his chest. He looked into the little red face, suspecting the babe couldn't see him any more than a puppy could, and breathed deep to fix her scent. "Water, I need water," he said, and Angrbotha already had the dipper at his elbow. He laced his fingers through it and let a few drops fall on his daughter's head, which made her wail like a siren—the more so when he marked Thor's hammer between her brows with a wet thumb.

"Alfgyfa," he said, thinking of Tin and her spear and her baubles, giving him back his life so he could be here, now, holding his child in his arms. Then he looked up at Jorveig, and quirked an eyebrow at her, trying for Ulfgeirr's rakish charm. "May I see Hjordis?"

❧

In the morning, Sokkolfr paid a boy to take a message to the keep—"to my mother," Isolfr corrected, and the boy nodded eagerly—while Ulfbjorn, Tindr, and the pups hiked back to the wolfheall to share the news with the werthreat. Isolfr expected silence from his mother, or at best a discreet return message memorized by the same boy. But Halfrid appeared at Angrbotha's door when the sun was no more than a span above the horizon, a basket of swaddling cloths in her hand and Kathlin and a maidservant flanking her.

Isolfr, sitting beside Hjordis on the bench before the fire, laughed as Halfrid swept past Angrbotha and took command of the house. His laughter startled Alfgyfa into wailing, and Halfrid shushed him with a frown as Kathlin—so tall now, a woman herself, but with her blond hair still falling free around her shoulders—came forward to claim her hug.

"Father allowed you to come?" he asked.

She blew hair out of her eyes. "Father's in Franangford, and with my betrothed husband there as well, there is no one to say us nay." She smiled at him. "Jonak says to say he sends congratulations and well-wishes and all the things he ought—he was so pleased with himself for being an uncle he couldn't sit still to think them out."

And Isolfr laughed with her.

He introduced Hjordis to his family, surprised at her uncharacteristic shyness. But by the time Hrolleif sent a messenger to summon Isolfr to the wolfheall, they were laughing and talking together, and Halfrid and Kathlin stayed behind when he and Sokkolfr had to go.

It was an uncomfortable leavetaking. They all knew that within the fortnight the Wolfmaegth would travel to Franangford, and the push to reclaim Othinnsaesc. And it was unavoidable that Viradechtis, a konigenwolf whose pups were half-grown and no longer needed her milk, would travel with them.

But necessity was what it was, and by sunset Isolfr had kissed his mother, and his sister, and his lover, and his daughter farewell, and had followed his wolf back to war.

Hrolleif didn't even bother to take him aside. He just congratulated Isolfr on the birth of the girlchild, told him they would be leaving for Franangford two days hence, and sent him to bed along with Viradechtis and her pups in the dark of the records-room. "You'll not have slept," he said, with a hard squeeze to Isolfr's shoulder. "And I need you fresh."

Isolfr didn't want to sleep. He didn't want to journey to Franangford, either, or face his father once he got there. But it was what it was. Still.

"Yes, wolfsprechend," he said.

Surprising himself, he slept.

❧

The march to Franangford remained in Isolfr's memory as a record writ in mud. Thick, gluey mud that caked trellwolf paws and legs and weighed down his boots until it felt as if he was trying to lift the world with each step. Thin oily mud, slick as ice, that brought men down like felled trees. Mud in his hair, mud under his fingernails; everything he ate tasted of mud, and the water they boiled left a fine layer of silt in the pot.

Their fourth evening out, once camp was set and Frithulf and Sokkolfr were arguing amiably about whose turn it was to clean and cook the rabbits that Kothran had brought them, Isolfr took Viradechtis down to the river and, despite the early-spring cold, insisted that they both wash. Otherwise, he'd have to listen to her trying to worry the mud out of her fur all night, which would mean that neither of them slept.

She grumbled but acquiesced, and even indulged him in a silly, splashy game of chase like a puppy. Then, cleaner and warm with exertion, he put his boots on and started for camp. Glaedir appeared at the top of the hill as they were climbing; with a glance at Isolfr—not so much for permission as acknowledgment—Viradechtis took off toward the big wolf at a run.

So much for the bath, Isolfr thought—and nearly ran into Eyjolfr halfway up the deep gully the river had dug for itself.

"Isolfr," Eyjolfr said and put out a hand to steady him, the gleam of his teeth in the dusk not reassuring. "Do you make a habit of wandering away from camp by yourself?"

"I'm not by myself any more than you are," Isolfr said steadily. Eyjolfr had not let go of his arm.

"The companionship of a wolf is not the same."

"I don't know what you're talking about."

"Don't you?" Eyjolfr's free hand came up to trace the line of his jaw. "I think you do."

"Eyjolfr—"

"There's no need to be shy, Isolfr. We both know we've been here before."

Isolfr stepped back, only to find himself pinned against a tree. He cast into the pack-sense; Viradechtis and Glaedir were hunting, coursing a spring-skinny deer.

"Will you always hide behind your wolf?" Eyjolfr said, both hands on Isolfr's upper arms now, his body pressed against Isolfr's. "If you do not want me, Isolfr, you should say so. Don't lead me on and then make a mockery of me in front of the entire werthreat."

"I didn't—"

"Why else would you let Skjaldwulf have you first?" Eyjolfr hissed, and his mouth came down hard, a bruising, punishing kiss.

Isolfr twisted his head away. "It was Viradechtis' choice."

"Do you really think I will believe that Viradechtis would do *any-thing* against your wishes?"

"Eyjolfr, please. She is konigenwolf. And I would not—"

Eyjolfr kissed him again, using his weight and leverage to hold Isolfr where he wanted him, using the tree to keep Isolfr from being able to plant his feet. He could feel Eyjolfr's sex hard against his hip, and the pack-sense was nothing but deer blood and triumph. He couldn't get enough air, and he tasted blood where Eyjolfr's teeth had caught his lip. He made a desperate, convulsive effort and wrenched free, only to fall over his own feet.

He landed hard, awkwardly. Eyjolfr said coldly, "I do not appreciate being toyed with, Isolfr."

"*Please.* I didn't. I swear to you."

"No? You don't find your power heady?"

Eyjolfr advanced toward him, and Isolfr scrabbled backwards, unable to find his feet or catch his breath. He could—he could fight, with fists or the knife at his belt. He could. And with the fear and fury he felt now, Viradechtis would think him truly endangered, even through the taste of her kill, and she might savage Glaedir where he stood. The big silver wolf would not defend himself against a konigenwolf.

"You don't enjoy watching the men of the werthreat make fools of themselves over you?"

"Viradechtis—"

"That's always your answer, isn't it?"

"What other answer would you have him give, werthreatbrother?"

Skjaldwulf's voice. Eyjolfr whipped around like a startled cat; Isolfr fell back into the leaves, panting. Skjaldwulf stood at the head of the gully, black Mar at his side.

"Skjaldwulf," Eyjolfr said, breathing hard but composed. "This is no concern of yours. Isolfr and I were merely talking."

Skjaldwulf started down, picking his way. Mar bounded past him, shoved by Eyjolfr hard enough to stagger him, and came to snuffle gently at Isolfr's face and hair.

"And your 'talking,'" Skjaldwulf said, "looks very much like something else—something which will get your throat torn out, Eyjolfr, and don't think otherwise. You are lucky Viradechtis and Glaedir have found that deer, and I suggest you go butcher it. The camp will appreciate fresh meat."

"I would not have—"

"Wouldn't you?" Skjaldwulf said with terrible mildness.

It hung there, unbearably. Isolfr shut his eyes, let Mar lick his ear and neck.

Skjaldwulf said, "He's not some wench to be wedded and bedded. And he is brother to a konigenwolf and not to a bitch like Ingrun. If you don't understand the difference, I suggest you ask Randulfr to explain it to you. Now, go on with you. That deer's waiting."

Eyjolfr went, in a slither of mud and dead leaves.

Silence. He could not lie there all night. Viradechtis would find him. Sokkolfr would worry. He picked himself up, pushing Mar gently aside. Swallowed hard against shame and said, "Thank you."

"Did he hurt you?" Skjaldwulf said.

"Bruises," Isolfr said and managed a shrug. Swallowed hard again. "I should have hit him back."

"Isolfr." It was too dark now to see Skjaldwulf's face, and Isolfr was glad. "It is not your fault."

"No? I did, you know. I let him. . . ." He couldn't finish the sentence, couldn't speak past the shame knotted in his chest.

"Isolfr." Skjaldwulf's hand touched his shoulder—gently, but Isolfr couldn't control his flinch, and Skjaldwulf drew away again. "Eyjolfr is wrong. A mating is not a *wedding*, and permission once is not permission twice. Please don't—"

Then Viradechtis was there, with impeccably awful timing, nearly knocking both of them over. Her thoughts were full of anxiety—though no real understanding of what had happened, and Isolfr breathed again—and she began nudging Isolfr back toward camp in a no-nonsense fashion. If he'd been small enough, she would have picked him up by his scruff and carried him like one of her pups.

"Thank you," he said to Skjaldwulf again, and let Viradechtis have her way.

Skjaldwulf made no mention of it that night, nor any other. But when they were gathered around the fire, wolves and men stuffing themselves on venison so they would not have to carry it, it was Eyjolfr who asked Skjaldwulf to sing. And Skjaldwulf glanced at Isolfr before he agreed, waiting for Isolfr's nod.

An apology tendered and accepted, after the manner of wolves.

The next night and the night after, they were harried by trolls, but small parties only. The wolfcarls had placed picket lines and patrols, of course—it would do no good to reclaim Othinnsaesc if a trellish army swept down on one of the lightly defended villages or wolfheallan in the absence of the guardians—but a small band could creep where an army could not. They could not keep the trolls out entirely.

They lost no one. Isolfr didn't even fight, but Frithulf was sentry during the second attack, and he and Kothran and Tindr pulled down two trolls by themselves before Ulfbjorn roused the camp. It was Isolfr's deepest frustration, that he knew why the trolls were coming down from the north and that he could not tell.

The journey was otherwise uneventful.

Grimolfr was waiting for them when they reached Franangford, and even though Isolfr knew he must have posted a watch, he was still impressed by the wolfjarl's attention to detail. The Franangford wolfheall was full to overflowing, and wolfless men, wolfcarls, and wolves were billeted in keep and village alike. The village teemed with warriors and civilians, all the machinery of war that existed to support the fighters.

Isolfr and Viradechtis, however, were billeted in the wolfheall proper, along with Hrolleif and Vigdis. Most of the konigenwolves and their brothers would travel with the army, but not the youngest—because she was precious—or the eldest, Aslaug—because she was frail—or the strongest, Vigdis and Signy, although having those two at close quarters would be less than a joy.

No one said why, but Isolfr knew.

Because one wolf would not make a difference in whether the pack failed, and if the pack failed, it was the strongest konigenwolves who must live.

Spring was an awkward time for waging war: too muddy for wagons, too wet for sleds and skis. There was more than enough work for everyone. There would be supply lines, and organizing them would be one of the duties of the wolfcarls and wolfsprechends left behind at Franangford.

The day after they arrived, between helping Ulfgeirr arrange provisions on muleback, manback, and wolfback for those who would be traveling to Othinnsaesc, Isolfr snuck glances at Skjaldwulf, who was nearby, sorting horse-harness by size and need for repair.

Skjaldwulf had kept his distance since the evening in the forest when he'd come to Isolfr's aid, and Eyjolfr had been positively conciliatory—more like his old, insightful self, his wit a little freer now that he wasn't trying so very hard. But oddly, it was Skjaldwulf that Isolfr found himself thinking about. He wanted to be wolfjarl, of course; who wouldn't? And if Viradechtis chose Mar again, then he would be, even if Mar was not the boldest or biggest wolf.

Viradechtis raised her head from where she lay, barring the door with her long furry body, and followed his gaze. Isolfr found Mar looking back at him, and Skjaldwulf followed it with a glance and a smile.

No secrets among wolves. But then Isolfr felt something, or Viradechtis gave it to him, with the smell of sunlight that was her love and regard, and the sharp sulfur of hot springs that was Mar's name. And he almost choked on the scent, because what she gave him was Skjaldwulf, filtered through Mar, and it was unmistakable. Although Mar would be quite pleased to be consort, Skjaldwulf didn't want to be wolfjarl.

He wanted Isolfr, and he would take the damned job that went with it, if he could win it, if that was what it took.

Stammering an excuse to Ulfgeirr, Isolfr rose, and stalked with his wolf out into a windy morning, clouds tattered and the air half-green with the scent of rising sap. A long walk: he needed to learn the village in case he had to defend it.

He was halfway down the high street when Othwulf found him. "Greetings, Isolfr!" he cried against the leaping wind. Viradechtis bounded forward, tail wagging delightedly, to exchange wolfish greetings with Vikingr.

"Greetings, Othwulf," Isolfr returned, although he could not quite make himself meet his uncle's eyes. He felt raw—had felt raw since Eyjolfr had accosted him, and it was worse now, knowing how Skjald-wulf felt, knowing that there was something in *him* that was . . . even mentally, he choked over the word "desirable." And with Viradechtis' re-gard for Vikingr so obvious that she might as well have hired a herald to proclaim it, he felt his face turning crimson and prayed Othwulf would assume it the effect of the wind.

"I hear your sister's second litter does well," Othwulf said.

"Yes," Isolfr said, struggling to conduct himself like a wolfcarl, a wolfsprechend-in-waiting, and not some virgin bride. "Yes, they remain in Nithogsfjoll—as does my daughter."

"Your daughter?" He looked up then, a glance, to see Othwulf beam-ing at him, and received a terrific, but unmistakably delighted, clout on the shoulder. "Congratulations, Isolfr! It is splendid news!"

"Her name is Alfgyfa," Isolfr said.

"Will she go to the heall?"

"I know not. Her mother's sister is childless, and my mother—" He grinned, remembering the invasion of Angrbotha's cottage. "My mother seems prepared to cherish her grandchild."

"As well she ought. And your father?"

Isolfr shrugged. "He is here, in Franangford. I do not know if he has been told."

"You have not told him yourself." Not a question.

"I have not seen him."

Othwulf sighed. "I would wish this could be buried. I told him, you know, in the Iskryne, that you were no insult to his honor. I told him that if I had a son half so worthy as you, I should be the proudest man in the North. But he would not hear me. Twisted my words so I nearly cried feud on him."

"Feud?"

"I do not mind if he thinks me a lecher and a monster," Othwulf said. "The bad blood between us is of long standing, and even did we wish to, I do not think we could wash it away. But that he should think you . . . No, I will not say it."

"You need not," Isolfr said, and managed a rueful half-smile. "Father has never scrupled to speak his mind."

"Damn him," Othwulf muttered. "But I am glad this head of conversation has arisen."

"Oh?"

"I hear that your sister will be forming her pack soon."

"Yes," Isolfr said.

"Isolfr." Othwulf's hand on his shoulder forced him to look up. "Vikingr and I will not be standing up for her."

"No?" Isolfr said and hated the way his voice squeaked with mingled relief and doubt.

"No." Othwulf shrugged, smiling. "I have no particular wish to be wolfjarl of anywhere, and I would not force myself on you when you so clearly find the prospect distasteful."

"I—"

"I can read the pack-sense, Wolfmaegthbrother," Othwulf said. "And while your sister would clearly be pleased to have Vikingr put to her—" Viradechtis, who was attending carefully, her eyes bright, hit them both with *male-wolfness* in agreement. Othwulf startled, then burst out laughing.

"Sister," Isolfr said crossly, red-faced again.

"She teases you, Isolfr. And I see why; you rise charmingly to her casting. I'm glad my own brother doesn't have her sense of humor." Othwulf glanced fondly at Vikingr, who laughed back, ears pricked. "In any case, I wished to reassure you."

Isolfr slapped his uncle's shoulder with the back of hand. "You're all a torment to me," he said, trying to hide his relief. "Have you any clever advice on what I could say to mend fences with your brother?"

"Your father?" Othwulf settled back on his heels and scratched desultorily at his beard. The lice were bad in crowded quarters, as Isolfr had already discovered, and the bathhouse insufficient to the needs of so many men.

"He does not wish to be known as such," Isolfr answered, with a shrug.

"Someday he'll feel differently." Vikingr nudged Othwulf's hand, demanding his ears scratched, and Othwulf obliged him. "When your fame outstrips his, he'll no doubt proclaim the connection widely."

Isolfr snorted, watching Viradechtis snuffle around his boots so he wouldn't have to meet Othwulf's eyes. "And what do I do in the meantime? Present myself for excoriation?"

Othwulf snickered. "Make the advance if you wish to, and be prepared that he may not accept it. Or turn now and walk away, and let it go." Isolfr started to protest, and Othwulf forestalled him with a raised palm. "You can't control him, Isolfr. But you can acquit yourself with honor."

Isolfr sighed, and stepped back. "Hel take him. I know."

⚮

Before the evening meal, however, the choice was made for him. Gunnarr Sturluson came to the gates of the wolfheall unattended, and asked to see him.

Isolfr went out alone. He saw his father's relief that the wolf was not with him and did not regret it, despite Viradechtis' displeasure. He knew also that she shadowed them at a distance. Twice, he'd been harmed when she was not there to guard him. She wouldn't allow it to happen a third time.

They walked in silence until they were down the long lane out of the village, away from the girls spinning in doorways and the clatter of the smithy, the reek of old blood in the mud by the butcher's door. They were under the arch of wide-spaced pines, springy needles and moist earth soft underfoot, before Gunnarr said, without turning, "Tell me how to regain my son."

"You never lost him."

He knew as he said it that it was the wrong answer, but he was unable to lie. A dark corner of his heart rejoiced in his father's frown; there was something in him that did not wish to be forgiven because it did not wish to forgive. He mastered it, and tried again. "A man's duty to his family is not lessened merely because he has another duty to follow—"

"When you have children—" Gunnarr began, and Isolfr cut him off with a laugh.

Mother has not sent to him. "If I treat my daughter as you have treated your son, Father, then may Othinn strike me, and no man recover my bones."

Gunnarr turned to look at him, a twig crunching under his boot—the damp dense sound of winter-rotten pine. The scent of resin sharpened the air, and branches creaked like fiddles bowed at random. The pause was long, and he still knew Gunnarr well enough to see him chewing the news with care and swallowing it bite by bite.

And choosing to speak of something else.

"He may yet," Gunnarr said. "He may yet strike us all. The gods are angry, N—" He coughed. His lips were chapped, peeling in thick yellow shreds. He popped a louse against his thumbnail and flicked it away. "Isolfr. We're losing the war."

Isolfr drew a deep, hopeful breath. It steadied him, so he took another. "Over all our dead bodies," he said, calmly, to hear his father's bitter laugh. The sound seemed stretched between them, a tenuous link, easily snapped.

Gunnarr snorted, and spat on the springy loam. "You're to stay behind, you and the wolf?"

"I am," Isolfr said, frowning.

Gunnarr nodded. "You'll see to your mother if it comes to it, then. And Kathlin and Jonak."

Isolfr sorted answers a moment, decided against reminding his father that Jonak was heir, and old enough to bear a man's part. Decided also against saying that he considered it an offense to his mother to suggest that she would need "seeing to," if worse came to worst. Halfrid knew as much about honor as any man, and she was no fool besides.

He said, "I will die defending her if that is the only way."

Gunnarr answered with a grunt, and took another three steps in silence before he said, "You have a daughter."

"Barely a fortnight old," Isolfr answered, but he didn't volunteer her name.

And Gunnarr did not ask.

Five days later, in a cold spring rain, the Wolfmaegth marched on Othinnsaesc, and the wolfless men went with them. Isolfr and the wolf-sprechends did not watch them go—bad luck, and they could all feel the luck running against them already. And in any event, they had more than enough to keep them busy.

It was not comfortable, living in a wolfheall with four konigenwolves. Aslaug was white-muzzled, lame with arthritis, half-blind—but she was still konigenwolf, and she would tolerate no impertinence from the younger bitches. Vigdis and Signy liked each other no better than they had at the Wolfmaegthing, and all three of them recognized Viradechtis, young and without a pack of her own, as a threat. They listened to their brothers, as Viradechtis listened to Isolfr, when they urged them counter to their instincts, but the konigenwolves were not happy, and this meant that the wolves of Franangford's defense were not happy either. Snarls and snapping were common, fights not infrequent. Isolfr learned more than he had ever wanted to know about doctoring trellwolves, but he could not help the warm glow of pleasure that kindled in his chest when Hrolleif remarked that he had a gift for it.

"And you stitch more neatly than any of us," Signy's brother Lei-tholfr added, watching while Isolfr tended to a triangle-shaped tear in the skin over the shoulder of a Thorsbaer wolf. "The gods know, I've seen enough hamhanded wolfjarls and wolfsprechends to last me the rest of my life. And Ormarr and Stafnulf are grateful, aren't you, Stafnulf?"

"Yes, Leitholfr," Stafnulf muttered, hastily dropping his gaze from Isolfr's face.

Isolfr did his best to get used to the way the younger wolfcarls stared at him when they thought he did not notice. He knew what they were thinking, and would have even without the pack-sense to tell him. Word had spread—for there were no secrets in the Wolfmaegth—that the youngest of the konigenwolves would be looking for her consort soon, and the young men were dreaming. Isolfr did not blame them, but it was uncomfortable being the center of so much attention, uncomfortable knowing that as much as they were thinking about their wolves' chances with Viradechtis, they were also thinking about having him, Isolfr, lie down for them. He caught glimpses of himself in the pack-sense, filtered through wolves and wolves: pale and cold and unapproachable. If Grimolfr's name to the wolves was black iron, then Isolfr's own was ice, the cold, pure ice of the Iskryne.

He was amazed, even when he was blushing hotly enough to disprove their comparison, at the sharpness of their observations, their ability to make judgments. For no wolf in the Wolfmaegth had seen the Iskryne before last summer's campaign, yet that knowledge was in the pack-sense now, the cold sharp smell of the ice of the Iskryne. And when they thought of that smell, the Wolfmaegth thought of Viradechtis' brother.

Spring wore slowly toward summer; the konigenwolves grumbled and snarled but maintained their truce. The wolfsprechends organized and planned, laid in stores, drilled their wolfcarls. Aslaug's brother, who had been wolfsprechend of Ketillhill for almost forty years, said that, aside from trolls, the worst danger they faced was bored men, bored wolves. Patrols were a necessity, and the men and wolves were kept busy on messenger duty to the wolfheallan, crofts, and villages, and hunting and requisitioning provisions for the army. Isolfr had had no idea of the scale of the logistical operation required to support an army of this size; it was nothing like a raiding party or a Viking band.

Summer was traditionally the time of harvest and relaxation. There was no such luxury this year. The trolls were dug in deep under Othinnsaesc; the news that returned with the waves of wounded was not encouraging, and left Isolfr half-frantic with frustration over not being there to fight beside Frithulf, Sokkolfr, and Ulfbjorn—yes, and Grimolfr, too. The men and wolves of the North had managed to reclaim what remained of heall and manor—wooden buildings had burned, but stone shells remained—but the trolls were into the sea-caves and had had the whole winter to warren the town. They burrowed silently, master sappers, and could emerge anywhere, any time, with only crumbling earth and collapsing walls to warn the men above.

At midsummer, it was decided, the Northmen would make a push and try to purge the warrens once and for all. Nobody said it out loud, but everyone knew: the stalemate had to end by winter or the trolls had won.

NINE

On the third day after the solstice, more wounded began to arrive at Franangford. It was horribly like a spring flood; first a trickle, then a stream, then a torrent, then simply the grim struggle to keep from going under and never mind the force one struggled against: men cursing, wolves crying with pain, screaming—dreadful screaming—as those whose trollbites had festered had to have their injuries lanced, and sometimes an arm or leg removed entirely.

It was ghastly work, butchery, no respite, no peace, and Skjaldwulf had said Isolfr's name three times before Isolfr realized who he was.

"Skjaldwulf!" He looked anxiously, first at the man, then for his wolf. Skjaldwulf wore his shield-arm in a sling, and Isolfr could see from the hunched outline of his shoulder that something was still amiss in the joint. Mar had a terrible bite, swollen and clearly festering, on his shoulder. He was whining softly, but from the way he kept bumping anxiously at Skjaldwulf's unbound hand, Isolfr saw his distress was for his brother, not himself.

Isolfr met Skjaldwulf's eyes momentarily, not meaning to, and had to look away. His face was pinched in pain, but traces of a smile lingered at the corners of his mouth. *I am not worth it,* he wanted to say, but bit back. That was not his decision to make, any more than it had been Viradechtis' choice whether Isolfr would stay with her. Instead, nervously, he said, as he had been saying to wolfcarls for days now, "I regret that I must cause you further pain."

"Aye," Skjaldwulf said, eyeing Isolfr's collection of lancets and salves with some dismay. "Before you make me forget though, I was charged most strictly to bring you greetings from your shieldmates."

"Are they well?"

"Better than Mar and me," Skjaldwulf said, with a lopsided grin that had all his hidden sweetness. "Frithulf says to tell you. . . ." He frowned in concentration, and when he spoke it was in an imitation of Frithulf so uncannily good that Isolfr almost looked around for his friend: "Ulfrikr snores so loudly we use him to scare off the trolls."

Isolfr felt himself smile, small and stiff. "Thank you, Skjaldwulf. Do you wish me tend you first, or your brother?"

"See to Mar," said Skjaldwulf. "His hurts are worse than mine."

As Isolfr worked, applying hot compresses to bring the poison up before he lanced the wound, he asked Skjaldwulf to tell him how the campaign fared. It was easier, if he did not have to meet the wolfcarl's eyes, and he knew Skjaldwulf needed something to distract him both from his own pain and from his brother's.

At first, he despaired of ever breaching the wall of Skjaldwulf's reserve. But then he hit on the idea of asking how the two of them had come by their injuries, and then, at last, Skjaldwulf began to talk with some ease. The voice he used was trained, fluid—not his own awkward phrases, disjointed by silence. He sounded like a skald, as he did sometimes, and Isolfr moved himself to wonder again what he might have been if he had not been a wolfcarl.

"We entered the tunnels with torches," he said, falling into a rhythm as slow and natural as breathing, while Isolfr drained the stinking pus from Mar's swollen shoulder, scrubbed the dead flesh away, and packed the wound with boiled moss, and herbs. The fur had already begun to drop out around the edges of the bite, but the fever didn't run through the wolf's body; the only heat was in the flesh near the wound. That gave Isolfr hope; the poison was not in the blood. "Through stinking troll-havens sought them, down into darkness, companioned by wolves."

"You're already making a song," Isolfr accused, and Skjaldwulf laughed, but lightly, hitching as if it pained him.

"Shall I try a plainer rendering?"

"No," Isolfr said, binding his dressing tight over Mar's dark coat. Mar groaned in appreciation, as if the pressure eased the pain of his wound. "You'll need the distraction. Now you," he said, and gestured to Skjald-wulf's injured arm.

"The collarbone's broken," Skjaldwulf said. "I can't raise the arm. I think it's broken too, and the ribs may be as well. You'll have to help me with my shirt."

Isolfr wiped the blood off his hands with a damp rag. "Has it come through the skin?"

"No," Skjaldwulf answered. Together, they got his tunic off, and Isolfr could plainly see how the bone in his arm was shifted, the skin bruised fiercely there, down Skjaldwulf's chest and shoulder and over his ribs.

"I'll have to set this," he said, and sent a village boy for Ulfgeirr. He was not strong enough to hold Skjaldwulf steady as well as straighten the bone.

Ulfgeirr came, and swore when he saw the injury. "Did a wall fall on you?"

"No," Skjaldwulf answered, as Isolfr took hold of his good arm and braced his shoulder against the wall. "A roof. Don't send it through the skin, werthreatbrother."

"Wouldn't dream of it," Ulfgeirr answered. He laid thumb by thumb on Skjaldwulf's arm, and with a deft wrench of his hands brought them level. Isolfr felt bone grind and click through his palms and did not count it cowardice when Skjaldwulf screamed. Mar growled, hard by his werbrother's knee, and Skjaldwulf managed to drop his good hand and soothe him.

"They mean me no harm," he said, when the whiteness of his cheeks gave way to a raw-looking flush. Mar whined, but fell back on his elbows and dropped his head across Skjaldwulf's foot.

"Well," Ulfgeirr said, with a frown. "It's good you're not an archer, but it should heal well enough for a shield. *If*," he added sternly, "you let it heal. If you break it half-healed—"

"I know," Skjaldwulf said. "Wrap it along with the ribs. It's best if I can't move anything."

But Isolfr traced the dark bruises under his fingertips, on Skjald-wulf's sword-arm shoulder, ignoring how the other man shivered. "These are wolf teeth."

"Mar dragged me free when the tunnel came down. And now you've made me tell it out of order, Isolfr."

"I'll hush," Isolfr said, bending for a roll of linen to wrap Skjald-wulf's chest and ribs as Ulfgeirr patted his shoulder and moved away. "Tell as you will."

"We fought our way down into the warrens," Skjaldwulf said in more normal tones. "We fortified and traded men off at every opportunity, sending them into the light to rest and be fed. The trolls had warrened from rock and the caves up into the earth under the village, and we fought them bitterly back. Our blood and their blood flowed before us as we descended. We splashed through gore. The way was slick and awful."

Isolfr had to lift Skjaldwulf's arm to wrap the ribs under it. Only the hitch in his breathing showed his pain. "Tell me more," Isolfr said, as much caught in the spell of the story as hoping to distract his patient.

"As we descended, we found ourselves fighting sows—as in the Iskryne, you remember?—and we knew we were coming to the heart of the warren. There were kittens, too, and once we got down to the bedrock, they'd started working the stone in those patterns of theirs. They mean to—ow!—to stay, Isolfr." He paused, breathing slowly through his nose.

"Do you want ale? Or something stronger?" *Idiot*, Isolfr thought. He should have offered at the outset.

"No," Skjaldwulf said. "When you are done, perhaps. Or perhaps Mar and I will rest a little, and then see what we can do to help." He frowned at his arm. "This will keep me from fighting for a month or four, but I can still sing."

"I think a song would be welcome." Isolfr reached for another strip of linen, and continued winding. "How did the roof come into it?"

Skjaldwulf closed his eyes. "We broke through the sows and the trellwitches, and found another rank, bigger warriors than any we'd seen, and with them a troll twice the size any troll has a right to be." He paused, breathing shallowly, too quickly, and leaned his head back on the wall. Sweat beaded, broke, and ran together on his forehead, and his skin under Isolfr's fingers was clammy. "The trolls brought it down," he said. "When they saw we were going to win through to their king. They brought the roof down on their own heads to save their king. Again, as they did in the Iskryne."

Queen, Isolfr almost said, thinking of something one of the svartalfar had said—and then remembered that he couldn't explain how he knew, and finished binding Skjaldwulf's arm over his tightly-wrapped ribs in silence. "There," he said, and—steeling himself—brushed the hair off Skjaldwulf's forehead. "Mar, make him sleep now."

The black wolf looked up at Isolfr with pale, cool eyes and, grinning, promised that he would.

⚘

Skjaldwulf was already a week on his way to Nithogsfjoll along with the rest of those too wounded to fight when Frithulf made the trip from Othinnsaesc, bearing tidings. He told Isolfr that not a troll had been seen on the surface or heard delving since the mines caved in, and the men and wolves remaining were starting to breathe easier. He and Kothran sat with Isolfr and Viradechtis by the fire, drinking mulled ale muddled with ginger and honey. His scars hadn't faded, but whatever salve Jorveig had given him seemed to be returning flexibility to the skin;

his smile was straighter than it had been. *And if it had been me,* Isolfr thought, *would half the wermaegth still be wooing me?*

A useless question. Whatever beauty he might possess was nothing compared to Viradechtis. He snorted into his ale.

"What are you thinking?" Frithulf asked, leaning against his arm.

"Just counting my dowry," Isolfr answered, with a nod to the wolves.

Frithulf chuckled. "Think of the fun we'll have come next summer," he said. "You'll be wolfsprechend, and I shall be your no-account, troublemaking friend. You'll be eternally busy rescuing me from the fathers of the maidens who swoon across your path, ripe for the plucking."

Their laughter drew no sideways glances in the half-empty wolfheall; the mood had grown lighter over the course of a week without wounded. The summer nights were still no more than a dimming of the light and men's hearts turned toward hope. Frithulf and Isolfr slept side by side, as in the old days, bracketed by wolves, and Isolfr allowed himself to believe that they might soon be going home.

They were not privileged to sleep long. Dawn was no more than a suggestion in high summer, a hesitation of the pale sun in its endless circuit of the sky. Isolfr was roused in that hour by shouting voices and the clash of metal, startling to his feet before he realized he'd dragged Frithulf with him. The voices were strained, angry, fearful. In firelight, he dragged his trews on and jammed his feet into his boots. Frithulf handed him his axe before his head was even clear of the neck of his jerkin, and Viradechtis and Kothran flanked them as they ran for the door amid a dozen other men and wolves.

They emerged to chaos. Trolls were everywhere, in among the outbuildings of the wolfheall, and Isolfr ducked an axe-blow and riposted unsuccessfully before he won free of the roundhall door. Frithulf was at his left hand still. They charged, making way for those behind them: the gravest danger was to be trapped inside, vulnerable to fire.

And the trolls had fire. Smoke rose beyond the walls, telling Isolfr that Franangford was already burning. He cursed and stumbled on a not-well-seated boot, managing to keep his head on his shoulders only because Viradechtis hamstrung the troll who struck at him. It went down with a crash, and he half-severed the lumpy greenish arm with which it wielded its enormous club, and then gutted it as he climbed over it, looking for the next. As he did, he saw how it fought in light; a hooded cloak and slit-eyed goggles like those men wore against snowblindness shielded its piggy eyes.

"Bet they can't see their flanks very well," Frithulf yelled, regaining his side.

"Like a man in a helm," Isolfr agreed. They advanced into the courtyard, cobblestones slick with blood, fighting as they went. They saw no wyverns, blessedly, but there were trolls enough for everyone, and Isolfr could see more pressing through the broken gate, overrunning the defenders there. "Damn. *Damn!*"

"It's all the fucking trolls in Othinnsaesc!" Frithulf started for the gate. Isolfr followed, running, axe raised as he shouted something wordless and white with rage. Other defenders ran to join them, wolfcarls and wolves forming an impromptu charge, and somehow Hrolleif was with them as they hit the wall of trolls, Vigdis snarling at his side.

They had no shields and there was no shield-wall to strike. The thunder of charging men, the impact that could lift you off your feet, was replaced by whistling axe blades and the thud of clubs on wolfcarl bodies. Something struck Isolfr across the face, teeth and brains, a blow that stroked his hair and killed the man before him. Then he was among the trolls, ankle-deep in gore, just as Skjaldwulf had described. He screamed, and the trolls were screaming, and the force of blows struck and blows parried made his arm ache and rocked him from side to side. He looked up once to see a trellsow looming over him, and saw her fall when Hrolleif took her head with a stroke that confounded understanding. Other than that, there was the blood, and he fought now beside Frithulf, now beside Ulfgeirr, and then beside wolves and men whose names he barely knew, men of Thorsbaer and Bravoll and he knew not where.

They won out of the compound, away from the wolfheall, but it was already in flames behind them, and then they were fighting in the village, men-at-arms and village boys and women beside them, or screaming and being dragged, being burned, being killed. He saw Grimolfr, great Skald with him, the length of the high street away, and then shouting men, shouting wolves, a great black shape he recognized as Vikingr. More trolls, from the other direction, from Othinnsaesc, and wolves and men in pursuit of them, among them, shouting and slaying.

Isolfr knew what must have happened, then. Trolls from the north—fresh trolls, come to relieve besieged Othinnsaesc—and the Othinnsaesc trolls themselves had burrowed out beneath the encamped men and flanked them, to come down on Franangford from two directions at once. They must have devastated the sentries and destroyed the patrols. There had been no warning, though the men at Othinnsaesc had pursued.

The scent of char and the scorched metal of blood scratched his throat. He saw it all, saw Grimolfr and Ulfsvith Iron-Tongue among wolfless men and wolfcarls fighting side by side, holding the street. Holding a route for their escape, his own little band of villagers and wolfcarls and wolves. Signy leapt forward as silent as plague, brought a troll to the ground, tore its throat and kept moving into the band of enemies between them and the men from Othinnsaesc. Viradechtis, a moment later, covered her flank, and Isolfr followed, the center of the leading part of a wedge. He shouted. He slew. He never felt the blow that left his shield-arm hanging numb and useless by his side, but he had no shield, so it did not distress him. He saw Vigdis come up to fight at Signy's side, Kothran running beside her. He saw Hroi emerge from among the trolls so black with blood that he looked like Mar, grinning through blood, shaking blood from his ruff and jaws, ready to lead them home. He saw trolls die, pebbled hides split open, gaping black like rotted fruit. He saw Grimolfr's torn lip and bruised cheek as the wolfjarl grabbed his arm and almost threw him into his father's embrace, saw Gunnarr put himself between Isolfr and Ulfgeirr—who limped on a leg gashed so badly that Isolfr could have put his fist in the wound—and the trolls.

He did not see Hrolleif fall.

✣

They came to Bravoll in tatters and shreds, a wolfcarl carrying his wolf across his shoulders, two wolfless men leaning on each other, Vigdis and Skald, one on each side of Grimolfr, keeping him upright.

Hrolleif was dead. There was no need to ask; Isolfr felt it all through the pack-sense, saw the memories of the wolves who had borne witness. Vigdis was keening, back in her throat; Grimolfr kept rubbing his eyes, as if he had not realized they were blurring because of the tears running down his cheeks.

Isolfr and Frithulf, Viradechtis and Kothran, formed the center of a loose knot of survivors: Ulfgeirr leaning on Nagli, Hroi limping on three paws and Sokkolfr, his hair matted to his back with blood, patiently encouraging him, refusing to let him fall behind. Kari and Hrafn were with them, too, and two young Ketillhill wolfcarls whose names Isolfr could not remember. One of them had lost his wolf, and they were both blank-faced with grief and shock. Littermates, Isolfr picked out of the pack-sense, like Viradechtis and Kothran, and did not wonder at the shield-mates' shared grief.

Tindr was dead, his spine broken and his body half-severed by the blow of a trellish axe. Ulfbjorn walked beside Sokkolfr and Hroi, his face blank behind soot and blood, and those of the Nithogsfjoll wolves who could make the effort would come up to him, nudging gently at thigh or hand, and Isolfr felt their love, their concern. Ulfbjorn was part of their pack, and they wished him to know it.

Sometime in that terrible march, Eyjolfr—who with Leitholfr carried the rough sling in which Signy lay, both her left legs broken—sent Glaedir to stay by Ulfbjorn, and Glaedir faithfully herded Ulfbjorn the rest of the way to Bravoll, so like a sheepdog that it would have been funny if it had not made Isolfr's eyes burn with tears.

The defenders of Bravoll were at least ready for them, the konigen-wolf coming gravely to greet them, despite the protesting squeaks of her new litter. She and Vigdis and Viradechtis touched noses, and the strong thought of *mother* in the pack-sense allowed Isolfr to let go, just slightly. Vigdis and Viradechtis would give way; dominance at Bravoll belonged to its queen.

They had to take it in turns to doctor each other, Frithulf assessing Isolfr's arm—not broken, he could move his fingers again, but horrendously bruised, black and purple and blood red, and it was a fortnight before he could raise it—as Isolfr stitched shut Ulfgeirr's thigh. Isolfr and Leitholfr setting Signy's legs while Ulfgeirr coaxed Hroi to let him tend his wounds. It was heavy between the wolfsprechends that Signy's chances were poor; if she had not been konigenwolf, she would already be dead. But Aslaug had died at Franangford, troll blood dripping from her muzzle, and they did not have enough konigenwolves that they could give up on Signy.

"I've always said she's the most stubborn bitch in the Wolfmaegth," Leitholfr said, touching her ears gently. "Perhaps that may work in our favor this time."

And Grimolfr grieved, although he never spoke of it, and he worked with Ulfsvith Iron-Tongue, Gunnarr, and the other jarls and wolfjarls on Bravoll's defense. Vigdis and Skald did not leave his side, and all the Nithogsfjollthreat grieved with him, but Isolfr knew none of them except perhaps the wolves truly understood the depth of Grimolfr's hurt. Hrolleif had been shieldmate, werthreatbrother, lover, wolfsprechend: there were not words, he thought, for what Grimolfr and Hrolleif had meant to each other, and he found himself wishing that Skjaldwulf were there, for if anyone could find a way to speak Grimolfr's grief, it would be he.

Isolfr thought his own grief for Hrolleif small and bittersweet beside that, and could not bring himself to speak of it either, even to Frithulf and Sokkolfr. Especially to Ulfbjorn, who moved like a man in a dream.

There was one small joy in the midst of the horror. Hrolfmarr, who had been Kolli's brother, and wolfless since, was chosen by one of the Bravoll konigenwolf's cubs, who clambered over tithe-boys and anyone else who might come between them to get to him.

Ironically, in the issue of Grimolfr's sorrow—in this one small thing as in no other—Isolfr's wishes were met. Skjaldwulf appeared at Bravoll three weeks later, at the head of a band of men and wolves that was larger than it should have been, to leave the remaining keeps and wolfheallan protected. Isolfr thought he understood the logic well enough. Mar's shoulder had healed to proud flesh and scar tissue, and though Skjaldwulf's arm was still splinted, he moved the shoulder freely. If he let Ulfgeirr and Isolfr keep his ribs wrapped tight, it caused him no pain that he would admit, and his presence—and his voice—brought a certain grim determination to sell themselves dearly to the wolfcarls and the wolfless men both.

It was plainspoken Kari who said it, one night as they sat by the fire. Winter was coming. And there was nothing between Franangford and Bravoll to stop the trolls.

Isolfr felt his oath to the svartalfar like a stone in his throat. He knew why; he knew why the trolls came. He knew what they were fleeing. If he had thought that information would help Grimolfr and Ulfsvith plan a defense, he could not be certain he would have held his tongue, all honor and his sworn word aside. Would he make himself an oathbreaker, lower than a kin-slaughterer, to save his brothers?

Although he knew it was wrong, he also knew that he would. If it would have made a difference.

But it wouldn't, and so he held his honor and his tongue.

Viradechtis came into season before the equinox. *Too soon*, Isolfr thought, although Hrolleif had warned him it might be so. And he could feel it himself, what Viradechtis felt, that with Aslaug dead, Signy nearly, and Vigdis without a wolfsprechend and showing no inclination to choose one, the Wolfmaegth had an emptiness at its heart, and it was an emptiness that Viradechtis could no more ignore than she could stop breathing.

The mating was different this time, as Hrolleif had also said it would be. When it was clear, to wolves and men, that Viradechtis' heat was coming, a meeting was called, a wolfmoot of every threat that had a presence in Bravoll. Isolfr sat beside Grimolfr, feeling as conspicuous as a spring garland on an ice giant, while threat by threat the wolfcarls were given the chance to announce their desire to enter contention, to stand up for Viradechtis and her brother.

Othwulf did not stand, as he had promised. Eyjolfr did, and Skjald-wulf, and a number of the wolfcarls who had courted Isolfr at the Wolf-maegthing a year and a half ago, including Vethulf of Arakensberg and his odd-eyed brother. Isolfr was surprised when Kari stood up, but grate-ful besides. He thought he could deal very well with Kari as his wolfjarl.

The mating, Grimolfr said, could not be held in Bravoll. Isolfr thought a moment, thought of the condition of the threat during and af-ter a mating, thought of the wolfless men (thought, his belly going cold, of his father), and agreed wholeheartedly. "We must go, then." And he managed a crooked smile. "As with her first heat, only . . ."

"Just so," Grimolfr said, and met Isolfr's eyes for a moment before he looked away. "Bravoll has the same sort of arrangement we do, for their bitches' first heat. Apparently, it's the site of the old wolfheall—'old' in this case meaning your grandfather's day—so there should be plenty of room. The yearlings' brothers have agreed to lead the way and to take the part our tradition appoints."

"They are very kind," Isolfr said.

"Isolfr." Grimolfr stopped. Skald nudged his broad muzzle under his brother's hand, and Grimolfr began rubbing along the wolf's jaw dis-tractedly. "I know the first mating was hard for you—"

"I will be fine, wolfjarl," Isolfr said. "I will not run craven."

"I didn't think you would," Grimolfr said dryly. "But I know that Hrolleif would have had advice for you, and I wish that I could give you his words. It is not the same, a mating of this kind, but I am not brother to a konigenwolf. I do not know what to warn you of."

"Thank you," Isolfr said. "But I think . . . I think Viradechtis has her plan. And where she leads, I follow."

"'Tis ever the way of it," Grimolfr agreed. "Tell one of Bravoll's yearlings he's to run back with news as soon as there's news to tell."

"I will," said Isolfr and went to find the things he would need.

A bedroll, a change of linen, Jorveig's invaluable salve: Sokkolfr found him in the storeroom packing those things and his roll of medical supplies into a bag, while Viradechtis sniffed interestedly at everything in reach of her nose.

"Isolfr, I'm sorry."

Isolfr sat back on his heels. "For what?"

"For not . . ." Sokkolfr's lips tightened; then, in the manner of wolves, he said simply, "I would stand up for you, if I thought Hroi could win."

"Sokkolfr . . ." But Isolfr did not know what to say. Hroi sat in the doorway behind them, and Isolfr could feel the old wolf's aches, his tiredness. And he felt, too, that if Sokkolfr had wished it, Hroi would have entered the fray for Viradechtis—and for Isolfr—though man and wolf both knew he would lose. *I do not deserve this,* he thought, as he had thought of Skjaldwulf's devotion. He managed, after a moment, to smile up at his friend. "You know I want you as housecarl anyway."

Sokkolfr smiled back. "Ulfbjorn and Frithulf and I, we will wait for you." And he extended his hand to bring Isolfr to his feet.

֍

Fortunately—or so Isolfr thought—the old Bravoll wolfheall was several miles east of the current wolfheall, rather than west toward Franangford. He walked beside Asvolfr, the leader of Bravoll's young men, who had volunteered to guide the mating party, and with some patience—*all that practice with Sokkolfr,* he thought and hid a smile—he managed to coax the youth into talking to him; he learned that the wolfheall had been moved some fifty years ago, when the traditional distrust between heall and manor had been dissolved by the widow of the jarl taking the heall's wolfsprechend as her lover. Their children were all heall-bred, one of them becoming a wolfcarl himself, and the young jarl of Bravoll had observed that it was foolish and inefficient for the wolfheall to lie so far from the manor and village it was meant to protect. The previous jarls—who, like Isolfr's father, preferred not to admit that they relied on the wolfheallan for anything—had liked it that way. The young jarl had had the wolfheall moved and built the new stone one after the modern fashion, with rushed floors and chimneys and mortared walls warmed by tapestries.

The site of the old heall was thus perfect for the purpose of isolating a bitch in her first heat—or, in this case, having an open mating without disrupting the wolfheall's defenses. Everyone knew where it was; the path to it was easy and broad, and the old heall-site itself was level and spacious and had a number of walls remaining, at least in part. "Plenty of shelter," the boy said, and following his glance at the high gray clouds, Isolfr understood why that was a consideration.

They arrived enough before dusk that setting up camp was not a problem. Asvolfr said, awkwardly, "How long do you think it will be?"

"I've no more idea than you do," Isolfr said ruefully. "Have you witnessed a mating before?"

Asvolfr nodded. "Not our konigenwolf's, of course, but the second bitch went into heat right after she did, and we—" He jerked his head indicating the other yearlings. "We bore witness."

He said it with the same mixture of awe and horror that Isolfr remembered from the first mating he had seen. "This will be different," he said to Asvolfr, as Hrolleif had said to him. "She chooses her consort now." He had to swallow hard, but made himself say it: "It will not be as bad."

Asvolfr nodded again, his eyes wide and grave.

"You and the other yearlings stay out of the way, no matter what happens or how badly a wolf is hurt," Isolfr said. That was something Leitholfr had told him, a quick word in the mad bustle of parting. "With the rut-madness, it will be hard for the wolves to tell friend from foe, and in a mating like this one, they will be eager for blood. You, and especially your pups, could be savaged. When it is *over*, then do your doctoring." He smiled at the boy, and after a moment, Asvolfr smiled back.

❦

Isolfr made his camp in what must have been the corner of a storeroom, where there were still two stone half-walls to give shelter and as much privacy as he could hope. Viradechtis' heat began to build in earnest as the sun went down; Isolfr found himself praying as he knelt awkwardly on his bedroll to make the first application of Jorveig's salve, a blanket draped around his shoulders because he did not want the wolfcarls to see this process. Praying that this time it would break quickly. He wished it done with.

Viradechtis laughed at him from where she sat, ears up, surveying her suitors. She was enjoying herself and was glad to have *male-wolfness* to think about instead of *stench-of-trolls*.

In that, Isolfr admitted, she was not wrong.

Asvolfr and his tithe-mates brought Isolfr supper; he ate what he could, which wasn't much, wrapped in his blankets not against the chill of the night air but because his arousal was already pressing the front of his trews, and foolish though it was of him, he did not want the yearlings to see.

A fight broke out, somewhere in the darkness. Viradechtis watched and listened. Isolfr fought the urge to back himself into the corner, to protect his flanks. *It will be one man,* he told himself. *As with Sokkolfr and Hroi. One wolf. One man.* Hrolleif's voice in his head again: *wolfjarls can be taught.* But this first time, he was at the mercy of what his wolfjarl knew *now*. He remembered Eyjolfr's brutal kiss, remembered his anger. And he wrapped himself more tightly, pretending that his shivering was due to the cold.

The night passed somehow. Isolfr dozed and woke and dozed again. There were more fights, and Viradechtis made one or two sorties into the midst of the dog-wolves. Not merely teasing, but almost taunting them. "Sister, you are cruel," Isolfr said at one point, mostly asleep, but he knew Viradechtis wasn't listening to him.

He came awake, abruptly and entirely, at dawn, when the world resolved from black and charcoal gray into visibility. His sex was like iron between his legs, painful with Viradechtis' need, and he sat up to see that a semicircle of wolves had surrounded him while he slept.

The last clear thought in his head was to hope that the yearlings were safely out of range.

He freed himself from his bedding, and the shirt that was all he had worn to sleep in, and felt more than heard the moan of the assembled wolf-carls. They wanted him, as their brothers wanted Viradechtis; Viradechtis' heat had come down upon them all.

A snarl rose up from someone's throat, deep and thready, and Isolfr could not help flinching at the sudden explosion of fur and claws and teeth that rolled into the open space in front of Viradechtis. And then he did back into the corner, as the entire gathering of wolves seemed to turn on each other, their brothers entering the fray behind them.

Isolfr caught bits and pieces of what happened. He saw Mar standing off two smaller wolves from Vestfjorthr, saw Glaedir take Hrafn down. He saw two wolves he did not know locked together in a fury, the one with his teeth firmly in the other's ear. Violence and blood, and he pressed himself into his corner, feeling more defenseless than he ever had in his life, knowing that the wolfcarl who made it past Viradechtis would take him, whoever it might be. He was the prize in this combat, where Viradechtis was both prize and prize-giver. Her choice, not his.

The ranks of the contenders thinned out, though Isolfr did not know if it was slow or fast. He saw, very distinctly, the moment when Kjaran drove Glaedir out of the circle, as Vethulf lifted Eyjolfr entirely off the ground and threw him, sliding and skidding, across the grass and the old uneven flagstones; Skjaldwulf, his bad arm clutched close to his side, knocked the wind out of a beefy wolfcarl from Kerlaugstrond with a hard and well-placed kick. And then, with seeming suddenness, it was just the two of them: Mar and Kjaran. Behind them, Skjaldwulf and Vethulf. The two wolves started to circle. Skjaldwulf's face was white with pain; Mar was bleeding from a set of claw-slashes across his muzzle. But they weren't backing down. Isolfr could feel it, in the madness that was the pack-sense. Kjaran would have to kill Mar to get to Viradechtis. And he realized, woolly-headed, that the other was true as well: Mar would have to kill Kjaran. *This* was what made a wolfjarl and what made a konigenwolf's consort—the will to die for the pack. And where Glaedir was lacking that will, perhaps, or was still too young, these wolves were not. Mar and Kjaran were both snarling, a weird duet, and the entire wolfmoot of suitors was watching.

No, he thought, muddled, starting forward, not knowing what he meant to do, only knowing that he did not want Mar hurt, and he didn't want Kjaran hurt, either. *No more death.* But his sight was blurred and dark, his body the wrong shape, too gangling and too tall, not enough legs and centered wrongly.

Isolfr's feet caught in his blankets and he fell, startled by the hardness of the ground into a cry.

Both Skjaldwulf and Vethulf turned toward him, Mar and Kjaran raising their heads, and Viradechtis made a strange, deep chuffing noise, neither a bark nor a snort, bizarrely satisfied. She bounded forward, a leap as exuberant as a puppy's but perfectly aimed and balanced for the sixteen-stone predator she was, and landed between Mar and Kjaran. And then, with a great and spurious air of gravity, she turned to touch noses, first with Kjaran, then with Mar.

Isolfr lay awkwardly as he had fallen, unable to gather either his limbs or his wits; Skjaldwulf and Vethulf were giving each other the most bewildered look, as if they did not understand why they were not at each other's throats. Then Viradechtis made her chuffing noise again, impatiently this time, and herded Mar and Kjaran toward Isolfr's corner.

And Isolfr knew, although he did not understand it and had not known it was possible. Viradechtis had chosen them both.

The rut-madness, banked for a moment by Viradechtis' choosing, roared over him again. He fumbled desperately for the salve, pushing the jar into Vethulf's shaking hands as his first wolfjarl joined him on the blankets. Isolfr rolled over, presenting himself as shamelessly as did the konigenwolf. There was nothing left in him but the need, the burning, and he moaned in frustration when he was touched with slick fingers. But Viradechtis was still teasing Kjaran; there was still time, and Vethulf seemed determined to take it.

Skjaldwulf's hands, with their scars and knobbled wrists and knuckles, came down over Isolfr's forearms. He could hear his second wolfjarl murmuring to him, although he could not make out the words. There were no words; there was only *need*. He pressed back, his breath coming in sobs, and Viradechtis swept her tail aside, giving Kjaran permission to mount.

Isolfr felt Kjaran as clearly as he felt Vethulf, but he also felt, as Kjaran pushed and Vethulf entered him, Skjaldwulf drop a kiss, very gently, on the top of his head.

Then there was only the madness, the glory, of Vethulf's strength.

He could feel Viradechtis' joy in Kjaran, feel why she had chosen as she had. And Vethulf was powerful, but not brutal; his hands did not clamp on Isolfr's hips but caressed his back, his shoulders. One slipped underneath him, found the thwarted agony of his sex, and within moments Vethulf had Isolfr screaming at every stroke, screaming with a ferocious passion that he had not known before, not even with Sokkolfr, not even with Hjordis. The pack-sense unfurled before him; this time he did not escape his body into it, he *joined* it, joined Viradechtis and Kjaran and Vethulf, and felt their desire and need and striving. His climax almost struck him senseless, and Vethulf and Viradechtis and Kjaran were there.

He felt Vethulf's hands stroking his hips and thighs, felt him—still gentle—move away. Skjaldwulf said, and now Isolfr could follow the words, "My wolfsprechend, will you roll over?"

Isolfr could not argue. He rolled onto his back, heard Skjaldwulf and Vethulf murmuring together, and then Vethulf's hands were urging him to lift his head as Skjaldwulf knelt between his spread thighs and reached for the salve.

Isolfr's head was pillowed on a blanket on Vethulf's lap, and Skjaldwulf bundled blankets beneath his hips, coaxing him to raise his legs, to let them rest on Skjaldwulf's shoulders. Bemused, Isolfr did as he was told as Mar and Viradechtis washed each other's faces, and then as the fire began to build again, he felt Skjaldwulf's fingers, greasy with salve, stroke past his stones, push up inside him, and *oh, oh yes*, and he threw his head back, his hands knotting in the blankets, and he brought his hips up to meet Skjaldwulf's first thrust. He heard Viradechtis bay her approval, almost felt Mar's forelegs against his own ribs, Vethulf's hand stroking his hair, Skjaldwulf's lean, fierce strength, and Isolfr keened through his teeth and met Skjaldwulf, thrust for thrust, fearless at last.

❧

ine, Isolfr thought, drowsily, and then, as he lifted his head, identified the sentiment as Viradechtis'. She sprawled lazily on sun-warmed flags in the late-summer light, her head pillowed on

Kjaran's gray rump, watching Isolfr with bright, alert eyes and a disconcertingly smug expression.

Never let it be said that wolves don't gloat or laugh.

Someone warm was pressed against Isolfr's back, a contrast to the coolness of the morning. He turned in the blankets, saw Vethulf regarding him with a pale, steady gaze. "Are you well?"

Isolfr stretched experimentally, and found himself far more well than he had expected. He nodded. "Where's Skjaldwulf and Mar?"

Vethulf dragged a long arm out of the blankets and pointed east. "They went to kill breakfast. We're supposed to make a fire."

Isolfr propped himself on his elbows and glanced around. There was blood on the stones, a tuft of fur pinned against a gorse bush by the steady breeze. They were alone. "They're gone."

Viradechtis and Kjaran raised their heads as Mar appeared at the top of the broken wall. He jumped down, his injured shoulder taking his weight well, and Skjaldwulf followed a moment later, an unlikely spidering of limbs. A brace of rabbits and two grouse hung from his hand. "Not all of them," he said. "I don't see a fire."

"We were getting to it," Vethulf said, with a bit of an edge, and curled to his feet. "There's a picket?"

Skjaldwulf looked at Isolfr, directly enough to make Isolfr glance down, his face hot. "I hope our wolfsprechend is pleased with us," he said. "Because his shieldmates and another half-dozen of the Wolfmaegth are out in the forest, preserving our privacy."

Viradechtis laughed smug delight all through the pack-sense, and showed her belly to the sun.

"Word must have gotten back to the wolfheall," Isolfr said into the blankets, guilty over having forgotten to remind the yearlings to send a message. He jumped when Vethulf laughed, and looked up.

Vethulf shrugged. "It's no different than the marriage you would have had if you'd stayed in the keep," he said. "No more privacy and no less, and a good deal more sympathy in the morning."

I don't need sympathy, Isolfr thought. He bit his lip. The last thing he needed was to start off this arrangement was a quarrel. *As if we'll live long enough to*—No. He owed Viradechtis more than surrender and death.

Somebody had thought to bank the fire before nightfall, and there were still coals to be coaxed into flickering life while Isolfr helped Skjaldwulf clean the game. The wolves snapped the innards and heads up happily, and didn't complain when Skjaldwulf presented them with a share each of raw rabbit and grouse.

Breakfast was accomplished with remarkable speed. Isolfr drew water from the old uncapped well and heated it with the wild mint and honeybalm that grew through crevices in the flagstones to make a tisane. They dressed and ate in silence. Their escorts stayed out of sight until they were within hailing of Bravoll, and then wolves and men came out to meet them, lining the streets. Isolfr found himself blushing fiercely, cursing his fair skin as he walked the length of the high street between his wolfjarls, their wolfbrothers jaunty and cheerful, tails waving like banners behind them.

He could not remember the last time he had heard the Wolfmaegth cheering.

TEN

Viradechtis was now konigenwolf of Franangford, though Franangford itself was destroyed, and the remnants of the Franangfordthreat were almost embarrassingly grateful to have a konigenwolf,
willing and eager to prove their loyalty. Other wolves chose Viradechtis'
pack, in the days after her mating: Hroi and Kothran and two other
wolves, followers of Mar's, from Nithogsfjoll; four wolves from Arakensberg; a wolf from Thorsbaer; one of the yearlings from Bravoll. And
Ulfbjorn, wolfless now, but still a man of the Wolfmaegth. Isolfr found
himself wolfsprechend in truth and for the first time listening to a pack
that was not Nithogsfjoll.

Much was the same, of course, and that was reassuring, but he had
never realized before how much Vigdis and Skald colored the pack-sense
of Nithogsfjoll. Viradechtis was at once sharper and lazier than her
mother, and where Mar was a sense of strength like bedrock, Kjaran,

canny, observing, was as definite in the pack-sense as his scent-name promised.

It was ironic that of Franangford's four bitches, the only one who had survived was Viradechtis' daughter Thraslaug. Sokkolfr—housecarl without a house—spent a day in negotiation with the other threats, and at the end of it Thraslaug went to Othinnsaesc, along with two of In-grun's sons (Grimolfr throwing himself willingly into the negotiations on Viradechtis' behalf), and Amma, the second bitch of Othinnsaesc—though Vestfjorthr-bred herself—came to Franangford.

She was a rangy, tawny-gray bitch, younger than Viradechtis, and her brother Brokkolfr, who had the dark coloring and intense blue eyes common to the western seafarers, seemed inclined to treat Isolfr as a mentor. Amma had had her first litter in the spring; her first open mating was still before them.

What am I supposed to tell him? Isolfr thought miserably. *Remember to prepare yourself. Don't fight. I'm told it gets easier with practice. Oh, very helpful.*

Much of the time, he felt he was drowning. Skjaldwulf was a vast fund of knowledge of how a wolfheall was run, and Vethulf, with something of Kjaran's knack for simply appearing on the spot when trouble was brewing, was better than Isolfr would have expected at keeping young wolves and young men in line. His scathing tongue played no little part in that, and Isolfr spent a great deal of time in placating both his own wolfcarls and the wolfheofodmenn of other threats—and in trying to prevent fights between his wolfjarls, who were not easy with one another. They humored him, as a general rule, but he could not help the image in his own mind of two trellwolves, warriors and hunters, condescending to play with a half-grown pup.

Or, in even worse moods, a pair of brother viking-jarls cosseting their shared wife.

He thought of Hrolleif, and determined—silently—that that was not how it would be.

Surprisingly, Grimolfr was the one who offered him the most guidance, and who was the first to treat him as an equal—whether out of his own loneliness or another motivation, Isolfr wasn't sure. "They don't want to hear from me," Isolfr complained to him one particular afternoon after the killing frost had come. They had labored like thralls or women in the wheatfields, and Isolfr was happy for a morning of rest, walking with the wolfjarl through scythed stubble that glistened like cheap silver-gilt under a layer of ice crystals. In the afternoon, he would haul wood with the rest of the men, but for now they had a little peace. Viradechtis reveled in it, running beside her sire across the rutted ground. Isolfr stepped up his pace, arms swinging. "I'm not fragile. I do not wish to be—"

"Coddled?"

"Placated," he answered, savagely kicking a pine cone that had somehow wandered out into the field. It would all be harrowed under anyway. Soon, maybe tomorrow. Before the earth froze. Isolfr wondered if any of them would live long enough to go hungry before spring. "I wish . . . " he began, and then remembered, and bit his lip.

"I wish he were here as well," Grimolfr said. "There's no shame in it. He could counsel you better than I."

"*He* never had two wolfjarls wrangling day and night," Isolfr answered. "They can agree on nothing, and the pack knows it."

Grimolfr laughed. He bent without breaking stride and scooped up a clod. It was nearly dry, breaking easily between his fingers. "Vethulf-in-the-Fire and Skjaldwulf Snow-Soft—is it any wonder? You know what Viradechtis has done, don't you?"

"Ensured herself endless attention," Isolfr said. The sunlight brightened his wolf's barred hide, catching crimson highlights on her fur as she turned her head to laugh at him. She showed nothing, yet, of the cubs growing inside.

"Made sure your wolfjarls will not take you for granted," Grimolfr answered. He pitched the remains of the clod away, overhand, and both wolves took off after it, running flat out and low to the ground. Viradechtis slammed into her sire's shoulder hard when he began to outpace her, tripping him so they both tumbled, a tangle of red and black and gray rolling across the field. "She can refuse either one of them next time, you realize. Or choose another entirely. They won't be easy with each other, until she either chooses or they become comfortable that she *won't* choose. Until then, they're both very aware where the power lies."

Isolfr looked at his wolf in a sort of awe. After a flurry of a wrestling match, her father had permitted her to pin him, and lay on his back, both forelegs folded neatly in surrender. "The manipulative little—"

"She's a regular strumpet," Grimolfr replied. He jostled Isolfr's shoulder. "I don't think you have anything to worry about with regard to your place in the pack."

"Vethulf is—"

"Bite back," the wolfjarl said. "Your bitch has teeth, and so do you." When Isolfr looked at him, he grinned, showing his own long yellow teeth. "They need your regard, Isolfr. You can demand their respect."

Isolfr didn't answer. They had reached the woods, and paused there, in the last warm sunlight at the edge of the shade, and looked at one another. Isolfr swallowed, his throat painful, and said, "What will we do when winter comes?"

Grimolfr sighed. "I don't know," he said, and shook his head. "Pray the trolls find other game."

๑๖๏

Isolfr prayed. He didn't think Othinn would hear him, not a prayer for mercy. A womanish prayer, but then, he stood as a woman's—a konigenwolf's—voice, didn't he? So he prayed on Viradechtis' behalf, and he prayed to golden Freya, who might have mercy on a mother, and on a father of a daughter.

That night he dreamed of the Iskryne and the svartal named Tin. He dreamed words in her mouth, and blazing weapons in her hands, and he dreamed a troll lying dead before her and a konigenwolf standing astride it, teeth gleaming, eyes shining with a rainbow light. He awoke in his blankets before dawn, hearing Ulfbjorn's familiar snoring on his left-hand side, and slid from between men and wolves, barefoot. Even Viradechtis never stirred as he padded over cold earth and rushes, between his packmates, and nodded to the sentry outside the door as he left. It was Yngvulf the Black, Arngrimr sprawled on the flags across his toes, keeping his boots warm. They were both wide awake, breath steaming in the morning, and Yngvulf nodded to Isolfr as he passed. "No shoes?" he asked softly, once the door had shut.

"I won't be long," he said, and paused there, arms folded across his chest against the chill. The sky grayed behind tumbled clouds. Before a bright edge of the sun peeked over the trees, it was heralded by the brilliant arch of a double rainbow, so bright and defined it seemed as solid as a ribbon in the hair of a girl.

"Freya's necklace," Yngvulf said, casually. He cleaned his ragged fingernails with his knife. "I've never seen it so bright."

"Maybe she has not forgotten us," Isolfr said, and knew his dream for the message it must be.

⚭

Later, Isolfr told himself bitterly that he should have known. He should have known there was no way in the world that his wolfjarls would listen to him when he said he needed to go north.

It did not help that when Skjaldwulf said reasonably, "Why?" Isolfr could not give him an answer.

And Vethulf was not inclined to be reasonable at all. He reminded Isolfr first that they were fighting a war, if he hadn't noticed, secondly that the Franangfordthreat needed its wolfsprechend, thirdly that Viradechtis was pregnant—"or did you not notice that part, either?"—fourthly that winter was coming, and he didn't know how they did things in Nithogsfjoll, but around here people generally tried to *avoid* traveling in the winter, and fifthly, "do you *want* to be killed and eaten by trolls, you idiot?"

And Isolfr, without a word he could honorably say in his defense, stood and listened and felt his face burning redder and redder. He was not, perversely, comforted when Skjaldwulf said, "Vethulf—perhaps *not* in front of every wolf in the Wolfmaegth?"

"Then we will discuss this in private," Vethulf said through his teeth, and although there was nothing Isolfr wanted less, he followed him into the storeroom which Viradechtis seemed inclined to favor for her pups, and which thus had become unofficially the Franangfordthreat's equivalent of the records-room in Nithogsfjoll.

Skjaldwulf closed the door behind him—making the room rather crowded with three men and three wolves, but the wolves would not allow themselves to be shut on the other side of the door.

"Isolfr," Skjaldwulf said, "you're not a yearling boy anymore. You can't just walk off into the wild when it suits you."

"It isn't—" Isolfr began, and bit his tongue. He had not meant to mention the matter at all, at least until he had some arguments mustered—*something* that would explain without breaking his oath—but Viradechtis had seen his intention to leave her behind and had protested so strenuously that Mar and Kjaran both heard her, and the inevitable next step had been Vethulf appearing, bristling like an affronted cat, to demand, "What nonsense is this?"

Isolfr said now, as much to Viradechtis as to his wolfjarls, "It is something that I must do."

"But *why?*" Skjaldwulf said, and Vethulf said, "Have you run utterly mad?"

"I cannot answer. Please." He looked from one to the other, from Vethulf's exasperation to Skjaldwulf's unyielding silence. "Can't you just trust me?"

"Not when what you're proposing is suicide," Vethulf said. "Isolfr, do you not see? You *cannot* do this. You are needed here."

"I know that, but . . ." He turned to Skjaldwulf. "You know I do not shirk my duty."

Skjaldwulf frowned, but before he could speak, Vethulf said bitterly, "Yes, of course. Set Skjaldwulf against me, as you have been doing these two months. Will you not fight your own battles, wolfsprechend?"

Will you always hide behind your wolf?

And he surprised no one more than himself when he shouted at Vethulf, "I cannot fight you! Call me cowardly or womanish or whatever you like, but I cannot fight as you do. You must know as well as I do that I will never win."

In the silence, a wolf whined, but he did not know who.

"Isolfr," Vethulf began, but Isolfr cut him off.

"No. You have made your opinion clear, both of you, and there is nothing more to say." And he said with flat anger to Skjaldwulf, "Let me out."

Skjaldwulf, eyes troubled, stepped aside, and Isolfr shouldered the door open and left, Viradechtis trailing him anxiously through the heall and out into the cold gloaming.

Where he all but fell over Frithulf, who opened his mouth to say something, then, uncharacteristically, closed it again. There was silence between them a moment, as Isolfr clenched and unclenched his hands and blinked angrily against the tears standing in his eyes, and then Frithulf stood up, shoving Kothran unceremoniously aside, and laid his hand on Isolfr's shoulder.

"What can I do to help?" said Frithulf.

And Isolfr, feeling as if someone else moved his tongue and shaped his words, murmured, very softly, "Pack me a satchel, Frithulf. And tell no one."

⊙⌾⊙

Viradechtis could not go. Vethulf, for all his unkindness, was right about that. She was pregnant, and it would start to slow her down before too much longer. Not to mention the risk to the pups, and the risk to a precious konigenwolf. Isolfr was nothing. Viradechtis was the world.

He couldn't bring her.

Which meant that Isolfr would have to do something that he had never heard of. That he was not sure could be done.

He would have to lie to his wolf.

The problem was that he wasn't sure the svartalfar would even speak to him without his konigenwolf. Silver and Tin had made it very plain who in the partnership they considered the leader—*just like everybody else*, he thought savagely, ignoring Viradechtis' whine when she could not understand his fury—but he had to try.

He had a sign from the goddess Freya. *Goddess of whores, how singularly appropriate*—no. He forced himself to kill that thought, like killing a troll kitten so it did not grow into a troll. He knew, no matter how angry he was, that Skjaldwulf and Vethulf did not think of him as a whore, any more than anyone had thought of Hrolleif that way. Wishing to protect him was not the same as considering him a child or a woman . . . *and truly, if they saw you as a whore, they would not* care *to protect you.*

As if he didn't already feel badly enough, Vethulf came to him that night to apologize. It was not something he did gracefully, or well, but he did it, his face nearly as red as his hair. Isolfr, knowing what it cost him, wished with all his heart that he could explain. But he could not, and so he said only, quietly, "Thank you."

And Vethulf gave him an abrupt nod and stalked away.

☙

S end a message to Hjordis for me?" he said to Frithulf later, in their furs, before their wolves or Sokkolfr and Ulfbjorn joined them.

"What would you have me say?"

Isolfr hadn't thought that far ahead. "I—damn. My regards, and concern for her health and Alfgyfa's. Tell her when the war ends, I'd like her to come to Franangford. I don't know. Lie to her, tell her everything's well."

"Do you think the war is going to end, Isolfr?" He'd never heard Frithulf sound so small. "I mean—"

Yes. Not just end, but end with any of them living. "That's the reason I have to go north," he said. "But I promised not to tell anyone why." He sighed. "You'll have to watch over Viradechtis for me."

"Don't be silly," Frithulf said. "Get Hroi and Sokkolfr to do it."

"Frithulf?"

Frithulf snorted, rolled over, and buried his face under his arm. "If you think I'm leaving you to die alone in the snow, you need to think again."

"You'd rather die with me?" Isolfr muttered.

His shieldmate's shoulders rose in a shrug. "We'll leave in the morning," he said. "It will take them longer to miss us if we leave by daylight, and after Franangford, no one will remark if we take our axes. I'll see if I can't get Sokkolfr to do something about packs, and I'll get Hroi to take

Viradechtis hunting. We'll wade the river north. The water will break up our scent."

Isolfr, frankly, hadn't thought it through half so well. He cursed softly, under his breath.

"See?" Frithulf said, jauntily. "You'd never survive without me." And feigned sleep before Isolfr could think what to say in reply.

❧

The astonishing thing was that it worked as Frithulf had planned it. When he found the time to talk to Sokkolfr, Isolfr did not know, but when they crawled out of their blankets in the morning, Hroi's presence in the pack-sense was full of thoughts of deer and rabbits and—canny old creature that he was—Viradechtis beautiful in the hunt. By the time she'd finished shaking herself awake, her eyes were bright and her ears high with the thought; she looked toward Isolfr, half asking, half pleading, and he said, "Go on, sister. I've other work."

Which was truth, perfect literal truth, and he used that like a shield.

She wanted to hunt. He felt her call to Mar and Kjaran, heard Vethulf's laugh, and the four wolves raced together out of the heall and toward the dense preserves south and east of Bravoll.

Kothran licked Frithulf's face, and Sokkolfr said in an undertone, "I've left packs for you in the hollow stump just beyond the north gate. I'll take care of your sister, Isolfr. Frithulf, you take care of him."

"I can take care of myself," Isolfr protested, but he was laughing as he said it. "Sokkolfr—"

"Yes?"

Isolfr hesitated, but there was duty and duty, and he knew his duty in this. "Tell Skjaldwulf and Vethulf that I am sorry. But I must . . ."

"You don't have to explain it to me," Sokkolfr said, with the same exasperated patience with which he had long ago told Isolfr to stop behaving like a wolfless man. "Now go on with the two of you."

They left, moving through the cheerful early morning bustle of the Wolfmaegth. Frithulf said, "You've got to figure the Bravoll konigenwolf is looking forward to getting her territory back."

Isolfr grinned. "She *sighs*. She looks at Viradechtis, or she looks at Vigdis, and she just *sighs*. All the way up from her toenails."

"How's Signy doing?" Frithulf asked. "I know Leitholfr doesn't look very happy."

"He's not sure she can hold the pack, even if she recovers. Thorsbaer's second bitch is strong. And eager."

"Could she be konigenwolf for Thorsbaer?"

"That's why Leitholfr is unhappy. You know. If it was just him and Signy, he'd petition to join Nithogsfjoll or maybe Vestfjorthr. Either Bekkhild or Vigdis could accept Signy as their second bitch and make Signy accept it, too. But he doesn't think Groa can hold Thorsbaer and . . ."

"The Wolfmaegth is precious short on konigenwolves," Frithulf finished grimly. "We'd better hope your sister decides to throw one this winter. And that the other bitches follow. Either that or—if we *survive* the winter—we'll be back to raiding the wild packs like they did in Hrolfmathr Hlokksbrother's time."

The thought was not a pleasant one, and they were silent through the north gate. They found Sokkolfr's hollow stump without incident and shrugged the packs on. Isolfr looked up and found Frithulf looking at him.

"You sure?" Frithulf said.

"As sure as I've ever been," Isolfr answered and started grimly walking north.

They were only barely out of sight of the gate when a voice said, "Ho, wolfsprechend," and Kari stepped out of the trees, closely followed by Hrafn.

"Kari," Isolfr said and wondered if there was any way the wolfcarl would accept Frithulf's wood-gathering story.

"You're going north," Kari said.

Well, never mind lying. "Yes. And if you move quickly, you can rouse Vethulf and Skjaldwulf in time to stop me."

"Why should I do that?" Kari leaned back into the underbrush and pulled out a pack of his own. "Hrafn says the konigenwolf has seen svartalfar."

Isolfr felt his jaw drop. "*Hrafn* has seen svartalfar?"

"No. But his mother had, and she taught her cubs to respect them." And Isolfr remembered the way the svartalfar had spoken of trellwolves, as creatures known and honored.

Kari said cautiously, "The konigenwolf did not *tell* Hrafn of the svartalfar, but—"

"There are no secrets among wolves," Frithulf said. "Although apparently there are among men. Svartalfar, Isolfr?"

"I swore to them I would not tell anyone," Isolfr said helplessly.

"And you've kept your promise," Frithulf said and patted his shoulder. "You didn't tell me or Kari anything." He cocked a bird-bright eye at Kari. "So, wildling. Clearly you seem to think the wolfsprechend should take you with him."

"These woods are Hrafn's territory," Kari said. "Jorhus was some five days north of Franangford, when it existed at all. My brother and I know the land, and I would wager I know more than either of you about living in the wild north in winter."

"He has a point," Frithulf said to Isolfr in a mock-aside.

"It was never that I did not want company," Isolfr said. "It was merely that I could not tell anyone why I went. If you wish to come, Kari, you are both welcomed and thanked. I admire Frithulf's willingness to die with me, but I don't want to put it to the test."

Kari smiled his shy smile and said, "Let's go."

They walked all day, steadily, at first wading over rounded stones through ice-cold water for hours, and then walking over moss and through stunted pine, while Kothran and Hrafn raced and bounced and showed every sign of forming a lasting friendship. The wolves also hunted, returning periodically to their brothers with rabbits and grouse, and once Hrafn, with the air of one conferring a tremendous favor, stopped in front of Kari and spat out a duck's egg, whole and entirely undamaged, onto the ground.

Frithulf was tremendously impressed and spent much of the afternoon trying to convince Kothran to learn Hrafn's trick. Kothran, who had his sister's sense of humor, just laughed at him.

The reminder of Viradechtis started an ache in Isolfr's chest, made worse in the late afternoon when he felt Viradechtis realize he had left without her. He knew they were too far from Bravoll, but he heard her howls nonetheless, and felt her casting for him, casting for him and failing to find a scent, along with the entirety of the Franangfordthreat. He clenched his fists and ground his teeth and kept walking, though it was like leaning into a scouring wind. Kothran came and bumped his thigh, and Isolfr felt ridiculously both better and worse. It was good he had Kari and Frithulf with him, because the effort of walking away from his wolf darkened his vision at the edges.

He put his head down, and pushed on.

As the shadows began to thicken, Kari said, "We should look for a place to camp," and repeated something similar to Hrafn. Frithulf and Isolfr traded a look, and Isolfr thought that if they did survive this journey to the Iskryne, and the winter, and the war, he would have to find out what else Kari and Hrafn could communicate to each other that ordinary wolfcarls would never think to try.

Then he stopped dead in his tracks, his heart slamming up into his mouth, as a dense well of shadow beneath a holly tree blinked great amber-gold eyes and moved out into the path. He and Frithulf were shoulder to shoulder before they even realized what they were doing, and Kari had moved sideways, calling to Hrafn in the pack-sense.

And then very strongly, they all felt, *Silly puppies*, and the massive beast resolved into Vigdis.

"Vigdis," Isolfr said, his voice barely a croak. "What are you doing here?" Frithulf was leaning on him, muttering breathless obscenities into his shoulder; Kari said, "She must have been tracking us all day. And Hrafn never . . ."

Puppies, said Vigdis, both fond and disdainful. Her eyes met Isolfr's, and she gave him a very clear picture of a svartalf talking to a konigen-wolf. There were men in the image, but they were small, their scents weak and unimportant.

"How did you know?" Isolfr said, and wasn't sure what question he was asking: how Vigdis had known he was going to talk to the svartalfar, or how she had known that they would speak only to a konigenwolf.

She just looked at him, ears pricked, tail waving, and far back in her eyes he saw the laughter that had been almost quenched since Hrolleif's death. "Grimolfr's going to *kill* me," Isolfr said, and Vigdis bumped his hip, staggering him.

"He'll have to get behind Vethulf," Frithulf answered, voice shaky. "We've become a conspiracy."

Kari stepped onto the path, Hrafn at his side, and now they were three wolves and three young men. "We weren't before?"

It had a hollow sound, but they all laughed nonetheless.

eLeveN

Of the trip north, at least it could be said that it was better than the mad and futile race to Othinnsaesc. They marched into the teeth of winter, each day's travel colder and harder than the last. Kari and Hrafn made it possible, and more than once Isolfr blessed his luck that they had kenned his intentions and chosen to come. Luck, or intervention; when Isolfr asked how they had known, Kari shrugged and said he'd dreamed it. So maybe the rainbow had been meant for more than one of them.

It was almost eerie, how few trolls they saw. Either the trolls were confident that they had driven the men out and men would not be returning, or they were traveling less openly than they had been. Isolfr didn't complain, especially as the nights grew in length and they walked by the light of the aurora or the moon more often than not.

They slept—when they slept—in a pile of men and wolves, and

every morning Isolfr woke to find himself flat on his back, pinned with Vigdis' massive head across his ribs—a position he'd seen Hrolleif in so many times that first it hurt, and then it was funny, and then it came to feel almost like a blessing. There was no wavering of his bond with Viradechtis—and indeed, he had never heard that a bond could shift when both bondmates were alive unless wolf or man left the wolfheall for good—and he knew, sometimes, when the pack-sense was particularly clear to him, that Vigdis didn't really think of him as a member of the werthreat at all. She thought of him as an ice-white puppy. She thought of them all as puppies, of course, Hrafn and Kothran as much as their brothers, but Isolfr was *her* puppy—hers more strongly even than Kothran was—and he remembered with odd clarity that moment in his father's hall when she had turned her head and seen him for the first time. He remembered the way her gaze had felt like a troll-spear, a mortal blow. And he thought, a little light-headed with the cold and the short rations, that if he had been born to the world as his mother's child, then surely he had been born to the Wolfmaegth as Vigdis'.

He could feel Viradechtis sulking at him, and he didn't blame her. She would have tracked him, he knew, if it hadn't been for Frithulf's trick with the river. As it was, she was bewildered and hurt—no, devastated. And there was nothing he could do to comfort her except give her his re-assurance and love.

The pack-sense didn't limit itself to Viradechtis, unfortunately. He could feel quite plainly that Skjaldwulf and Vethulf were furious with him, and that a good deal of that fury was being brought to bear on Sokkolfr and Ulfbjorn. The greatest surprise, however, was that Grimolfr was absorbing more than his share of the wrath, which didn't endear him to the Franangford wolfjarls. But Grimolfr could not be made to back down. Isolfr couldn't know what he *said* to Skjaldwulf and Vethulf, but over the course of a fortnight he felt Grimolfr's obduracy temper their anger into resignation, concern, and outright worry.

He only wished he could believe they were wrong.

Most of what the travelers had in their packs was clothing. There wasn't anywhere north of Bravoll where they could have traded for fur coats or woolen clothing unless they detoured east to Nithogsfjoll, and they would never survive the Iskryne without them, even with fire and the wolves. Isolfr huddled in the wonderful warmth of a greasy sweater that Hjordis had nalbound from yarn spun of musk oxen, sheep, and goat's wool, and blessed his woman's name. The mittens were excellent too. Two pairs, packed with the shed undercoat of trellwolves, and he thought he might keep all his fingers, even the nails.

At least this time they didn't have to fight their way into the mountains. Traveling without an army, they moved faster, and light-footed through the pass without drawing the attention of trolls or the wild trellwolves.

Whether the goddess was truly watching over them or not, they made it into the pass before the storms came down. Isolfr wished Viradechtis were with them, or even that he dared permit her to perceive where he was. If she'd known, he wouldn't have been able to keep her from following—alone if necessary, over the hundreds of miles that had spread between them. He didn't want to think what she would do to Kjaran or Mar if they got between her and her goal, if she ever came to know it.

Five cold weeks in, frost on the fur ringing their hoods, their lips bleeding despite anointings with bear-grease and butter, they came to the broken gates of the trellwarren where Isolfr and Viradechtis had met Tin.

The svartalfar were waiting at the gates. They stood just inside the mouth of the tunnel, where the weak winter sunlight could not reach them, the torches in their hands catching sparks off the jewels in their hair and ears and off the wicked blades of the weapons they carried.

"Isolfr," Frithulf said very quietly, "they don't look friendly."

"They, um, aren't."

"You could have mentioned that before."

One of the svartalfar thumped the butt of its spear on the smooth stone of the tunnel floor. "Isolfr Viradechtisbrother, you have broken your vow."

"I told no one," Isolfr said. "My companion, Frithulf Kothransbrother, accompanied me without knowledge of my intent, and Kari Hrafns-brother," laying stress as strongly as he could that all three of them were wolfcarls, "was told in a dream to seek the svartalfar. I would not have brought them into the tunnels with me." He stepped heavily on Frithulf's foot to forstall protest. "I have told them nothing of what lies beneath Trellheim."

"It is true," Kari said. "He has not. And we will likewise swear not to speak of you, if you wish it."

"What good is that?" said the svartalf. "We already have proof that men do not honor their oaths."

"*I told no one,*" Isolfr said. "And I have come back only out of desperation, for the trolls are destroying us, and if we do not have help, neither wolfthreats nor wolfless men will survive to see the spring."

The svartalf flicked its ears and said, "You say this as if you imagine we would grieve."

৩৵৩

It was the one thing he had not expected. He had been prepared to bargain, to plead; he had been prepared to sell himself to work in the svartalfar mines if that was what it took. But simple obdurate hostility . . . The svartalfar had stayed only long enough to inform them that if they entered the tunnels of the trellwarren, they would be killed, and then disappeared. It did not seem to matter to the svartalfar that they had a kon-igenwolf with them, nor that the trolls were a common enemy to both races. They perceived no need of men to balance the threat.

In silence, Kari led them away from the trellwarren to a spot suitable for camping. "Not that it will matter," Frithulf said when they had windbreaks staked up and a fire laid with the last of their rationed wood. "From the looks of the sky, we're going to be buried under two feet of snow and dead as salt fish by morning."

"And Grimolfr will come to Hel's palace to kill me himself," Isolfr said gloomily. "I am sorry. I did not think. . . ."

"You expected them to behave as men would behave," Kari said. "As the wolfless men have behaved."

"I suppose I did. I should have known better."

"It wasn't a bad idea," Frithulf said. "If they know how to use weapons as well as they make them, they must be terrors in a fight. And it stands to reason they'd know more about trellwarrens than we do."

"Yes, a good idea, except that it was doomed to failure before I set foot outside Bravoll. I am an idiot, and I've condemned you, too."

"We chose," Frithulf said. "There's no point in torturing yourself. You rolled the bones and lost. That's all."

The first flakes of snow were falling, and Isolfr was wondering if he could apologize through the pack-sense to Viradechtis and Skjaldwulf and Vethulf and Mar and Kjaran and Grimolfr and the entire Franang-fordthreat and everyone else he had betrayed in his folly, when Vigdis' ears pricked, and Kothran and Hrafn both came to their feet, tails wagging.

"Eh?" said Frithulf and turned to get up, then froze, absolutely still as stone, as the point of a svartalfar spear caught him under the chin.

"Isolfr," said Frithulf, with commendable calm, "your friends seem to have decided not to wait for the snow to kill us."

"Tch," said the bush behind the spear, and a svartalf stepped forward into their rude shelter. "You have a different konigenwolf with you this time, Isolfr. I trust your sister is not ill?"

"Tin?" Isolfr said. The svartalf smiled, and he recognized the copper and silver tracery that inlaid Tin's teeth. "Have they changed their minds?"

"The smiths and mothers do not change their minds," Tin said and rolled her eyes. "But come, introduce me to your companions."

"Please do," Frithulf said faintly. Tin gave him a small nod and shifted her spearpoint away from his throat.

Isolfr gave Tin their names, finishing with Vigdis, ". . . who is my sister's mother. My sister does not come because she is heavy with pups."

"Ah," said Tin, and bowed to Vigdis, as she had not bowed to any of the others. "A konigenwolf and mother of a konigenwolf. This is a mighty queen indeed, Isolfr Viradechtisbrother, and the elders will—" she used a word Isolfr did not know, and one that was heavily overlaid with the harmonics of the svartalfar voices "—when they learn of that."

"Will what?" Frithulf said.

"Lose pride?" Tin said experimentally. "It is what you feel when you come before the Masters with your Master-piece, and they strike it a single blow in a certain place, and it breaks as if it were a child's toy made of sticks and slag ore. You are revealed not to know as much as you ought, and not to know as much as you thought you did."

"Did you . . . ?" Isolfr began, remembering that she had said something about testing the last time he had seen her.

She laughed. "No, it is not an example from personal experience, thanks be to the mothers of my mother. But tell me, Isolfr, why did you come?"

"I told the elders," Isolfr said. "The trolls have destroyed two wolfheallan already. If we cannot find some other way to fight them, we are doomed."

"And you think we svartalfar have answers for you?"

"You fight them successfully. And I dreamed . . ."

He hesitated, feeling even more like a foolish child, but Tin tipped her head, her eyebrows rising, and flicked her ears in a way he thought was meant to be encouraging. "What dreamed you?"

"I dreamed of a thing my wolfjarl told me," he said, and even in the midst of fear and bitterness, even with the guilt and anger he still felt, there was a surprising warmth in claiming Skjaldwulf as his. "He said that in the caves beneath Othinnsaesc, when the men made their strongest push against the trolls, he saw a troll bigger than any he had ever seen—bigger, he said, than any troll had a right to be. And he said the other trolls brought the roof of the cave down rather than letting men or wolves get near it. But in my dream, you were there, standing next to the troll, and you said," he could feel his cheeks heating but pushed on, "*A trellqueen is not a woman*, and your words were a spear, a spear made of flame, and on that spear the great troll died. And when it died, all the other trolls howled and fell down dead. Although I do not know what any of it means, I know that in my dream the trolls died because of the words of a svartalf. And we are desperate. If I die here, now, it does not matter, because I would just die before trolls otherwise, and my child and my sister and my pack with me."

Frithulf cleared his throat. "Why didn't you kill them all? Why drive them out to harass us?"

"Not safe," Tin said, with a shrug. "It's one thing to harry their flanks, drive them along, gnaw their toes until they leave. Easy. Far different to hound them to bay and wipe them out. It would cost us dear, in lives and in the smiths those lives will not become, as nipping their heels to chivvy them along does not. Wolves ought to know that."

"So you push them down onto us," Isolfr answered, bitterly.

"Save your arguments. I agree we owe you a debt. Though we knew not that they'd pushed you back so far." She frowned, her feathery brows drawing together over her knife-bridged nose.

"We have nowhere to go," Kari said, softly. "My whole village—" He stopped, shook his head, his throat working, and turned back to the fire.

Tin fell silent, or as silent as Isolfr had ever heard a svartalf fall. Her throat swelled only a little under the collar of her cloak, a thrumming sound vibrating behind closed lips as she thought. "This is our doing," she said, finally. "If the smiths and the mothers see it or not. We have brought this doom on you; on svartalfar shoulders rests it."

"But the . . . the mothers and the smiths. They won't help us."

She smiled. "But I'm a smith now," she said, her voice ringing on harmonics of earned pride. She patted her belly under the cloak. "And by next winter, now that I have my Master's rank, I may be a mother too. And I say we will." Her meandering crook-lipped smile turned into a frown, and she tapped one metal-laced fingernail against her teeth, filigree clinking on inlay. "We must win them over. And we must prove that you are brother of a konigenwolf, and better than meat for trolls."

"Tin—"

"Hush," she said, and settled under her cloaks and wraps until she looked like a pile of disreputable rags with a beaded wig stuck on top and her nose a bent stick poking out from the front. Her long many-jointed fingers curled around the haft of the trellspear propped before her, and she moved no more than a statue might.

Isolfr sighed, and turned away to make her tea. When he returned, she looked up in surprise, propped the trellspear against her shoulder, and then took the steaming cup gravely between her palms. "I thank you the hospitality of your fire," she said, formally, and bowed without standing. Isolfr wondered how tall she would be, if she could ever unkink that knobby spine.

"It's our pleasure," he answered. The jewels in her hair caught the light as she sipped the tea.

"So," she said. "Do you think you *can* kill a trellqueen, Isolfr Viradechtisbrother?"

"I don't know," he said, honestly. "How do I get to one?"

❦

The answer, apparently, was *follow me*. While she explained, the harmonics of her voice whistled like the winds that seared through the pass. She made the wolfcarls hold her cloak so they could stay by her, and it was as well she did, because the snow made them as blind as newwhelped cubs. Hrafn broke trail ahead, Vigdis and Kothran behind him to broaden it, and the svartalf and the wolfcarls staggered in their wake like geese spread out in a wedge.

"Your dream was right," Tin said. "You must kill the trellqueen at Othinnsaesc. As long as she is alive, the trolls will swarm to her place of warren like bees to their queen. There is one queen left in the Iskryne; we have killed two and driven one south. That must be the one your wolfjarl saw in the new warren. I lead you now to the Iskrynequeen."

"And if we kill her?"

She turned to him, a flash of her teeth around the edge of her hood. The trellspear made a stout prop, and she a strong anchor, but Isolfr wished they could have brought snowshoes or skis from the wolfheall when they fled. Foolishness, of course. There was no way to keep that secret, not before snow lay on the ground. "You will impress the smiths and the mothers, and even the warriors. Perhaps even our sceadhugenga, our old one.

"Do not mistake me; the trellqueen will not die easy, or we would have killed her by now, even though we do but harry. She is the troll of trolls, and older than any memory of my people. The others are but her daughters. But she *is* mortal. She can die. Only, the mothers will not risk the lives it would take." Tin *tsk'd* between jeweled teeth.

"And then what?"

"Perhaps my people will help you then."

"I meant the trolls," Isolfr clarified, and waited while she considered, bobbing her head.

She hummed, and went on, "The trolls may make another, if they have kittens young enough. But if you kill the kittens and the trell-witches, then there will be no new trellqueens. The warren will die."

"We'll kill all the trolls," Isolfr said, not certain he could credit it.

"If you kill this trellqueen and the one in Othinnsaesc. Yes. It is only queens who can breed. All the trolls of the Iskryne will die."

Isolfr stumbled. He kept his grip on Tin's cloak, though, and her momentum pulled him up and steady. Vigdis was abruptly beside him, and he buried his mittened hand in her ruff, just because she was there, and warm under the snow crusted white over her shoulders. Isolfr didn't speak, and Kari didn't look at him, but the wildling grunted, and then muttered, "Good."

⚭

Isolfr's toes were unfeeling in his boots by the time Tin led them to a tunnel entrance they never would have found without her. It was too small for trolls—barely big enough for wolf or man—and hidden in a thicket.

"A rabbit hole," Frithulf said.

"For a half-cooked rabbit," she answered, and brushed past him, ducking her head as she bustled underground. "It's an escape tunnel," she said. "Come on."

The wolfcarls exchanged glances, and it was Isolfr who shrugged and went to his hands and knees to follow. He hadn't exaggerated when she found them in the snow. They were as good as dead already, and it was warmer underground.

When they were all inside, Tin produced flint and steel from under her cloak, and fetched a pair of torches from a shadowed niche out of sight of the cave entrance. She gave one to Frithulf, with a caution not to burn himself—and then a snipped-off laugh when he took a half-playful swipe at her.

"You *have* got spirit," she said. It didn't even sound grudging.

"Why are you helping us?" Isolfr asked, unable to keep the question behind his teeth any longer. Could it be as simple as guilt over the svartalfar's responsibility for the exodus of the trolls?

Tin showed him her snaggle-toothed grin. "A weakness for baby animals," she answered, but the effect was ruined by her glance down the dark tunnel, over her shoulder. "Hurry," she said. "We must be careful of alfar as well as the trolls. I do not care to die on a warden's spear."

"No, thank you," Frithulf said, and Kari leaned into the pack-sense with the need to be quiet. Vigdis snorted—she did not need telling—but Hrafn and Kothran both flattened their ears submissively.

They moved silently, three men, three wolves, and a svartalf, and they moved fast. Isolfr could tell when the tunnels of the svartalfar gave way to trellwarren—and he would have known even if they had not had to climb through a hole like that which had first made him wonder about stone mice in the Iskryne: the stonework changed, the heights and angles changed. Frithulf was walking much closer to him than he had been, and he could see sweat beading on Kari's face. He remembered that Kari had not been in a trellwarren before. And that Frithulf had.

"They, too, have Masters, you know," Tin said, and somehow the harmonics of her voice shifted so that the sound was no more than the words, not an echo, not a buzz, not even the hiss that the men would have been unable to flatten out entirely. "Later, if you are alive to hear it and I to sing it, I will tell you the edda of the Mastersmiths, and how Jasper of the Gold Kinship stood against the trellsmith Guth."

"Trolls have names?" Isolfr said stupidly, and even though he spoke as softly as he could, they all winced at the noise. Tin gave him a beady-eyed glare, and he put his hand across his mouth to signify that he would not speak again.

She nodded, mollified, and answered his question: "They do not have names as we understand them, no. Nor as you understand them, I think. We must name them in our eddas for otherwise we cannot sing of them, but they are small names and have no power."

Which raised, Isolfr thought, as many questions as it answered. If, as she had said, they were alive later, he would have to remember to ask.

They descended lower and lower, the wolves slinking now as if they were as oppressed by the weight of stone and earth above them as the men were, and he could feel their growls in the pack-sense, although none of them made a sound. Tin said, "The trolls have not quite this shared mind that the wolves gift you with, but it is also a saying among my people that what one troll knows, all trolls know. Eventually, we will not be able to proceed unnoticed no matter what we do, but in the meantime, when we encounter trolls, the more quickly they can be killed, the better."

Never follow a running troll.

They encountered two solitary trolls. The first Vigdis took down almost before any of the rest of them had seen it, and Tin bowed and said, "Thank you, konigenwolf." The second turned to flee, but was pursued and died on the point of Tin's spear. Frithulf and Isolfr shared a glance; it would not do to forget how horribly strong the svartalf's ropy, gnarled limbs were, no matter that Tin's head did not come up even to Kari's shoulder.

"Come," Tin said. "Our luck cannot run clean much longer."

Indeed, two cramped, steep switchbacks later, they came upon what was clearly a picket. Four trolls, and while three stood their ground, the fourth ran, making a high-pitched ghastly ululation as it went.

"That's the alarm, then," Tin said. "It is war." And she disemboweled the largest of the trolls, while Vigdis and Kothran took down the second, and Isolfr buried his axe halfway through the throat of the third.

Past the wide spot of the sentry box, they ducked into a side corridor and followed Tin through a crevice barely broad enough to admit the trellwolves' skulls. They found themselves in a series of globular chambers, each widening from one entrance and narrowing to the next, though even at their most spacious they could not fit three men abreast. It was awkward going; the wolves could get through only by wriggling, and Isolfr thought he and Kari and Frithulf would soon be as cramped and twisted as Tin. But it prevented the trolls from massing against them, and Tin could spider through a hole and check for trolls on the other side before the wolfcarls joined her. "These aren't troll caves," Frithulf whispered, when they paused for breath. "They could not fit through here."

"'Tis a new warren," Tin answered, with a glance of surprise and respect. "They were driven from their old steadings by yours and mine. The trellwitches are still working down these rocks, and it is why their defenses are weak. It is fortunate I am new to my Mastery and not yet broadened with smithing and bearing, and you are not so broad as svartalfar smiths."

"Magic?" Isolfr asked, remembering to keep his voice low.

"Of course," she answered. "You don't think trolls delve like honest stonemasons, do you?"

Isolfr thought of the pulse and cling of their shaped stone walls, and shuddered. No.

"I played here as a kindling, and knew the way, but I was not certain it was open still."

"What would you have done if it hadn't been?" Kari, his voice strange and thin. Isolfr could feel in the pack-sense how much he did not like the close walls and the dark.

She shifted her grip on her spear. "Died."

Slow, bloody going: they were all bleeding and painted with the dark vileness of trellblood by the time they dragged themselves through the last hole of the series into a tunnel more like those they were used to. Harsh shrieking resonated from the other end of the tunnel. "That is the trellqueen," Tin said, "calling her sisters to defend her. We must hurry."

His limbs were rubbery, but Isolfr ran at Vigdis' heels down the tunnel. He felt the others beside him, even though the tunnel seemed to slip and mutter around him as he ran, the thud of his feet jarring spine and skull.

They rounded a tight, boxy corner, and ran directly into the presence of trolls. A dozen of them, barring the base of a dais heaped with hides, and a great brazen throne.

Trolls, and a wyvern as well.

At least where the winged snake was there was room to maneuver, and light. Twisted bronze torches lined the wall, burning stinking fuel on twisted wicks. Isolfr thought it was tallow, badly rendered.

He was not sure it came from cattle, and from the snarl baring Tin's glittering teeth and drawing her leathery face into lines, she wasn't either. Vigdis' growl mounted in her throat to a scream such as he'd never heard a trellwolf make before, and she launched herself at the warriors between them and the Iskrynequeen.

Skjaldwulf was right, Isolfr thought as Hrafn and Kothran gathered themselves and sprang, and he heard Frithulf cursing behind him. *No troll should be that big.*

She was so large that he could not imagine her moving through the tunnels above. If he had not heard Tin say this was a new warren, he would have imagined it had been centuries since she had moved from this room, imagined that she must have hollowed it around herself to accommodate her size. She made Vigdis look the size of a dog, and even Ulfbjorn would have seemed a child beside her.

Of course, he thought, looking at her great knobbed, taloned hands. The trellwitches twisted the stone so she could come here, and then closed it up behind her to keep her safe.

Isolfr moved forward because it was the only thing he could do, although his mind was yammering, *We cannot kill this thing, nothing can kill this thing, at Ragnarok she will still be here, gnawing her holes in the bones of the earth.* She did not rise or gesture. Her howl ended; her head lowered on its thick neck. She stared at them through eyes that caught the torchlight and splintered it red and gold and green.

Her warriors and her wyrm moved forward, and Isolfr lifted his axe and ran behind his brothers to the battle.

He remembered the fight in images, brutally sharp and queerly senseless. Vigdis with her teeth sunk in the wyvern's thick neck, dragging it down so Tin could bring her trellspear into play. The jolt of his axe in his hands when it came down on bone, on meat, on bronze. Kari fought like a thing possessed—berserk, senseless with war-rage. *So he survived Jorhus. So we may yet survive this war.* Isolfr knew the gush of blood across his hands, the stench of trellmeat, the agony of a torn shoulder, of a taloned claw across his forehead and cheek, the sting and blindness of blood washing his eyes. *You won't be so pretty now, Isolfr,* he thought, and looked around to find that there were only two trellwarriors left, and Tin, Kothran, and Frithulf had them in hand.

Isolfr tasted blood when he grinned, and surged forward in Kari's wake as he, his wolf, and Vigdis charged up the steps of the dais. Isolfr shouted, and Vigdis yowled, and as they came upon her, the trellqueen deigned to rise from her chair. She lurched forward, the wolves upon her, and the mountain itself seemed to shift under her tread. She was sure-footed in the pile of hides and ingots around her throne; Isolfr and Kari tripped and skidded. She swung one massive arm, Hrafn dangling from it with all his teeth buried in her forearm, and Isolfr saw her bulging belly, the grotesque and leaking swollenness of her teats.

The Iskrynequeen was pregnant, and he remembered what Tin had said, that only the queens could breed, but if the trolls had young kittens, they could make queens. For a moment, sickened, he thought of Viradechtis and the pups growing in her belly, back in Bravoll, but the pack-sense threw Franangford at him, Hrolleif dying, Aslaug dying. Pregnant bitches had died at Franangford, and at Othinnsaesc, and the trolls had not hesitated, not—as the svartalfar had said in contemplating the destruction of men—grieved.

He heard his own rising shriek, a noise as terrible as Vigdis', and as the trellqueen turned her head, bellowing, Hrafn still dangling from one arm, Vigdis snarling and snapping and aiming for the hamstrings, Isolfr darted in, braced his feet, and swung with all his strength at the crest of the Iskrynequeen's belly.

He saw the axe hit, saw the gout of black blood, and then he saw the trellqueen's arm begin a swing, a fist like a morningstar aimed at his head. He started back out of the way, but his feet fouled among the furs, and as he scrabbled for balance, his still-entangled foot tipped him backwards over the edge of the dais. He had just sense enough to cast his axe aside before the stone collided with his skull.

☙❧

Isolfr?"

Frithulf's voice.

"Come on, Isolfr, we need to get out of here. And I'm not carrying you." A slap, hard enough to sting.

Isolfr moaned protest, dragging one hand up to catch Frithulf's wrist. "Don't hit me."

"So you are in there! Come on, brother, open those pretty gray eyes. Vigdis, you want to give me some help here?"

A wolf tongue, hot and wet and accompanied by breath reeking of troll blood, began to wash his face. Moments later, it was joined by a second, and the pack-sense said Kothran, who liked washing Frithulf's face best, but would lick a werthreatbrother and gladly. Wolf-spit stung in his cuts. His face felt flayed.

"Ah, gods! Frithulf!" He floundered into a sitting position, ending with one arm hung around Vigdis' neck. She snuffled his ear and then began washing that, too.

"I knew that would get you," Frithulf said with evil satisfaction. "Now, come on. Tin says we can't let you sleep here."

"Did we . . . is everyone . . . ?"

"That monster is dead," Frithulf said, "and you're our worst casualty, though Kothran will be limping for a few days. And I think Kari's broken some fingers and I want you to look at them, so get up, Isolfr, and let's get moving."

Isolfr lurched to his feet, although his head was pounding and he could only open one eye. "Is there bone showing? I don't know what we'll do for splints down here—"

"Shhh. Lean on me. Kari'll do fine until we're back to Tin's people. She seems to think they'll help us now."

"But only if there is enough of us left to be helped," Tin said. "Can he walk?"

"Vigdis and I will keep him up," Frithulf said grimly. Isolfr wanted to protest that he was perfectly capable of keeping himself up, and was Kari really all right? But the cavern was swimming in front of his one good eye, and the floor kept bucking and lurching beneath his feet. He buried his fingers in Vigdis' ruff and followed where she and Frithulf led.

There were long stretches of their climb back to the svartalfar's domain that Isolfr could not later remember. He remembered being left against a wall like a rag doll while the other six butchered three trell-witches who would not even turn from their working to defend themselves, remembered Tin saying dryly as she dragged him to his feet one-handed, "And now perhaps the mountain will not fall down on our heads before we have a chance at a bath."

He remembered them coming to a room—for Tin was taking them a different way and he wondered why but could not find his tongue to ask—in which six stunted trolls lay dead, each with its fingers tightly clasped around the hilt of the knife protruding from its stomach. Kari's voice said softly, "What happened here?" and Tin answered, "These were her males. They lived only to breed with her, and as she died, so died they also."

"*These* are male trolls?" Frithulf said.

Tin tched impatiently. "And what else should they be?"

But if Frithulf answered her, Isolfr did not hear him, his wits wandering again, and the next thing he knew clearly was Frithulf saying, "Duck. *Duck*, dammit, Isolfr. Bend your head," and he realized his friend was trying to urge him through another mouse-hole in the stone.

"'M not a stone mouse," he said muzzily.

"Of course you're not," Frithulf said, "but you're really starting to worry me."

"His brain has been rattled," Tin said from the other side of the hole. "He will be well, with rest."

"Yes, but he can't rest here. Vigdis!" And Vigdis' head appeared through the hole; she leaned forward and took Isolfr's forearm very gently between her jaws, and began tugging.

"Vigdis not a stone mouse," Isolfr said.

"No, she's a trellwolf, and on feast days she flies to the moon." Frithulf's hand on the back of his head, pushing, and Vigdis pulling, and it was too much work to argue about it. Isolfr climbed through the hole. *Good puppy,* said Vigdis, warming him down to his toes, and Frithulf and Kari followed him through.

"He can't go much farther," Frithulf said to Tin.

"He won't need to," she said, and her voice opened up again into its full range. "The sceadhugenga will know the trellqueen has fallen, and I imagine by now the elders will have noticed I am gone."

"So we'll either be greeted as heroes or kidnappers," Frithulf said. "Splendid."

"You are men, and young ones at that. You could not make a Master-smith of the svartalfar go anywhere she did not wish to. Now come. These halls stink of troll."

More walking, and Isolfr was stumbling, even though the floors were remarkably smooth. He felt as if the trellqueen's furs were still tangling his feet. The pounding in his head was echoing all down his spine, and he could feel his knees wanting to buckle.

"Isolfr," Frithulf said, "you weigh a hundred stone."

"Do I? Sorry," and he tried to straighten, but nothing was working.

Frithulf swore and said, "Kari, I think I'm going to need you to get his feet."

Are they running away? Isolfr wanted to ask. He would have believed it, as odd and distant as they felt.

But then the tunnel was full of light, and he tried to get a hand up to protect his eyes while svartalfar voices boomed and hummed and chimed around him. Without Vigdis to steady him, though, he could no longer tell where the floor was, and although he knew for a moment that he was falling, there was nothing he could do about it. *Sorry, Frithulf,* was the last coherent thought he had for some time.

❦

When he woke clear-headed, after an interval of fevered dreams and terrible worry, he was lying in his own bedroll, but the surface beneath him was smooth pale gray stone. The fire was burning in a sunken circle of the same stone, and even he could recognize the beauty of the masonry under the soot.

"Are you come back to us, Isolfr?" Tin asked. He turned his head to find her crouching beside him, leaning on her spear.

"Have I been gone?"

"You frightened us something awful," Frithulf said from beyond Isolfr's feet. "The sceadhugenga said the wyvern's poison was inflaming your wounds, and we had to grind up the most vile smelling paste I've ever met in my life to draw it out."

"You said my brain was rattled," Isolfr said to Tin, frowning, trying to piece his memories together in a way that would make sense.

"It was," she said. "But the fever was the danger."

"The sceadhugenga said you might be left wit-addled," Frithulf said, coming to crouch on Isolfr's other side. "I asked how we'd tell the difference, but just got bones shaken at me."

"Bones?"

"The sceadhugenga's honor," Tin said. "When each sceadhugenga dies, the next adds one vertebra to the strand."

"Whose vertebra?" Isolfr asked, although he had the feeling he might not want to know.

"The dead sceadhugenga's, of course. It is how the lore is passed."

He'd been right about the knowing.

"You are lucky," Tin said. "Chrysoprase is of the oldest lore-line, and knows more of healing than anyone I have met. He says you will not lose the eye, either."

"Oh good," Isolfr said weakly.

"And he's stitched you up beautifully," Frithulf said. "It should scar very cleanly." There was no bitterness in his voice, although Isolfr would not have blamed him if there had been.

He stretched his hand out and Frithulf clasped it briefly, warmly.

"What about Kari?" he asked, remembering. "Didn't you say his fingers were broken?"

"One broken, two sprained. He's got a paw like a seal's flipper right now, but the sceadhugenga did nice work on him, too. And the wolves are very well. If the svartalfar keep feeding them as they have been, we may have to roll Kothran out of here like a beer barrel."

"The elders are most embarrassed at having been discourteous to a konigenmother," Tin said, and the gravity of her voice was belied by the wicked twinkle in her eyes. "Moreover, Silver spoke for you—which is more than I would have expected of her—pointing out that you did not swear not to return here, but only swore not to speak of us to others, which you did not, and not to bring harm to us, which you manifestly did not. And you have—" Another of those svartalfar words Isolfr did not know.

"What?"

"That's what I said," Frithulf put in.

"It goes very badly into plain speech," Tin said. "You exceeded your oath."

"I did?"

"If I've understood them correctly," Frithulf said, "you swore not to bring harm to them, but by killing the trellqueen, we actually brought them good. Tin says it would have taken them months, if not years, to find the opportunity to do it themselves, and by then the trellwitches would have made another queen. So you did more than you swore to do, and it—"

"It embarrasses the elders," Tin said. She cocked her head, regarding him with her small, bright eyes. "You must understand, we are a cautious people, of oaths and bargains. And thus we are very careful to deliver what we promise, but delivering *more* than one has promised is considered the mark of a mother and it is not treated lightly."

"And it's a bit of a blow to them that we did this thing—I won't try to pronounce it, I thought Silver was going to laugh herself sick when I tried—when half the time they can't even remember not to call us beasts."

"Your position," Tin said, and cocked her head the other way, "is now more favorable for gaining the svartalfar's help."

"Why are you doing this?" Isolfr asked her.

This time she did not turn him aside. She shrugged and said, "You have killed the Iskrynequeen, and I believe you will kill the young queen as well. My people as well as yours will be free from a fear that we have known, mother and daughter, all our lives. My mother and my mother's mother, and the full hand of my siblings, all were killed by trolls."

"But you couldn't have known we would succeed," Isolfr persisted.

Tin smiled at him, brilliantly, and said, "I gambled."

☙❧

Chrysoprase was a gnarled little being who could have ridden on Vigdis' back the way Isolfr had ridden his little gray pony Stout when he was still too small for a man's horse. He came shortly thereafter, and poked and prodded the flesh around Isolfr's stitched wounds. When he was satisfied, he crouched back on his heels and grunted, his brindled sideburns feathering in the faint ceaseless breeze through the caverns.

"You'll do," he said, and rattled the silver rings on the tip of the staff he carried in place of a trellspear. "You'll heal as well as the rest of them." He shuffled back; Isolfr, crouching, fought the bizarre urge to drop to his hands and knees and follow at a crawl. Chrysoprase's lips were thinner and crookeder than Tin's, and there were no inlays in his teeth. He took a breath, and spat his next words out as if he was spitting on a woman's fresh-swept floor: uneasy defiance. "And what would you have of my people, Konigenwolfsbrother?"

Isolfr had not been ready for it. He blinked, and hunkered down on his heels. "Help," he said, finally. "Only what I came here to ask. Help against the trolls. And soon, as soon as possible. We've already been in the mountains too long." He didn't say what he felt, the clear glass-edged fear.

"Humph," Chrysoprase said. He thumped his staff on the stone. "We'll see." But Isolfr rather thought he meant, *yes.*

TWELVE

They came back to Bravoll before the solstice, three wolfcarls and three wolves at the head of a svartalfar army. The svartalfar traveled fast, even over snow and with the winter at their back, blowing hard. They had horses—ponies—no bigger than the trellwolves, shaggy and seeming accustomed to cold and ice and the dark underground. The ponies ate palmfuls of grain and stamped their feet, shaking ice from their fetlocks, and did not complain.

Isolfr, for himself, rode a sledge more often than he liked—Tin and, surprising him, Silver required it of him, and of Kothran as well whenever the white wolf limped. From his privileged seat, Isolfr watched the svartalfar, and healed. Chrysoprase pulled his stitches out after a week, although Isolfr's face still hurt when he frowned or—less often—smiled.

The svartalfar traveled swaddled in cloaks, hunched on the beds of the sledges when they could. It took them only twenty days to come to the pinewoods outside Bravoll, and they were expected when they came. Isolfr could not have kept it from Viradechtis, not with her worry eating at him with every clop of the ponies' hooves.

The whole wolfheall turned out to greet them. The fighting men—wolfcarls and wolfless—of Bravoll came to meet the svartalfar army, and the trellwolves came with them. Isolfr made sure he was standing for it; his injuries were healed as much as they would until spring, and he wasn't about to meet his wolf—and his wolfjarls, he thought, concealing a flinch—wrapped in furs and flat on his back like an infirm old woman.

You came home with an army, he reminded himself, turning over his shoulder to catch a glimpse of four thousand svartalfar, banners and trell-spears glittering in the winter halflight.

It didn't help.

The red-and-black-barred wolf bounding at the head of the pack, her belly bulging with pups, came close enough to Isolfr to catch his scent and then turned her back on him, ears flat, making a display of her wrath. Mar and Kjaran at least sniffed his hand before snubbing him. And his wolfjarls—

He forced himself to meet their gaze evenly, aware of Skjaldwulf and Vethulf drawing up short before him, side by side, matched in their gait and matched in their hesitation. Isolfr felt as if his face burned, as if each etched claw-mark was on fire once more.

He actually thought he might have bolted, if Frithulf hadn't been beside him, driving his nails into Isolfr's elbow through sweater and shirt alike.

There was no way he could bemoan his scars in front of Frithulf. It shamed him even to remember them.

He leaned into his friend's touch for a moment and then shook loose, pulled forward, Tin appearing at his side. *You've made her respected*, he thought, but that wasn't quite right. *She* had made herself respected. She'd gambled and she'd won.

And Isolfr was happy to name her an ally and a friend. "Skjaldwulf," he said, forcing his lungs to breathe, to support the words that wanted to fall soundless from his mouth. "Ve . . . Vethulf. This is Mastersmith Tin, of the smith's guild and the Iron Kinship, daughter of Molybdenum of the lineage of Copper. She comes in your defense." Isolfr swallowed, and waved over his shoulder with a broad, sweeping gesture he hoped might be worthy of a ballad. "She's brought her family."

They stared at him. And Skjaldwulf said, "Your face—"

"A trellqueen," he answered, and bit his lip to keep from apologizing for not being as beautiful as he should have been. *Idiot*, he thought. The scars should have been a secret relief.

"Isolfr—" Vethulf began, and Isolfr braced himself for the dressing down. But Skjaldwulf knocked Vethulf's arm with an elbow, and then pulled Isolfr into an almost brutal embrace that Vethulf lunged into a moment later, both of them pounding his back and shouting until Frithulf stepped in and grabbed the wolfjarls' arms and said "His ribs were cracked, you fools—"

It didn't matter. Even the pain didn't matter, because Viradechtis finally deigned to come and lean against his hip. And as she did so, her mother sat in the snow beside her and began painstakingly washing her face.

They were home.

They had come home in time.

⊚⅄⊚

Even Ulfgeirr couldn't find much to complain about with regard to the sceadhugenga's doctoring, although once they were back at the wolfheall he did make Isolfr sit on a wooden bench and peel off coat and jerkin and sweater and tunic and shirt so he could see how the wounds had healed all down. He grumbled and muttered, especially when he found the still-sore swelling over Isolfr's ribs that Frithulf had wrapped tight for him, but in the end he sat back and patted Isolfr's shoulder and said, "He made a better job of it than I could have."

Isolfr smiled—it hurt less every day—and bent down to show that he could, and, incidentally, to rub his hands in Viradechtis' coat. She lay on her side, belly like a snow-smoothed hill; he ran his hands down her to feel the puppies squirming under her skin. Five or six, he thought; a big litter, for spring. Maybe there would be a konigenwolf.

He tipped his head toward the jarls, wolfjarls, housecarls, svartalf Masters, and wolfsprechends milling around the far side of the fire, and said, "How bad has it been?"

Ulfgeirr sighed and handed him a clean shirt. Isolfr pulled it on over gooseflesh. His hands were chapped and mottled with chilblains; the journey had been fast, but it hadn't been easy. Nevertheless, he managed the laces, and pulled his jerkin on over it, wincing as he raised his arm. After two months outdoors, even the drafty chill of the heall felt like luxurious warmth.

"That bad?"

The housecarl shrugged, and absently reached down to tug Nagli's ears. The red wolf sighed and pushed against his knee, and Isolfr felt sudden panic. "Ulfgeirr, where's Sokkolfr and Hroi? And Ulfbjorn?"

"Relax," Ulfgeirr said. "Sokkolfr broke a leg in the last raid. He'll be fine, but he's . . . convalescing in the home of a Bravoll widow-woman who finds him charming for some reason. I don't think he'd complain about a visit when our council's done. And Ulfbjorn's around here somewhere. He's probably shy of all the fuss and waiting to say hello in his own fashion. That's the good news. Signy, though"—he shook his head—"won't last the winter. She's taken a bone fever. And we lost the last patrol we sent toward Franangford, but otherwise the trolls have been quiet. Ulfsvith thinks they may be sapping, but that seems a great distance to dig."

"They have magic," Isolfr said. He stood up, rocking his foot under Viradechtis' head to awaken her. She protested, but heaved herself to her feet. "Ask Tin about it. They can . . . make the stone crawl to their whim. They are shepherds of stone."

Ulfgeirr looked at him, and then bundled his doctoring things into a scrap of leather and stuffed them under his furs. "Come on," he said. "They're waiting on us."

⟨⟩❦⟨⟩

T he council proceeded more smoothly than Isolfr could have hoped. The svartalfar were inclined to listen to the wolfheofodmenn, and the wolfheofodmenn and wolfless men both were in awe of the svartalfar and their army. In awe, and—Isolfr thought—a little in fear. The svartalfar forces seemed vast, the forest of gaily decorated and be-medallioned hide tents they had erected on the snow-covered fields outside Bravoll housing twice over the remaining forces of assembled heall and keep. It made the men uneasy—even more uneasy, when they learned that half the warriors were women, as, in fact, was the leader of the expedition.

A few hours with Tin, however, and they seemed to forget she was anything but a brother warrior, no matter how strange her small hunched shape or what her clothes concealed. She drank ale and ate bread and cheese with as much gusto as any wolfcarl, and seemed to appreciate their raw humor—or, at the very least, could feign it.

Frithulf and Kari were not present. Apparently, the wolfheofodmenn had extracted their story while Ulfgeirr was fussing over Isolfr's injuries, and sent them off to rest. As for the council meeting, Isolfr mostly contented himself to watch, and tried not to blush so hot that it couldn't be mistaken for the red cast of the firelight on his skin every time Skjaldwulf or Vethulf cast a glance or a smile at him. He was, he found, tremendously tired, and the horns of ale were not helping. He barely managed not to glance at his father; they had not spoken since Gunnarr saved his life in Franangford, but he knew Gunnarr knew that Viradechtis was konigenwolf in her own right now. He didn't want to see how his father would look at him, or his wolfjarls.

And really, he had nothing to say. He was not a tactician like Grimolfr and Ulfsvith Iron-Tongue and Gunnarr—and even Othwulf, who was *not* a wolfheofodman, but who was among the wolfcarls and soldiers summoned once it was determined that they *would* attack the trolls, and the discussion turned to how—and the trip north had proven that. He had not planned. He had not thought.

He'd done nothing but gamble his life, and the lives of three wolves and two friends. And it was only the grace of the goddess—and Tin's unexpected friendship—that had brought them home alive and with an army at their backs. So he sat silently, blessing his good fortune, and bit his thumbnail to keep from scratching at his scars. He missed Hrolleif with a great numb weight he had almost forgotten. Vigdis slept by the firepit, Skald draped across her back, and the sight made his eyes burn like a woman's, like a child's. He closed his eyes and pretended to half-doze to hide it; the warm weight of Viradechtis compressed his feet.

He almost jumped off the bench when a heavy hand fell on his shoulder. He looked up, expecting Vethulf or Grimolfr, and was startled to see his father's beard and cheek. Gunnarr didn't look down, but his fingers flexed tight, denting the leather of Isolfr's jerkin.

"Wolfjarl!" Gunnarr ordered, as Isolfr stiffened against his grip. Vethulf was already coming to his feet, his hair catching gold and orange highlights off the fire, one hand dropping to rest on Kjaran's withers as the gray wolf rose beside him like a shadow. Skjaldwulf was turning too, and Grimolfr—and every wolfjarl in the place, frankly—but Vethulf was closest, and it was he that Gunnarr stared at.

In the tension taut between the men, Isolfr heard the rattle of Tin's beads as she reached for her spear.

"Yes, Lord Gunnarr?" Vethulf asked. He didn't look at Isolfr either, but Isolfr put his foot lightly on Viradechtis' shoulder to keep her down anyway. If there was going to be a fight, he didn't want his pregnant wolf engaged.

"This man's injured," Gunnarr said. His hand fell off Isolfr's shoulder. "He's had a march and a fight and a march, and you've fed him nothing but cold ale and bread. Is this the way you see to your wolfsprechends at Franangford? Because at Nithogsfjoll, we'd call it shameful."

Vethulf stepped back, fish-faced with astonishment, and Kjaran, beside him, dropped to a sit and flipped his tail around his toes. The silence lasted heartbeats, and then was shattered when Grimolfr began to laugh. "Would we?" the Nithogsfjoll wolfjarl asked, and shook his head. "Aye, I suppose we would, at that. Go on, Vethulf, Skjaldwulf," he said, as Gunnarr stepped away, back into the circle of men. "Put your wolfsprechend to bed. We're as good as done here anyway, if we're all agreed that we march in two mornings."

Skjaldwulf was grinning, too, as he came over to brace Isolfr to his feet. Vethulf, scowling, was close behind, and Viradechtis, Mar, and Kjaran all crowded so close that Isolfr was nearly knocked down again. Around them, men and wolves rose, stretched, began to separate again toward their beds.

Isolfr met Skjaldwulf's eyes for a moment, swallowed hard. "I am sorry."

"For what, wolfsprechend?" Skjaldwulf said. "Mar, move your bones."

"For . . ." He stumbled a little, and Vethulf was there on his other side, holding him up. "I swore an oath that I would not speak of the svartalfar. And I couldn't . . ."

The words weren't there.

"You behaved with honor, if not necessarily with wisdom," Vethulf said tartly. "And you did bring an army. And gutted a queen troll, Kari says. You're the hero of the day, Isolfr. They'll sing you in Valhealla."

"I'm no hero," Isolfr said. The world was blurring and swimming, and he had to shut his eyes, letting wolves and wolfjarls guide him. "Please don't be mad at me."

"We're not mad at you, you daft creature," Vethulf said. Even in his leaden exhaustion, Isolfr couldn't mistake the fondness in his voice. "Skjaldwulf, tell Isolfr we're not mad at him."

" 'Course we're not mad at you," Skjaldwulf said. "Worried only."

I'm sorry, Isolfr tried to say again, but they lowered him onto a bed, a straw tick and pillows and quilts and furs, and it was as if a knot unraveled. The last thing he knew was Viradechtis grumbling as she hoisted herself onto the bed with Skjaldwulf's assistance.

❧

Isolfr woke to sunlight pooling on the flagstones and for a moment was aware of nothing except the blissful sensation of finally being warm enough. He blinked around and found Viradechtis nested in the furs be-side him, Mar and Kjaran draped across the foot of the bed in a compan-ionable tangle of limbs, and when he turned his head the other way, Skjaldwulf propped up on one elbow, watching him. Beyond him, Vethulf was sitting up, braiding back the long red rivers of his hair.

"This must be the biggest bed in Bravoll," Isolfr said, awed, and Skjaldwulf laughed.

Vethulf said, "Technically, it's two beds. We lashed them together when it became clear that Viradechtis wouldn't make do with less than both consorts and both wolfjarls when she slept. It's worked out quite well, really."

"Oh," Isolfr said and looked away. He already missed his place against the wall, Sokkolfr and Ulfbjorn on one side and Frithulf on the other. His eyes stung again; he bit his lip, and the ropes creaked under the strawtick as he slammed the back of his hand against the head of the bedstead. And Sokkolfr had his widow-woman, and—

And Frithulf and Ulfbjorn would manage, if Ulfbjorn decided to come to Franangford with him. Maybe they'd take Kari as a shieldmate. He needed shieldbrothers, Kari did, and Hrafn needed a pack-within-the-pack.

Think like a wolfsprechend, Isolfr told himself, to dull the pain of loss. Viradechtis whined, pawing the bedcovers, and Skjaldwulf touched his face gently. "You did what you felt you must, and in truth I think you have saved us all."

The consequences are what they are, Isolfr thought, but he turned away.

"Skjaldwulf has been a great comfort these past two months," Vethulf said drily. "How are you, Isolfr?"

"I am well," Isolfr said, with a shrug. "My ribs will ache a while longer yet, but . . ." He glanced at them, looked away. "I am not as pretty as I was."

"Do you think that matters?" Skjaldwulf said, and this time the gen-tle touch of his fingers was on the scarred side of Isolfr's face.

"Does it not?"

"Not to me," Skjaldwulf said.

Vethulf leaned across Skjaldwulf, said, "A man can find a pretty face anywhere, if he cares to look." And to Isolfr's abiding astonishment, Vethulf kissed him. Then rolled back, stood up, said, "There's a deal of work to be done, Skjaldwulf."

"Oh, aye," Skjaldwulf said, winked at Isolfr, and began extracting himself from the bed. Mar and Kjaran hopped off the foot, stretched, shook, and looked at their brothers with the bright eyes of wolves who are quite sure it's time for breakfast.

"You stay here," Vethulf said to Isolfr. "Rest and mend. I'll send someone with food. And you can figure out how you're going to convince Viradechtis to let you go to Othinnsaesc without her."

Isolfr looked at the wolf snoring amid the blankets and furs and said, "That will be a trick, won't it?"

❧

I t was Ulfbjorn who brought Isolfr breakfast: porridge with honey and the best thing Isolfr had tasted in as long as he could remember. Ulfbjorn sat beside him, too, while he ate, and caught him up on the gossip and small doings of the Franangfordthreat in his absence. And when Isolfr had done, Ulfbjorn said, "Would you like to visit the bathhouse? I can help you, if you need."

"Did Vethulf assign you as my keeper?" Isolfr said.

"He asked if I would mind helping you," Ulfbjorn said. "I was pleased to have something worthwhile to do."

Isolfr winced. "Sorry. I didn't—"

"Broken ribs are enough to make anyone fretful," Ulfbjorn said placidly. "And Frithulf tells me you took a bad knock to the head, as well."

"Yes. And, yes, the bathhouse is a wonderful idea."

"Come, then," Ulfbjorn said, and gave him a hand to steady him as he stood.

Viradechtis, having licked Isolfr's bowl clean, got off the bed as well, indicating plainly that Isolfr could go where he liked, so long as he didn't think he was going to leave her.

Isolfr luxuriated in the bathhouse while Viradechtis lay outside by the door, out of the heat. Ulfbjorn combed his hair out for him and re-braided it, and Isolfr was astonished to realize he had a wolfcarl's braids now, each as thick as two fingers and reaching nearly to his waist. Not a jarl's son anymore, wolfsprechend. *No, just a fool.* He snorted to himself, but he felt better, and when Ulfbjorn asked what he cared to do, he said, "I want to visit Sokkolfr. If you're busy, you needn't . . ."

But Ulfbjorn grinned. "Ah, Sokkolfr and his widow-woman. No, it isn't a long walk, and yes, he would be glad to see you."

It was a brilliantly clear day, the sky blue and high and cold. Viradechtis waddled when they walked, and he said to Ulfbjorn, "Perhaps I've lost count of the days, but should she not have borne her pups already?"

Ulfbjorn shrugged. "She is a little late, but Grimolfr said to remind you when you worried that she has always had long pregnancies. And we think she's been waiting for you."

"Oh." He felt himself blushing and said to Viradechtis, "Silly wolf."

She snorted at him, a snort uncannily like her mother's; Ulfbjorn and Isolfr caught each other's eye and both burst out laughing.

As Ulfbjorn had said, Sokkolfr's widow-woman lived not far from the wolfheall. She was stout and apple-cheeked, and Isolfr was at first taken aback by the throng of children who seemed everywhere underfoot. But when the youngest, a bright-eyed little creature, barely toddling, stretched out her arms toward Viradechtis and cried, "Doggie!" with unmistakable delight, Isolfr began to understand why Sokkolfr might be happy here.

Indeed, Sokkolfr, in a bed by the hearth, though pinched a little with pain, looked almost dream-dazed with happiness. And Hroi, tail waving sedately to and fro as his coat was combed by two little girls, seemed to agree.

Sokkolfr's delight at seeing Isolfr was wholehearted, and got him scolded for trying to move his bad leg. The widow shooed her children out, and Isolfr and Ulfbjorn sat down on the hearthstone to talk to

Sokkolfr while Viradechtis lay with her head pillowed companionably on Hroi's flank.

Isolfr found that explaining about the svartalfar did not get easier with practice, although it was easier that it was Sokkolfr he was talking to, who never passed judgment. Sokkolfr in his turn described the circumstances of his broken leg, with particular emphasis on how Hroi had stood over him howling until two wolfcarls from Vestfjorthr came to fetch him on a travois.

Then Sokkolfr looked down, fiddling with a bit of loose binding on one of his blankets. "I sent to Hjordis as you asked. She is well, and your daughter is well."

"But?" said Isolfr, for Sokkolfr's reluctance was plain.

"She says she cannot come to Franangford, though she is glad you wished it of her."

"*Cannot?*" Isolfr said. "Why?"

"Her duty is to her family," Sokkolfr said, with a quick, unhappy, sympathetic glance at Isolfr. "To her mother and sister, and they need her. In Nithogsfjoll, not Franangford. And . . ."

"Say it," Isolfr said wearily.

"She is being courted. She says she will say yes. But she says she will send Alfgyfa to be heall-bred if it is what you wish. And she says she is sorry."

"She has nothing to be sorry for," Isolfr said, and was pleased at the steadiness of his own voice. "She is not my wife. She swore no oaths."

"Isolfr . . ."

"Thank you, Sokkolfr. I am glad to know they are well." He stood up, looked to Ulfbjorn. "We should be getting back, do you think? I'm sure there is work for willing . . . *damn.*" He pressed the heels of his hands hard against his eyes, as if he could block the tears by main force.

Hroi whined. Viradechtis raised her head, then pulled herself to her feet and came to nudge demandingly at Isolfr's midsection. *Cub?* she said anxiously, having picked that much out of the pack-sense.

"No, she's fine," Isolfr said, rubbing Viradechtis' ears. "She is very well. It's all right, sister." And he did not look at Ulfbjorn or Sokkolfr, so that they would not see his eyes.

❦

The first thing that greeted Isolfr's ears as he stepped through the door of Bravoll wolfheall was the sound of his wolfjarls wrangling. He dropped into the pack-sense without thinking, found Kjaran's dry canniness waiting for him, and even as he was striding across the hall toward them, Kjaran was showing him what the argument sprang from. Not the words, though Kjaran followed men's speech as carefully as Viradechtis, but the fact that both wolfjarls were strained to the breaking point between the war and the displaced state of the Franangfordthreat and the long absence of their wolfsprechend. Isolfr could feel the damage done to the threat by his truancy, just as he had been able to feel the Nithogsfjollthreat slowly unraveling when Hrolleif was gone.

There is work to be done, he said to himself. *And now that we have a chance not to lose this war, perhaps there will be time in which to do it.*

He had chosen, he acknowledged, coming up beside Skjaldwulf and Vethulf. He could not unmake his choice or choose differently. And truly, he thought, no matter how badly he had handled it, he had not chosen wrongly.

The raised voices broke off abruptly; Vethulf and Skjaldwulf turned to look at him. "Wolfjarls," Isolfr said.

"What are you doing up?" Vethulf said.

"Keeping you from each other's throats, apparently," Isolfr said. He smiled at them and did not let himself wince at the twinge in his cheek. "And you two are . . . brawling like fishwives in front of the Wolfmaegth?"

They looked at each other sidelong, like sheepish little boys. Then Skjaldwulf nodded. "I'm afraid so. We've fallen into bad habits without our wolfsprechend to tend to us." There was a wicked glint of mischief in his eyes.

Isolfr sighed.

It was going to be a long winter.

THIRTEEN

In the end, Isolfr did not march with the armies to Othinnsaesc. Ulfgeirr thought it would be ill-advised, and more than that, when Viradechtis caught his intention, she sat down in the middle of Bravoll wolfheall and howled. Howled and howled, like a new-weaned pup, until Mar and Kjaran, and then Kothran and Hrafn and Hroi, and then the entire Franangfordthreat was howling with her.

So Vethulf looked at Isolfr, and Isolfr shrugged. It was settled; Isolfr and Viradechtis stayed in Bravoll along with Sokkolfr and the other wolfcarls and soldiers too injured to fight—and after a day and a night of chaos, the remaining complements of heall and keep marched on Franangford with the svartalfar army beside them.

By the end of it, Isolfr was so tired that he fell into bed—his old place by the wall in the coldest corner, and not the bed in the alcove that Vethulf and Skjaldwulf had built for Viradechtis—and slept the brief afternoon light away, and much of the night that followed. Viradechtis had taken to snoring as her time grew closer, but even that didn't keep him awake, though she insisted on sleeping in his arms.

He didn't mind. He felt small and alone. And it had occurred to him that with all the wolfheofodmenn and the jarls gone, Bravoll—heall, village, and keep—was his responsibility, and he had perhaps a dozen wolfcarls to hold it with, counting Sokkolfr who wouldn't be going anywhere soon.

He arose before dawn in the empty wolfheall, more worried than rested, and distracted himself from Viradechtis' irritable pacing by organizing patrols. The wolfcarls took boys—and girls: Isolfr wasn't above learning from the svartalfar, when it came down to it—from the village; any child who could ski was pressed into service, with strict instructions to flee home as fast as possible if he—or she—saw anything that could be remotely considered a troll.

While Isolfr settled himself to wait, Viradechtis went into labor. She spent hours dragging furs and pillows from her enormous bed to the back corner of the storeroom, behind the barrels of salt-fish, and growling at any wolf or wolfcarl who came too near.

Leitholfr, the only other whole-bodied wolfheofodman remaining in Bravoll, sent one of the boys tithed to the most recent Bravoll litter to find Isolfr, and when Isolfr came, at a dead run, Leitholfr looked up from the death-vigil he was keeping by Signy with a strained smile. "I will come with you if you wish it, but. . . ." His mobile face fell into stillness, and he touched the dull, matted fur of Signy's head with such distracted, heartbroken love that Isolfr said, against the clamoring panic rising in his chest, "No, it is not necessary. It is her third litter, after all."

"Aye," Leitholfr said. "Signy has borne ten." He shook himself. "It is your wolfjarls who should be with you."

"And they knowing even less than I do," Isolfr said and managed from somewhere to find a smile. "If something seems to be going terribly amiss, I shall ask at least for your advice, but otherwise, no. Please. Stay with your sister."

They separated with a glance that lasted a little too long, and Isolfr caught himself looking over his shoulder at the older wolfsprechend as he bent again over his wolf. She shifted her head to press it against his knee, and Isolfr quickly looked away. A thought struck him, one that was a little bit stunning. Vigdis had not chosen a new bondmate, but she also showed no signs of leaving Skald and the wolfheall. She couldn't keep Nithogsfjoll without a wolfsprechend for long, especially once the war was over.

Could she be waiting for Leitholfr? Was a trellwolf—a konigenwolf—wise enough to plan *that* far in advance? It left him with a shiver up his spine when he thought about it too hard, and instead, he went to Viradechtis' side to keep her from shredding the furs she was arranging into a nest.

The new Bravoll wolfheall was a stone building, more a keep than a roundhall like Nithogsfjoll, with rooms and corridors and three levels—four at the corner towers. All that fastness would benefit nothing if the trolls undermined it, of course, and right now all it meant was that he had corridors and stairs to hurry.

Viradechtis looked up as he came into her chosen den, teeth bared, and then relaxed, hackles dropping, shoulders slumping, when she caught his scent.

"You have been busy, I see," Isolfr said, and she laughed back at him, even through her discomfort. He rumpled her ears and she leaned into him, and he knew that things were right between them again. She wanted him here, trusted him to be here, and for the first time in days—months?—he wanted to be exactly where he was, doing exactly what he was doing.

All at once, everything seemed easier.

She made a low whuffing sound, neither a sigh nor a moan but a demand, and nosed at her pile of bedding. "I know," he said, and crouched beside her, helping her arrange the furs. "No soft dirt floors here. I'm sorry."

She gave him a canny look, and if wolves could frown he would have sworn it was one. He caught her irritation, a brief flash of warmth and familiar smells, cold-iron and cold-ice. He stroked her ears as she sank down onto the furs and the blankets, panting.

He was homesick, too.

Yearling brothers came to the door periodically during the afternoon and evening, their eyes as wide as war-shields, to ask if he needed anything or wanted anything or if the konigenwolf wanted anything. He smiled at their awe and asked several times for fresh water for Viradechtis and once for supper for himself. And Viradechtis paced and grumbled and told him how bored she was, as well as uncomfortable and aching.

Cubs, he reminded her, and *Cubs,* she agreed with a long-suffering sigh that nearly made him cough ale out his nose.

Perhaps Freya was still looking down on them; it could have been much worse. There were six pups, the largest dog a brindle, and the second-largest and third-to-last born a gray bitch who—blind, grubbing, rowing with undeveloped legs—promptly began shoving her brothers away from Viradechtis' teats. "Konigenwolf," Isolfr said, and sat back among the bloody furs. There was no mistaking it, even so soon; now he understood how Grimolfr and Hrolleif had known from the moment of Viradechtis' birth what she would be.

"You have done well," he said, as his wolf flinched from another contraction and then turned to nose her pups. Viradechtis looked at him quizzically, angled eyes bright, panting. He touched her nose, and she grinned, as if to say, not done yet.

The fifth pup was stillborn, the cord wrapped around its neck, and nothing Isolfr could do would rouse it. *Grimolfr could have saved it,* he thought, as he swaddled the small body in scraps of the furs Viradechtis had mauled and laid it outside the storeroom door. But Grimolfr wasn't there and perhaps even he couldn't have cheated Hel for that pup.

The sixth—small, perfectly formed, the pale color of spring butter— was a second bitch. Isolfr shook his head and said, "If the whole pack is of your line, little girl, where shall we go for breeding stock?"

Viradechtis laughed at him, and settled herself for a long, smug adoration of her five living pups: the gray bitch, the tawny bitch, two dog-pups as black as Mar, and the big brindle.

In a coincidence, as beloved of poets, Signy died before the sunset, but not before Isolfr gave the gray pup her name.

❧

They burned Signy and the dead pup together. Isolfr stood at Leitholfr's elbow, ready to support him, but the former wolfsprechend seemed almost relieved that the vigil was done. It had been a long, cruel winter for him, and Isolfr knew how much of his wolf's pain he had felt. And he needed to be strong, now—there would be time for grieving in the spring, when the army returned. When they knew that they would live.

Messengers came with some regularity, and it was to Leitholfr and Isolfr that the seemingly endless, fiddly task of arranging the logistics fell. In the wake of two years of war, provisions were scarce, and travel in winter a nightmarish near-impossibility. They managed, somehow—sledges drawn by unhappy, exhausted horses, men on skis with tump lines dragging sleds across the worsening snow, the women of heall and village and keep sending whatever they could to the men who had left them behind to fight for their lives. Even Viradechtis' pups grew thin, though Isolfr saw to it that she got half his rations as well as her own, and Leitholfr and Hroi took to hunting when they could, while Sokkolfr stumped about the great hall on crutches, cursing his still-unsteady leg.

The svartalfar and the men liberated Franangford—if liberated was the right term for a village that had been burned to the root-cellars—and Vethulf sent Kari and Hrafn back and forth with bulletins at every opportunity. Kari didn't seem to mind; he was comfortable traveling in the cold and, as he reported with an elaborate shudder that hid a very real discomfort, "They're fighting in the tunnels now."

Isolfr agreed. If he never saw a trellwarren from the inside again, it would be far, far too soon.

Their solstice celebration was a slender group—Kari and Hrafn, Sokkolfr and Hroi (who had moved back into the wolfheall as soon as Sokkolfr's leg healed enough for him to get around on it), Isolfr, Viradechtis and five squeaking, staggering pups arranged in a basket by the hearth in the great hall, Leitholfr, and the three yearlings who were not on patrol, as well as the noncombatants remaining in Bravoll, village and keep, from the blacksmith's five-year-old son all the way up to Inge, the venerable and terrifying mother of the jarl, who held the keep in his absence.

The keep's crippled fiddler, old Thorsbjorn, played over the meager feast, and on the swept floor of the wolfheall women danced with little boys and half-grown girls. Isolfr danced once or twice as well, but mostly sat with Sokkolfr and their wolves by the fire.

"I don't know what we'll do for tithe-boys, either," Isolfr said, gesturing at the pups. The boys should have been there already, sneaking glances at the basket, sniping and teasing each other over the possibilities of who would bond one of the bitches. Instead, all the boys of an age were already in Franangford or marching on Othinnsaesc. Old enough for the wolves was more than old enough for war.

Sokkolfr followed his motion and said, quietly enough that Leitholfr—who was tending the winter-skinny boar turning on the spit over the fire—would not hear it, "We'll have whatever's left when they get home. There will be wolfcarls who have lost their wolves, as well."

Isolfr shook his head and looked down under the weight of Sokkolfr's earnest stare. "They seem so much younger than we—"

Sokkolfr grinned, and reached down to stroke Hroi's ears. "We managed," he said. Which Isolfr could not argue.

Isolfr patted his friend on the shoulder and pushed himself to his feet. "Rest your leg," he said. "I'm going to check the solstice fires."

Sokkolfr nodded, but Isolfr felt him watching as he left. It was all right; he'd be back shortly. He just felt the need to make sure the fires would last through a night when the sun did not rise.

He made the rounds of the fires, shivering: north, east, south, west, exchanging formal blessings with the fire-watchers as he went. A broken-armed wolfcarl to the north with a pair of eager town-boys; two widow-women to the east; two more wolfcarls to the south, one of whom had lost his sight and the other his right leg below the knee; Thorlot, the Bravoll wolfjarl's lover, to the west, with her eldest son. She was the daughter and sister and widow of blacksmiths and knew a good deal of practical smithing herself; Isolfr had had cause to be grateful to her more than once already, and the winter only half over. She was a big woman, her forearms and shoulders muscled like a man's, her face unexpectedly beautiful. It occurred to him, seeing her lit by the solstice-fire, that this was what the waelcyrge must be like, and he shivered a little at the thought.

They exchanged the blessings, the boy blushing mortified scarlet when his voice cracked halfway through, and Thorlot said, "How goes the night, wolfsprechend?"

"Well, I thank you. And you?"

"Cold." She grinned. "Will you share a cup?"

"Gladly," he said, ridiculously pleased at the invitation.

She had mulled wine and a stack of wooden cups. "'Tis for the patrol when they come in," she said, "but I always take care to make more than enough." She and Isolfr saluted each other and drank, while her son checked the solstice-fire with earnest concentration.

"How do your sister's cubs?" Thorlot asked.

"Very well," he said, and could not stop the smile that spread across his face. "They'll be opening their eyes soon, and then matters will become truly exciting. I remember what Viradechtis was like—"

He broke off. He had been, purely out of reflex, watching the forest over Thorlot's shoulder as they talked, and he saw a small figure on skis break from amid the trees and make for the palisade, going at a tremendous clip. "That child's going to break her neck."

Thorlot turned, her son coming up beside her, and thus they were all watching when the girl pulled up, waved her arms frantically, and shouted, "Trolls! Two miles west! They're coming up out of the ground!"

"Sound the alarm," Isolfr said to Thorlot and her son; he himself scrambled down the ladder so fast he nearly broke his own neck and took off running full-out for the wolfheall.

☙❦❧

bunting trolls through the woods at night in snow is . . . unpleasant. Isolfr and Viradechtis, with every other wolfcarl, wolf, and wolfless man who could fight, labored through the shadows and the branches, wading through the drifts of snow like cattle at a mud wallow. Isolfr had tried to get his wolf to stay in the wolfheall, but the pups were old enough that she *could* leave them for a few hours, and she had not listened to any of his arguments. He had done what he could: appointed Sokkolfr to watch the pups and followed his sister into the night.

He had expected warriors, but these were trellsmiths, trellwitches, half-grown kittens. The warren was emptying, and Isolfr killed them with a lump in his throat so big that it hurt to breathe around. Two miles. They'd tunneled to within less than two miles of Bravoll.

The whole warren could have been on them at any moment, the earth opening under his feet, trolls in the keep, in among the cubs and women—

It had been a very near thing.

It was still a near thing, too near for comfort. The trolls fought wildly, and Isolfr knew they were animals at their last point of retreat. But more than that, they fled before him; anywhere he and Viradechtis appeared, they broke, and were cut down as they fled.

They *were* fleeing, panicking, and Isolfr's heart lifted a little with what that must mean about affairs at Othinnsaesc. He was praying, as he killed troll after troll, Leitholfr on one side and a wolfcarl from Kerlaugstrond on the other, praying for his wolfjarls and his shieldmates, for the konigenwolves who fought at their wolfsprechends' sides, for Grimolfr—even, to his surprise, for his father. Whatever he had felt for Gunnarr as a child—love, awe, hero-worship—was gone, but he found that he preferred the thought of his father alive and storming in Nithogsfjoll to the thought of his father dead and bloody on his funeral pyre.

It will do, he said to himself, and killed a trellsow, one of the ones he'd learned to recognize as a smith. And thought of Thorlot, who might be a better blacksmith than her father or brother or dead husband, or than her son would be, but who would never be anything more than wife, sister, daughter, mother. *At least* she *was honored,* he thought, wrenching his axe free of the trellsmith's ribs. He didn't mean Thorlot, and he did not know whether he was angry at his own kind for their blindness or angry at the trolls for making him see how blind they were.

The trolls and the svartalfar—Tin who barely recognized the word *woman*—and he killed the next three trolls in a black and causeless fury.

And then the line of men stopped moving forward, and Isolfr looked around; their vicinity, for the moment, was clear of trolls. His sister stood near; she tilted her head to look at him and said wistfully, *Cubs?*

"I told you so," Isolfr said, but they were both exhausted, and the trolls were not fighting well. The absence of one konigenwolf and one wolfsprechend would not tip the balance.

He said to Leitholfr, "Viradechtis wants her children."

Leitholfr smiled and said, "You did tell her so. Go on with you, then."

Isolfr nodded, said, "Come, sister." They started back toward Bravoll, through the snow and the bitter cold. They were tired, Viradechtis' jowls rimed with blood and Isolfr's mittens stiff with it, but in this cold it was death to sit or even to stop and rest for a moment, leaning against a tree.

They had gone maybe three-quarters of a mile when they heard the noise. It was a tiny sound, piteous, and they both thought, *Cub?*, Isolfr wondering for a crazed, panicked moment if somehow Signy had gotten out here, all by herself in the cold and dark.

The next moment he knew that was nonsense, but by then he could see the source of the noise.

A trellwitch, crouched in the snow, a muddle of rank furs and dull bronze, clutching to her breast a troll kitten. The kitten was crying, and when the trellwitch looked up, Isolfr was astonished to see tears in her mad red eyes.

Viradechtis growled and gathered herself, and Isolfr reached to unsling his axe.

The trellwitch said *please*.

Isolfr flinched back; his hand closed on Viradechtis' ruff before he thought. The trellwitch did not speak as men spoke, nor in the images of the pack-sense. She did not have a voice, as he understood such things, the word seeming to be formed out of darkness and stone and smelting fires and things that did not ordinarily make words. And it was not exactly a word; it was merely the closest she could come.

please said the trellwitch again.

He should have killed her. Taken her head off, disemboweled her—or simply let go of Viradechtis. Should have killed her and smashed the kitten's skull with the heel of his boot. But he was tired of death, tired of blood and slaughter and pain, and the trellwitch was rocking the kitten gently, soothing it with her crooked, knotted claws even as she stared at him. She was afraid, and if trolls could grieve, she was grieving, and yet she stayed where she was and tried to communicate with him.

"I cannot let you live," he said to the trellwitch. "Your people will slaughter mine."

slaughter the trellwitch said, amid flashes of fire and screaming, of Othinnsaesc. He saw for a moment what men looked like through troll-eyes. And shuddered away from the seeing.

Othinn, god of wolves, god of men, expected he would show no mercy. Othinn was a god for the strong, who granted no more than a man or a pack could take, and defend.

"I cannot," Isolfr said. "I am sorry."

And he *was* sorry, although he could never have explained it to anyone. Sorry because she found him as loathsome and terrifying as he found her—Viradechtis a great *thing* with flaming eyes, himself a spidery wrong-angled creature pale as a rotten corpse—sorry because the trolls were caught between the men and the svartalfar, and although it was no doing of his, it was no doing of hers either. Sorry because she loved that kitten as Viradechtis loved her cubs. Sorry because he could feel her fear and her desperation and the howling loneliness that gnawed her. Her queen was dead, her sisters were dead, the world was empty to her—and he knew that this was the first time in her life she had ever had to think of herself as a single creature.

kitten she said, as Viradechtis pushed toward her, and Isolfr held onto the wolf's ruff when it would have slipped through the clenched fingers of his mittened hand.

Trellqueen, Isolfr answered, the Iskrynequeen vividly in his memory. Beside him, Viradechtis, growling, leaned forward against his grip. She was not trying to make him let go of her, not yet, but he could feel her patience wearing thin.

kitten the trellwitch said desperately, and he understood. This was the only kitten, the only daughter of the Othinnsaesc queen, the only remaining daughter of the blood of the Iskryne. And he understood, in all the things that clustered around the trellwitch's approximation of language, that this meant even more to trolls than it did to men or svartalfar, that if this kitten died, a whole wealth of craft and lore died with her, the race-memory and daughtermind and history and shapings of trolls who had delved so far under mountains as to touch the giant Mimir's hair, and wrought black cities underground.

Trellqueen, Isolfr said, and thought of the destruction of Franangford, Hrolleif and Tindr and Signy and everyone he knew who had been killed by trolls, Tin's siblings, Kari's grief.

The trellwitch flinched a little, and he caught a scrap of confusion in her thoughts. Trolls knew that men did not have queens as they did, did not share the daughtermind. It baffled her, that men could care so about creatures who could not share their self.

He had never thought that trolls could grieve; the trolls had never thought that men could grieve.

"I owe my people—" he said, and there had to be something wrong with him, he was apologizing to a *troll*. "I cannot let a trellwarren grow again here."

away the trellwitch said. And then again *away*. She drew herself in, trying to shield the kitten with her body.

Viradechtis moaned.

"You have nowhere to go," he said. "And I know that you would lie to save that kitten's life."

away the trellwitch insisted, and he caught clouds of meaning, shreds of clarity. The Iskryne trolls knew of other troll warrens, other lines. *sisterkin* the trellwitch said, and although he could not make sense of the concept, he understood what she was telling him. She would take the kitten to one of these other warrens where the Iskryne line and lore could be preserved.

"You would not return to the Iskryne later?"

dead said the trellwitch, meaning that the Iskrynequeen was dead, meaning that the Iskryne was a place of death, meaning that the Iskryne was dead to trolls. Although he knew she would lie to him if she could, he also knew that she was not lying. She did not want to return to the Iskryne or to the caves beneath Othinnsaesc. She wanted to find her own kind again, wanted *sisterkin*, *daughtermind*, and she wanted the kitten to live.

And, though Othinn might curse him for it—god of wolves, god of war—and though Viradechtis whined beside him, leaning against his will, already tasting the trellwitch's blood in her teeth, he could not bring himself to blame the trellwitch.

It was not the god of wolves who had saved him, him and the wolf beside him, his daughter and Viradechtis' cubs. Not the god of war.

It was the patroness of smiths, the goddess of witches, and of whores.

"Teach her that we can also love," Isolfr said, and dropped his axe to hold Viradechtis hard, with both cold hands, while the trellwitch fled into the snow.

FOURTEEN

Franangford and Othinnsaesc had to be rebuilt from the tumbled stones, and it would take more than the summer—especially as heallan and keeps alike desperately needed the spring for planting to recover from two bad years. Food was more needful than shelter, and the Franangford wolfheall would be little more than a stockade and a circle of tents when Isolfr and his wolfjarls took up residence, along with the new Franangfordthreat. Sokkolfr would be housecarl, as he and Isolfr had planned; he and Frithulf and Kari remained Isolfr's shieldmates, his friends, his *pack*, as they had been.

While they stayed at Bravoll still, some nights Viradechtis wished to sleep with her consorts, but some nights she wished to sleep with her brother and her mentor and the black wildling, and where she chose to go, Isolfr chose to follow.

And Skjaldwulf and Vethulf did not complain. They seemed delighted when he came to their bed—and they continued to share, for Kjaran and Mar insisted on it—but accepting when he did not. They had reached some sort of peace with each other at Othinnsaesc; Isolfr did not ask for details, knowing it would be unkind. Though they still butted heads, and brawled—like fishwives, Isolfr told them—through the wolfheall, no one could doubt that affection underlay the insults, especially when Kjaran could not be troubled to turn from washing Mar's face to see what the matter was.

Isolfr had spoken to them, when they returned from Othinnsaesc full of Skjaldwulf's tales of the trellqueen, terrible-taloned, maw-handed mother of monsters—"it took two men to bring her down, though Frithulf tells me the one you slew in the Iskryne was larger."

"Um," Isolfr said.

"Two men," Skjaldwulf said, grinning, "and when the monster fell and they turned to clasp hands over her corpse, there in the strange-chambered warrens and caverns of what once was Othinnsaesc, I vow to you, Isolfr, they were the two most surprised men in the North of the world. For there was Gunnarr Sturluson on one side, black to the brow with the blood of trolls, and there on the other—"

"No," Isolfr said, guessing.

"Yes! And there on the other, Othwulf Vikingrsbrother with the trellqueen's ichor still wet on his axe."

"What did they do?"

"What could they do? They clasped hands over her corpse. And then Gunnarr spent three hours in the bath house, washing like a cat that's fallen in the honey pot."

Isolfr managed to retain his dignity until Skjaldwulf's own lips began to twitch with repressed laughter. And then they were holding each other up as they choked on mirth, Skjaldwulf's arm tight across Isolfr's shoulders, Isolfr's eyes streaming, while Vethulf looked on in feigned disapproval.

But it hadn't been the trellqueen, or even his father, that Isolfr had wished to speak of. He thought he'd had enough of trolls for one life, and he thought he'd hear the story a thousand times anyway, if the gods granted him the years in which to hear it.

It is the manner of wolves to say what they mean and say it plainly, and he said to them plainly that he wished them to treat him as a werthreatbrother, no more and no less. "I am not fragile, and I am not a child." He glared at Vethulf. "Call me 'lad' again, and I'll have your stones."

Vethulf tilted his head and tucked his chin like a wolf protecting his throat. Skjaldwulf intervened before the red-haired wolfjarl could step forward, though, and said in his quiet voice, "We do not think you fragile, Isolfr. We would have to be blind as well as fools to think so. I did not want . . ." He spread his hands helplessly, and his love was all through the pack-sense, honey stirred into tisane.

Isolfr understood; it softened his heart but not his resolve. "Then think of me as a wolf. You would never seek to . . . to *coddle* Mar as you have sought to coddle me."

Skjaldwulf's turn to look taken aback, but Vethulf burst out laughing and tossed his braids over his shoulders. "Can I still call you a daft creature?" he asked, and Isolfr was almost offended, and then realized that he was being teased, that that was Vethulf's way of signifying agreement.

He grinned at his wolfjarls and said, "That will suit me very well."

And things were better. To his surprise, neither Vethulf nor Skjaldwulf pressured him to lie down for them, though they made no secret of desiring him. They could not have kept their desire out of the pack-sense if they had wanted to, but they did not court him. He was afraid, at first, that Vethulf would corner him as Eyjolfr had, but he did not, and Isolfr came to understand as winter turned to spring, that he *would* not, that Vethulf, for all his sharp tongue and arrogant self-confidence, did not see other men as less than himself, and there was a generosity in him that finally showed Isolfr why Viradechtis had made him wolfjarl.

Eyjolfr himself chose to join the Franangfordthreat. Isolfr had been startled enough when Randulfr said that he and Ingrun wished to stay— but he was pleased, also, and it made sense, for Ingrun was easily second bitch at Franangford, and Amma had none of Kolgrimna's stubbornness. But when Glaedir came up beside Ingrun, he could not help looking to Skjaldwulf—who gave him a nonplussed shrug and said, "Eyjolfr? Do you follow your wolf?"

"I do," said Eyjolfr, and added a bit stiffly, "I bring no quarrel to Franangford, with wolfjarls nor with wolfsprechend."

The pack-sense said he meant it. "Then you are welcome," said Isolfr.

That was indeed a day of wonders, the day before the Nithogs-fjollthreat began their long trip home, for Vigdis, to no one's surprise more than Grimolfr's, chose Ulfbjorn as her new brother. It was a good choice, despite his youth; the big man was steady of heart and even-tempered, and even Ulfrikr Broken-Nose had the sense not to call *him* womanish.

And it was wonderful as well for the look on Grimolfr's face, when he had to tilt his head back—far back—to glower up at his wolf-sprechend.

When the snow still lingered—gray at the edges of meadows and deep under the trees—the svartalfar marched home. Tin took her leave of Isolfr privately, and left him with a gift he hadn't expected—a war-axe shaped by her own hands. Not her Master-piece, of course, but an axe made by a Mastersmith nonetheless.

"If you hang it on the wall over your mantel," she said, troll finger-bones rattling from the rings lining her long pointed ears, "I will know, and I will come and take it back."

"Are you wishing me war, Mastersmith?" He smiled to soften it, and laughed when she showed him her teeth.

"With no trolls in the North," she said, "it would have to be war with the svartalfar."

He sighed, and sank down in a crouch, the axe laid across his knees. It was a beautiful thing, art and destruction wrought in one bright killing curve, the broad steel blade inlaid with bronze and silver coils. "My people will fear it. Fear your people, I mean."

"Use that to keep the wolfheallan strong," she said, and reached with bony fingers to pat his hand. "Even the smiths and mothers will speak to queen-wolves. Get your lover to put it in a song, so people remember. If they fear us, there will be no war."

"He's not my lover," Isolfr said.

She raised an eyebrow, a long feathery, shaggy sweep. "You're his beloved. Both of them. I saw enough on the war-trail to know." Then she laughed, and took her hand off his and pushed his chest like a wolf-cub nudging playfully. "We don't get to pick who loves us, you know. And better to get him to write the song than be remembered forever as 'fair Isolfr, the cold.'"

He scrubbed a hand across his face, roughness of beard and scars and the smooth skin of the unmarked cheek. "Is that really what they call me?"

She smiled. "You frighten them, Viradechtisbrother. You went down under the mountain and came out again, twice, and the alfar call you friend. They'll have you among the heroes before you know it. And you can seem quite untouchable—'ice-eyes, and ice-heart, and ice-hard, his will.'"

"Othinn help me. It *is* a song already."

"Isolfr Ice-Mad," she said, and when he winced, she shrugged.

He snorted and looked down, pretending he was testing the edge of the axe on his thumb. "There are worse names."

"Don't tempt your gods," she admonished.

"It's a goddess I ought to thank." Viradechtis looked up from her place by the fire, and gave him a dark, opaque stare. He knew what she was thinking—the trellwitch, and the kitten. He hadn't told anyone about them, and he wasn't about to tell Tin.

Viradechtis would forgive him eventually. She would have to; he was hers, and she was his—unto death and the hall of heroes, if Othinn would still have them—and they'd each forgiven worse.

"Goddess?"

"My dream of trolls and you and fire," he said. "A gift from Freya."

Tin laughed. "Ah, yes. You know svartalfar made her necklace for her? So our songs say."

"So do ours," he said. And they said she sold her body to earn it, too, but then, what choice did women have? Even goddesses. Even queens.

"Tin—"

"Yes?"

"What you said about war, and the wolves, and teaching men to fear the svartalfar."

"Yes." She settled back, and folded her hands.

"I am the father of a daughter," he said formally, recalling Hjordis' words: *if you wish me to send her to be heallbred*—

"I have heard." Her eyes caught the light, quartz-bright. He thought she knew already what he was about to ask.

"When she is of age, may I send her to you, to be apprenticed as a smith? It seems to me . . ." He hesitated, coughed to clear his throat, began again. "It seems to me that we will need people, men and svartalfar, who can speak between the races. And if my child is a smith, and later a mother—"

"Ah." Tin rocked on the balls of her feet, medallions and talismans clanking on her gorgeously embroidered clothes. "Ah, yes, and the daughter of Isolfr Ice-Mad, Isolfr Viradechtisbrother, yes—"

"Yes," he said.

"Yes," she promised. He almost thought the brightness in her eyes was about to spill down her creased cheeks, but instead she clasped his hand again. "Yes. Send her to me. I will make it right with the smiths."

"And the mothers?"

She laughed and showed him the inlays on her teeth. "The *mothers* will understand."